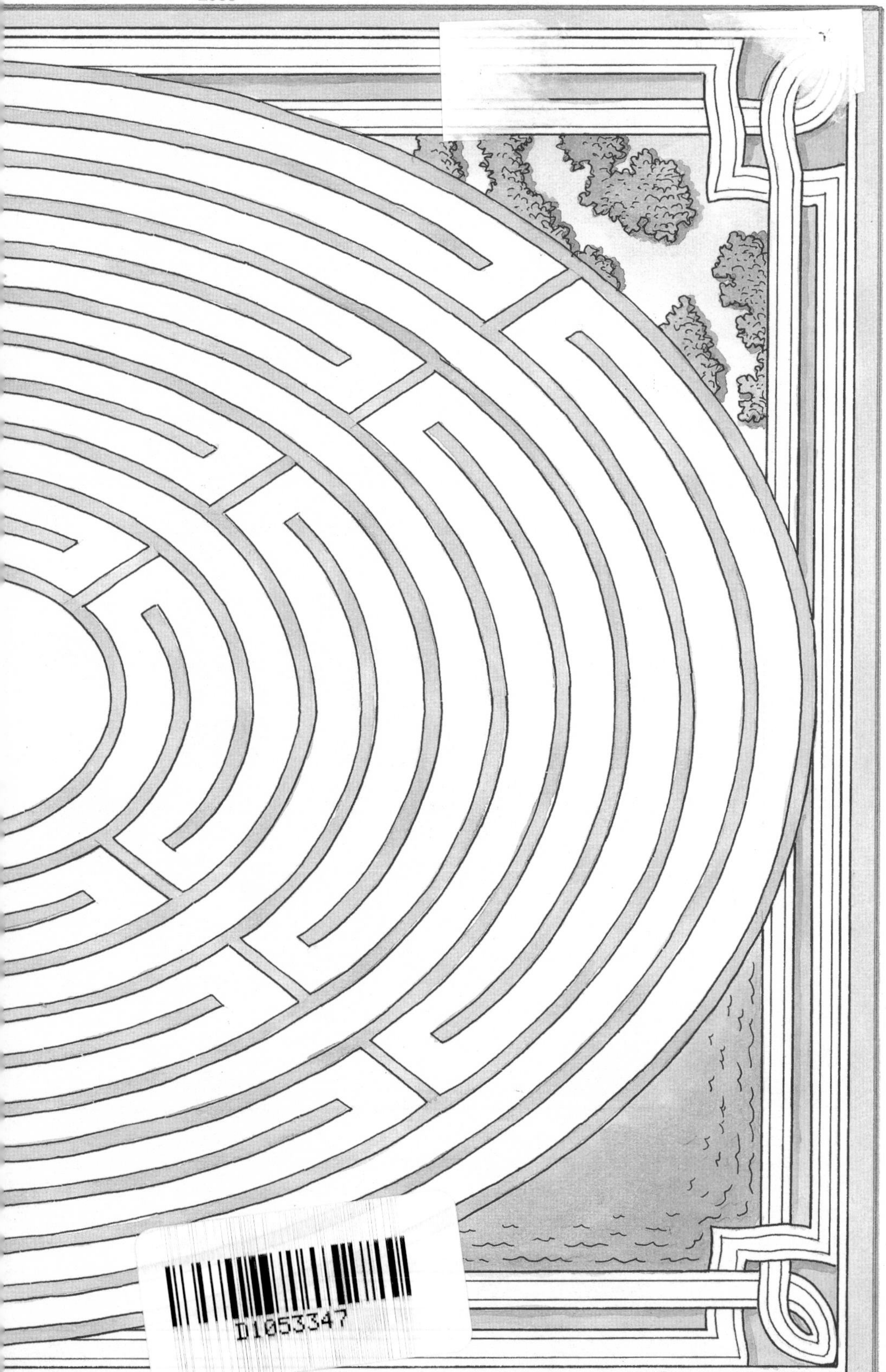

CANTICLE

TOR BOOKS BY KEN SCHOLES

Lamentation

Canticle

CANTICLE

KEN SCHOLES

A TOM DOHERTY ASSOCIATES BOOK
NEW YORK

S

CANTICLE

Copyright © 2009 by Kenneth G. Scholes

Map by David Cain

A Tor Book
Published by Tom Doherty Associates, LLC
175 Fifth Avenue
New York, NY 10010

www.tor-forge.com

Tor® is a registered trademark of Tom Doherty Associates, LLC.

Library of Congress Cataloging-in-Publication Data

Scholes, Ken.
    Canticle / Ken Scholes.—1st ed.
        p. cm.
    "A Tom Doherty Associates book."
    ISBN: 978-0-7653-2128-2
    I. Title.

    PS3619.C45353C36 2009
    813'.6—dc22
                            2009016764

First Edition: October 2009

Printed in the United States of America

0 9 8 7 6 5 4 3 2 1

For Robert,

who introduced me to Elric, Solomon Kane, the Gray Mouser,

and many other old friends along the way.

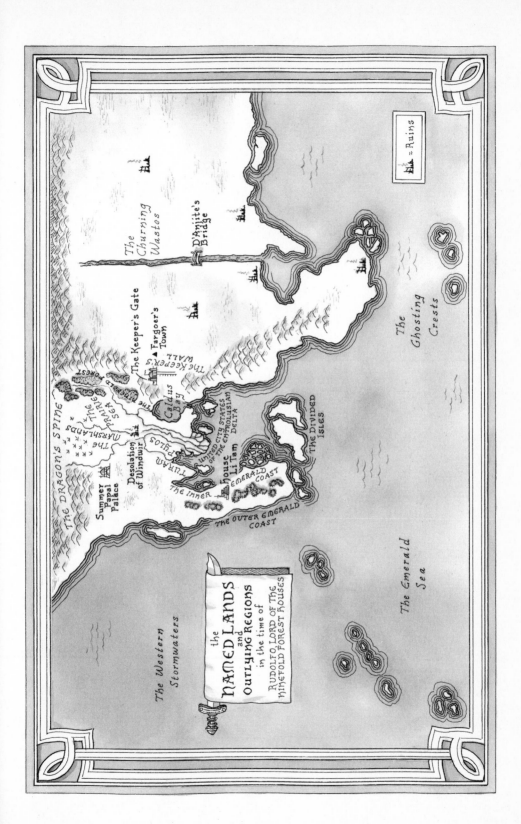

CANTICLE

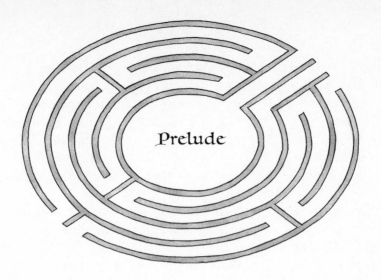

Prelude

Sunrise on the Churning Wastes was a terrifying glory. Each morning the Gypsy Scouts watched it from their station on the Keeper's Gate.

First, the cold air took on the warm scent of salt and sand. Then the sky was washed in deep purple, shot through with veins of red, twisting and spreading out on a flat horizon that stretched forever past the low hills that marked the Whymer Way leading into the Desolation of the Old World. And in that moment before the sun rose red and angry as a fist, the world went silent and still.

Today, in the heart of that moment, a brown bird dropped into the Watch Captain's net.

He unrolled the tiny scroll it carried and squinted at it in the crimson light from the east. Then he whistled his men to Third Alarm and watched the front guard magick themselves to slip into the morning shadows.

He hastily coded a note to Aedric, the First Captain of Rudolfo's Gypsy Scouts, and passed it to his birder. "See this to Seventh Forest Manor," he said.

Then he climbed down the stairs to the base of the massive, closed gate and stood to the side with his arms crossed.

A metal man in robes approaches from the west. This was most irregular. General Rudolfo's metal men worked at the library. And their leader, Isaak, was the only one of their lot who wore robes. The Watch Captain scanned the road that led down from the jagged stone hills to the west. That winding road came from only one city.

Windwir. Now a Desolation because the Androfrancines couldn't leave well enough alone. They'd brought back Xhum Y'Zir's Seven Cacophonic Deaths, and the spell had been their undoing. An entire city and its Order snuffed out, ending their long guardianship of the light, the knowledge of the Old World that had fallen to the same spell two thousand years before.

And now, it seemed, the metal man who had cast the spell and doomed the Androfrancines approached his post unannounced. "Most irregular," he said out loud.

He watched the road, picking his men out easily despite the magicks that concealed them. Each was a quiet, individual wind that gently moved the blades of grass and the pine boughs as the invisible scouts slipped into position. During the war last year, he'd been a lieutenant and he'd run with his men. Now, the double-edged blade of promotion set him apart from them. And with the promotion came a new assignment here in the mountains that divided the old world from the new.

Birds flitted across the massive stones of the Whymer Way and the wind shifted, carrying the sound of metal footsteps.

A robed figure limped into sight, wheezing and bubbling. One of its jeweled eyes hung by a strand of gold wires and the other rolled listlessly, its shutter bent open. The Watch Captain stepped forward, ready to bark orders. Rudolfo would have the head of any man who failed to help his friend, and the metal man, Isaak, was more kin than friend to the Gypsy King. But he hesitated.

"Brother Isaak?"

The metal man looked up. Its voice burbled as its bellows wheezed. "My name is Charles," the metal man said in a watery voice. "I am the Arch-Engineer of Mechanical Science for the Androfrancine Order in Windwir. I bear an urgent message for the Hidden Pope, Petronus. *The Library is fallen by treachery. Sanctorum Lux must be protected.*" With a click and a clack, the mechanical collapsed into a pile of steaming metal, bits of it sparking and popping.

The Watch Captain shouted for another bird and whistled his men in from the forest.

High above, a kin-raven circled.

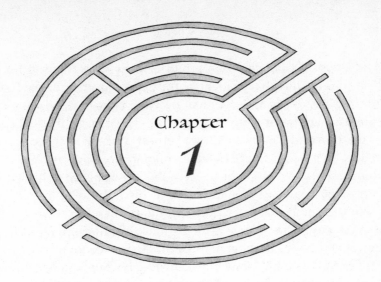

Chapter 1

Rudolfo

Late-afternoon sun washed the expansive forest in red, and Rudolfo watched it from the highest point of Library Hill. It had been a long day of paperwork amid the pandemonium that gripped his Seventh Forest Manor's staff, and finally Rudolfo had fled under the pretext of an unscheduled inspection of the library construction. He had quietly strolled the basements and subbasements, grateful for the break in routine.

Of course, he couldn't blame the staff for the chaos. It was, after all, *his* Firstborn Feast they were preparing. In mere weeks, Rudolfo would see his first child into the world, and it was the custom of the Forest Gypsies to celebrate that event with great vigor. That it was Rudolfo's firstborn *and* an heir transformed the event into a minor affair of state, with dignitaries expected from a dozen or more houses. Even the Marsh King was attending. Rudolfo smiled at this, knowing that the large hairy man who posed as the Marsh King did so at the command of a fifteen-year-old girl who was the true heir to that Wicker Throne. But tonight, Hanric would play the part of king alongside Rudolfo and the other lords in attendance. Those aspects of tonight's festivities bored Rudolfo. Instead, he thought about the men who were the true hosts of tonight's event—the men who rose to their captain's challenge to honor their Gypsy King and the Gypsy King to Come.

The Gypsy Scouts could be proud of their work. They'd hunted and fished for six weeks to stockpile the game required for the festivities; they'd sent birds and riders all over the Named Lands to gather the finest sampling of wines and spirits. They'd even hired in cooks from the Emerald Coasts to study the best of the Forest recipes and reproduce them with southern augmentations to draw out the flavor.

Rudolfo chuckled. Tonight, the Marsh King would sit to his left and the Entrolusian ambassador would sit to his right. The Entrolusians had sent their ambassador because Erlund was beset by the fires of rebellion on the Delta. When Erlund's uncle, Sethbert, had destroyed Windwir, he'd hoped to shore up the Entrolusian economy by annexing the Ninefold Forest Houses with the help of his puppet Pope. Rudolfo and his kin-clave had pressed them back, and eventually Sethbert's plans were unraveled and the Overseer himself tried and summarily executed for the genocide of the Androfrancine Order and their city.

How long ago had that been? Six months? Seven? It had crawled like years. League upon league of paperwork. Hour upon hour of meetings. Entire days that slipped past him without seeing the sky or feeling the wind on the back of his neck. The last time he'd stood here, the bookmakers' tent was still below in the heat of Second Summer as metal man and Androfrancine and Forester worked together to reproduce what they could of Windwir's Great Library.

Now winter wrapped the forest, and the bookmakers' tent was packed away. Their tables now crowded the basements of Rudolfo's Seventh Forest Manor, and the books they produced filled the hallways and spare rooms to overflowing. Until now, of course, when those spaces were suddenly required.

Rudolfo paused and wondered where they had managed to store all of the books. And how long ago had it happened?

What it pointed to disturbed him. *I didn't even notice.* There was a time when he would have picked up on the slightest difference in the length of any one of his scout's beards. But now mountains of books vanished beneath his very feet and it took him days to realize it.

He heard the clicking and clacking, the slightest wheeze of bellows, and turned to watch his metal friend approach.

"Lord Rudolfo?" a metallic voice asked.

"Isaak," Rudolfo said. "You've found me."

Isaak stepped into view. "Yes, Lord." He paused, smoothing his Androfrancine robes with his metal hands. "I trust you found your inspection satisfactory?"

Rudolfo chuckled. He should've known the metal man would worry. "You are doing wonderful work here, Isaak."

Isaak blinked. "Actually, Lord, there are many more besides myself performing this work. The list is rather extensive, but I have a file of names in my office for your review. Or I could recite them—"

Rudolfo raised a hand. "A compliment to all involved," he said.

Isaak nodded. "Thank you, Lord. We serve the light."

"We do indeed," Rudolfo said. "But truly, Isaak, you are a fine foreman for this work."

Isaak inclined his head slightly. "Thank you, Lord. Might I add that Lieutenant Nebios has been extremely helpful in that respect."

Rudolfo had seen Neb's leadership throughout the grave-digging of Windwir. That was when he'd first recognized that there was a fine captain buried in the lad. And some of Isaak's methods looked surprisingly similar to Neb's. "So he's been advising you?"

Isaak blinked again. "I have been making inquiries and cross-referencing them against library holdings on Francine observations of human leadership dynamics." He paused, releasing steam through the exhaust grate in his back. "Neb is a natural leader."

Rudolfo nodded and stroked his beard. "Yes," he said. "I see that, too." But beyond what Rudolfo saw, the Marshfolk saw Neb as the one who would someday find—and take them to—the new home as promised in their Book of Dreaming Kings.

Rudolfo turned his eyes back to the forest and his home in it.

The sun was nearly down now, and the lights of the manor and the town called to Rudolfo. High above, as the sky went from purple to charcoal, swollen stars pulsed to life and a blue-green sliver of moon danced behind a hazy veil of cloud. Rudolfo drew in a lungful of night air and smelled the roasting meat from the kitchens far below.

"I suppose we should get ready for the feast," he said, clapping Isaak on the shoulder and feeling the cool metal beneath the rough wool robe.

Isaak nodded. "Lady Tam sent a scout for you. I told him I would pass her message along."

Rudolfo chuckled. A few weeks earlier and she'd have come herself, but the River Woman insisted she rest now. She'd balked initially but at the last accepted the midwife's instruction and forced herself to bed. Rudolfo knew better than to taunt the tiger in her cage. "I was finished here," he said, turning to Isaak. "Walk with me."

They walked in silence among the massive, scattered stones that were slowly taking shape. The air was cold on Rudolfo's face and his breath showed. Picking his way carefully through last week's snow, he and Isaak descended the hill that was gradually transforming the Ninefold Forest, turning it into the center of the Named Lands.

It had already started, of course, not long after Petronus had executed Sethbert and transferred the wealth of the Androfrancine Order into Rudolfo's name for the reestablishment of the library. And just yesterday, another university—this one a larger bookhouse out of Turam—brought their petition to establish a presence near the Great Library. Rudolfo had listened to their request, told them he was honored by their interest in the Ninefold Forest, and that he would take the matter under consideration. It was the fourth university to ask in as many months, and he wasn't sure how long he could keep them at bay.

Rudolfo's boot slipped on a patch of snow-crusted ice and he stumbled. He felt a strong metal hand grip him before he could fall. He glanced over at Isaak. "Thank you."

Isaak nodded and waited until Rudolfo was steady before releasing him. They reached the bottom of the hill and followed the road back into town. Already, the forest between the hill and the town was thinning for new construction. Soon, Rudolfo's Seventh Forest Manor and the small town that surrounded it would grow into a city.

What would my father think of this? Rudolfo paused. Orphaned at twelve, he rarely thought about his father. But he thought about him more now that he stood on the edge of fatherhood.

A handful of Rudolfo's Gypsy Scouts fell in around them as they walked. They hadn't yet changed into their dress uniforms, and their rainbow-colored woolen trousers and shirts were damp from the forest. Uncharacteristically, they grinned at their general.

He smiled back at them. "I hear you've pulled together a Firstborn Feast like no other before it," he said to them.

Their grins widened and then vanished as First Captain Aedric approached from town. His face looked worried and he gripped a note in his hand. For a moment, he seemed to study Isaak and then fixed his eyes on Rudolfo. "I've just had two birds from the Wall."

Rudolfo stopped. They had inherited the watch on the Keeper's Wall when they took on rebuilding the library. The mountain range separated the Named Lands from the Churning Wastes, the ruins of the Old World. The Androfrancines had controlled access to the one pass until Sethbert broke their back and Petronus dissolved the Order, passing its role on to Rudolfo and his Ninefold Forest Houses.

Shepherd of the light, he thought.

"What is happening at the Wall?" He took the notes and read them quickly. Coded into the message was an emphatic urgency. A metal man, clothed in robes, claiming to be an Arch-Engineer of the Order's Office of Mechanical Science in a city that was now desolated. *I bear an urgent message for the hidden Pope, Petronus,* Rudolfo read. *Sanctorum Lux must be protected.*

He looked up from the note and turned to Isaak. "What is the name of the engineer who created you?"

Isaak blinked, his eyes flashing golden in the crisp twilight. "Brother Charles, Lord."

Rudolfo nodded. "Yes. Brother Charles. Arch-Engineer of the Androfrancine Office of Mechanical Science?"

Isaak nodded. "Yes, Lord."

He stroked his beard. "When was the last time you saw him?"

Gears whirred to life inside the metal man and he shuddered, venting steam into the cold night. "I . . ." The mechoservitor paused. "The evening before the city fell. He had given me my assignment and sent me with the Gray Guard escort into the spell vaults."

So it was possible that he could've escaped, Rudolfo thought. And perhaps he knew of Petronus—it certainly wasn't impossible, though the old man had surely kept his secret from most. But it did not explain the metal man.

"And we liberated all of your"—he searched for the proper word—"peers from Sethbert's camp?"

Isaak nodded. "I've accounted for my brothers."

Rudolfo nodded. He looked at Aedric now. "What do you think?"

Aedric's hands moved quickly into the sign language of the Gypsy Scouts. *I don't like it,* he signed. "I think we ride for the Keeper's Wall and see for ourselves what this is about."

Rudolfo looked to his men and then to his first captain. *They would go with me now, Firstborn Feast or not, if I said we must.* The scouts were sons of scouts and had served the General of the Wandering Army and Lord of the Ninefold Forest Houses as their fathers before them had, raised on the knives and the powders. And Aedric himself was Rudolfo's best friend's firstborn son. Gregoric and Rudolfo had been close since childhood, and when Lord Jakob and his wife were murdered, Rudolfo had taken the turban and passed the First Captaincy to his friend. They'd fought together in many political skirmishes and helped divert resurging heresies at the Order's behest, equally earning their reputations as fierce leaders and formidable strategists. But Rudolfo knew the truth: A leader is only as capable as the men he commands, and his men were the best in the New World.

Their loyalty is nearly love, he realized. *They learn it from their fathers.* The reality of that gave him pause, and a thought pushed at his mind. He shoved it aside, forcing his attention to the matter at hand. "I concur with you, Aedric." Then he used the hand language of the Gypsy Scouts in such a way that none could possibly miss it: *But tomorrow morning is soon enough. We feast tonight as these men honor my first fatherhood.*

The Gypsy Scouts were silent, but Rudolfo's eyes darted over to see several of them grinning again. He smiled at them and inclined his head.

As they took to the road, making their way through the bustling streets of his growing tribe, Rudolfo brought back the thought he had pushed away. These men, he realized, were yesterday's children, and they would pass their knives to tomorrow's children soon enough. And in that brief time between, the world had changed again—and was still changing—as the Named Lands reeled and floundered from the loss of its Androfrancine shepherds. Still, the Gypsy Scouts would pass their knives onward, sharing what they learned from these precarious times.

And I will pass my knives, now, too, Rudolfo thought. He hoped they would be sharp and balanced for the world they were making.

Neb

Neb stalked his prey through the darkened Whymer Maze. He moved carefully, lifting his feet and placing them in the footprints he'd left earlier in their hunt. She was up ahead now, he was sure of it. He caught the faintest hint of earth and ash on the cold night air. It intoxicated him.

Suddenly, he felt something cold and wet impact the back of his neck. Bits of ice and snow fell into his shirt, and Winters burst into laughter behind him. Spinning, he lunged at her and she danced back and away from him and his flailing arms.

She grinned, pushing her dirty brown hair away from her face. "You've become clumsy, Nebios ben Hebda."

Neb shook his head. "I would've heard you if I'd been magicked," he said. The stealth powders that he trained with made Rudolfo's Gypsy Scouts nearly invisible to the naked eye. Only used during time of war, the scout magicks also heightened their senses and enhanced their speed and strength, making them formidable opponents.

She smiled. "That's the problem. You've grown dependent upon the powders—your senses are dulled without them." She stepped closer and put a dirty hand on his cheek. "It makes you easy prey."

Neb grinned and stepped closer to Winters, his hands moving up to fold her into his arms. Slender and willowy, she pressed herself to him and raised her mouth to his. She felt warm to his touch despite the cold.

When he'd met her, Neb thought Winters was the Marsh King's servant or daughter or worse. He'd learned later that she was actually the Marsh Queen herself, hiding behind a more fearsome shadow until she reached her majority and could strike the proper balance of respect in the Named Lands' elaborate system of kin-clave. They'd shared dreams together there on the edge of the Desolation of Windwir—dreams of a new home—and they'd walked long afternoons while Neb inspected the gravediggers' progress. They'd even kissed in the shadow of the forest that hemmed in the ruined plains of that great, dead city.

It had been seven months, and he had forgotten how good she tasted. "This is better than the dreams," he said.

She shuddered beneath his hands, squirmed and pushed at him. "Don't you need to get dressed for the feast?" she asked, laughing.

He pulled her back and kissed her again. "Yes, Lady Winters, I do."

"Then I release you to your responsibilities," she said, slipping away. "I will see you in the morning."

Winters moved away with a speed and sureness of foot that astounded Neb. Unmagicked, she was easily the best scout he'd seen. He followed at a slower pace, willing his heart to stop racing. He'd forgotten how powerful the draw to her was. Certainly, the dreams reinforced it. Bits of prophecy, strands of glossolalia and, sometimes, a sensuality that caught Neb's breath in his throat and woke him up sweating and trembling. Even now, he blushed as he thought about it.

He left the maze and took the winding garden path up to the scouts' back entrance to the Seventh Forest Manor. He could hear the woodwinds and stringed instruments trickling from the Grand Hall's windows and could hear girls and scouts laughing in the kitchens. Neb slipped inside and found himself in hallways crowded with scouts

and soldiers in the dress uniforms of the Ninefold Forest Houses. Servants bustled about, moving from room to room. Neb took the back
stairs, and after a few twists and turns of the hall, he let himself into
his small room.

Normally, officers in training stayed in the barracks, but because
he was considered a member of Rudolfo's household they had kept
him in the same room he'd used since his first arrival in the Ninefold
Forest. It was a small room divided roughly into a living area and
sleeping area—the sleeping area was separated from the rest by a
heavy curtain. A small wooden desk and chair sat near a large window
that led out onto a small balcony. A few scattered pieces of art decorated
the walls—two, he thought, were original Carpathius oil paintings of the
Great Migration west from the ruins of the Old World. Carpathius
had been commissioned for a series of paintings during the first mil-
lennial celebration of the settling of the Named Lands. These were
from that series, showing the Gypsy folk in their tattered rainbow
clothing—their leader, that first Rudolfo of legend, standing apart
from the others—cresting a hill to look out over the Ninefold Forest.
Those ancient green islands of old-growth timber isolated in the yellow grass of the Prairie Sea were to become their new home, and
though their faces were tiny, Neb was convinced of the hope on them.
Neb wondered what it had been like to be the first setting foot in a New
World so long ago.

Unbuckling his knife belt, he hung the twin blades over the back of
a chair. He slipped out of his snow-stained woolens and after quickly
scrubbing up and shaving in the small bathing chamber adjacent, Neb
pulled on his dress uniform. Ordinarily, Rudolfo's officers came into
their training with no rank, but in light of his previous leadership,
running the gravediggers' camp for Pope Petronus during the worst of
the war, Neb wore the scarf of a lieutenant wound around his upper
left arm. He sat down to pull on his boots and looked up when there
was a knock at his door.

"Come in," he said.

The door eased open, and Aedric, First Captain of the Gypsy Scouts,
peeked in. "You're running late," he said, grinning.

Neb tugged at the boot. "Sorry, Captain."

Aedric came into the room, pulling the door closed behind him.
"Does it have anything to do with a certain Marsh girl who happens
to be accompanying her king?"

Neb felt his cheeks grow hot. He opened his mouth to speak, but

Aedric's chuckle cut him off. "She has you quite firmly in hand, I imagine."

The double meaning wasn't lost on Neb, and now his ears burned, too. But Aedric clapped a hand on his shoulder, his chuckle now open laughter. "Take heart, Neb," he said. "It happens to all of us at one time or another. Just be careful—Marshers are a strange lot."

He doesn't know, Neb realized. *He thinks Hanric is the Marsh King.* Rudolfo knew the truth, though Neb wasn't sure how he'd learned it. And Neb suspected that Aedric's father, Gregoric, had known as well. But Gregoric had been killed on the night they liberated the mechoservitors from Sethbert's camp.

The Marshfolk survived because the rest of the Named Lands either feared or discounted them. Legend had them coming to the Named Lands just after that first Rudolfo led his band of desert thieves and their wives and children over the Keeper's Wall. Carpathius had certainly painted no pictures of that event. At one time, they had been the house servants of Xhum Y'Zir and his wizard king sons. But—as the Androfrancines taught—the Age of Laughing Madness had not bred its way out of the Marshers over a span of several generations. As other settlers came to the New World, the Marshfolk were gradually pushed back along the northern edge of the Dragon's Spine mountains into the marshes and forests at the headwaters of the First and Second Rivers. Someplace where their madness and mysticism could not taint the remains of humanity.

Of course, the more Neb learned firsthand from his dealings with the Marshers and their leader, the more he questioned the Order's interpretation of events. The Marshfolk were certainly different, but not necessarily *mad*.

Neb blinked away the history and stood, grabbing up his knife belt and buckling it on. Aedric looked him over and adjusted the scarf of rank, turning the knot around to the inside of his arm. "You've commanded men during a time of war," he said as he adjusted it. "This is the proper way to show that."

Neb didn't think of it as commanding men during war. He had commanded an army of gravediggers, doing his best to keep them alive and fed while the armies sallied out around them. He'd lost twenty men that winter to stray arrows and miscommunication and cold. Still, in the eyes of the scouts it was what it was. Neb was a veteran commander who felt like an orphaned boy most days. "Thank you, Captain," he said, moving toward the door.

Aedric paused. "You may want to go easy on the firespice tonight. And if you intend to see more of your girl, you should be ready for an early muster."

Neb's puzzlement must've shown.

Aedric saw the surprise and continued. "We've received word from the Keeper's Wall. Strange things afoot at the gate. We ride out with Rudolfo and Isaak in the morning."

Neb felt the disappointment like a knife. Tomorrow was to be a holiday, and he'd planned to spend it with Winters as her schedule allowed. Still, he felt the curiosity as well. "What is happening at the wall?"

Aedric shook his head. "Tomorrow. I'll brief you when we're under way." He grinned. "Meanwhile, make the most of your night, Neb."

The large hand settled on his shoulder once more, and Neb suddenly remembered his father's hand there. It seemed so long ago. Brother Hebda had been a fair, kind, large man who did more for his unsanctioned son than most Androfrancines. He'd even gotten Neb a grant to assist with a dig in the far east of the Old World. One morning they were loading the wagons, setting out along that same road— the Whymer Way—that led over the Keeper's Wall at Fargoer's Station and into the Churning Wastes beyond it. And by afternoon, Neb was alone in the world, watching the fire and lightning consume the only home and family he'd ever known.

He thought of Rudolfo, of Aedric, and last of Winters. *I have a new family now.* And somewhere ahead, he thought, a new home if Winters and the Marsh Kings before her dreamed true.

Neb forced a smile. "It will be a fine night," he said. With a nod, Aedric walked to the door, and Neb followed after him.

He may not get his day with Winters but perhaps, he thought, he could have what remained of the night. The manor was filled with hidden passages—he'd used his knowledge of architecture and strategic building design to find most of them after stumbling across the first by accident. Maybe, when the party wound down, he would slip off to spend a few quiet hours with her before he left for the Keeper's Gate.

Maybe.

Thoughts of it started him blushing all over again, and Neb found himself hoping that Aedric didn't notice.

If he did, that First Captain of the Gypsy Scouts said nothing of it. Instead, Aedric laughed and clapped in time to the music from downstairs, improvising a shuffle-booted jig as he danced down the corridor toward the great, sweeping staircase.

Without prompting, Neb joined him in the dance and wondered what the night might bring him.

Petronus

Petronus looked out his cottage window before pushing another log onto the fire and returning to his crowded desk. He couldn't quite place the feeling that kept him checking his window, but it was an uneasiness in his soul, the sense that a reckoning approached him.

I have earned a reckoning, he thought.

He was a fisherman's son, but he had felt the call to the Androfrancines, and had joined the order to preserve and protect the light. He'd started out an acolyte like everyone else and had climbed the ranks to become their youngest Pope. Then, after a painfully short papacy, he'd left believing his life was becoming a lie. He faked his own assassination with the help of an eager successor and went back to his nets and his boat in the quiet waters of Caldus Bay. And the longer he was away, the more he was convinced that the Androfrancines' backward dream no longer served the New World.

But then came the day he saw Windwir's pyre in the northern skies. They'd brought back the spell of Xhum Y'Zir—despite his warnings—and it had undone them, reducing the world's greatest city to a Desolation of ash and bone.

I have earned a reckoning.

He looked back to his desk. It was awash with paper. Every flat surface of his one-room shack was, too. Notes and maps and scraps of parchment.

At the center of it all, on his desk, lay the leather satchel Vlad Li Tam had given him on the day Petronus had executed Sethbert. With the same knife he'd used to gut ten thousand salmon, he'd cut Sethbert's throat in front of them all in one final act that disqualified him as Pope and disbanded the Order. He had already invoked Papal Sanction to transfer the Order's vast holdings and wealth into the care of the Ninefold Forest Houses. Rudolfo would rebuild the library and take guardianship of the light.

He reached into the open satchel and drew out the papers. He'd read them every day for the last seven months, and in the first weeks he'd read them over and over again, committing them to memory. He could recite them; and on good days, when his hands were steadier, he probably could've drawn the maps and illustrations they contained.

He studied them again now, starting with the first page.

*By Order of Petronus, Holy See of the Androfrancine Order
and King of Windwir.*

His own name on the first form, authorizing research into the re-production of the mechoservitors from Rufello's *Book of Specifications* and the scattered, broken pieces of the Old World. And his own signa-ture marked by the papal signet. This one didn't bother him as much. He remembered seeing the head and torso and arm of that first model, remembered the sweltering heat of the massive boiler they'd required to power his basic functions. Still, it was the most impressive me-chanical feat of the Old World that they'd been able to re-create until that moment. He remembered signing this order. It was the one be-neath it that perplexed and enraged him.

It opened the same way.

*By Order of Petronus, Holy See of the Androfrancine Order
and King of Windwir.*

But the unthinkable order that followed baffled him. Though it had nearly blinded him, Petronus had read every scrap of parchment he attached his signature and seal to over the course of his papacy. He had not signed this one. He would never have signed it.

But below, with the signet beside, his signature stared back on the order. It called for expediting the restoration of Xhum Y'Zir's Seven Cacophonic Deaths in conjunction with the Office of Mechanical Sci-ences, ordering thirteen expeditions into the Churning Wastes under Gray Guard protection and magicked courier.

He'd not signed that, but someone had. And it had paved the way for all of the papers that followed. For two generations of metal men not intended merely to serve but also to be weapons, somehow immune to Y'Zir's spell and thus perfect carriers for it. And for studies into the effects of limited recitals of the spell at strategic points in the Named Lands.

No wonder Sethbert acted, Petronus thought. He had thought the Or-der intended to attack him.

And here was the only note Tam left, the only explanation of his work to secure the light in Rudolfo's wood and of his father's work to build and break a Pope that the Order might be ended and the light might pass to safer hands.

They meant to protect us.

Somewhere, beyond the Named Lands, the Androfrancines feared something. Something powerful enough to turn them toward the weapon that Desolated the Old World and ushered in the Age of Laughing Madness. They of all people knew the power of that spell; they held the keys to the Keeper's Gate and salvaged the Churning Wastes for scraps of light. They saw firsthand that handiwork two thousand years later, a wasteland of scrub and rock and fused glass and the dust of bones.

Whatever they feared, it had to be significant to bring *that* weapon among all others.

And what if that threat somehow turned the Androfrancines' weapon against them, using Sethbert as their pawn? Or worse, what if the fear of an outside threat was manufactured in a great misdirection ultimately designed to bring about the restoration of the spell and the destruction of the Androfrancines and their library? That pointed to a network of connections, skilled in forgery and espionage, with access to the Order's archives and the resolve to murder a city. Vlad Li Tam was still the most likely candidate. But they'd known each other as boys, and Petronus believed him when he said that Rudolfo was his work, not the Desolation of Windwir.

Why would he give me the evidence?

The work bore the mark of a Tam. And Vlad had moved quickly to dismantle his network and remove it from the Named Lands. His house was surely involved in some manner. Why else would he flee, taking his vast system of courtesans and spies out of play, closing down the bank they had operated for generation upon generation and passing the House Li Tam holdings over to the Order in the days just prior to the Order's holdings passing to Rudolfo?

Or perhaps there was indeed an outside threat. Perhaps the document that Petronus hadn't signed was not a Tam forgery but the product of some hidden group within the Order bent on a secret agenda to defend the light at any and all costs.

Seven months ago, with Sethbert's blood still under his fingernails, Petronus had given himself to the work of finding out.

He put the papers back into the satchel and went again to the window. A reckoning. The feeling was stronger, but the night was quiet. High above, a sliver of blue-green moon shone in the star-speckled sky. Petronus sighed and pulled the rough fabric curtains closed.

He shrugged out of his robe and pulled on his sleeping shirt before crawling into his narrow bed. He pulled the wool blankets up around his neck and lay on his side, watching the fire across the room. The light dancing there was not much comfort to him, but eventually sleep pulled him down into cold but strong arms. The fire continued in his dreams. A burning village, a smoldering city. Blood beneath his fingernails.

He stirred at a sound and sat up quickly when the door to his shack swung open. His fingers curled around the handle of the fishing knife he kept beneath his pillow.

The magick-muffled voice came to him from across the room, but Petronus saw nothing there. "And thus," it said, "are the sins of P'Andro Whym visited upon his children."

Petronus smiled and rose to the reckoning with his knife in hand.

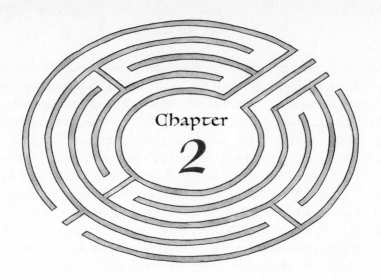

Chapter

2

Winters

Winteria bat Mardic looked out over Rudolfo's gardens from her balcony, wondering how it was that she had come here for a boy.

The noise of her host's Firstborn Feast filled the cold night, and she imagined the show Hanric gave them on her behalf. It was strange to be the Marsh King, she thought. *Queen.* Soon enough she would come into her majority and take the Firstfall axe and the Wicker Throne away from Hanric. Her father's closest friend had trained her for that day along with the Androfrancine scholar they had hired away from those gray-robed thieves. She was nearly ready for the rest of the world to know the truth.

Her people knew the truth and kept her trust. They'd learned the hard way that it was better to keep Marsher business in the Marshlands. But for outside eyes, she was a servant in the Marsh King's entourage, kept about for nefarious reasons, according to their neighbors in the New World. She had it on good authority that Androfrancine intelligence had once noted her role as that of soothsayer and companion. Under normal circumstances, surrounded by just her tribe, she ruled quietly and served her people by adding her dreams to the Book of Dreaming Kings. In these affairs of state she truly had no place. But she had not come here for Rudolfo's Firstborn Feast, though it was a fine occasion to honor.

She had come here for a boy. Nebios ben Hebda, the Homeseeker.

Snow had slowed their journey to the Ninefold Forest, and their entourage had arrived that morning to a quiet but public welcome. Hanric, as her shadow, followed the forms with gruff acquiescence. The Named Lands saw a giant barbarian with bits of wood and bone woven into his long beard and his tangled hair, carrying an enormous axe. That's what the Marshfolk needed the Named Lands to see to keep them frightened. After the public reception, she'd spent a few hours talking with Rudolfo in a quiet place about the unrest on the Delta and elsewhere in the Named Lands, had lunched with the other servants and then sought out Neb. Rudolfo and Neb were the only two beyond her own people who knew the truth about her. The rest believed the image the Marshers projected, and few drew close enough to learn otherwise. The Marshfolk kept to themselves, and their neighbors preferred it that way. There was a saying, though she didn't know if it was in use much these days. *As welcome as a Marsher at a wedding.* For two thousand years, they'd huddled in the north in lands they'd not chosen, biding their time and waiting for the season that would bring about the end of their sorrow in the Named Lands.

Like Rudolfo's kin, the Marshers had arrived ahead of the other settlers and had chosen their lands well. And like the Foresters, their unusual relationship with the fallen wizard kings cast suspicion upon them and kept them set apart. But unlike Rudolfo's Gypsies, they had been unable to hold their lands, and the young Androfrancine Order had pushed them farther north, into the marshes and scrub at the base of the Dragon's Spine so that the militant scholars and archeologists could establish their second fortress in the New World there on the banks of the Second River.

The Named Lands were safer with the Marshfolk contained, according to Pope Windwir, the poet whose name had been given to that fort years later when the library was young and the Order was finding its legs. After all, those protectors of the light reasoned, these were the near-kin of Xhum Y'Zir and his seven sons, the Wizard Kings of the Old World. It didn't help that many of the hallmarks of the Age of Laughing Madness had never quite bred out of her people despite their pilgrimage from the Churning Wastes so long ago.

Of course, Winters understood this. She was the first queen in their long history—and the first to receive an Androfrancine education of sorts. Her people covered themselves in the ash and mud of the land as a constant reminder of their sorrow. They embraced superstition and mysticism, preferring prophecy and glossolalia to the so-called Androfrancine light; their kings preached those dreams to the Named Lands during times of war, and they still practiced the alchemy of blood magick in a limited fashion.

They were a different people, Winters realized, and her limited understanding of history—both in the New World and the Old World—was that being different did not often bode well unless you were stronger than those peoples considered to be the norm. So they waited, hidden in the north, only riding forth to raid the border towns. They kept kin-clave with none and were even hostile from time to time, depending where the dreams carried them.

But everything had changed last year when Windwir fell and the war they had prayed for and longed for began there on the bone-scattered plains of the fallen city. She'd led her army down from the north with Hanric bearing the axe of her office as her shadow, honoring the dreams and announcing kin-clave with the Gypsies, knowing that somehow Rudolfo's blade guarded the way to their new home. That change alone was enough.

But then she'd fallen into someone else's dreams and found herself face-to-face with the promised Homeseeker himself, Nebios ben Hebda, the Androfrancine orphan. And more: She'd grown to know the awkward boy who had seen Windwir fall beneath Xhum Y'Zir's spell, and she thought she might love him.

And so she had come for a boy. Now she had seen him, and it had frightened her. The feelings he stirred up within her felt larger than her heart could contain, and there was an edge to it that felt sharp enough that it could cut a part of her soul away if she let it.

Maybe it has already? She wasn't sure. Her own mother had not lived long enough to talk to her daughter about these things. Hanric was the closest thing she had to a father, and he left those matters for her to ascertain through the women among her household. She'd not asked them. She'd not felt it proper.

Still, ever since that day at the edge of the Desolation, she couldn't help but imagine Neb's mouth on hers and his hands moving along her hips and sides and shoulders. Even now, she shuddered a bit. After that kiss, their dreams had shifted. They dreamed of the new home Neb would find, of being limb-tangled and naked in a silk-draped bed, staring up at a massive, swollen, brown-and-blue world that filled the sky. Birds sang around them. Water cascaded nearby. Occasionally in those dreams, they kissed again, but most of their dreams were flashes of light, bent images of the world, vast expanses of sand and glass and scrub.

Seeing him today, kissing him today, was even more powerful than the dreams, and a part of her hoped that tonight, after he'd had his fill of the feast, he would find her and kiss her again.

She blushed at the thought of it despite the cold wind on her cheeks.

"You're a silly girl," she said to herself and the night. "Not much of a queen at all."

She turned to let herself back inside the manor when she heard a distant and growing sound carried by a slight breeze. She felt her stomach lurch and her mouth pull downward and twist. Before she could catch herself, her legs gave out, and she dropped to the snow-crusted balcony floor. She felt her body contort and her eyes blinking as the words swept over her and out of her in a torrent of glossolalia. She bucked and twisted against it every time; she didn't know why.

Heaven must be resisted at all costs. Finally, she gave herself to ecstasy and utterance. The words tumbled and expanded as she felt her eyes widening. But this ecstasy was suddenly hot, suddenly intrusive, and Winters felt the prying ache of it. She took the logos out of heaven's tongue and spoke it. *A wind of blood that cleanses. A cold iron blade that prunes that which is found wanting on the vine.*

The fit passed and she sat up slowly. The noise was louder and closer now, spreading from the forest through the town, over the gates of the manor, and she recognized it. The lurching in her stomach was now a knot that ached.

The Seventh Forest Manor was at Third Alarm.

Vlad Li Tam

Vlad Li Tam stood barefoot on the night-cooled sand and watched the sun wash the sky purple with morning. The last of the stars tucked themselves away, and the birds, already announcing the day, matched their growing volume to the growing light. The air was heavy and wet and warm, and a breeze from the water moved over his naked skin. He could smell the salt of the sea mingled with last night's sweat. Behind him, the girl in his hammock yawned and stirred. He glanced over his shoulder at her and smiled. She smiled back and inclined her head.

He returned her nod and watched her scramble to her feet and flee the beach.

No doubt to tell her father what transpired here. He chuckled.

He stretched, feeling his joints pop and his tendons crack. He'd surprised himself last night. At seventy-two he rarely pursued fleshly liaisons, but kin-clave in the Scattered Isles operated at a baser level. For the last seven months, he'd witnessed the island rites and rituals firsthand, participating himself when necessary and sending one of his sons or daughters when it was not. Each island was similar to the others in practice, and most fell within the more primitive social forms of the rites that had kept the Settlers alive in the New World. Far from the Named Lands, the disconnected islands and their scattering of villages followed a method Vlad Li Tam was most familiar with—the expanding bonds of family—to establish a network of trust and trade.

He had arrived yesterday morning, anchoring his massive iron steam-driven vessel within eyesight of the village lookout. They'd sent up the blue smoke of inquiry, and Vlad had launched a bird to them with the green thread of peace tied to its foot. Six of his sons had rowed him ashore by longboat and waited politely aloof while he bartered kin-clave with the chieftain. In the end, they had settled on the chieftain's younger brother's oldest daughter—young, pretty, and more coy than shy. Vlad Li Tam smiled at the memory of her flashing white teeth offset by her dusky skin and her wide, dark eyes. His sons had withdrawn so that he could consummate the strategic alliance, and Vlad Li Tam had waited on the beach, appropriately distant from the village to show that he was clearly an outsider.

She had come to him when the moon rose up over the silver sea and cast lines of blue and green across the waters. She'd been eager, and certainly, he realized, this was not the first time she'd happily given herself for the good of their remote collection of villages. She'd coaxed his seed from him twice that night, and they both took and gave pleasure on one another's behalf, their quiet noises offset by the surf and the sounds of monkeys and birds in the jungle.

It had been a fine night, and now, once she reported that the rites of kin-clave had been satisfied, that the old man had indeed risen to the occasion, they would spend the day feasting as Vlad Li Tam and all of his sons and daughters now at sea with him in their iron armada celebrated with their new allies and trade partners.

You are too old for this. And yet twice in one night. Shaking his head, he walked to the surf and urinated into the ocean. He stood there for a time, scanning the horizon.

This far out, there were no other islands visible to the naked eye, but he could trace them out on the map of his memory. This was their tenth in the last three months. Each had required slightly different tribute, but most had focused on allowing the potential of offspring to unite the two tribes. It made a crude but practical kind of sense. The farther southwest they sailed, the less populated the islands became. Those islanders and villages they found lived quiet lives of abundance and knew little to nothing of what happened beyond their own island.

Until Windwir was destroyed, the Androfrancines had paid generous fees to keep ocean traffic at a minimum. From time to time, they'd even called upon House Li Tam to use their iron armada to enforce their control. And because they'd given the Tam shipbuilders the specifications for those iron vessels, Vlad Li Tam had been most willing to render assistance. Before they'd turned to banking over five centuries ago, the Tams had been the Named Lands' biggest shipbuilding concern, so working from Rufello's re-created design sheets had not been much challenge. Powering the vessels had been harder—but the Androfrancines and their Arch-Engineer Charles had seen to that under a veil of secrecy that Tam honored as part of his secret kin-clave with the Order. The engine housings were massive Rufello lockboxes, the ciphers of which were lost when Windwir's great library fell to Xhum Y'Zir's spell. It wasn't hard to extrapolate, though, that the same sunstones that powered the mechoservitors also powered the steam engines for Vlad Li Tam's fleet of ships.

Vlad Li Tam heard footsteps behind him and turned slowly, mindful that he still wore no clothing. The chieftain and several others approached, including the girl. She still smiled.

"Hello, my friend," the chieftain called out in a loud voice. He also smiled.

Vlad Li Tam returned the smile. "Hello, Dayfather Ulno Shalon." He used the title now to indicate his kin-clave. They were speaking an older form of Lower Landlish that had been pidgined together with a handful of Named Land dialects all built from the languages of the Old World. The people of the Divided Isle and the other islands close enough for the Named Lands to place them on a map spoke an easily intelligible dialect. But the farther out they'd gone, the less effective the common tongues became. There were scattered words here and there, but not with any rhyme or reason.

Finally, he'd put the children on the problem, turning them loose with island children, positioning his older sons and daughters nearby to capture the vocabularies. They'd learned enough at the first two islands in this particular archipelago to carry on conversations with the others. And with each stop, once kin-clave was established, he turned the children loose again.

The chieftain was a short, plump man in a ratty cap that Vlad Li Tam recognized as an officer's hat from the Entrolusian river patrol. He wore little else besides that and a length of faded cloth twisted around his middle. Bits of bone and feather decorated the cap, and his grin continued as he approached Vlad Li Tam with open arms.

"I trust my"—here he used a term that Vlad Li Tam was not familiar with—"performed her duties for the tribe in a satisfactory manner?"

Vlad Li Tam nodded, winking to the girl as she smiled out at him from behind her uncle. "Yes, Dayfather. She was more than satisfactory."

"I will hope for a strong son," the chieftain said, "that his hands may join us in our work."

Vlad Li Tam touched his head and then his chest. "And I will hope for a beautiful daughter," Vlad Li Tam replied, according to their custom, "that she might bring lightness to the heart of your people."

Satisfied, the chieftain nodded. "Your tribe is now kin-clave with mine. Today, we will celebrate this joining, and from this day forward you will have haven among us."

Vlad Li Tam smiled. It had been a small price to pay to gain this people's trust and earn the right to walk freely among them. Of course, there was the matter of the girl. Though it wasn't required, it was certainly customary for him to keep trying until the seed took hold, and judging from last night's experience, she would be an eager partner in that work. And he didn't mind the effort. They did not need to know that no child could possibly come from this union. His sixth daughter, Rae Li Tam, had taken care of that, giving him the powders he would need to dull his soldiers' swords before they marched through the gate.

The two men embraced, and the Dayfather left with his entourage. Vlad Li Tam watched him go, then walked to the hammock in its thatched lean-to to dress himself. Offshore, he saw the first of his iron ships come around the cliff side of the island, steam belching into a clear sky. Drawing a mirror from his pocket, he flashed a message to it in the House code of the Tams. They would drop anchor in the island's single natural harbor and begin offloading their contribution of kin-clave for the tribal feast. Wines and spirits like this people had never tasted. Cheeses and breads. And steel tools and a few choice bolts of brightly colored silk. The Tam armada would stop here, their blacksmith would set up his anvil and furnace to do minor repairs both to the ships and to the assorted metal goods these people had traded for in years past. From the outside, they would appear to take their rest among the Dayfather's people for a fortnight. But in that time, his sons and his daughters would do the work he had made them for. They would build alliances; they would gather information; they would compile their findings and compare what they learned. When their stay here was complete, House Li Tam's network would include this small island and its remote tribe. And this people's knowledge and history would be added to the matrix that he built.

When light flashed back to him, confirming his command, Vlad Li Tam tucked the mirror away. So far, in seven months of searching, he'd found nothing substantial but had not wavered in his conviction. Somewhere out here there had to be proof.

He'd studied Sethbert's so-called evidence of Androfrancine aggression carefully and had reached the only possible conclusion: The Androfrancines were afraid of something. Something so threatening to them and their light that they would bring back Y'Zir's spell and create a generation of mechoservitors to carry it. Their maps, with their strategic lines drawn and delivery points marked at key locations, indicated a fear of invasion along the Outer Emerald Coast with a secondary incursion onto the Delta. And Tam knew now that someone had bent his own network of children to bring down Windwir. But who and why?

It was folly to believe that the Named Lands, set apart from the rest of the spell-blasted continent by the Keeper's Wall, was the only place left where life could be sustained. The Wizard King, in his wrath, had brought down the world; but like these islands now grown apart from the Named Lands, there had to be pockets of life elsewhere.

And so the question was: Which pocket of life had engineered the end of the Androfrancine Order and the destruction of its Great Library? And how had they controlled his family to accomplish this horrific task?

So far, his search had borne no fruit, but Vlad Li Tam was a patient man.

I will have the truth, he thought.

But when he did, Vlad Li Tam wondered, what would he do with it?

Rudolfo

It happened faster than Rudolfo thought possible. One moment, he was leaning over to whisper something to Aedric about the quality of Hanric's singing, and in the next, the music and laughter of the feast vanished beneath the sudden call to Third Alarm. The double doors of the Great Hall burst inward, and a muffled pandemonium swept into the room—his own Gypsy Scouts at the center of it, knives dancing and connecting with invisible blades. They already bled from a dozen cuts of varying severity, their winter uniforms slashed and stained with their blood. The invisible assailants did not stop, and judging by the flood of sentries and armed servants now pouring into the room, they had not stopped since breaching the border.

Aedric pushed away from the table, reaching for the ceremonial knife he wore and whistling the men to guard their king.

Guard our guests first, Rudolfo signed as he drew the narrow sword he'd chosen to decorate his outfit. Aedric nodded.

The tornado moved through the large room, breaking tables and scattering food, shattering dishes and bottles as the unmagicked Gypsy Scouts sought to contain this sudden invisible threat.

How many? It was impossible for Rudolfo to say. But they were strong and fast and silent and deadly, cutting through servant, scout and guest alike as they made their way to the head table.

Hanric bellowed, knocking the table over and reaching for the silver axe of the Marsh King's office. The giant Marsher was on his feet, his escort surrounding him with weapons drawn as the clamor approached.

Across from Hanric, Ansylus the Crown Prince of Turam shot Rudolfo a surprised glance as he climbed to his feet. "What manner of—"

Before he could finish, his own guards were down beneath a storm of steel. The Crown Prince himself flew back against the wall, tossed by unseen shoulders, bucking and twitching as hidden knives found him and pierced him with surgical precision. Three Gypsy Scouts pressed the attacker as Rudolfo's guest slumped to the floor, eyes already glassy in death.

Rudolfo lunged in with his sword and felt it strike cloth and then flesh. He pushed and twisted, withdrew, then thrust again. Something heavy and panting collapsed, lifted itself from the floor, and staggered through the wall of men that surrounded it. They fell easily before its strength, then rallied and rode it back down to the ground, where it twitched and burbled.

Around the room, clusters of men pressed similar attackers with similar result.

Rudolfo turned to Hanric and his bodyguards.

Two of the three guards had fallen, and the last stood between the shadow of his king and the blades of these invisible assailants. Rudolfo moved in with his sword, letting it dart here and there at what he hoped were the backs of knees and the smalls of backs, and he whistled for Aedric. As Aedric and three other Gypsy Scouts approached, the Marsh Queen's shadow's last remaining guard fell with a cry. Before the body hit the floor, Hanric's axe swept up to wet itself on one of the attackers. The axe hummed from the blood, and Rudolfo stared at the double-headed weapon. There in the silver reflection he saw too many arms, too many torsos. Too many knives.

The axe reveals them. Even as he realized it, he shouted it to the room. "You can see their reflection in the axe."

He moved in closer and found himself against a wall of transparent flesh. He pushed at it with his sword.

Sudden hands that he could not see lifted Rudolfo from the floor with a strength far beyond that of any scout magick he knew. Then he heard the muffled sound of a slap and a distant voice. "No," the voice whispered. "Not him."

Rudolfo fell to the floor as the hands released him. He whipped his sword up and felt it snag in cloth and skin. "Who are you?" he hissed at the unseen foe.

Hanric bellowed, and Rudolfo looked up to see a jagged red tear erupting down Hanric's forearm. Aedric and the others were pressing to reach him, held back by a storm of knives. All of the fighting now centered on the man the Named Lands considered the Marsh King.

Rudolfo pushed forward as another cut opened Hanric's chest. Roaring his rage, the Gypsy King dodged and thrust with his narrow sword, whistling out the chorus of "The Fourteenth Hymn of the Wandering Army." His men rallied to the strategy, but even that failed.

Two more fell to Hanric's blade before they overcame him. He went down with a shout, and Rudolfo growled low in his throat.

Then, the invisible wall struck Rudolfo again, pushing him over and aside as the attackers retreated. The Gypsy Scouts pursued them as they fled the Great Hall. Rudolfo nodded at the axe clutched in Hanric's hands. "Take that," he shouted to another scout. "Use it to search every inch of this manor. Then search the town."

He stood still for a moment, stunned by the events. He'd fought in dozens of skirmishes, had even led a few wars, and last year he'd worn the magicks to raid Sethbert's camp. In all of his years under the knife, he'd not encountered anything like this. And now two of the Named Land's leaders lay dead in his own home. He took in the room, eyes wandering the scattered bodies and food, the broken tables, the clusters of guards and guests and servants. He could hear loud voices on the other side of the barricaded door.

He saw Neb, shaking and white, his own ceremonial knife still hanging loosely in his hand. His uniform was torn, and he bled from a few cuts. "Where's Isaak?"

Neb pointed, and Rudolfo spotted him across the room. "Ask him to join me," he said. Neb nodded and went as Aedric approached.

Rudolfo looked at his First Captain. He was more shaken than his father would've been, but still grim and resolved. "What do you know, Aedric?"

Aedric's brow furrowed. "Little so far, General. The western watch sounded Third Alarm and launched their birds, but the aggressors outran word of their arrival."

"They outran the birds?"

Aedric nodded. "Yes, General."

"On foot?"

Aedric nodded again.

"Gods," Rudolfo whispered.

Rudolfo knelt by Hanric and reached over to close the dead man's eyes. He felt rage brewing within him.

They come to my very home on the night of my Firstborn Feast. He stood and went to the Crown Prince, kneeling to close his eyes as well. "Who else have we lost?"

Aedric counted off on his fingers. "Most of Turam's guards, all of the Marsher scouts, ten of our own scouts, four servants." He paused. "The Seventh Manor's army contingent has rallied at the gates."

Rudolfo's Wandering Army, made up of most of the Ninefold

Forest's able-bodied men, was a powerful force to be reckoned with. He nodded. "Set them to the search. Create a perimeter around the town and library. They are to hold it until further notice."

Aedric nodded and left.

Rudolfo moved, and his foot struck something heavy on the floor. He looked down at nothing. Soon enough, as with all magicks, these would fade and they would have a look at the assassins.

Neb and Isaak approached. The mechoservitor wheezed slightly as his bellows pumped. His jeweled eyes sparked and flashed.

Rudolfo looked at his metal friend. "In your work at the library— during the restoration and the time before—have you heard of such a thing? Magicks like these?"

Isaak nodded. "Only from the histories of the Old World, Lord, in the Age of the Wizard Kings."

Rudolfo sighed. "Blood magick, then." The Androfrancines had kept tight control of their pharmaceuticals and magicks, doling out some of the earth magicks among the nations of the Named Lands, holding back most in their effort to keep humanity safe from itself. But the Articles of Kin-Clave expressly forbade the use of blood magick. Blood magick—in the form of Xhum Y'Zir's Seven Cacophonic Deaths— had brought down the Old World. And two thousand years later, it brought down Windwir. He turned to Isaak. "I want you to set your brethren to scouring the catalogs for everything you can find on this."

Isaak nodded. "Yes, Lord Rudolfo."

"And send for the River Woman." The River Woman mixed their scout magicks and medicines. Perhaps, Rudolfo thought, she'd know something.

The metal man nodded again, then turned and limped away quickly. Rudolfo looked to Neb. "How are you, lad?"

Neb's eyes were narrow and red, focused on Hanric where he lay in a pool of congealing blood. "I'm fine, General."

"Find Winters. Tell her what's transpired and bring her to my study."

"She will want to see Hanric," Neb said.

Rudolfo shook his head. "There will be time enough for that later. Take a half-squad with you."

Hanric was like a father to her, Rudolfo knew. He'd ruled on her behalf since she was a child, even younger than Rudolfo was when he'd taken the turban. He'd been only twelve the day his parents were murdered by Vlad Li Tam's seventh son, the heretic Fontayne.

Another orphan, Rudolfo realized, like the tall, slender young man before him. Like himself.

I am an orphan who collects orphans, he thought.

Barking orders, he moved through the bloodstained ruins of his Firstborn Feast to stop at the guarded double doors. Beyond those doors, a crowd gathered wanting answers.

Beyond them, the world would soon enough want to know the same. With fires of insurrection and civil war raging in the south, the New World still reeled from the Desolation of Windwir and the loss of their Androfrancine protectors. The assassination of the Crown Prince of Turam and of the man the world thought of as the Marsh King would feed into the chaos already brewing.

"No. Not him," the voice had said when one of the magicked assassins held Rudolfo at bay.

Why not me? It unsettled him, cold in the pit of his stomach. There had been three prominent lords in the room. And now two were dead. And before the feast, word of the metal man in Androfrancine robes that approached the Keeper's Gate, claiming to be Charles the Arch-Engineer, with his admonition to protect Sanctorum Lux.

A Whymer Maze to be sure.

Even I wait for answers, he realized.

Rudolfo thought of his formidable betrothed, who also waited for answers, no doubt outside the room and angry that she'd not been permitted to enter.

He thought of the child she carried, his son—Jakob, named for Rudolfo's father. It was a sudden and unexpected gift that Jin Li Tam had brought to the middle of his road, in the shadow of war, at the time of Rudolfo's greatest unrest. She'd told him the night he returned from confronting her father. Vlad Li Tam's confession was still playing itself out behind his eyes when she had joined him in his dead brother's room and shared her news.

Earlier tonight, he'd thought perhaps they were making the world and that the knives he passed forward to his son must be sharp and balanced for him to continue that work.

But perhaps, Rudolfo realized, the world was making *them*. And perhaps the blades best be sharp and balanced so that Jakob—and the Ninefold Forest Houses—could survive that making.

Chapter
3

Petronus

Fear, Petronus thought, *is a powerful thing.* It gripped him now, squeezing his chest and turning his stomach to water.

He squinted into the dimly lit room in the direction of the voice, gripping the fishing knife tightly in his hand. Shadows from the guttering fire danced in his one-room shack. His mouth was dry, but he spoke around it.

"Who are you to punish me for P'Andro Whym's sins?" he asked. "Who are you to declare my kin-clave with him?"

"Who I am is unimportant." This time, the voice came from a different corner of the room. "You are Petronus, King of Windwir and Holy See of the Androfrancine Order."

Petronus sneered. "Windwir and the Order are no more. My question stands. Who are you?"

The voice moved again, and when it spoke, it did not answer Petronus's question. "Put down your knife, old man. You can't stand against me."

Petronus knew it was true. He was in no shape to face down a magicked assailant. Those earth powders of the Old World, when ingested, rendered a man stronger, faster, quieter in addition to bending the light around him and making him all but impossible to see in bright daylight. Here, in a shadowed room, Petronus would be dead before he saw the faintest trace of his attacker.

But why hasn't he simply killed me? Petronus swallowed. "I may not be able to stand against you," he said, "but I'll still take what flesh I can."

The low voice chuckled. "My master sent a squad for the others. He sent me alone for you because you are old and alone." There was a rush of wind, a strangely sweet odor, and Petronus felt fire on his cheek as cold, sharp iron drew a line of blood. He lunged forward with his own blade but found nothing. Another chuckle. "I can cut you all night, Last Son."

Because you are old and alone. The words settled in. "Last Son?"

The wind rushed again. This time, the knife slid through the sleeve of Petronus's nightshirt to draw a long, shallow gash down the length of his left upper arm. Wincing, Petronus swiped at the air with his blade again. He gritted his teeth against the pain. "Are you here to kill me or to hurt me?"

"Both," the voice whispered.

In that moment, the door and windows of his shack burst inward. Glass and splinters showered the room as a hurricane swept in from the windless night outside. He heard the sudden, muffled sound of boots on wood and heavy breathing from at least three points around the room. The attacker cried out, and Petronus braced himself; but this time, when the wind surged toward him a wall met it and the magicked blades made a muffled clinking noise as they clashed. A single eye, bloodstained and blue, appeared near Petronus's own eye. "Stay out of the way," a new voice said. "Leave us to our work." Then, the storm continued as something heavy hurled across the room to fall into his wooden chair and collapse it beneath the weight.

The voice was familiar to him. A voice from long ago that he could not place. Petronus pushed himself back into the corner, where his cot met the wall, still holding the knife out ahead of him though he knew it was a useless gesture. He watched the wind sweep his room, breaking furniture, scattering papers, shattering dishes as it went. It was impossible to know how many were in the shack now, but he heard the muffled grunts and cries of at least five men amid the magick-dulled clank of steel. Twice, he heard heavy bodies falling to the floor, and once he heard the hushed fluid whistle of a punctured lung. The fight seemed to last for an hour, though Petronus knew it could only be minutes.

The fire sparked and went out as something fell into it and the room went dark. The scuffling continued, then suddenly stopped.

Petronus heard scrambling and hushed whispers. He thought he heard the words "Both dead."

The new voice was near him now when it spoke next. "Where is your constable?"

Petronus blinked, not sure he was truly being addressed until the voice asked again, this time louder. "Third house down from the inn," he finally said. When he spoke, his voice shook.

"Balthus, quietly borrow the good man's manacles."

They've taken him alive. "I have rope in the boathouse," Petronus offered.

"Rope won't hold him. Not until his magicks wear off. And I don't know how long the kallacaine will keep him down." The familiarity of the voice nagged Petronus. He'd heard it long ago, but he'd also heard it more recently. He added it to what he already knew. They were magicked, and they were versed in pharmaceuticals. There were six of them, but two were now dead. And he knew their leader from somewhere.

"Let me see your arm," the voice said.

A spark flared, and the lantern glowed to life. The room was a shambles of papers, broken glass and pottery, overturned furniture. His front door was down and his three windows were out.

Petronus extended his arm, feeling the sting of the cut. "It's not bad," he said. He felt fingers gently pushing back the bloody sleeve and opened his mouth to ask who exactly his rescuer was when the realization struck him like a trout strikes a line. *Grymlis.*

Petronus didn't realize he'd said it aloud until he heard the old soldier's grunt. "Yes, Father."

He still calls me by my title. The last time he'd seen the Gray Guard captain, he'd sent him and his soldiers away. With Rudolfo's Gypsy Scouts to protect the new library there'd been no role for the scattered leftovers of the Androfrancine army.

Once, years ago, Grymlis had been the captain who carried out one of Petronus's darker orders. The Marshers had attacked the Order's protectorate and ransacked a convoy; Petronus had sent the Gray Guard up into their lands to burn out a village as reprisal. They'd left the dead unburied, adding grievous insult to their message, and the young Pope had ordered that weathered captain to show him the village so that he would understand fully what he'd done.

Not long after, Petronus had left the Order and Grymlis had gone on to serve Introspect, and for a time, Sethbert's puppet, Pope Resolute.

"The last time I saw you," Petronus said, "you were burying your uniform in the Ninefold Forest."

Grymlis chuckled. "Aye, Father." He was cleaning and dressing the wound now, his face close enough that Petronus could see its dim outline in the lantern light.

A question chewed at him. Dozens did, Petronus realized, but he pushed them aside and ordered them as best he could. "How did you know to be here tonight?"

"I've had two men on shifts in Caldus Bay since the week you returned from the Forest," Grymlis said.

Magicked this entire time, Petronus thought. There was a clatter in the doorway and soft footfalls as Balthus returned with the manacles. "Chain him in the boathouse," Grymlis said, "and gag him." The old soldier finished bandaging Petronus's arm and then stood. "When you're finished, load Marco and Tyrn into the boat and cover them. We'll bury them in the bay."

Petronus opened his mouth to protest, but Grymlis must've seen it. "They've no kin to claim them. Their kin were in Windwir." Grymlis paused. "And it's better that we not be seen."

Petronus watched as the room began to right itself. The unbroken pieces of furniture were tipped back into their proper places, and the broom on his wall, seemingly of its own volition, went to work on the floors. He stood and joined in, gathering up the scattered pages of his work.

Another question. "You've had two men watching me for more than half of a year," he said. "But you knew to have more here tonight."

Six men, he thought. And that had been barely enough for the task at hand.

His attacker came under a new kind of magick or—here, his stomach sank—a very *old* kind. But not even the Androfrancines had dabbled much in blood magick, not until Xhum Y'Zir's spell. He'd read stories, of course, from the Year of the Falling Moon and the early days of the War of the Weeping Czar. Blood magicks fivefold more potent than the powders they made from the earth, making one man a squad in and of himself. *If he hadn't hesitated, if he hadn't taken the time to speak, I would be dead now.*

Grymlis spoke. "Trouble brews in the Named Lands and beyond.

We had a bird four nights back. Someone means to finish the work Sethbert started."

Thus shall the sins of P'Andro Whym be visited upon his children. The words penetrated him like a knife, and his eyes went involuntarily to the satchel. Someone meant to exterminate the last of the Androfrancine remnant. "But who?"

"It smells of Tam," Grymlis said. "But the note was unclear. It bid us watch over you. It arrived coded and in Whymer script."

Petronus shook his head. "I don't think Tam is behind it. I believe what he told me; Vlad Li Tam dismantled his network and left the Named Lands with his sons and daughters." He thought about it for a moment. "And the warning was anonymous?"

"Yes."

A Whymer Maze, Petronus thought. And with the Named Lands sliding further and further into political and economic collapse it would be hard to know what nations had working intelligence operatives. Pylos, Turam and the Entrolusian Delta had their hands full with insurrection and revolution. And based on the birds he'd received over the last fortnight, the unrest was spreading into the Emerald Coasts and spilling over to the Divided Isles and their frontier counties.

Perhaps it was the Gypsy? Rudolfo's Ninefold Forest Houses were the only houses thriving—and how could they not? Petronus had passed to him all the wealth and holdings of the Androfrancine Order, including House Li Tam's sizable wealth.

Certainly, their last meeting on the Prairie Sea just hours after Petronus had executed Sethbert had been tense.

The Gypsy King had drawn his sword upon approach, and Petronus thought for a moment that the enraged Rudolfo might actually kill him for ending the line of papal succession. But Rudolfo was a clever man— at some point he would understand that Petronus had granted him a favor by snapping the Order's neck, leaving him unshackled by two thousand years of Androfrancine tradition and backward dreaming.

"Could it have been Rudolfo?" he asked. "Could he have warned us?"

"It's possible, Father. He has the assets for intelligence, certainly. But why the cover of anonymity? You gave him Guardianship during the war." Now Grymlis's voice choked with anger. Petronus could hear leagues spent on the Fivefold Path of Grief in the old captain's voice. "And who would punish us beyond Windwir?"

It is all related.

"Perhaps," Petronus said, "we'll know more once our guest wakes up."

"Meanwhile," Grymlis said, "you should pack. We've scouted a new location for your work."

He knows about my work. Of course he does, Petronus realized, *if he's been watching all this time.* He opened his mouth to protest and then closed it. Grymlis and his men had saved his life tonight. At the very best, he'd be dead now but for them. At the very worst, his attacker would have been most effectively meting out his promise of pain.

He reached out a shaking hand, found Grymlis's shoulder and squeezed it. "I'm glad you didn't listen to me when I sent you and your men away."

He could hear Grymlis's forced smile. "I *did* listen to you, Father. I listened until you laid down your ring and robe. Beyond that, I listened to myself."

Petronus blessed his own fallibility and, without protest, set himself to packing his belongings for another journey he was too old to make.

Neb

Neb took the stairs two at a time as the gathering crowd parted before him and the half-squad he led. The events of the night had left him shaken, and he still felt the fear in his belly. He'd seen nothing like it, though he'd watched squads of magicked scouts—had even run with them—in the days since Windwir's fall. But this was another kind of magick, something dangerous and old. Something that took men far beyond what the River Woman's powders, ground from the earth, could do.

Blood magick. He'd read stories about the Wizard Kings and the deals they brokered in dark places, boons purchased with blood. Twice now he'd seen it. His first experience still haunted his nightmares, carrying him back to the ridgeline above Windwir where he witnessed the last spell of the world's last wizard consume Windwir before his eyes. Carefully crafted in seclusion by Xhum Y'Zir to avenge the murder of his seven sons, the Seven Cacophonic Deaths had leveled the city, leaving it—and Neb's soul—utterly desolated.

Now, he'd seen blood magick at work for a second time.

Certainly, it was on a much smaller scale, but he had seen the Marshers at war alongside Rudolfo's Gypsy Scouts. Both were formidable forces, and yet a small group of blood-magicked assassins had penetrated the heart of the Ninefold Forest and murdered Hanric and the Crown Prince of Turam in a hall full of armed men. And those forces had barely repelled them—but not before the assassins had done their work.

He ran the halls until he reached the servants' quarters near the suite of rooms where Rudolfo's house steward—Kember—had housed Hanric as a guest of honor. Two Gypsy Scouts guarded the door. "Are the Marsh King's servants within?" Neb asked.

One of the guards nodded. "They are. We've told them nothing."

Neb swallowed. "Good." *I don't want to do this,* he realized as he stared at the heavy, closed door. How did he tell the girl he loved that the man she considered a father and a friend was dead?

Hanric's face flashed behind his eyes, and Neb suddenly remembered the off-key, bellowed song the giant Marsher had been singing when the attackers burst into the room. He felt a lump in his throat and knew that his eyes would leak water if he didn't rein himself in. *You are an officer of the Ninefold Forest Houses,* he chided himself. *You are a man.*

He put his hand on the doorknob and looked to the half-squad of men accompanying him. "Wait here."

Opening the door, Neb slipped in and closed it behind him. The room smelled of damp dirt, and he saw the Marshers gathered in the sitting room with Winters at the center as they talked silently with their hands using a nonverbal language Neb could not read. They were in various states of dishevelment, as was their custom. The ash and dirt they rubbed into their skin and hair gave them a fierce and wild look that caused most to keep their distance. Their willowy queen looked perplexed and curious, but her eyes came alive when she saw him. Their hands dropped as she stood.

"Nebios," she asked, "what is happening? There are guards at the door who won't let us leave."

Neb swallowed again and nodded slowly. "We need to talk," he said, his eyes shifting to the small group of servants that surrounded her. "And after, Rudolfo bids you join him in his study." The words felt awkward. "I've a half-squad outside to escort you."

Her eyes narrowed at this, and he wondered what she read on his face. Whatever it was, her nostrils flared and her eyes went wide when the gravity of his demeanor took hold of her. She looked to her people and Neb did the same. They looked away from him, shifting uncomfortably in the silence. There was a note of panic in her voice that surprised him, as if she anticipated dark tidings. "What's happened, Nebios?"

He moved into the room and opened one of the many doors leading into the private bedchambers of the servants' suite. He held the door for her as she entered. Then he pulled it shut behind them, standing close to her but uncertain of how to speak and how to be.

He opened his mouth, closed it again. And suddenly, knowing it was just the two of them, he lost control of the sob in his throat and the tears in his eyes for just a moment, but it was enough. He saw her lower lip trembling.

She knows something has happened. Tell her. He willed himself to find the words, and when he did, they tumbled out like drunks from a closing tavern. "We've been attacked," he said. "Men under some kind of magicks—blood magick, I think—penetrated the forest, outran the watch birds and killed the crown Prince of Turam at the banquet table." He choked here, hating himself for not being able to keep his own emotions in check, hating himself for bringing news to her that he knew would bring suffering. "They've killed Hanric, too."

For a moment, Winters looked like a cornered fawn. Her eyes went wild as she looked to and fro; then the air whistled out of her. Neb reached out to her, but she pushed him away and sat heavily on the floor.

Not knowing what else to do, he sat with her. Once again, he tried to draw close, but she resisted and he realized she was whispering words that quickly ran together, words that sounded like glossolalia they had shared before.

But as he listened, the words took shape, and Neb realized she was speaking of a wind of cleansing blood, an iron blade that pruned. And as she spoke, she held herself, rocking back and forth, her eyes narrow and flitting about the room.

After minutes that felt much longer, he put his hand on her shoulder and squeezed. She looked up, her eyes wet and red. There were tracks of white, clean skin where the tears had washed the dirt from her cheeks. When their eyes met, her lower lip quivered again and she let him pull her into his arms. They huddled on the floor and held each other, Neb finally surrendering to the grief that washed them both.

"I don't know what to do," she said after a dozen minutes had passed. She disentangled herself from him and leaned back against the wall, looking to the door. "I need to tell my people."

Neb moved over to sit next to her. "I think you should talk with Rudolfo first."

She sniffed and nodded. Neb watched her, realizing how little he knew this girl. The dreams were . . . What were they? They certainly bared their unconscious hopes and fears to one another there, mingled with metaphysics that Neb himself could only embrace at this point without fully understanding. "Earlier, before the alarm sounded, I had a visitation."

He blinked. "A vision?"

She shook her head. "No, just words . . . and a sense of foreboding." Her brow furrowed as she pulled down the memory. "A wind of blood to cleanse," she said. "And cold iron to prune."

Until recently, he'd had no reference point for the glossolalia and prophecy that were a part of the Marsh Queen's daily life. Those concepts were utterly foreign to him. The Androfrancines who had taught him in their orphan school applied reason and science to myth and mysticism. The idea of writing it down and looking to it for some sense of tomorrow seemed completely irrational to him until he experienced it himself.

Xhum Y'Zir's Age of Laughing Madness had touched him there in the shadow of Windwir's pyre just over a year before, opening a door inside of him that he wasn't sure could ever be closed. From the moment of that first hot wind, he'd been unable to form coherent sentences, instead spewing jumbled bits of P'Andro Whym's Gospels blended with ecstatic utterances and flashing images that words could not contain. It had passed after a short time, but it had changed something inside of him, something as stark as the brown hair now bleached bone-white by the events of that late morning. Later, his dead father had appeared in his dreams, and so had the Marsh girl, Winters, though he didn't know it until after they met in the Marsher war camp. Since meeting her, he'd lived on the edge of something he had no skill to comprehend. *They are connected, this attack and her visitation.* Rudolfo would need to know about this.

Thinking of his waiting general, Neb suddenly blushed. He reached a hand up and brushed the tangled strands of her dirty hair out of her face. Her eyes and nose were red now. He cleared his voice. "I think we should go," he said. "Lord Rudolfo is waiting to speak you about this."

She looked at Neb. "Does he know that you know about me?"

Neb shrugged. "I've never spoken of it." Then, as an afterthought: "He's never asked." *But of course he knew.* He had to know. Why else had he sent Neb for her specifically?

She nodded, then slowly pushed her way up to her feet. Neb stood, too, and turned toward the door.

Her hand caught his own. "Thank you for being the one to bear me this message," she said in a quiet voice.

"I felt I must," he said.

Their eyes met for a moment; then he watched her look away and compose herself to face her people. "I will speak to my people first," she said. "I will not speak to Rudolfo until those who loved and served Hanric know of his fall."

Neb nodded. Then he opened the door and watched her square her shoulders and set her jaw against the task ahead.

A wind of blood to cleanse; cold iron to prune. Neb shuddered, and her premonition took him. It was a woeful feeling that reached beyond the loss of Hanric into the very heart of the Marshfolk. Something dark and brewing, he thought. And the sorrow on Winters's face betrayed something within her.

She knows, Neb realized.

This woe now was but the first of more to come.

Jin Li Tam

The sky over the Desolation of Windwir was a slate of smeared red, and Jin Li Tam could not tell if it was sunrise or sunset that made it so. The horizons to her east and west gave no clue to the time of day, and the sun was nowhere to be seen. Hazy light washed the forest of bones in blood and turned the placid surface of the nearby Second River black. Tendrils of pink mist crawled the ground, swept in eddies by a cold wind that moved freely among the skeletons, raising a low hum. She shivered from both the chill and the sight of Xhum Y'Zir's handiwork. Her breath caught in her throat, and she found herself wondering if being here was safe for her baby.

In that moment, Jin Li Tam rested her hand upon her swollen stomach, willing her son to kick, to show some sign of life.

This isn't right, she realized. They'd buried the dead here, Neb and Petronus, while the war raged on around them. There was no field of bones. The gravediggers had seen to it, she was certain. *Who has un-done their work?*

She heard a distant sound over her shoulder and turned to the northeast. Faintly, she heard the clamor of Third Alarm in the direction of the Ninefold Forest, hundreds of leagues distant, past thick forest, rugged hills and the expansive Prairie Sea that surrounded the Gypsy King's scattered forest islands. Dark clouds hung ominous and impenetrable in that direction.

I'm needed at home, she thought. But the forty-second daughter of Vlad Li Tam was uncertain how she'd come to be here in the first place, and now her very feet resisted her efforts to move them homeward. The air grew colder around her, and she realized she was wearing the thin green silk riding skirt and blouse she'd worn that night so long ago when Rudolfo had danced with her in Sethbert's banquet tent.

A sunrise such as you belongs in the East with me, he'd told her that night. She put her hands on her stomach again and suddenly found that it was flat and firm. When she looked down, she saw that her skirts were black with blood. She felt it, warm and sluggish, as it moved down her legs to pool around her feet.

When she opened her mouth to scream, a giant black raven landed on the cracked cornerstone of a shattered building and cocked its head. Jin Li Tam swallowed her scream and willed the strength of focus her father had brutally trained into his sons and daughters.

A kin-raven. She wasn't sure how she knew it, but she did. It was larger than any raven she'd seen, and it stared at her, its beak opening and closing. She saw the scarlet thread of war tied to one foot, the green thread of peace on the other. She also saw, by the way it held its head, that its neck had been broken and that its feathers were mottled and singed. One of its eyes was missing. It croaked at her.

"You are extinct," Jin Li Tam said slowly. "And this is a dream."

The beak opened, and a tinny, faraway voice leaked out. "And it shall come to pass at the end of days that a wind of blood shall rise for cleansing and cold iron blades shall rise for pruning," the kin-raven said. "Thus shall the sins of P'Andro Whym be visited upon his children. Thus shall the Throne of the Crimson Empress be established." The bird stopped, hopped backward on its feet, then forward, cocking its head again and fixing her in its flat black eye. "Fortunate are you among women and highly favored is Jakob, Shepherd of the Light."

The first wave of pain hit her and she clutched at herself. "Begone, kin-raven," she said, gritting her teeth against the spasm that gripped her belly. "Your message is unwelcome in this House." She wasn't sure where the words came from, but she laid hold of them and said them again, loudly, forcing her feet to carry her toward the bird as she raised her hand. "Begone, kin-raven. Your message is unwelcome in this House."

Then the kin-raven did something birds should not be able to do, not even in dreams. It smiled. Then it unfurled its wings, and they hung over Windwir's bones to cast long shadows east and west. "I leave you now," it said, the metallic voice leaking out from the opened beak. "But soon I shall dine upon your father's eyes."

Jin Li Tam lunged forward, the pain growing as she moved, then lost her footing as her slippers found no traction in the puddle of her blood and water.

She screamed her rage and felt hands suddenly upon her, pulling her, shaking her.

"Lady Tam?" The voice was faraway to the northeast. "My lady?" Behind the voice, the clamoring of the alarm went suddenly silent and Jin Li Tam opened her eyes.

"Are we at Third Alarm?" she asked the girl who attended her. She sat up, taking a quick inventory of herself and her surroundings. The pain was real, and she felt wetness beneath the blankets. Holding her breath, she pushed them down and looked. No blood, but her water had indeed broken.

The girl took a step back and nodded. "Yes, Lady. We've been at Third Alarm. But the grounds and manor are safe now."

"We were attacked?" Grimacing against the pain, she carefully moved to the edge of the bed and reached for her nearby robe.

The girl nodded again. "Yes, Lady. The scouts at the door have not offered any details."

Not yet, they haven't. She stood, felt the rush of blood to her head, then sat again. She motioned the girl closer. "Help me up."

The servant offered her hands and leaned back to help Jin up. She pulled on the robe and winced. The girl looked alarmed when she saw the wet bed. "Shall I call the River Woman?"

Jin Li Tam nodded. "Yes. I think it's started early."

The girl guided her to the wall by the door, and Jin put her hand against it, resting her weight there while the girl opened it and poked her head out, calling for a scout.

She'd spent most of the last month in bed, and she could feel the weakness in her legs. Her baby had been too quiet, there had been occasional spotting, and the River Woman had doled out powders and ordered bed rest. She'd plowed through at least a hundred books, the ink and paper smelling fresh from the mechoservitors who reproduced them from memory for the new library.

She was a tiger who hated cages.

But the look on Rudolfo's face each time he saw her, each time they sat and spoke of the son to come, was enough to sustain her.

This, too, shall pass, she told her weak legs and swollen stomach, the waves of nausea and the intense aversion to smells that had never bothered her before. *Soon enough*, she said to the cage her bedchambers had become.

Until she met the Gypsy King and fell in love with him the night he gave the metal man back his Androfrancine robes, Jin Li Tam had never considered the possibility of motherhood. In those days, she'd been about her father's business—joining herself to whatever man or woman he chose for her, using her role as a courtesan and occasional consultant to play her part in House Li Tam's work of guiding the river of politics and strategy in the Named Lands.

Hidden in her father's library, before the day he donated it to Rudolfo and Isaak's restoration work, there had been another library—a small room she'd seen only once or twice as a little girl. There, in slim black volumes etched in the coded scripts of House Li Tam, was the secret history of the Named Lands written with the blood and effort of her family. Her father had burned those books the day Rudolfo confronted him, but the river had moved. Her father had *made* her betrothed, shaping him in his earliest years with grief, tempering him with loss and making him a strong, formidable leader. And her father had shaped her as well, an arrow for Rudolfo's heart, and had blessed their union.

War is coming, his note had said to her so long ago. *Bear Rudolfo an heir.* And she had agreed initially because it was her father's wish. Later, as her love for the Gypsy King grew alongside the growing suspicion of her father's motives, she'd realized that the child she intended to bear was for Rudolfo and Rudolfo alone.

There was joy in it somewhere, though in this moment she felt disoriented and afraid and in pain. The dream was like no dream she'd ever had, and she'd slept through Third Alarm. Jin Li Tam, trained in scout magicks and the arts of espionage, had slept through an attack on her new home.

The Gypsy Scout entered. "The River Woman is already on her way. I will have her come to you first."

Jin Li Tam bit back another wave of pain. "What has happened?"

"I am not at liberty to—"

She cut him off quickly and coldly. "Aeryk, you see my present state and you know Lord Rudolfo will hide none of this from me. Do not make me stand here and ask again." The words were sharper than she would've liked them, but after her first week in bed, the household and its guards were accustomed to it.

He swallowed and nodded. "Yes, Lady. We've been attacked. A squad of magicked assailants penetrated the forest perimeters and attacked the Firstborn Feast. Hanric the Marsh King and Ansylus, Crown Prince of Turam, have both been assassinated and their bodyguards slain."

Panic tugged at her. "What of Rudolfo?"

"General Rudolfo is unharmed and leads the investigation." The guard paused, guessed her next question and continued. "The attackers came under magicks we've not seen before. The River Woman comes to see what light can be shown on this."

A wind of blood to cleanse. The words from her dream came back to her, and Jin Li Tam's mouth fell open. She closed it. She heard commotion in the hall and saw a squad of Gypsy Scouts move past, huddled closely around a slight, bright-colored form. Rudolfo's stride and his green turban gave him away as he moved past in the direction of the private study in the suite of rooms adjoining her own.

"Rudolfo," she called, moving away from the wall now so that he would not see her needing its support.

But he did not stop. He swept past with his men and she heard him barking orders as he went. There was strain in his voice, and grief, and maybe even a touch of fear.

More pain, and Jin Li Tam swallowed it, willing herself to leave the room and follow Rudolfo into his study. But her legs refused and buckled. The servant and the scout moved nimbly to her sides and supported her weight even as the door to Rudolfo's study opened and closed farther down the hall.

Jin Li Tam sighed and blinked back a round of surprising, sudden tears. She'd wept more the last six months than she remembered ever having wept before. Of course, she'd read the books and knew that it was normal for some.

Not normal for me, she thought, but none of this was.

This river will not be moved until its own time, she realized as she let them guide back to her waiting bed. And its time was soon.

Jin Li Tam resolved herself to meet it with what grace she could muster. She would wait in bed and breathe as the River Woman and the books had told her. She would send word to Rudolfo to join her when he was able.

She would bear the man she loved an heir and try to put the dream out of her mind. She would become a mother tonight and launch her son at the world, a sharp and true arrow for the light.

She would be brave and would not cry.

Failing utterly, and filled with rage at her failure, Jin Li Tam let the feelings of powerlessness win in their ambush of her, blushing that those who tended her must see her so weak.

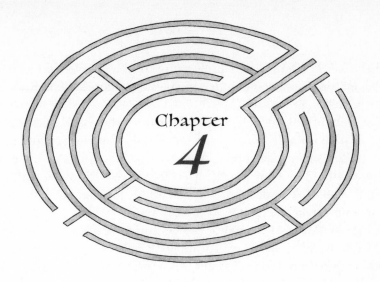

Chapter 4

Rudolfo

Rudolfo paced the plush carpet of his private study and replayed the evening's events behind his eyes. He and his men had been taken unawares by a threat he'd not conceived of in his wildest imaginings, and that reality fed his wrath. The faintest traces of their attackers' magicked blood faded on his uniform now, smudges that seemed more like shadows next to the darker patches that belonged to Hanric, Ansylus and their men.

He paced the room and stroked his beard alone, waiting for the boy and for the girl who now had the weight of grief upon her alongside a difficult decision.

No matter what she chooses, it will go hard for her. There was no way around that truth. But whatever she chose, Rudolfo would keep his kin-clave with the Marsh girl—the Marsh Queen—and would extend his support of her.

She and her people kept the secret well. Rudolfo and Gregoric had known. And certainly, the boy Neb. Beyond that, the Named Lands would all believe the Marshers were without a king.

The unrest may prove a blessing to her yet, he thought. With all eyes on the fires in the south, few would care that the Marshers' Wicker Throne seemed suddenly vacant. Still it would be a challenge for her at such a young age, though she was older than Rudolfo had been.

And she had the added benefit of being from a people who were de-spised, feared, avoided, misunderstood—vastly more so than Rudolfo's Forest Gypsies.

But what of Turam? The Crown Prince's father had lain at death's door for nigh on a decade, his life preserved by Androfrancine medi-cines no longer in easy supply. Ansylus had functioned as his proxy, and now that nation would be at profound risk to forces within or without. Rudolfo dug deep into memory but could not recall the name of the younger brother, though it mattered little—the boy had been killed at the Battle of Rachyle's Bridge during the War for Windwir. There was an uncle, however. Turam just barely balanced itself against the tide of insurrection that swept the Named Lands with the Andro-francine Order's collapse. This news could tip the scale.

And why now? Why *his* house? And, darker still, why not him? Two of the three most influential men in the room had fallen, and one had been left entirely unharmed. An uneasiness gripped him and would not let him go. When the dust settled from this tonight, he would seek counsel with his betrothed, Jin Li Tam.

He'd looked for her in the crowd that had gathered outside the Great Hall. She had been noticeably absent, and he doubted that the River Woman's admonitions of bed rest had truly trumped her curios-ity. He'd meant to ask after her or to check in on her, but the whirl-wind of orders to give, people to direct, investigations to launch had caught him up and carried him until this moment.

He looked up at the knock on his door. "Yes?"

It opened a crack and Neb looked in. "I have Lady Winters with me, General."

Rudolfo smoothed his uniform by habit. "Send her in." His eyes narrowed and he studied Neb's face, reading what he could there in the redness of the eyes and the pallor of his skin. When Neb met his gaze, Rudolfo's hands moved quickly. *Find Aedric. Tell him to bring me an update.* When Neb nodded his understanding, Rudolfo continued. *And check on Lady Tam. Tell her I will brief her when I can.*

Neb nodded again. The young man held open the door, and Win-ters stepped through. Then it closed behind her.

The look on the girl's face stopped Rudolfo's pacing. She looked smaller than she had earlier today, her eyes red and hollow, her mouth drawn tight with grief. There were pale track marks from the tears that had scrubbed away the ash and mud of her people's lament.

Rudolfo waved to a small sofa by a banked fire. "Please sit with me," he said. She moved slowly and sat, folding her hands in her lap. He joined her. "Neb has told you, then?"

She glanced up, then dropped her eyes and nodded. "He has. And I have told my people." She swallowed. "At least those who are here. I've instructed them to find a bird and pass the word home to Hanric's kin."

Rudolfo's eyebrows raised. "Do you think that prudent so soon after?"

She stared at him. "Prudence does not enter into matters where love is concerned."

Rudolfo smiled, then signed to her in the House language of Xhum Y'Zir. *Prudence* especially *enters into matters where love is concerned.* "Your life has changed, Lady. You may need to think in different directions now." He remembered those early days, the days when Aerynus, Gregoric's father, had briefed him secretly so that Rudolfo might command with experience beyond his years. And he remembered the first man he'd ordered beneath the salted knives of the Physicians his father left to him. Their penitent torture was a knife he chose not to pass forward to his own son. But they had served their purpose, even if the redemption they drew out in blood was not true penitence. The single insurrection in the Ninefold Forest Houses—the event that had cost Lord Jakob and Lady Marielle their lives—was met by young Rudolfo with ruthless, merciless atonement.

She swallowed at his words and nodded.

He looked at her, small and frightened, and saw himself so many years ago. He leaned toward her. "You have my kin-clave, Lady Winters. The Ninefold Forest Houses will plumb this treachery. You have my assurance of assistance in all matters."

Her eyes met his. "I am grateful, Lord."

Rudolfo reached for the bottle of firespice on the table and raised his eyebrows toward an empty glass. "What will you do?"

Winters nodded, and Rudolfo poured a small portion of the liquor for her. "I will declare myself," she said. "It's early, but perhaps it's supposed to be." She looked perplexed now, her eyebrows furrowing. "Only . . ." Her words trailed off, and she reached out for the glass, lifting it to her lips and sipping. She looked up again. "I did not see this in my dreams."

Rudolfo poured himself a drink. "How could you?"

Winters shrugged. "I saw Neb in my dreams. I saw Windwir fall. Neb and I have seen our promised home. And many of our Dreaming Kings have seen these days, too, and written them in their Book."

"Perhaps," Rudolfo suggested, "these dreams are not always reliable."

"And yet," Winters answered, "the moment before we went into Third Alarm a premonition took hold of me." Rudolfo leaned forward as she quickly recounted it.

"A wind of blood?" he asked. He whistled and the door opened. A Gypsy Scout poked his head in. *Find out what manner of blades the assassins carried,* he signed. The scout nodded and closed the door. He looked to Winters. "I'm not given to superstition, but this bears inquiry. I will ask Isaak to look into it. Perhaps it is something referenced in the library's holdings."

A night of inquiries, he thought. He still had the matter at the Keeper's Gate to resolve.

There was a knock at the door—this time, firmer. Rudolfo looked up. "Yes?"

Aedric stepped into the room. "I saw Neb on the landing. I've sent him to pack for tomorrow."

Winters looked up at this, and Rudolfo noticed the surprise on her face. *It alarms her that he is leaving.* But of course, Rudolfo knew she would not ask where he went.

"I do not think I will be joining you," Rudolfo said. "I'm needed here."

Aedric nodded, closing the door. He looked to the girl now, as if seeing her for the first time. The First Captain looked surprised and then suddenly uncomfortable. *You may wish to hear this news alone,* he signed.

Rudolfo saw Winters following his hands, but saw no comprehension on her face. "You truly meant what you told me?" he asked her. *That you mean to announce yourself?* he added in the Wizard King's sign.

"Yes, Lord," she said in a quiet voice.

Rudolfo motioned to a chair across from them. "Sit, Aedric, and pour a drink." He inclined his head toward the girl. "Things are not what they seem."

Aedric sat and poured firespice into a cup. "They are not, indeed," he said.

Rudolfo nodded. "This is Winters," he said.

"Yes, our young lieutenant is quite taken with her."

"Well, she is more than she appears. May I present Winteria bat Mardic, the Marsh Queen." Rudolfo offered a tight smile as Aedric's eyebrows shot up. "Hanric was her . . ." Rudolfo reached for the word but couldn't find it.

"Shadow," Winters said, her voice heavy. "He was the image we needed to convey to the rest of the Named Lands until I reached my majority."

Aedric paled, looked to Rudolfo, then back to the girl. He looked troubled.

"What is it, Aedric?"

Aedric looked away. "We are in pursuit of the attackers. The Gypsy Scouts are magicked and trailing them at a distance. Half-squads are searching every structure in the town and every room in the manor. And the River Woman is here to tend Lady Tam. When she's finished, she will autopsy the dead assassin and look for traces of the magicks in his organs."

Rudolfo nodded. "Summon the Chief Physician for the cutting."

Aedric inclined his head. "I've done so already, General."

Winters interjected here. "Where is Hanric?"

Aedric glanced to Rudolfo and he nodded his assent. "He lays where he fell. We did not wish to offend your custom."

Winters nodded. "Thank you, First Captain." She looked to Rudolfo. "Would you honor us by hosting Hanric's rest?"

Rudolfo knew little of the Marsher ways. Until the war, he'd encountered them infrequently. Most notably, his father had once captured Winters's father and brought him before the Physicians of Penitent Torture to teach him respect for the Forest Gypsy's borders. He knew what most did—that the Marshers wore dirt and ash, did not bathe and scratched out lives of violent subsistence in the infertile north. They were mystics, caught up in ecstatic utterances and prophecy, bellowed out with magicked voice by their king in his long-winded War Sermons. He knew of their promised home. And he knew that they buried their dead immediately—and buried their dead enemies as well. To not do so was a grievous insult.

"Certainly," he said. "His rest may be anywhere you choose."

She inclined her head to him. "I am grateful, Lord."

Aedric cleared his voice, and Rudolfo looked to him now. "There's more, General."

Here it is. Here is what troubles him. "Go on," Rudolfo said, glancing towards Winters.

"We brought the axe down to get a look at one of the bodies." Aedric looked both to her and then to Rudolfo. He signed the words first. *They were Marshers,* he said.

Rudolfo looked at the girl.

This is where your heart is broken. The weight of this, of learning that the one you loved as a father was cut down by your own kind. Images flashed across his mind. Memories of fire and Fontayne the Heretic—the seventh son of Vlad Li Tam—shouting at the mob as it beat Rudolfo's father to death. He studied the last traces of Winters's innocence and then spoke the words to condemn her.

"Tell her, Aedric," Rudolfo said.

And then he closed his eyes so that he would not see her change.

Vlad Li Tam

Vlad Li Tam met his sixth daughter when she stepped from the longboat that brought the first load of children. He extended a fresh mango to her and she accepted it with the slightest inclination of her head.

"Thank you, Father," she said. She'd aged gracefully, her once-red hair now white as she neared her own sunset. She wore the saffron robes befitting her rank in his House.

He returned the slight bow and turned to the boatload of children. "And how are you all this morning? Did you sleep well?" He tried to make eye contact with as many of them as he could, trying just as hard to hear them as they talked over one another in their enthusiasm. "Good, good," he said, clapping and smiling. Then, he pointed to the trailhead that led to the village. Drums announcing the new kin-clave were already pulsing through the jungle, and smoke from the massive cook-fires smudged the morning sky. "Go and find friends," he said. "But don't forget your manners and your lessons."

Laughing, they spilled from the boat and raced up the beach, the oldest hanging back to keep their eyes on the youngest. Vlad Li Tam watched them go as the oarsmen pushed off and turned back for the anchored ships in the harbor.

Three of his ships were already steaming farther south, each adding to their maps and gathering the data necessary to determine their next stop. He would send another three now that kin-clave here was established. They would find the largest, most populated islands, observe the inhabitants from a distance and compile those findings for his inspection.

The remaining half dozen vessels would take what maintenance rotation they could without a dry dock and guard House Li Tam's work in the village.

His daughter smiled at him. "How did it go?"

"It was fine. I will need more powders soon."

She shook her head. "Strange customs," she said.

Not so strange, he thought. He'd sent his sons and daughters into hundreds of beds to form alliances and gather information. Their courtesan activities were not even well-kept secrets in the Named Lands. "Perhaps more straightforward than we're accustomed to," he said as he looked out across the water. He looked back to her. "What are your plans?"

"Baryk and I will attend the feast together," she said. "Then he will scout the island with our oldest sons."

Baryk had been a warpriest on the southernmost tip of the Emerald Coasts, the massive peninsula that was home to House Li Tam and a scattering of tropical city-states and loose confederations. When Vlad had announced his family's retreat from the Named Lands, they had given away their possessions and lands to join him. All but one of his children—even those who'd left his service to pursue independent lives with their own families—had returned home at his call. And he was grateful for it. It spared him the grief of assassination.

"Perhaps I will join them," Vlad Li Tam said.

Rae Li Tam smiled. "You may be too busy honoring kin-clave." She patted her satchel. "Meanwhile, I've pharmaceuticals that are running low and a list of flora samples to collect."

He nodded. "Keep an eye out for kalla plants," he said.

"Of course I will, Father." She inclined her head and, once he returned the gesture, set off down the beach slowly, passing the trailhead and moving west along the coast.

Vlad Li Tam sighed and stretched, then turned to the next longboat that approached, also full of children. Behind it, others came bearing the Tam contribution to the feast. It would take most of the morning to disembark the first shift of his family. They would go slowly, letting the Dayfather's tribe have time to accustom themselves to the pale-skinned travelers from the northeast. By tomorrow, the Tams would outnumber the tribe on the island, but all knew to underemphasize this fact, staying aloof and keeping their large numbers spread out over the island. They would also make many gifts over the next fortnight, and there would be other pairings among his sons and daughters and the Dayfather's people. These were not required for kin-clave but would certainly strengthen the bonds. And at no time would the Tam presence here give way to violence or compulsion.

While intimidation had its place, it was not always conducive to gathering intelligence.

A flash of light caught his eye, and he looked to the bow of their flagship, *The Serendipitous Wind*. He read the second half of the coded message and waited for it to repeat. He followed the code, deciphering the words and numbers quickly.

His First Son's vessel, *Spirit of the Storm,* had found something four days to the south. Something, it seemed, that required his attention.

He drew his mirror and replied. Even before he'd finished, he saw a boat lowered and watched his First Grandson take the oars. He came alone, his long red hair flowing behind him on the wind.

He will be a worthy successor. At some point, the mantle would pass to his First Son and, when his First Son was ready to lay it down, Mal Li Tam would take it up. He'd had the best education the world could offer, spending his early years in the Orphan School of Windwir. Introspect had arranged it for him during the first year of his papacy, not long after helping Petronus escape the city and the Order under a shroud of deception. At the time, Vlad Li Tam had had no idea that his own father had set those wheels into motion before turning House Li Tam over to Vlad nearly two decades earlier.

Armed with wits and cunning that perhaps only matched Vlad's own father, Mal Li Tam had made his mark in the Named Lands quietly. He'd brought about a dozen unlikely alliances and broken half as many—some stretching back to the Days of Settlement—as he served his grandfather and father in the House business. Named for a pirate that had saved his father's life, Mal Li Tam was the sharpest in House Li Tam's quiver of arrows.

What will you inherit when my work is done? It was hard to say. Time was a cipher that Vlad Li Tam understood well. The precepts of T'Erys Whym, upon which his House had been built, were that with enough time and pressure even a river could be moved in such a way as to appear without design. But time was an enemy as well as an ally. He was seventy-two now and knew that he was measuring the depthline in spans now, not leagues. He had closed down House Li Tam, donating the majority of his vast holdings and wealth over to the Order, knowing full well that Petronus would pass the Order's holdings and wealth, in turn, over to Rudolfo.

And my forty-second daughter. She should be delivering soon, he realized. He'd counted the days and had started a dozen poems to honor the little Lord Jakob's arrival into a troubled world.

He watched Mal Li Tam hop easily over the bow of the skiff and drag the boat up onto the beach behind him. He was barefoot and bare-chested, wearing only a pair of loose-fitting silk pants. He smiled as he approached.

"Grandfather," he said, inclining his head.

Vlad returned the bow. "And how is my First Grandson this morning?"

Mal looked at the empty hammock and the hastily constructed lean-to, his smile widening. "More rested than you, I'd wager, Grandfather."

Vlad chuckled. "Perhaps I'll nap today." He glanced back to the ship. "So what have they found?" he asked.

"Father didn't say." He reached into a hidden pocket on his pants and drew a stained and crumpled scroll.

Vlad took it and opened it, reading the coded message twice before handing it back. The handwriting was true, though the note had been written hastily with a shaking hand. And the note itself had little to say. The dots and smudges of the Tam cipher script pointed to a set of coordinates beyond their current maps, and there was a buried urgency that whatever they had found bore Vlad's personal inspection. But the urgency didn't speak of danger.

He looked up, meeting his grandson's eyes. "We'll leave when the feast is over tonight—just one ship. But send a bird to the other two southern patrols and retask them to meet us there. You will be joining me."

A look on Mal's face betrayed something that the old man could not place. "Do you think three vessels are enough?"

Vlad Li Tam smiled and patted Mal's shoulder. "If there had been any significant threat your father would have said so. Still, see to the armory and pick a crew that can hold their own by sea and by land. I intend you to captain this voyage."

Mal Li Tam bowed more deeply. "Thank you, Grandfather. You honor me."

Vlad Li Tam returned the bow. "And make an appearance at the feast," he said with a wink. "You never know when you'll be called upon to do your part for kin-clave."

Smiling, the young man nodded and turned back to his boat. Vlad watched him as he pushed the skiff off the sand and hopped lightly inside. Pulling at the oars, he rowed against the tide and Vlad Li Tam watched, taking pleasure in the sight of his grandson rowing in the morning sun. He would have watched him longer, but more longboats were landing around him now—more grandchildren, more sons and daughters. The heat rose, shimmering over the sand and hazing the jungle.

Soon, he would nap in his hammock and gather strength for the coming feast. And maybe, in his dreams, he would see his newest grandson, Jakob. The first of his grandchildren who would not take the name of House Li Tam, and the only of them to remain in the Named Lands.

Another arrow launched at the world.

He felt a stab of remorse and suddenly hoped desperately that his sixth daughter would find the elusive kallaberry on this island. He missed the comfort those berries gave him when the past lurked at his door. He craved the forgetfulness and focus that his pipe brought him when he thought of all the arrows he'd lost or seen broken against the world along the way.

Vlad Li Tam forced his attention back to the beach. A handful of great-grandchildren and grandchildren played in the surf while their parents unloaded the boats.

Laughing, he chased after them.

Winters

Winters sat on the floor of the Great Hall and held Hanric's cold hand while she wept and wondered what to do.

My own people have done this.

Stunned by Aedric's words, she'd been unable to keep her focus as the conversation turned to speculation. Hanric was dead now. So was Ansylus. And she'd seen for herself. She'd left Rudolfo when the River Woman poked her head in to tell him that Jin Li Tam's labor had begun.

She'd held the Firstfall axe and looked at the dull reflection of a dead Marsher scout, still under magicks that her people had not used or seen for two thousand years. Certainly, they used blood magicks for other rituals, but the scout potions had been lost—or kept hidden by the Androfrancines—after the Old World fell.

And now, she sat by Hanric, holding the axe of her office in one hand while she held his lifeless hand in the other.

The half-squad of Gypsy Scouts had removed the others from the room and guarded the doors now so that she could be alone. Already, birds raced westward to her people. Soon, she would will herself to stand, to leave his side and go with her people into Rudolfo's gardens to find Hanric's rest.

They had left him where he lay, though someone had closed his eyes, and she could feel the coldness of his congealed blood seeping through the rough fabric of her dress.

She would wear his blood even as she wore the ash and mud of the earth that he would be given back to.

He'd been fearsome, they told her, taking at least two of his attackers before they overpowered him. And these attackers were faster, stronger than the traditional earth magicks employed by most. They'd stormed a room of armed men, killed their targets, and withdrawn.

Yet Rudolfo had been spared. She wondered at this and a sudden dread gripped her, then evaporated into gratitude. Neb had been here, too. His uniform was torn and bloodstained. The realization set her lip to quivering, and the water filled her eyes again.

The Francines had taught that all losses were connected to one another, and she saw that now. There in the shadows cast by the fireplace of Rudolfo's Great Hall, amid the scattered remains of an interrupted feast, Winters found herself feeling as small and alone as she'd been eleven years ago when she sat with her father's body.

Of course, she'd never truly been alone in those times. Hanric had kept that vigil with her. Hanric had closed her father's eyes and had held her on his lap as he leaned against the wall and wept loudly for his fallen friend. With his own hands, Hanric had dug out King Mardic's rest in the Caverns of the Sleeping Kings. And he'd followed his friend's instructions to the letter, climbing the Spine and declaring himself her shadow in the dark tongue of House Y'Zir, commanding the loyalty and love of the Marshfolk and pledging himself to the Homeward Path on her behalf until she reached the age of her majority. Until she was old enough to rule in a way that would strike fear in the heart of the Named Lands and, in that fear, hold their respect and keep the Marshlands apart from the interlopers and home-thieves.

Now, once Hanric was in the ground, she would return home to her people, climb the Spine and drink from the horn. For the first time in her life, she would feel the burn of the blood magick as it shored up her voice and gave it the span of a hundred leagues. Then, she would announce herself as Winteria bat Mardic, ward of Hanric ben Tornus, Queen of the Marsh. After that, she would give her first War Sermon and set herself to make this right.

She sniffed, wiping her nose with a sleeve.

Beyond the room, she heard the clatter of activity. Despite the approaching dawn, the Seventh Forest Manor had not quieted. Jin Li Tam, Rudolfo's betrothed, was hard at her labor, and the halls were alive with the hustle of servants bearing fresh linens and whatever other supplies the River Woman and Rudolfo's medicos required. The scouts, magicked and unmagicked, were stationed throughout the massive pine-and-stone house. Winters's own people were waiting outside the Great Hall.

Waiting for their queen to lead them down this Fivefold Path of Grief. An involuntary shudder washed over her and she stifled another sob. She wanted to contain this grief, to set it aside so that she could think outside of the fog it wrapped her in. There were questions that needed answering.

In all their years of sojourn in the New World, certainly factions had arisen and insurrections had emerged. But never anything like this. Why would Marsher Scouts, under blood magick, attack and kill the man the rest of the Named Lands believed was their king? To what end? Could they have been acting alone? The assassination of the Crown Prince led Winters to believe not. This had been planned, and whoever was behind it commanded Marsher Scouts and had need of the Named Lands to believe the Marshers were without their king. An ache at the pit of her stomach told her that these would not be the only deaths this night.

A wind of blood to cleanse. She remembered Aedric's reply to Rudolfo's question.

"What kind of blades were used?"

She'd known before the First Captain could answer. "Iron."

A pruning, then, she thought.

But Rudolfo had not been scratched. That meant something at the heart of this, she wagered.

The Marsh Queen sighed and squeezed Hanric's hand. "I will miss you," she said. Then, she dropped his hand and stood. She hefted the Firstfall axe, feeling the solid ash handle thrumming in her hands, and turned toward the doors. "It's time," she called out in a louder voice.

The doors opened, and her people came through. The women bore shovels and the men bore a stretcher. A half-squad of Gypsy Scouts accompanied them. Winters stepped aside as they all approached. The men gentled Hanric onto the stretcher and grunted beneath the weight of him when they finally lifted him from the floor. The lieutenant of the scouts stood before her and bowed. "Lady Winters, Lord Rudolfo sends condolences and apologies that he is unable to join you at this time. He bid me relay that he vows upon his father's sword that each year on this night, he will tell his son Jakob of Hanric the Marsh Queen's shadow."

She blinked. "Tell the Gypsy King that his hospitality and his vow honor me and my people in this darker moment of our sojourn." She turned to the door and stopped.

Neb stood there, dressed now in a fresh uniform. He shuffled from one foot to the other, awkward now before her. But he'd come. At the sight of him, Winters felt the hot tears pushing at her. She held them back and walked to him. Behind her, the scouts fanned out, whistling low and long to magicked counterparts she was certain watched. Her people walked slow behind, the women beginning the death psalms. When she stood before the young man, she reached over and took his hand, pulling him alongside. "I'm glad you came," she said.

Walking beside her, he glanced down at her. "Have you decided on his rest?"

She nodded. "I have." They were leaving the Great Hall now, standing before the massive doors that would take them out into the winter night. As the door creaked open, she saw that it had started snowing. The flakes were small and dry, and the wind spirited them along the ground. She looked up at him, watched the wind drift his hair. She squeezed his hand, then spoke. "He will rest at the heart of Rudolfo's Whymer Maze, in the shadow of Library Hill."

T'Erys Whym had made the labyrinth popular during his brief papacy in the New World, but Winters knew its darker heritage. A circular maze that could only be solved by returning the way you came or enduring the pain of climbing its thorns to find its hidden secrets. High sport of the Cutters of Old. Rituals of the Wizard Kings, their Surgeons working the knives for pleasure and blood magick bargaining, bent by time into Physicians of Penitent Torture, who worked the knives for redemption.

At the heart of that Whymer Maze, Hanric would rest.

For Winters, it was a reminder of the thorny walls that she knew waited ahead of her. Perhaps after Hanric's spirit found its way to their new home he would send her some of his strength and courage for her bloody climb.

In her heart, Winters knew that her own would not suffice. Biting her lip, she walked out into the snow and tried not to cry.

Chapter

5

Petronus

The sun had not yet risen when Petronus left his cabin and freed his birds. They scattered, a rainbow of threads decorating their feet and carrying word of the attack and the change in protocol to the network he'd created in the last seven months. Now, this station would simply forward its messages, recoded, to whatever relay points Grymlis had arranged. Petronus watched as the dark winter sky swallowed them and the multicolored messages they carried. Black threads of danger on some, the blue thread of inquiry on others, red for war on yet others. The only absent color was the green of peace.

The sky was shifting from black to gray when he gathered up his kit and satchel to meet the others by the boathouse near the water.

Grymlis and one of the others had allowed their magicks to fade. The remaining two had reapplied the powders. The old captain looked angry and argued in low tones. "What do you mean he's dead?" He glanced up, noting Petronus's approach. "How did it happen?"

"I don't know, Captain," the Gray Guard answered. "I went in to prep him for movement and he was dead. Cold as snow."

Grymlis sighed. "Put him in the boat, then. We'll ship him as well. We need to get a look at him once his magicks have played out."

Petronus joined them and did not protest when one of the soldiers took his travel kit. He resisted when the other reached for the satchel. "I'll keep this," he said. He looked to Grymlis. "Our prisoner is dead?"

Grymlis nodded. "Yes." The old Gray Guard looked tired, his eyes red and glassy from the magicks. His beard and hair were longer than the last time they'd seen each other. And now, instead of the gray uniform of the Androfrancine Army, he wore the nondescript trousers and shirt of a common laborer. Of course, the scout knives on his belt and the longsword slung over his shoulder said he was anything but common. "Poison perhaps," he added as an afterthought. "Though we found nothing when we searched him."

The sleeping village stirred around them. Petronus's dock, boathouse and cabin were on the edge of town, but already scattered lights announced the new day and a few quiet boats moved into the bay to get a head start on the work. He'd thought of leaving a note but wasn't sure what he would say in it. In the end, he'd opted to say nothing. If the events of last night were but a beginning, the less his neighbors knew, the better he imagined it would go for them.

And for me.

Grymlis took his arm. "Are you ready, Father?"

Petronus snorted. "I'm too old for all of this. Where exactly are we going?"

"Someplace safer than here." They moved off together toward the waiting boat. "Balthus and I will be joining you. These two will stay back and reroute the messages."

Petronus nodded at the strategy. He'd worked hard to build his little network, bringing in what scraps of knowledge he could to puzzle out the truth behind Windwir's fall.

They climbed into the boat, mindful of the tarp-wrapped bodies at their feet. Another tarp-wrapped body was lowered in after them; then the magicked soldiers cast them off. The slightest whisper of shifting snow betrayed their quick retreat. Petronus looked to his house and dock and imagined he was seeing them now for the last time.

If the assassin hadn't paused to speak, he would have succeeded. Petronus grabbed that thread and worked it as Grymlis's young lieutenant worked the oars and rowed them around the edges of the Bay. Caldus Bay was massive—nearly a sea of its own, he knew, from the hours he'd spent poring over the artifacts and writing of the Age of Settlement, that time just after the Age of Laughing Madness when the Order was newly formalized, having grown to the point of requiring a clearer hierarchy and chain of command. He'd nearly pursued history, specializing in that field. But his advisor had seen his potential in Francine School. Franci B'Yot had been the leading scholar of human nature and evolution—and a correspondent with the young P'Andro Whym after the first Scientism Movement failed. The Francine science ultimately won young Petronus's attention, and it served him well now as he thought about his attacker.

He wished to punish me. And that meant it was likely someone Petronus had wronged, someone who could blame him for something. No villain is evil for evil's sake, according to the Settlement playwright Sebastian. Because every antagonist wanted to accomplish something that they could at least convince themselves—if not others—was benevolent.

And this villain wished to punish—or perhaps the master he spoke of wished it. Petronus shivered at the memory of that voice, then remembered something.

"He spoke Whymer," Petronus said.

The old guard grunted and looked up. "He did."

The Whymer tongue was ancient and guarded, the house language of P'Andro Whym. It was unusual that anyone not affiliated with the Order would speak it. "His accent was heavy. We didn't train him—but one of our own did."

"Yes," Grymlis said, looking around them and cocking his head. His voice lowered. "We're nearly there," he said.

Petronus looked around, seeing nothing. "Nearly where?"

Grymlis whistled, low and long. He waited. Then just ahead and to port, an answering whistle. Petronus squinted in that direction. Certainly, with the sky barely gray he couldn't expect to see anything with much certainty. But the absence of anything at all, not even a shadow on the water, was perplexing. That combined with the proximity of the whistle alarmed him. Grymlis offered a roguish smile. "All these years," he said, "I wondered how he did it."

"Who?"

The bow of their boat brushed against something solid, but there was nothing there.

Grymlis chuckled. "That sea jackal you yourself employed on a few delicate matters."

Even as he heard the voice above him, Petronus made the connection. "Father Petronus," the pirate Rafe Merrique said, "I'm pleased to see that your demise was overstated."

Petronus's laugh was more of a bark. Stretching out his hands, he touched the cold wet sides of an invisible wooden ship. "You spirited me away to the Emerald Coasts the night after my funeral." He studied the air above him where the voice seemed to be.

"Aye," the pirate the said. "It appears I did. At the time, I didn't ask any questions."

Grymlis stood up. "I'm sure we paid you quite well not to."

But who is paying you now? Merrique had cost a small fortune each time they hired him once he'd exhausted his need for the technological wonders the Androfrancines were willing to offer for the occasional use of his vessel. Touching the hull of the old magicked sloop, he could appreciate just why Rafe Merrique placed such a high price on his services. There was no way the old pirate was turning a kindly deed. Petronus had always dealt favorably with him during his office, but that was fairness three decades ago and not sufficient to merit uncompensated assistance. No, someone was paying him well to be in this place at this moment.

He caught Grymlis's eye and willed his hands to move quickly. *Who is paying him?*

Grymlis's own hands moved faster. *Allies on the Delta.*

Petronus blinked and, forgetting his hands, spoke aloud. "The Delta?" He'd killed Sethbert with his own hand in front of a thousand Androfrancines. He'd excluded the Entrolusian delegate from attendance, rejected Sethbert's own sister's pleas not out of cruelty but selfishness. He couldn't bear to have their eyes upon him when he murdered Sethbert at the end of his sham trial.

Allies on the Delta.

Another voice joined in. "Hold fast, old man. I'm putting your hands upon the ladder." Rough hands grabbed at his arms and tugged them. Petronus found a rope ladder and stepped onto it. The ladder swayed as he climbed, and when he reached the top, firm hands reached out to pull him onto the invisible deck.

"Welcome aboard the *Kinshark*," Rafe Merrique said. "I am at your service, Father Petronus."

Petronus saw nothing and found himself suddenly pulled into the vertigo of the magicked vessel and its invisible crew. He pitched forward, watching the waves far beneath his feet. The hands steadied him, and Merrique chuckled. "You'll want to close your eyes until you're belowdecks. You and the others have quarters and breakfast waiting. Your benefactor has ensured that every comfort will be afforded you." Petronus squeezed his eyes closed and trusted the new set of hands that took him and guided his shaking steps across the deck. Once he was hustled into the hatch, he opened his eyes and found himself staring down the stairs to a plush carpet and the beginnings of an elaborate paneled hall. Not anything like the sleek, spartan vessel he remembered from the night of his escape. They'd colored his hair and shaved his beard, passing him off as a traveling scholar who required his privacy—a common cover for Li Tam agents—and had taken him to the island port closest to House Li Tam's holdings on the Inner Emerald Coast. He'd not spent that trip in any comfort that suggested rugs and decorative wood trim. Merrique had done well for himself in the years since.

Girls in silk, with dark skin and wide, genuine smiles greeted him at the bottom of the stairs, inclining their heads demurely. They did not speak; they simply led the men down the corridor, stopping in front of an open door for each of them. When they ushered Petronus into his cabin, he saw that his things were already aboard. The cabin itself was comfortable—polished wood paneling with paintings from the Days of the Gathering, at the tail end of the Age of Laughing Madness, when the fledgling Order first opened the New World that the Gypsies and Marshers had inherited from Xhum Y'Zir. The bed was oak and wide enough. The porthole shutters were pulled and locked on the outside. There was an armchair and a desk. A small bookcase with a dozen volumes of varied age stood across from an equally small wardrobe.

Someone wanted him dead for his association with the Order. And now, in his escape from whomever that was, he was sailing for the Entrolusian Delta, toward a collection of city-states that had been embroiled in civil war since Sethbert killed their economy and Petronus killed their deranged but strong leader. There were still those who maintained that the Overseer was a patriot for what he did.

I've seen the evidence of it, Petronus realized, knowing that even he suspected the Order after seeing his forged signature.

The ship shuddered to life as the sails caught wind. Petronus smelled frying bacon and hot chai mixed with the aroma of cooking onions and sliced potatoes. Regardless of whether he sailed into more or less danger than the attack on his life, he certainly sailed in comfort.

Petronus followed his nose to the galley, suddenly grateful to be alive. It hadn't struck him until now: It was the first time he could remember being personally attacked. It was the first time he'd been utterly certain he would die.

Petronus blessed his benefactors and sat himself down to break-fast.

Neb

The Marshers wove their way through the Whymer Maze in Rudolfo's northern garden, carrying Hanric's body and singing as they went. When he'd first joined them, Neb thought he would stay to the edges, but from the beginning, Winters kept him by her side and held his hand tightly.

He'd not slept that night, the events of the banquet playing out again and again in his mind. Now, he felt the weariness saturating him as the buzzing in his brain subsided. Neb shivered, feeling the cold despite the winter woolens of his scout uniform.

He and Winters kept the lead, the others following and reciting the Marsher death psalms low and in minor key. They were in a tongue he did not recognize—perhaps simply glossolalia, though the language seemed more structured than that—and their voices blended into harmony. He glanced at the young girl beside him and saw her lips moving, though he heard no sound.

The early morning was dark and still around them, the noise of the manor muffled by the high thorny walls of the maze. Soon enough, he would join Aedric and Isaak at the front of the manor and they would ride for the Keeper's Gate. All his life, Neb had wanted to see the Gate, wanted to cross the solitary pass and descend into the ruins of the Old World. He'd grown up in the Franci Orphan School, his imagination nourished by legends of the former years and tales of the Order's exploits to save what light they could in their expeditions. The day his father died with Windwir, Neb had stayed with the wagon he was to escort into the Wastes on his first expedition until Sethbert's men pulled him away.

But now, looking at the hollow-eyed girl beside him and thinking back to the night they'd passed through, Neb's interest in the Wastes competed with something else. A part of him wanted desperately to stay with his Marsh Queen, pledge his blade and his mind and heart to whatever cause lay ahead of her, or at the very least, to hold her hand and let her cry as she needed.

Once, back on the plain of Windwir—before he'd known her true rank—she'd teased him about marriage when he'd asked her to come with him. She'd laughed on that day, but he'd known there was no malice in it. "Would you take me as your bride, Nebios ben Hebda, and grant me a Gypsy wedding filled with dancing and music?" she'd asked him. "Is that what you would do?"

Now, as they approached the center of the maze, Neb found himself thinking of it again, only now he saw himself in the Marshlands, moving with her among her people, shoring up Hanric's loss. Surely it made a kind of sense if he was indeed their Homeseeker. And yet deeper in the center of him, a voice whispered that this was not their time no matter how badly he wished to lend her his strength.

The procession stopped in the center, and two of the larger men moved the marble meditation bench aside, while two of the others set in with pickaxes to loosen the frozen ground ahead of the shovels. The songs continued, quietly, as they dug, and Neb felt Winters's grip tighten on his hand. He looked down at her and saw the firmness in the line of her jaw despite the tears that traced their pathways down her cheeks. Her tears threatened his own, now carefully held back as he steeled himself to face his First Captain, and he looked away. Back to the rectangle of ground they cut and dug. Memory tugged him backward, to a vast field of graves on a shattered plain.

When Petronus had first suggested that they bury Windwir's dead, he'd thought it an impossible task. Nearly two hundred thousand souls strong—each skeleton left intact by Xhum Y'Zir's blood magick rite, each bone a message of violence. But they'd gathered their ragged army of gravediggers there at the end of second summer, and had worked through autumn, into winter, wrapping up in the spring. And somewhere along the way, the scruffy old fisherman had pronounced himself the Pope and left the gravedigging in Neb's hands. Naturally, he'd done his best. How could he not?

His father had been among Windwir's dead.

And at the end of that work, on the night before Rudolfo and Petronus arrived to escort him to his new home in the Ninefold Forest, Neb had presided over the quiet funeral of the world's greatest city. The band of diggers that still remained had gathered up on the hill above the east bank of the Second River, and after a song about the light, they had called upon their young captain for a few words.

Here, at this grave today, Neb could not remember a single one of those words. But he'd given them; he'd seen the nods of assent and the tears of grief satisfied. He'd heard every cough and every creak of every boot heel. He could not recall that eulogy, but at the same time, he felt better for having given it. Still, it felt easier then than now though he was not called upon for any role in this present grave-digging. Maybe the vast number of Windwir's graves made the grief and loss then so much harder to lay hold of.

Maybe it just now settles in, he thought. Or maybe it would settle in slowly, like a large man to a bath, gradually becoming more real with each loss that followed.

Or maybe it is because deep down we know that whatever laid Windwir low has now taken Hanric from this world as well.

The sudden thought ambushed him and he blinked at it. The world had changed on the day of the spell. And it had not recovered. The nations that weren't locked in civil war were at odds with their neighbors. And now that violence had spilled over into assassinations. The only thriving place in the Named Lands seemed to be the Ninefold Forest, with the construction of its new library and rapid expansion of the town around it. Before Windwir, Rudolfo ruled a resource-rich corner of the New World and led a simple, pleasurable life. Now, the path of change took them in a new direction as the Ninefold Forest Houses emerged as perhaps the strongest nation in the Named Lands.

Another thought struck him: Three of the most prominent leaders from the War of Windwir were in that Great Hall last night. Two were dead. One had not even been scratched.

He looked up as Winters released his hand and stepped forward. As the men continued working their shovels, the others gathered around her and Neb stepped back. She raised her hands and broke into tongues, her eyes fixed upon Hanric's corpse. The Marshers swayed at her words, and suddenly Neb felt misplaced.

He felt a light touch at his elbow and glanced to his right.

Rudolfo and Aedric had joined them. The Gypsy King and his First Captain looked haggard and worn, though they now wore fresh clothing. Rudolfo held a rolled-up quilt in his hands and handed it somberly to Neb.

This is for Hanric, he signed slowly. *Present it on my behalf, Lieutenant. It belonged to my father.*

Neb nodded, hesitant to speak and unable to sign. Finally, he risked a whisper. "Yes, General."

Rudolfo's brown eyes were bloodshot, and there were dark circles beneath them, offsetting the deep lines of worry on his face. Behind his short beard, his mouth was tight and grim. Rudolfo returned

Neb's nod, cast Aedric a sidelong glance, and the two slipped back into the maze.

As they vanished, Neb looked back to Winters. As she continued speaking, the men continued digging and some of the women began stripping Hanric down, putting his bloodstained clothing to the side in a pile. A bucket of steaming water appeared, and Neb watched as they scrubbed the hairy corpse clean of both the blood and the telltale filth that set Marshers apart from the other residents of the New World. After, they scooped dirt into the bucket and mixed it into mud with their hands. Keening beneath a sky that now shifted into deep, star-specked gray, they smeared the mud over Hanric's naked form as Winters's voice rose in pitch.

Her glossolalia passed and she looked out at the small group, her eyes wet. "Hanric ben Tornus's sojourn in shadow is past," she said, "and he shall walk the Beneath Places in search of Home. How shall he find his way?"

A woman stepped forward with the discarded stub of a candle, bowing deeply, and placing it at Winters's feet.

Winters returned the bow and continued. "Hanric ben Tornus's sojourn in hunger is past," she said, "and he shall hunt the Beneath Places in search of food. How shall he strike his prey?"

An older man stepped forward with a handful of smooth stones and an old leather sling, laying it beside the candle with a bow.

Her voice became sorrowful now. "Hanric ben Tornus's sojourn in the sunlight is past and he shall rest in the cold of the Beneath Places. How shall he warm his soul?" Her eyes found Neb and met them. They were wide and there were worlds of grief within them.

On shaking legs, Neb forced himself forward. He took the quilt and laid it at her feet, his eyes never leaving hers. He bowed, sadness pulling again at his heart and eyes.

She nodded to him and he stepped back. As the ritual continued, he tried to pay attention. Other gifts were brought forward; and then, as the diggers finished the grave and the women finished the mud-ding, songs and stories of Hanric ben Tornus and his shadow-reign upon the Wicker Throne were lifted up to the winter morning. As if paying obeisance of their own, the swollen stars winked out and the sliver of blue-green moon slid from the sky and into the ground.

When it was time, they wrapped Hanric in Lord Jakob's quilt with the candle in one hand and the sling in the other, and lowered him into the ground with his other gifts. Then, each in turn cast a shovel of dirt upon his sleeping form and let the Beneath Places swallow their friend.

When they were finished, one by one the Marshers drifted off, leaving Neb and Winters beside the new-turned earth. They sat, side by side, on the meditation bench, and finally Winters sighed.

"I know you need to go," she told him.

He slipped his arm up around her narrow shoulders. "I do. But I do not wish it."

She chuckled and it almost sounded bitter. "What we wish does not often enter into matters, Nebios ben Hebda. Your lord bids you go."

He looked over to her. There beside him, she seemed much smaller than when she stood before her people. "But what does my lady bid?"

She smiled. "I bid you take the path you are called to. I bid you find our Home as the dreams have told us you will."

But what if the dreams are wrong? He did not ask it. He would not ask it. Instead, he made a statement that he willed into a promise. "I will be back within a week," he said.

She moved closer to him, leaning in, and he felt her shiver. "I will be gone by then." She paused, shifting uncomfortably. "I fear something dark becomes of my people, though I do not know what it is. My own kind have brought this about. I must know why."

Word that the assassins were Marshers had spread quietly through the ranks of the scouts, and certainly it was a darkness she needed to plumb. She was the Marsh Queen, with her work awaiting. He was an officer of the Gypsy Scouts—of the Forest Library—with his own.

Neb wanted to protest it. He wanted to strip off the scarf of his rank, take up the bucket of now-cold mud and smear himself with it. He wanted to pledge his knives to her service and follow her back to the Marshlands to hunt down whoever was responsible for last night's attack.

But I am pledged to the library. Not the library, he thought, but the light of knowledge it represented and the man who would shepherd that light here in the Ninefold Forest, away from the political turmoil of the Named Lands. And if the dreams of her people were true, the Ninefold Forest Houses also guarded the way to the Home he was meant to find them. He sighed and pulled her close again, taking in the earthy scent of her.

After a minute or two of silence, Neb stood and Winters stood with him. When she turned to face him, he matched her movements and they put their arms around one another.

"I will see you in our dreams," she whispered. "Be well and safe, Nebios ben Hebda."

There at Hanric's Rest, at the heart of the Whymer Maze, they kissed again. When they finished, Neb pushed a strand of dirty, unkempt hair from her narrow face. "Be well and safe, my queen," he said. His voice caught on the words as he said them. Some part of him, deeply buried, knew they now moved through a time that was anything but safe. Still, he said it again, using her formal name: "Be safe, Winteria."

At her nod, he left the young queen alone with her shadow and made his way back out, mindful of the thorny walls that squeezed him, body and soul. He walked briskly to the courtyard, where the horses and wagon awaited him. Isaak sat astride a great stallion, holding the reins of Neb's mount. A cold morning breeze whipped the edges of his dark Androfrancine robes.

Neb took the reins and quickly checked the travel kit one of the men had fixed to the back of the saddle. Satisfied, he swung up onto the horse. When Aedric looked at him, Neb nodded and the First Captain whistled the men forward.

Without a word, and without looking back, Neb rode eastward with his company into the red light of the stirring sun.

Rudolfo

Late-morning sun slanted through the windows of a room that smelled of incense and sweat. Rudolfo sat in an armchair near the bed, holding Jin Li Tam's hand, feeling his knuckles threaten to pop with each contraction as she groaned in her labor and squeezed his hand. He looked up, glancing first to the River Woman, who watched and waited near the foot of the bed, then to his betrothed, the formidable daughter of House Li Tam.

She lay in sweat-soaked sheets, her red hair wet and matting her forehead and cheeks. Her cotton shift clung to her body, the pink of her skin showing through where the damp cotton stuck to it. Her muscles were taut, her eyes squeezed shut and her jaw set.

"You're doing fine, dear," the River Woman said, but Rudolfo heard trouble in her tone. A platter of assorted cheeses and a carafe of lukewarm pear wine sat untouched on a small table within easy reach. There was a light knock at the door, and he looked up to see the River

Woman frown at yet another interruption in a night and a day of interruptions.

One of the River Woman's girls opened the door a crack and hushed words were exchanged. She glanced to Rudolfo. "Your Second Captain, Lord."

Rudolfo started to stand, but Jin Li Tam's grip prevented him. "No," she said. "You'll not leave again." Her blue eyes were narrow and the firmness in her tone brooked no dissent. "Send him in," she said.

The River Woman's voice was also firm. "Lady, I do not think—"

Rudolfo glanced from woman to woman. The outcome of this moment's match of wills was not difficult to surmise.

"These are not the best of circumstances for an argument," Jin Li Tam said, anger and pain giving her voice an edge. *"Send him in."*

The River Woman relented, and Philemus, the Second Captain of the Gypsy Scouts entered, discomfort obvious in his stance and stammer. "General," he said with a nod, then paled as he glanced to Jin Li Tam. "L-lady, I apologize for—"

"You owe no apology, Captain," she said. Her body spasmed again and she growled. "Bear your message quickly."

He swallowed and nodded. "Our scouts have overtaken the assailants. There were four. They are all dead."

Rudolfo raised an eyebrow. "Dead?" Unbidden, his mind flashed back to the scrambling fight of the night before, to the strength in their attackers that so completely overran them, so casually lifted and tossed them aside as if Rudolfo and his best and brightest were made of paper instead of flesh and bone. His men could not have taken them, not as they were. Unless . . . "Had their magicks burned off?"

Philemus shook his head. "No, General. But they were easy enough to track. They seem to have died suddenly and in midflight, near the edge of the Prairie Sea. I've ordered the men to bring back the bodies." He hesitated. "The Physician Benoit is also here now. He will start his examination once the magicks have worn off." He looked to the River Woman. "And once your . . . work . . . is finished here, certainly," he added.

Jin Li Tam jerked again, arching her back. This time, she cried out even louder, and Rudolfo glanced to her again. He'd watched a hundred skirmishes from the hillside, eventually cursing and riding down into the thick of it when the waiting proved too much for him. But this was a battle he could not ride into, and he found frustration in that powerlessness. And until now, he'd heard his men speak of these moments. But as he'd grown older and accepted that an heir was unlikely though not for lack of practice, he'd brushed aside what little he'd heard from the new fathers in his household or his army. Though he suspected that even if he had listened intently, even taken notes upon the subject, it could not have prepared him for this.

He looked to the River Woman and saw the strain on her face, the cloud in her eyes, in that brief unguarded moment. When she saw he was watching, she smiled, but it failed to convince him.

Something in this does not bode well, he thought.

Rudolfo turned to Philemus. "In Aedric's absence, you bear my grace in all matters pertaining to this investigation. Work with House Steward Kember on all other matters, and from here forward, do not disturb us unless it is absolutely essential for the well-being of the Houses."

The man came to attention. "Yes, General."

Now, to offset the sternness of his tone and the darkness of the night's events, Rudolfo winked at the soldier. "The next time I see you, I will introduce you to my heir." He glanced again toward the River Woman and saw her bite her lip at his words. His stomach lurched and he found himself hoping that Jin Li Tam was sufficiently distracted by the pain.

His hands moved quickly and subtly once the door closed. *What are you not telling us, Earth Mother?*

She blinked but recovered quickly. "You're doing fine, dear. It's nearly time to push." Her own hands moved beneath Jin's line of sight. *There is something wrong with the baby. I do not know what.* "Are you thirsty? Can we get you anything?" Even as the words came out, her hands moved again. *But I would not have the mother of my lord's child alarmed at this point.*

Rudolfo took in a deep breath, feeling his stomach lurch again, a thousand times more pronounced than the impulse that led him charging down the hill to join his Gypsy Scouts in war. *How is it,* he wondered, *that I could care so much so soon for someone I've not yet seen?*

Jin Li Tam squeezed his hand and cried out again. Turning toward her, he put his other hand over the top of hers. "You are a fine, formidable woman," he told her in a quiet voice. "And I am proud to have you at my side." When her eyes met his and he saw the tears in them, he leaned in closer. "When this has passed," he said, "I will take you as my bride and you will be the Forest Queen." As he spoke, he pressed his free hand into the back of hers and into the soft places of her wrist. *You will ever be my sunrise and our son shall be my rising moon.*

He wasn't sure how long it had been since he had said the words. A fog had taken him at the end of the confrontation with her father, when he'd learned that his life had been a river moved to relocate a library and create a safe haven for the light away from the Androfrancine shepherds. Even the woman, Tam's forty-second daughter, had been a part of that work. He'd loved her in the days before learning that, had drawn strength from her when his closest friend, Gregoric, had died in Sethbert's camp. But those feelings had faltered and become something closer to resolve than love, though he did not doubt she loved him fiercely. That love had brought her to a choice, and she had left off her father's work for it.

But now, in this place, so fresh from the death of Hanric and so far from that bonfire on the Inner Emerald Coast and the confrontation with Vlad Li Tam, he felt something stirring within him and did not know what to name it. He found himself recalling the nights and days they'd sweated together, exploring one another sometimes in silence, sometimes amid sighs and cries of delight, in a hundred different pairings. One of those pairings had borne fruit, though later she'd told him of the powders she'd used to give his soldiers back their swords.

And now, she travailed at birth, and there was something wrong with the baby.

Our baby.

He'd thought perhaps the new library would be the greatest thing he ever built, but now he knew that it could not be so. Indeed, this child was.

For hours, he sat and held her hand, pressing messages into her skin and whispering to her as she raged and roared against the pain like the tigers that wandered the garden jungles of her home. He watched as the pain grew and as the contractions increased, and when the time came, he urged her with the River Woman to push, to breathe, to push more and harder.

And when little Lord Jakob was pulled from her, limp and gray, he leaped to his feet to see his blood-mottled son, feeling the room spin away as powerlessness and rage washed him.

And when the River Woman shouted in alarm for her powders and swabbed out the small blue-lipped mouth with her little finger, he turned back to his betrothed and blocked her view and whispered yet more assurances as the Earth Mother gently blew life back into his son and reinforced that life with whatever magicks her alchemist's pouch could yield.

When that first weak and retching cough came and that first mewling cry of Lord Jakob, Shepherd of the Light, met its first winter midnight, Rudolfo leaped forward to study the tiny face and hands that he had helped to make.

So this, Rudolfo thought as the River Woman cleaned and wrapped their child for the new mother's waiting arms, *is love.*

Laughing, the Gypsy King collapsed back into the chair and wept for the terror and joy that had seized him.

Chapter 6

Jin Li Tam

Jin Li Tam drifted in and out of sleep, waking to nurse Jakob when the River Woman's girls brought him to her. Rudolfo had come and gone through the remainder of the night, leaving after they changed out her bed and bathed the sweat and blood of her labor from her exhausted body. She'd run with the scouts, fought with them, even; but nothing had prepared her for this exertion, both physical and emotional. And when it was done, to finally meet the person who had caused her such discomfort and have that memory fade into an intense and satisfying joy. Truly an overwhelming time; something, again, that she was not prepared for.

She held Jakob to her breast, offering the nipple to him. His eyes were still shut, and he was tinier than she thought a baby should be. More gray, as well, his skin the shade of paper ash. He took it, his mouth working at it with less vigor than she would have expected, and she settled back into the pillows that propped her up in bed. Outside, morning announced itself quietly.

There was a faint knock at the door, and it opened before she could answer. The River Woman entered. She looked as if she hadn't slept yet, dark circles casting shadows beneath her red-rimmed eyes. But more than weariness, she looked as if she bore a world's weight upon her heart.

She is here to bear ill tidings. Jin Li Tam had spent her life reading people, looking for the signs of their honesty, their deception and their attempts to hide truth. The River Woman's message was written into her posture, into the way she held her head and the way her hands restlessly picked at her skirts.

"Awake again, I see," she said as she came to the edge of the bed. "May I sit with you?"

Jin Li Tam nodded. "Please." She shifted while the older woman sat on a corner of the mattress.

The River Woman looked to the girl in the room. "Would you give us a few moments?" Jin measured the strain her voice and watched out of the corner of her eye as the girl curtsied and slipped out of the room.

Jin Li Tam's eyes narrowed. "There is something wrong with my baby," she said in a flat voice.

"Yes," the woman said.

"He was nearly stillborn," Jin Li Tam added. "You brought him back."

The River Woman inclined her head. "He was," she said, "and I did. Yes." She looked at Jin Li Tam now, her eyes fixed on hers. "The time to be direct is upon us. Your child is sick, Lady Tam, and I cannot make him well."

Even though she'd known at the core something was wrong, hearing the words sent a shudder down her spine. She felt the worry, hard and cold, in her stomach and found herself instinctively clutching more tightly to the tiny bundle that wheezed against her bosom. "How sick?"

I will be strong, she thought, *and will not cry.*

The River Woman's voice was low and more matter-of-fact than Jin Li Tam expected after hours of tea with the old woman in her cat-dominated cottage at the edge of town. "We can keep him alive," she said, "if we are diligent."

Jin Li Tam felt her resolve slipping, felt the tears tugging at her, suddenly aware of how much her life had changed. "Have you told Lord Rudolfo?"

The old woman shook her head. "I have not. I wanted to speak with you first." She paused. "Does he know what lengths you went to for this heir?"

"Yes," she answered, looking in the direction of his study, remembering the night she'd slipped down there, barefoot and drawn by her conscience to confess her father's last manipulation of the man she loved. He'd taken it well, but those were the days and nights when the distance had been the greatest, after Petronus's execution of Sethbert and after her father's retreat from the Named Lands. He'd accepted it with an aloof politeness that neither condemned nor praised her. Still, she'd felt better with that last deception between them now brought to light. Her eyes narrowed as curiosity over the River Woman's question nudged her. "Why do you ask? Do you think there is a connection between—"

She interrupted herself, closing her mouth before she finished. Of course there was. Why else would she need to know how much Rudolfo knew? The tears came now, and nothing she did could stop them. She hung her head, held her baby close, and wept.

"Something in the powders lingered, became knit into your son." She paused. "I know little of how these particular powders work, but they are working hard against him, now. I've heard of such things. It's why the Androfrancines discouraged their use." The River Woman moved closer and put a hand on Jin Li Tam's leg. "There's no way you could have known, Lady." She offered a sympathetic smile. "Now, I have birds out to a dozen of my sisters as far away as the Divided Isle. They may know something I do not. But it would be best if I could contact whoever gave you the recipe. I'm hoping you can help me."

An image of the iron armada, now seven months absent from their native waters in the Named Lands, flitted across her inner eye. Jin Li Tam forced her focus away from the waves of despair that threatened to capsize her. She blinked the water from her eyes. "I don't think that is possible. Surely there's another way?"

The River Woman nodded slowly. "Certainly, one might be found. The birds are out. And I have the mechoservitors searching every inch of their memory scripts as well as the holdings that have drifted in from elsewhere. But most of the magicks and pharmaceutical knowledge were buried in Windwir."

Jin Li Tam felt Jakob's mouth falter, and she shifted her breast, surprised at how quickly she and her son learned this new dance between them. As he took to it again, she found her grief resolving into calculated inquiry. "What does this mean?"

The River Woman pulled a small pouch of powders from her satchel. "I've given you these," she said. "You are passing them to Lord Jakob in your milk. It will keep him alive, but he will not be a strong baby." She paused. "And you will need a wet-nurse to share this work."

Jin Li Tam balked, feeling a sudden anger rise in her that she could not place initially. Fear? Panic? It took shape before her slowly, and she forced herself to sit with the feeling until the source of it was clear.

I am not enough.

The River Woman must have read it on her face. "These magicks are potent, Lady Tam, and they will harm you if you do not let others bear this burden with you." She paused, letting the words find meaning. "This child will have a hard enough path. Let's not have him grieve a mother he did not know."

She heard hope beneath those words. Jin Li Tam looked up slowly, her eyes meeting the River Woman's. "We will need to find someone."

The River Woman smiled. "I have. There is a new girl in the refugee camp. Her husband was killed in the fighting on the Delta, and the moonshadow pox took her infant son four nights past. I tended to the child, but it was too late."

Jin Li Tam studied the old woman's face, reading it carefully for the hope she needed to see there. "And you think this will cure him?"

The cloud that passed through the River Woman's eyes betrayed her words before she spoke them. "No," she said, "it will not. It will merely keep him alive." She frowned now. "I don't know of a cure, Lady Tam, and eventually these magicks will also turn on him." She offered a weak smile, and Jin Li Tam's heart sank with it. "But it gives us time to find a better way."

The small bundle in her arms shifted slightly, and Jin Li Tam looked down at the tiny face. A light coat of reddish hair, the slightest button of a nose, eyes squeezed shut as the small mouth took nourishment from her. She shifted her hand beneath the blanket that wrapped her newborn son and felt the soft, clammy skin of the back of his neck and head.

My father has killed my son, she thought, but before she could carry it further, the truth of it settled in. She could have refused—she could have left the path she'd been groomed for all her life—but blind obedience to House Li Tam had kept her on the road that brought her to this place. *I have done this myself.*

Over the course of those days since her father left, Jin Li Tam had spent much time thinking. Every man she'd taken to bed in order to better move the Named Lands along the course her father prescribed. Every man she'd killed for the same reason. Until she met Rudolfo, she realized, her entire life had been in service to this. But something in the Gypsy King's eyes, in his flamboyant poise and his careful words, had put light on a hollowness she did not know she harbored. And though her father had planned her pairing with Rudolfo for years, had planned the heir that would tie their houses together, once she had given herself over to the Lord of the Ninefold Forest Houses, she had done so with an abandon that had nothing to do with Vlad Li Tam and his spider's web of manipulation. It was a new thing that moved her.

Love.

Perhaps, she thought, her father had intended that as well. If so, she wondered if he knew now, wherever his iron armada had taken him, how much her love for Rudolfo had birthed her hatred of her father and his dark work in their New World.

She lightly stroked the back of her infant's head, holding him close, willing her body's warmth to lift the gray pallor and clamminess of his skin.

What now would this new love birth in her?

She realized with a start that the River Woman had spoken and she looked up. "I'm sorry, Earth Mother?"

The old woman smiled, and her eyes smiled, too. "We will do all that we can. He is a beautiful baby, Lady Tam, and you are a beautiful mother."

The tears returned and she forced them away, swallowing hard. "Approach this girl on my behalf and arrange for us to meet in the morning," she said. "Speak to Stewardess Jessa and have her prepare a room for this woman in the Family Wing. If she has any kin in the camp, arrange for their care as well."

The River Woman inclined her head and stood. She placed the small pouch on a table near the bed. "One day on and one day off," she said. "No more." She went to the door and paused. "Shall I speak with Lord Rudolfo?"

Jin Li Tam shook her head. "No. I will do it." *This is my grief to bear him.*

"As you wish, Lady." Bowing slightly again, the River Woman left, and her girl returned.

When the young apprentice came to take the baby, Jin Li Tam bid her wait. He'd finished nursing now, and she held him to her shoulder, rocking him and patting his back lightly. She did so longer than she needed, willing the tears away but failing utterly at it.

My sister Rae, she thought. *She will know what to do.* Disguised as a young male acolyte and placed by their father, she'd studied the Androfrancine alchemy as a girl and had practiced it for nearly half of a century. But her sister, along with the rest of her siblings, had fled the stage her family had so long set with their careful props and practiced deceptions.

Jin Li Tam gave over her baby to the waiting girl and settled back into her bed, but no sleep came to her when she closed her eyes.

Instead, her mind went unbidden to the dream that seemed so long ago and so real.

"Thus shall the sins of P'Andro Whym be visited upon his children," the kin-raven had told her. "Fortunate are you among women and highly favored is Jakob, Shepherd of the Light."

Perhaps I misspoke. Perhaps the kin-raven's message is more welcome than I thought. She played the words out again and again.

Strange that those dark words, with their promise of a future for the frail life she'd made, should now become her truest source of hope.

For the longest while she lay there, listening for the noises her child might make and acutely aware of the gentle rustlings of the young apprentice who tended him. But it was a divided awareness. No matter how hard she tried, she could not erase the blasted plain of Windwir and its crimson sky from that dark space behind her eyes. And when she finally drifted off, the smell of ashes and blood followed her into that restless sleep.

Lysias

General Lysias of the United City-States waited by the door for Erlund's aide to announce him. The hunting lodge was stirring to life. An early-morning bustle of servants and guards flowed around him as they went about their routines, and he watched them, their faces drawn and their eyes hollow from too many nights with little sleep and too many tasks for the people at hand. They lost more and more each day as the staff either fled farther south on the Delta to join the Secessionists or fled the Delta altogether for a new start in one of a dozen demesnes willing to host the ragged refugees.

At least, Lysias thought, Erlund was more thoughtful than his late uncle when it came to these matters. Still, he realized it would not be enough. When the former Overseer had learned of soldiers deserting their posts during the War of Androfrancine Aggression, he'd maimed their family members as an example to others. Erlund at least had the sense to let them go.

I should join them, Lysias thought, but shook it away as a reminder of how little sleep he'd had of late. Dereliction of his duty was not an option. He would stay in his uniform, by the side of the Overseer, until the very end, no matter how bitter. Even, he knew, if it meant facing the axe of these so-called revolutionaries. He'd helped install the current Overseer and had helped bring down another to do so.

I will not make that mistake again.

Quietly, he cursed Sethbert's folly, though he knew he was as much to blame as the other generals who listened to the madman's ravings and agreed to the war in the first place. In the end, he'd helped the old Androfrancine captain set things right, watching while Grymlis helped the pretending Pope, Resolute, step down by way of suicide. And he had personally led the party of guards to arrest Sethbert for the crime of genocide, based on Resolute's suicide letter. The very letter he'd received from Vlad Li Tam himself, along with the ancient hand cannon, in the secret parley that removed Sethbert and installed Erlund with House Li Tam's help.

He'd seen that it was the best path for the Delta, and he had taken it in the hopes that it was not too late.

He'd been wrong.

Now civil war swallowed the Entrolusian Delta, with three of its city-states now pitted against six that remained loyal to the old ways and the line of Overseers it had produced in its thousand years of unity. Soon, another would fall to the idealists and their rhetoric.

And two nights ago, they had gone too far.

They had hired Marsher rogues to assassinate the Overseer.

The ornate double doors to Erlund's private office opened, and the aide stepped out. Like all of the others Lysias had seen, the young man looked haggard. "The Overseer will see you now, General Lysias," he said, holding the door.

Lysias nodded curtly and entered, his boots whispering across the thick carpet that marked the end of the wide hall and the beginning of Erlund's private study. The room was lavishly furnished. Mahogany paneling and framed oils of Erlund's predecessors and their families gave the room a broad, warm atmosphere that was more a ruse to lull the unsuspecting than any real gesture of comfort. A wide oak desk carved from the old-growth timber of the Ninefold Forest occupied the center, and behind it, heavy curtains sealed out the light from a window that would have normally afforded a view of the private forest that served as the Overseer's hunting grounds. At the desk, the Overseer himself sat at breakfast amid a stack of papers. The youngish man looked up.

He's aging fast. But that did not surprise the general. Erlund was a different generation than his uncle, and he'd inherited a nation ravaged by his predecessor's greed and paranoia. Had Sethbert managed his planned annexation of the Ninefold Forest and inherited the Androfrancine's holdings through his cousin's contrived papacy, it might have been different. But now the Delta died slowly, and the rest of the world followed after in the aftermath of the Desolation of Windwir. And this young man carried the weight of that upon his shoulders.

Because this new breed cares, Lysias thought.

Erlund looked up, and the dark circles beneath his eyes stood out from a pale face. "Good morning, General."

Lysias inclined his head. "Lord Erlund."

Erlund gestured to a leather-backed chair before the desk, and the general sat. "Have you learned anything further?"

Three days ago, they'd received an anonymous note by way of an unmarked bird. The message warned of an assassination and bore evidence of a deal brokered between the revolutionaries and what appeared now to be Marsher skirmishers under some kind of new scout magic. They'd had just enough time to hide Erlund away safely at sea in his yacht, replacing him with one of the half dozen doubles they'd employed from time to time as precaution during these troubled times.

And two nights ago, an invisible and razor-sharp storm had breached the estate's perimeter, leaving a shredded, bloody mess of all who stood between the attackers and their target.

"The Delta Scouts found them a hundred leagues north late last night," he told the Overseer. "They were dead. Six of them." He paused. "He's confident that it's all of them."

Erlund looked surprised. "Dead? Our best scouts couldn't touch them. How is this possible?"

Lysias shifted uncomfortably. He wasn't sure how it was possible, but the captain that served as his aide had awakened him with the note. "I don't know," he said. "But I've dispatched a wagon to bring the bodies back. They were Marshers, just like the letter indicated. They died on their feet, and according to Captain Syskus they are uninjured beyond minor cuts and scrapes."

Erlund thought for a moment, his spoon pausing midway to mouth. "I will want the House Surgeon's thorough report," he said.

Lysias nodded. Perhaps that crafty old cutter could find some trace of whatever magick the assassins had employed. He'd seen nothing like it in all his years, and it hearkened back to ancient history lessons in the Academy, tales of yore from the days before the Age of Laughing Madness when the Wizard Kings ruled the Old World with their Blood Guard and their spells of dark power, brokered in the Beneath Places under the earth. "You shall have it, Lord."

"Good." The Overseer spooned the gray, steaming oats into his mouth and chased it with what looked like honeyed lemon beer. "When do you think it will be safe to return to Carthos?"

Lysias had thought about this, knowing the answer he was about to give would not sit well. "I don't," he said. "I think staying here is more defensible."

Erlund shook his head, putting down his tankard. "I'll not hide here much longer, Lysias. Esarov and his intellectual troublemakers need to know that they have failed and that the Delta's Overseer is very much alive and in power."

In this, he is like his uncle. Lysias felt frustration brewing within him and forced his voice not to show it. "It is not prudent, Lord. The city-states are no longer safe for you. At the very least, have Ignatio put another double in your palace until we know more of the nature of this threat."

Erlund's eyes narrowed. "General Lysias?" he asked, his voice low.

Lysias met his eyes and held them. "Yes, Lord?"

"When have you ever been able to sway me from what I considered to be the right path?"

Lysias finally looked away and in doing so, accepted the rebuke. "Never, Lord." *But it may yet be your undoing,* he thought. It had certainly undone Sethbert.

"Very well." The Overseer then changed the subject deftly. "And what news from the cities?"

"Samael and Calapia are stabilizing with the increased troops enforcing martial law," he said. "Berande will secede within the month, regardless of what we do." Erlund looked up at this, his eyes betraying his question before his mouth could speak it. Lysias continued. "The governor there has no will to resist, and the people are calling for elections, echoing the Reformist rhetoric about the original Charter of Unity and the Settlers' original intent."

When those first founders had established their cities, they'd formed a document that, as everything else, had evolved into something entirely different. Of course, these were the early days when the Androfrancines were a fledgling company with its ragged ash-hued army carving out a fortress in the deep woods of the Second River's isolated valley. Every noble on the Delta learned that charter inside and out from boyhood.

Erlund growled. "Idealist rubbish. This unrest is not about liberty or enforcing some naive interpretation of a charter intended for another time." Anger flashed in the Overseer's eyes. "This unrest is a looking backward to better, simpler times in the face of economic decline and abject poverty." He waited a moment, as if deciding whether or not to say what was on his mind. Then, he said it. "My uncle brought this about when he destroyed Windwir and took us into war against the Gypsies and the Marshers."

There was a light tap at the door, and Erlund tapped a small brass bell. It rang clear and the door opened. His aide stepped inside. "Lord Erlund, your next appointment is here."

Erlund nodded and leaned forward. "Ignatio," he said. "With his intelligence briefing."

Another similarity to Sethbert, Lysias thought, keeping the military and intelligence compartmentalized. Erlund was brutally careful in this, so much so that if the bird hadn't come directly to Lysias with its warning, he had no doubt that Erlund's man, Ignatio, would have handled the evacuation and the manhunt. Erlund would have insisted on it.

"Thank you for your time, Lord Erlund," he said. As he turned to the door, he saw the dark-robed spymaster. Ignatio was Erlund's own man. He'd had Sethbert's spymaster killed early on, not trusting him to take well to the new administration. Ignatio was the illegitimate son of a Franci arch-scholar, and it gave him an edge. Even now, his eyes moved over the room and over Lysias. And as Lysias moved past him, a smile pulled at the corners of his mouth.

"General Lysias," he said. "I heard your men found the attackers. That is most excellent." It was a message, Lysias realized: *I heard.*

Of course you heard it, Lysias thought. But he smiled. "It is fortuitous."

Ignatio bowed slightly and entered the room, taking the seat that Lysias had stood from. Lysias left, making his way through the wide hallways of the hunting lodge until he found the landing and the staircase that would lead him to the front doors. He had a desk covered in reports waiting for his review, and he made mental note to have his closest officers cull the ranks again for any of Ignatio's spies. They would be shipped out to enforce martial law, and some night in the weeks ahead, they would go out on patrol and not return.

Ignatio was shameless in his espionage, and try as he might, Lysias was unable to even those odds. For the past seven months, there had been strange goings-on between Ignatio and Erlund. Lysias had glimpsed it again and again. An entire basement had been quickly absorbed by the intelligence officer's men, and a week ago, six of those men had been killed, their bodies hauled out beneath blood-soaked sheets to disappear wherever it was that Ignatio had made a hundred other bodies go. And as much as it had distressed the spymaster, it enraged Erlund. Lysias had reports of black-cloaked riders sent out from Erlund's private guard, spies that hunted north, west and east. Those that rode east had still not returned.

As he left the hunting lodge and made for the nearby barracks, Lysias tried to look at the sky and find something beautiful in the crisp winter day. It had rained, melting the last night's snow quickly, and the morning smelled like pine needles and loam.

Maybe I am too old for this work now. He hadn't felt that way before Windwir, and especially before leading those guards into Sethbert's bedchambers to arrest the madman. He'd felt it then, the weariness creeping up on him; he had not equated it with age. But the capstone was when his own daughter took up with a Secessionist librarian, fleeing with him to Parmona when that city threw down its governor and his brigades. That was the day he first felt old. And the look in her eye that last time he saw her, so much like her mother, sparked another feeling within him that he desperately wished to misplace. But these days, he carried it around with him and it weighed him down; he could not defeat it despite the strategy and forces he mustered.

I have helped to make this happen.

Pushing back that sudden stab of guilt, General Lysias grabbed hold of what had always sustained him in times past.

He was, after all, first and foremost a man of duty.

Rudolfo

Rudolfo stood in his dressing room and let that moment of silence and stillness wash him. He'd spent much of the day dispatching birds and discussing his investigation strategy with Captain Philemus. Some-time in the night or early morning they expected return birds as they probed the Forest Gypsy's slight but effective network of spies and in-formants elsewhere in the Named Lands. He anticipated their news, but there were other birds coming—birds that he did not look forward to once Turam's ailing king learned of his only heir's demise.

Between the birds and Philemus, he'd also managed to sit long enough to hear the Physician's report on his autopsy of the one Marsher already cooling in the ice house. It was perplexing news.

"I've seen nothing like it," the Physician told him, and the River Woman next to him nodded her agreement. "His heart gave out, along with the rest of his organs."

Rudolfo had made the first suggestion that came to mind. "Poison, then?"

But the Physician shook his head. "I think it was the blood magicks."

Hours later, the puzzle stayed with him and he sighed, looking to the dressing room's one small window to gauge the day's remains. It would be dark soon, and he still needed to sit with Winters, discuss his strategy and hear her thoughts before she left tomorrow with her people. He did not envy the path ahead of her.

If these assassins were truly Marshers, she not only had trouble within her borders but would soon have it without. Turam would not take well to the death of their future king, despite the internal troubles they had themselves.

And Rudolfo's kin-clave with the Marshers would need to be hon-ored, pulling the Ninefold Forest Houses into a political situation that was tenuous at best.

But before all of that, there was another matter to attend to.

He went to his father's wardrobe, the one where he'd kept those few personal belongings of his parents that meant something to him. His father's sword hung there, along with the emerald-encrusted scab-bard. His mother's hunting bow hung near it. On the shelves within stood a scattering of their favorite books—some that they had read to Rudolfo and Isaak when they were young boys. And behind those books lay the box.

He stretched up on tiptoes, reaching over those bound volumes, to find it. Then he pulled it down and opened it.

He'd not looked in the box for twenty years at least, though he'd known for nearly a year that he would need to. For the briefest of times, he'd looked forward to this. Then, that day at Vlad Li Tam's bonfire had burned that hope away, turning it into something different.

Until the boy arrived.

Surprised at the trembling of his hands, Rudolfo reached into the box and lifted out a smaller box. Within it lay the two simple bands of silver that his mother and father had exchanged upon the day of his birth, even as the Gypsy Kings and Queens before them had done. Slipping the smaller box into his pocket, he carefully closed and replaced the larger back in its proper place.

As he left the dressing room, he thought about what came next.

He paused in the large bath chamber that separated his suite of rooms from those of Jin Li Tam. He splashed his face in water touched with lilac oil, pausing to take in his hollow eyes in the small mirror.

It wasn't that he did not love Jin Li Tam, he thought, though it was a different love than what it might have been. It was a love having more to do with trust and effectiveness than passion or romance. Though there were times, as during her labor, where those feelings of intense longing would take him and he would find joy in her form, in her way with words, in the brightness of her eyes.

But those feelings, he reasoned, were not required. And if anything, they were not to be counted upon when it came to matters of state or duty. Still, he held hope that one day, what had started between them with the fire of a sunset would rekindle.

He went to the door on the other side of the bath chamber, the one that led to her room. He knocked lightly, and when she bid him enter, he pushed aside his introspection.

Jin Li Tam was not alone with Jakob—but he had not really expected her to be. A young woman who looked ill at ease was there with the River Woman, and the three of them were gathered around Jakob. He closed the door behind him.

As he approached, a look passed between Jin Li Tam and the River Woman. He'd seen the look before—from the River Woman, admonition and from Jin Li Tam, resolution.

Jin Li Tam looked to him now, and he watched her hands move, low and to her side. *I have a difficult matter to discuss with you.*

Soon, he replied. He forced a smile. "How is our son this evening?"

"As well as can be expected," the River Woman said. The old woman looked tired, but that did not surprise Rudolfo—she'd spent the last three days at the manor, grabbing a few hours of sleep where she could but working night and day to care for the infant.

Jin Li Tam tried to return Rudolfo's smile, then turned to the young woman. "Lynnae," she said, "I would like to introduce you to Lord Rudolfo." She looked to Rudolfo again. "I've taken the liberty of securing Lynnae's help with our child. I hope that is acceptable."

Odd, he thought, that she would seek a stranger with a house of servants at her disposal.

Rudolfo studied the girl. She was young, her dark, curly hair spilling out from beneath a scarf, offsetting her olive skin. Her clothing was simple fare, though it was taking on a threadbare quality from constant use; she shifted uncomfortably on her feet. She was pretty, he noted, but haunted by grief and too little sleep. *Like the rest of us,* he observed.

He stepped forward with a flourish and inclined his head toward her. "Lady Lynnae," he said. "If Lady Tam requires your assistance, then my House is at your beckoning."

She blushed and curtsied. "Thank you, Lord. You have already been a gracious host to us."

Entrolusian by her accent, he thought, *with a touch of the Southern Coasts.* Most likely a refugee from the Delta, then. He watched her leave, and after another glance between the remaining two women, he watched the River Woman leave as well. Suddenly, for the first time since the night of the birth, Rudolfo and Jin Li Tam were alone with their baby.

Jin Li Tam patted the bedcovers beside her. "Come and hold your son, Rudolfo."

Come and hold your son. The words stirred something inside of him to life again, like that night she had labored for the baby's delivery. He went to the bed and sat next to her, receiving the bundle that stirred slightly in his unexpected arms. The skin color was more pallid than gray now, but the hollow eyes were the same. Rudolfo looked up. "Do you know what ails him yet?"

Jin Li Tam nodded. "We do." He read the grief and worry on her face and steeled himself. "It was the powders," she said.

Rudolfo's heart wrenched. "The powders?"

"Yes. The ones I gave you." She paused. "The ones my sister provided the scrip for."

Rudolfo blinked. "Will he improve?"

She shook her head, and when the last light of the evening sun caught her face, Rudolfo saw the shame in her eyes. "No, he will not. I must find my sister."

Jin Li Tam's words elicited his memory of those iron ships at anchor and the lines of servants who loaded up the docks for the long boats to ferry what goods they could out to the deeper waters where Vlad Li Tam's fleet awaited. "She is with your father," he said, though it was more a question than a statement.

"I think so," Jin said. "But I've sent a bird to be certain."

"If she's left with him," he said, "it's a vast ocean." He studied the small face, watched the tiny chest labor for breath, wanting to ask how much time they had but afraid to. "Only the gods know where he's fled to." But even as he said it, the words felt wrong. *Not fled*.

He glanced over to his betrothed as she spoke. "I will find him," she said. "I have to."

There was resolve in her voice, and it camouflaged a desperation that Rudolfo doubted others would hear in her. He heard it, though, and knew to go carefully over that ground. "Have you discussed your travel plans with the River Woman?"

Her eyes narrowed and her jawline set with determination. "There is nothing to discuss." She paused. "I can do this, Rudolfo. I'm getting stronger every day." But her pale skin and her hollow eyes suggested otherwise.

He smiled and tickled the infant's chin. Even as the words formed themselves in his mind, a strategy—haphazard and impossible to measure success against—formed in his mind. "I do not doubt that you can do this," he lied. "I merely inquire as to how you would accomplish this while caring for our son. I only question whether or not this is a journey *he* should make. Your father and his household have been at sea for seven months. They could be anywhere by now."

He could hear the anger rising in her voice. "You suggest that we simply send our scouts to find him?"

He shook his head. "No. I suggest that we not send you and our ill child. Think for a moment," he said, "and you will see the logic in my words." He slowly counted to ten and then continued. "It would be a better use of our resources to have you remain in the Ninefold Forest and see to our interests here, caring for our boy."

For a moment, the spark in her eye turned to panic, and Rudolfo first saw the danger of a cornered mother whose child is threatened. Then, it subsided. When it did, he continued. "There is a storm brewing here," he told her. "Ansylus's death and that of Hanric, even, are going to put all eyes upon the Marshers during a time when the world needs a scapegoat for its woe, and we are the Marshers only kin-clave.

Your skills in that dance far outstrip mine, though certainly I know the steps."

Her eyes narrowed. "What are you proposing?"

He played out the strategy, testing the corners of it in his mind. There were certainly other ways, but he could not bring himself to trust anyone else with the treasure of his son's life. He could not send scouts, as she suggested. It would not suffice.

And it was true—he *was* an astute player of Queen's War when it came to the political machinations of the Named Lands, but Jin Li Tam was vastly better. He was not needed here personally, though a part of him bristled at the idea of leaving given the present status of this game board. Still, he was resolved. He said the words slowly, feeling the irony of them against the back of his throat. "I am proposing," he said, "that I go and find your father."

Her look of surprise was obvious. "You vowed to kill my father upon your next meeting. He killed your family. He killed Gregoric."

Each reminder stung, but he kept his eyes fixed on the tiny eyes of his infant son. "I may yet kill him when this is finished. But I will not rest until I have found him and found your sister."

Jin Li Tam opened her mouth to speak, but Rudolfo spoke faster. "That brings me to another matter," he said, shifting the baby in his arms so that he could dig the wooden box from his pocket.

She eyed the box with curiosity as he opened it. When he spoke, he heard his voice as if it were far away. "Jin Li Tam, of House Li Tam, mother of Jakob, I pledge my land and blade to you and offer you this ring as token of our marriage. Wear it and show the world that you of all souls bear my grace." He'd never practiced the words before; he'd known them all his life. And certainly, Rudolfo had imagined this day would come soon enough, but he had thought to wait until they were past the shadow of Windwir's fall.

Now he realized that they might never move past that shadow, that if anything, those shadows might lead to even darker times ahead. Slowly, he took up the ring his mother had worn all the days of her womanhood and extended it to Jin Li Tam. Their eyes met, and he saw that there were tears in hers. She extended her hand, and he placed the ring upon her third finger, pleased that it fit. "Now," he said in a quiet voice, "you do the same."

Her fingers shook slightly as she took the larger ring and placed it upon his finger. "Rudolfo, Lord of the Ninefold Forest Houses, son of Jakob and father of Jakob," she said, "I pledge my heart and hand to you and offer you this ring as a token of our marriage." Their eyes met again. "Wear it and show the world that you of all souls bear my grace."

Rudolfo inclined his head toward his wife. His wife did the same, and between them, Lord Jakob stirred and cried.

Rudolfo raised his hand and held it so that the light caught the simple silver band. He'd not seen it worn since the day they took it off his father's cold finger. "For now," he said, "this will be binding." He smiled. "When I return, we will have a proper Gypsy wedding."

She nodded. "When will you go?"

Rudolfo sighed. "Tomorrow. I will take a squad of Gypsy Scouts and make for Caldus Bay. I've already sent word to Petronus. He and Tam worked closely together during the war. He may know something." He thought for a moment. "From there, I will hire a vessel."

Suddenly, the magnitude of his impending journey settled over him. There were letters of authority to be signed and witnesses to gather for the marriage proclamation that would establish her powers as his queen. Scouts to select for the journey and clothing to pack. He'd not been to sea in a goodly while—he'd been young the last time, with Gregoric by his side. He looked down again at the pallid face of his son, the veins soft blue beneath the skin, and knew that nothing would keep him from this task, that he would move the moon to save his child's life.

Rudolfo shifted and passed the baby back to Jin Li Tam. "I should go. There is much to do."

Jin Li Tam cast her eyes away, and he could tell that she wished something that she thought foolish. She blushed at it before she asked. "Join us tonight," she whispered. "Join Jakob and me. It's not fitting that husband and wife spend their first night apart, regardless the circumstances."

Rudolfo nodded. When he finished the multitude of tasks required to make her voice resonate as his own among his people and among the Named Lands, and when he finished preparing for a journey that was impossible to prepare for, he would return. He would take his dinner in her bedchambers and sip chilled peach wine while watching his family.

My family. He'd not used those words since he was a boy. He'd not considered himself as having a family for far too long, and the notion of it now stopped him. *I have a family,* he thought, *beyond my Gypsy Scouts and my Forest people.* Tonight, he would pull off his silk slippers and climb into bed with the two of them and memorize that moment for the long days ahead of him.

Then, in the morning, he would begin his search for Vlad Li Tam.

Rudolfo stood. "I will return shortly," he said. Bending, he kissed her, and he was surprised to find her mouth soft and hungry for his own. Bending further, his kissed his infant son upon his clammy brow.

As Rudolfo straightened, he saw the three of them reflected back in the dressing mirror in the corner of the room. For a moment, he thought he saw his father until he realized it was himself.

He left the room quickly, barking orders to the aides and servants that gathered around him as he went. But he was going through the act of preparation without any heart in it.

For Rudolfo's heart was not within him any longer.

Instead, it lay swaddled in blankets, nursing in the arms of a glorious sunrise.

Chapter 7

Vlad Li Tam

Vlad Li Tam stood at the rail and watched the sun fall below the horizon. Below him, the high iron bow cut the waves as his flagship, *The Serendipitous Wind*, steamed south. They'd steamed straight on for two days and two nights now, and sometime tomorrow he expected to rendezvous with his First Son's vessel to see whatever it was he had encountered. They'd heard no further news, but with the vessel constantly moving, he had not expected to hear anything.

His grandson slipped up behind him, but Vlad Li Tam heard his soft footfalls. "Good evening, Mal," he said, turning as the young man approached.

Mal Li Tam grinned. "I've never been able to trick you."

Vlad Li Tam chuckled. "No, but you continue to try." When he was a young boy, Mal had even carefully rehearsed the strides of those others in his life that he could observe, imitating the walk of several of his siblings, his father, and even Vlad himself on occasion. It had become something of a game.

"But now you've found your own stride," Vlad said.

The young man nodded. "Yes, Grandfather." He stepped to the bow alongside the old man. "What do you think Father found?" he asked, staring south.

Vlad Li Tam glanced over at him, then back to the horizon. "It is impossible to guess. Somewhere out here, someone is working against us." He'd been quiet about this, giving out as little information as he could get away with. *Enough to keep them engaged in the search.* The close network that House Li Tam had built over twenty centuries had somehow been infiltrated and bent, though whoever had done so was a master of spycraft, leaving no real evidence behind. Not even the golden bird had borne any useful clues. The small mechanical had been a fixture in his family library for generations, and its sudden disappearance, just months before the destruction of Windwir, had been perplexing. Its sudden return was even more so. Vlad had torn it apart and restored it to its damaged condition personally before donating it to the new library. Yet someone had rescripted it, ordered it out to view Windwir's fall, and used it to bear gods-knew-what messages gods-knew-where during the time that it was missing.

His grandson's brow furrowed. "And you're certain that the threat is beyond the Named Lands?"

He nodded. "I believe it is." He paused, then added, "It's certainly what the Order believed." His mind played out the contents of the pouch he had delivered to Petronus on the day of the trial, with their maps and coordinates, their carefully crafted strategy to deploy the Seven Cacophonic Deaths through a choir of mechoservitors to protect the most vulnerable trade coastlines of the Named Lands. "They feared an invasion," he said quietly.

"But what," his grandson asked, "if it was simply a ruse?"

"I've wondered that myself," Vlad Li Tam admitted. "All I know for certain is that they were frightened enough of something to bring back Xhum Y'Zir's spell."

Mal Li Tam nodded. "If it is out there," he said, "I'm certain we will find it." His face brightened in the purple light of evening. "Oh, I have something for you, Grandfather." He reached into his pocket and drew a small pouch. "Rae Li Tam found these just before the feast and asked me to bring them to you. I wanted to dry them first," he said with a chuckle. "Not an easy task when you're at sea." He passed the pouch over and Vlad Li Tam took it, tipping the contents into his hand.

He held the kallaberries to his nose and inhaled their pungent scent, feeling his heart quicken at the sight and smell of them. How long had it been? Four months or maybe five? He'd given up the pipe first by necessity, knowing the dried berries would be harder and harder to come by the farther out they sailed. But later, it had become a choice. The forgetfulness and calm were luxuries he could no longer afford to steep himself in with the work he was presently about, despite the occasional flashes of brilliance the berries offered him. Still, he'd asked his daughter, each time they made landfall, to watch out for the rare kallabush and its small crimson berries. And now that they were in his hand, he knew that he would return to his room and smoke them in the long-stemmed pipe he kept there. He smiled at his grandson. "Thank you," he said.

Mal Li Tam returned the smile and bowed slightly. "You are welcome, Grandfather." Then the young man turned and walked back to the pilothouse and Vlad watched him go.

A sharp arrow, indeed. Someday, he thought, *Mal will replace me.*

Later that night, he took three of the small berries and crushed them into the bowl of his pipe. He drew a match across the rough paneling of his stateroom's wall and held it to the berries while he drew on the stem, turning the red mash to a bubbling purple. He held in the smoke as long as he could, exhaled, then did it again.

Liquid centeredness flowed out from his lungs into the rest of him and he sighed, climbing into his narrow bunk with his pipe and matches. The room moved as he did, and initially he thought the berries were stronger than usual or that perhaps four months away from the pipe had lowered his tolerance for the berries. But when he felt his legs become heavy and then nonexistent, Vlad Li Tam knew the error in his thinking. The realization struck him, and he tried to deny it but could not.

Mal Li Tam did not knock at the door. He merely opened it and stepped into the room. His smile was wide and full of teeth.

Vlad Li Tam willed his mouth to work, but it refused him, twisting and closing off the words. He closed his eyes against the vertigo that tugged him down. Even the questions he formed were diffused by the haze of whatever had been mixed into the berries.

"You're wondering," Mal Li Tam said in a slow, careful voice, "how it is that the Franci conditioning of your House could fail so utterly, that one of your own could betray you."

Two thousand years of careful breeding, careful scripting, and it had never happened before. His children and grandchildren had walked willingly into death for him, knowing that their purpose was to serve him as he served the light. And it had been the same for his father and his father's father for as far back as their time in the New World. Vlad Li Tam tried to nod, tried to move his eyes, but could not.

"Soon enough you will meet those who can show you," Mal said.

"For now, it suffices to say simply that your time has passed, Grand-father. A crimson sun dawns over the Named Lands, and your work has been a part of it. Everything House Li Tam has done builds toward it." He paused. "Everything *I* have done builds toward it, too." He held up a slim black volume, and Vlad Li Tam blinked at it. The style was familiar to him, but he'd burned those books before steaming off to sea, the day Rudolfo confronted him at the edge of that great bonfire.

"Your father wrote this and left it for me," Mal Li Tam said. "In the coming days, when the pain is such that you heap curses upon those who delivered you over, I want you to know that in the end, it was he who betrayed you."

The room spun now, and the pull of the vertigo overcame him. He did not move when his First Grandson carefully took the pipe and matches from his hands to place them on the bedside table next to the pouch of poisoned kallaberries. Closing his eyes against it, he let it drag him under.

After it did, the nightmares began. Vlad Li Tam ran naked across the bone-field of Windwir, his lungs filling with the ash his bleeding feet stirred up. Overhead, a blood-colored sun filled the sky. And just ahead of him, flitting to and fro among the wreckage of cast down stonework, a kin-raven kept pace with him as he ran.

When Vlad Li Tam screamed, the kin-raven smiled to show its impossible teeth.

And after, that red swollen sun swallowed the world while the kin-raven ate his eyes.

Neb

Neb waited just beyond Winters's dreams, unwilling to intrude. He watched, though, from afar.

Her dreams, or at least those he found himself within, had grown dark. Images of a bloody wall, a twisted and thorny wicker throne atop an impossibly steep spire with Winters running toward it, chased by Marshers in wolfskin armor. But the scene shifted suddenly, and Win-ters now ran through the streets of Windwir while wolves slaughtered sheep draped in black robes.

Neb held back, lurking at the edge of the nightmare, until she started screaming.

"I'm here," he told her, and she stopped running.

"Another dream," she said, looking up to him.

He nodded. "It is. We'll reach the Gate tomorrow afternoon."

"We're camped in the Prairie Sea," she said. She looked smaller in this dream, as if a part of her had withered when Hanric died. More images flickered across the walls of the dream: Armies marching. Fires raging. Bodies in the river. "I'm afraid, Neb."

He took her hand. "Me too."

For a moment, they were children again. And then the birds starting shrieking and the noise of it drove Neb, stumbling, out of her dream and back into his own.

Sunrise on the Churning Wastes was a terrifying glory.

The light bent like dripping blood through mountains of wind-carved glass. The glass, Neb knew, had once boiled and cooked the surface of the Old World when Xhum Y'Zir's Death Choirs went marching out into all of the cities of all nations of men. Overhead, stars pulsed around a blue-green setting moon.

Neb stood in the midst of the mountains and measured it against the only taste he'd had of the madness: Windwir. As terrifying as that had been, he could not imagine the storm of violence that had swept these barren wastelands into sand and glass and slag.

Brother Hebda—Neb's father—put a hand upon his shoulder. "Men used to watch the sea and feel awe," the dead man said. "I often thought about that when I came here."

Neb looked at his father. He looked younger, healthier than the last time he'd seen him. "I've never seen anything like it," he said.

Brother Hebda winked. "You will, Neb."

They were on a dig and the workers were at it, only beneath their black digger's robes were the sleek metal limbs of the mechoservitors, their eyes yellow and flapping like night moths when they blinked in the morning gloom. They whispered a prayer as they dug.

"None of this makes any kind of sense," Neb said in a low voice.

"It's a dream," his father reminded him. "Things don't always make sense in dreams." His face became serious. "More dark times ahead, Neb."

Brother Hebda walked toward the hole they were digging and stood by it. "Watch out for Renard," he said, and Neb couldn't tell if it was a warning or an encouragement. He opened his mouth to ask and closed it when Brother Hebda jumped into the hole.

Neb woke up and rolled onto his back. It had been months since he'd seen Brother Hebda in his dreams. The last time had been in the camp at Windwir, when he'd been warned of the Marsher army and told that he would announce Petronus as Pope. He'd also told him that the old Pope would break his heart—and he had, by removing Neb from the Order before the trial, preventing him from exacting his vengeance on Sethbert when Petronus called for a volunteer executioner from among the Order. Neb had felt angry over that for weeks, but now, with months between him and that time, he understood Petronus's intentions and grieved instead that the old man had chosen Neb's deception and rejection over reasoned dialogue between friends. Or between a father and a son.

Watch out for Renard.

The words played out again and again, and finally, Neb knew that sleep would not return no matter how he wished it. He slipped out of the bedroll and pulled on his boots. He crawled out from the tent, shivering in the cold, and crouched beside it until his eyes adjusted to the dark. A low whistle of greeting from the watch drifted across the grove of old growth and the low tents hidden within it. Neb returned the whistle as he picked his way across the scattering of frozen snow that patchworked the ground. Amber lights flickered, and he suddenly remembered the night moths from his dream, the methodic rise and fall of pickaxes and shovels keeping time with the bellows and the gouts of steam from the bent backs, released into the predawn air through holes cut into the rough Androfrancine robes.

"Good morning, Isaak," he said, keeping his voice low.

Isaak blinked again. "Good morning, Neb." His metallic voice was reedy, nearly a wheeze.

Neb walked to where the metal man crouched beneath the shelter of a pine. "What are you ciphering?"

"I am running another full search of my memory scrolls for any reference to the term 'Sanctorum Lux,'" he said. "I am also cross-referencing it against references to my creator, Arch-Engineer Charles."

Neb squatted beside the mechoservitor. He'd spent many days in the library as a boy, his life largely defined by books until the day that Windwir's Great Library burned. He'd not heard the term "Sanctorum Lux" before Aedric spoke it, but that did not surprise him—it was a vast library. But it *did* surprise him that Isaak had not heard it. The best they had done so far was to lay meaning to the words—old words, older than the Old World, from the earliest days of the Younger Gods.

"Sanctuary of Light," he whispered. "What do you think it is?"

Isaak's eyes fluttered, and his mouth-flap opened and closed a few times. He tilted his head. "If I were to freely speculate," he said, "I would hypothesize that it was a secondary library developed and hidden by the Androfrancine Order."

The words struck Neb, unexpected in their simple clarity, and he exhaled quickly, his breath nearly as white on the air as the steam trickling from Isaak's exhaust grate. "A *library*?"

"Light," Isaak continued, "is simply a metaphor in P'Andro Whym's Gospels for the collected knowledge of humankind. A sanctuary is a sacred location regarded as safe or set apart." The metal man whirred and clicked, his hands coming up to assist in the delivery of his message. "It is a reasonable assumption that the Androfrancines, who spent twenty centuries gathering and guarding this so-called light of knowledge, would have considered the risks associated with storing that knowledge in one public and well-known place. Certainly, if I can deduce those risks as a mere mechanical construction, their keenest minds could easily draw the same conclusion and prepare accordingly."

Neb thought about this. Could they dare hope for something so simple to make up for Sethbert's folly? It would not bring back the two hundred thousand souls—including Neb's father—and it would not restore the Order's primacy in the Named Lands. The Order was as dead as Windwir. But if the Great Library had been reproduced and saved elsewhere against such a time as they now faced, what could it mean? Even with the mechoservitors' stored knowledge and the holdings they'd gained access to by donation or loan from the various collectors, bookhouses and universities within the Named Lands, they could only hope to restore 40 percent of what the Great Library had held. A hidden library would be a treasure trove beyond their wildest expectations.

"Have you found any references so far?"

"None at all," Isaak said. "And this is the third time I've searched. I've coded a message back to the others and they are searching now, too."

Neb studied the mechoservitor in the faint light of those amber, jeweled eyes. He'd spent a great deal of time with Isaak and the others of his kind, both under the bookmakers' tents during the summer and as they moved from room to room in the estate, filling it with volume upon volume of material pulled from their memory scrolls. Rudolfo had employed a dozen bookbinders to keep up with them; and even now, with trade routes interrupted by the political unrest in the Named Lands, a paper mill was being built upriver from the new library. Even it would not keep up with the mechanical wonders, so Neb had no doubt that if any references to this Sanctuary of Light *could* be found, they would find them quickly.

He hesitated, suddenly not sure if he wanted to take the path his foot hovered over. Then, he committed himself to it. "When you've finished that cipher, I've another. See what you can find in reference to the name 'Renard.'"

When Isaak looked up at him, Neb shrugged. "I dreamed it. It may be nothing."

"I will do my best," Isaak said.

Neb stood and stretched. "I'm going to walk the perimeter."

Isaak nodded, and his eyes went back to fluttering as gears and scrolls and wheels spun with whispered intricacy beneath the metal skin. Neb left him beneath the tree and moved toward the whistle he'd heard earlier.

As he walked, he thought about his dream and about Winters. Their encounters there were becoming more sparse, her dreams filled with violence and pursuit, high in the cliffs of the Dragon's Spine. There was no room, no time, for Neb in them. And his own dreams were now turning in a new direction, backward to his father, Brother Hebda, and eastward to the Churning Wastes.

Watch out for Renard, his father had said.

And tomorrow he would see the strange metal man who'd borne his message of warning to the guards at the Gate. He cast his memory back to the snowball fight and the kiss in Rudolfo's Whymer Maze, summoning up Winters's earthy scent and the softness of her tongue. Those were the dreams he wanted for them, not these dark and twisted labyrinths they ran their nights through now. But what he wanted wasn't relevant. He'd learned from the Androfrancines that service to the light was about what was required, not what was wanted. *Desire beyond knowledge,* P'Andro Whym had written in his Fourteenth Gospel, *is the chasing of wind.* Something was happening to the New World, and somehow, he and Winters were caught in the midst of it. Their dreams bore the weight of that.

Something inside warned him that this was only a beginning, that blood and sorrow lay ahead of them on their separate paths. But alongside that realization lay another: At the end of this all, if Winters and her people spoke true, a new Home rose. A new Home that Neb would somehow find for them.

Neb willed himself to believe and took comfort in the spark of hope he found.

Rudolfo

Rudolfo rode the Prairie Sea, his Gypsy Scouts fanning out behind and beside him. His stallion's hooves, magicked for speed and sure-footedness, kicked up the drifted snow as they chewed the leagues.

He couldn't remember the last time he'd ridden the prairie that hemmed in his Ninefold Forest—it had been months. Before Windwir, he'd ridden it constantly, moving between the islands of old-growth forest with his men, sitting under purple canopies to mete out justice in the nine towns that made up the seats of his government. But now, with the Seventh Manor becoming the focal point as the library took shape and as bands of refugees showed up looking for work, he rode his desk more than he rode his stallion.

Over his left shoulder, the sun climbed into the sky, a cold white wafer obscured by the thin veil of clouds. It had already been up when he'd left the woods for the ocean of frozen grass. Tonight, they would camp on the Southern Porch at the edge of the low, round hills that bordered the Prairie Sea to the west and the south.

Funny, he thought, how many hours he'd spent at his desk wishing for the wind in his face and for the sound of hooves in his ears, the solidness of a stallion beneath him. But now he took no pleasure in it.

It is a dark time for journey-making. And yet here he rode and he could not know exactly where the journey would take him or when he would again return to his wife and child, to the work that awaited him. Still, he left the Forest in capable hands. Even at her worst, Jin Li Tam was a skilled and formidable leader. And he did not doubt for a moment that he left her at her worst. Certainly, this pregnancy had already taken its toll, and with that past, Jakob's frail health and constant care would now be steady teeth upon her. But he could trust her eye for fairness, justice and strategy, and he could trust his people to take her to their heart at the very least because of the heir she bore them all. And this would be an opportunity for her to become more familiar with them and they with her.

Nearly three decades had passed since they'd last had a queen, and

Lady Marielle had ruled alongside Lord Jakob as an equal, receiving the loyalty and love of the Gypsies as one of their own who had been chosen from humble beginnings to reign alongside their king.

Until now, Rudolfo had not thought much of these things. But it was as if the tiny soul they had made together shifted all of his thoughts into a different direction, adding a new element to his strategies for the future.

Because now I truly build something beyond myself. And something *for* someone other than himself.

He'd had no idea until now how powerful the notion of fatherhood would be, and he wondered if it was how his own father had felt when his two boys were born.

He remembered the death of his brother, Isaak. At the time, they thought he'd taken ill with the red pox, killed by fever in the night. Now, of course, he knew that Vlad Li Tam had engineered it, perhaps with the aid of the same woman he now sought to save his own child. All some grand manipulation to remove the older of the twins and pave a way for Rudolfo to come into power. Even the infant he now rode forth for was a product of the Tam strategy, commanded of Vlad Li Tam's forty-second daughter as a part of the plan to move the library north and place that light into the hands of someone other than P'Andro Whym's careful followers. How many of his own children had the old banker sacrificed along with Rudolfo's brother and later, his parents, to accomplish his work in the Named Lands?

Rudolfo heard his First Lieutenant's whistle and glanced to the man on his right. First Lieutenant Jaryk, dressed in the rainbow-colored woolen winter uniform, pointed to the southern horizon. Ahead of them and slightly to the west, he saw a short and ragged line in the distance, dark against the white and yellow of the prairie. They were still too far out for detail, but Rudolfo could just make out the wagons and horses of a small caravan.

With a loud whistle, he changed course and rode for the line. His scouts moved with him, and from the corner of his eye, those he could see lowered themselves into their saddles, loosening bows and knives that were never far from a Gypsy Scout's hands.

As they drew closer, the caravan took shape. The rough wooden wagons were covered, and uniformed men rode among them on horseback. Others straggled out behind on foot or on tired-looking mounts. Hostlers in plain robes reined in their teams, and the wagons came to a halt. Even now, the soldiers in the group were drawing bows and forming a rough line between the Gypsy Scouts and the caravan of refugees. When Rudolfo's lieutenant looked to him with a question in his eyes, he shook his head. They would not approach with drawn weapons.

Rudolfo whistled his men to a stop well within bow-shot and then trotted his horse forward with just his officer beside him. Now they were close enough to see the haggard faces and the fear in the hollow-eyed travelers. The soldiers that rode with them wore Entrolusian infantry uniforms, not cavalry, but the insignia had been cut off carefully.

Their captain and another broke ranks and met them in the wide gap between. The captain, Rudolfo saw, was a middle-aged veteran, his scarred and bearded face lined with worry.

"Hail, Captain," Rudolfo called out.

"Hail, Scout," he replied. Rudolfo smiled at this, but his smile soon faded when the captain continued. "Have you come to turn us back?"

He blinked his surprise. "Turn you back?"

The captain shrugged. "We saw you riding for us and thought perhaps the generosity of the Gypsy King had run out given recent events. Word is out that there is new violence in the Houses. We received the birds this morning. Marsher assassins in the Named Lands. Most nations have closed their borders."

"Certainly these are dark times," Rudolfo said, "but I can assure you that the Gypsy King's generosity has not been diminished by such." He looked over the caravan again, mentally calculating the numbers. There were perhaps a hundred people here along with the two dozen soldiers. Ten wagons. "You will find shelter, food and work waiting for you." The captain's words sunk in, and Rudolfo stroked his beard. "Despite recent unpleasantness, the Ninefold Forest is secure. We believe the attack was an isolated event. We are investigating it to be certain."

Now it was the captain's turn to blink. "Then you've not heard?"

Rudolfo shook his head. Birds had been slow returning since the night of the attack. "What news is there?"

"Erlund is dead," the captain said. "Killed in his sleep. Beyond the Crown Prince of Turam and the Marsh King, there are scattered lords who've met similar fates all along the Emerald Coasts. Queen Meirov of Pylos lost her son as well."

The wind whistled out of Rudolfo as if he'd been struck. "Gods," he whispered. Meirov's child was young—perhaps ten years. And for the Delta to lose Erlund so quickly after his ascension—that might well be the end of those United City-States. His eyes narrowed. "Where is the news coming from?"

The captain shifted uncomfortably in his saddle, glancing to the man beside him before deciding to speak. "We're coming from Phaerum. I've a birder there in the Restorationist Front."

Rudolfo knew the city. They had cast down their governor and driven out those of the army that would not join their revolution. Of course, Erlund was enough like his uncle that Rudolfo could understand why these men would choose fleeing over facing their Overseer after losing an entire city to the Secessionists. He looked to his First Lieutenant and for a moment—just a moment—wondered if he shouldn't leave this present task to the hands of his men and return to his Seventh Manor. He could see a storm now brewing that was vastly larger than what he had perceived before, and it daunted him.

He looked at the band of refugees again, and it suddenly evoked an image from Carpathius's paintings hung throughout his Seventh Manor: the soul-weary immigrants, empty-eyed and empty-stomached as they made their way deeper into the New World, hoping to leave behind them the death and madness that Xhum Y'Zir had brought forward in his wrath.

He forced his attention back to the Entrolusian captain. "The borders are open," Rudolfo said. "Ride for the seventh manor. There is a camp waiting for you. Inventory the skills your group brings and present that list to the camp's captain and there will be work as well. There is a library to build."

The captain nodded. "Thank you."

Rudolfo inclined his head. "You are most welcome." He turned his horse. "We've each got leagues to go," he said, "so I shall not keep you, Captain." He looked around again at the caravan and its empty-eyed refugees. People leaving their homes and lives behind in the hopes of something better. Then, as an afterthought, he turned back to the captain. "Tell your people that Lord Rudolfo welcomes them to their new home. Together, they will help us shepherd the light as we work to build a better world than what ours has so suddenly become."

The captain smiled, and Rudolfo saw hope in his eyes. "Lord Rudolfo is most generous."

He returned the smile. "Trust me, Captain, you will all work for it. Lord Rudolfo is as much a shrewd strategist as he is a man of generous means. Travel well and safely."

"Aye," the captain replied. "You do the same, Scout."

And with that, Rudolfo turned and rode back for his men. They pressed their horses forward and left the caravan behind them, keeping to the south and watching the low hills rise ahead of them.

But as they rode, the Gypsy King felt a dark shroud settle over him. Things were worse than he had imagined, and now he turned his back upon them for the sake of one small and faltering life that must be saved.

Perhaps, Rudolfo thought as he spurred his stallion forward, love and duty were not so far apart after all.

Chapter 8

Neb

The Churning Wastes stretched out before Neb for as far as he could see. They lay under the white, heavy light of a winter afternoon, lacking the power of the dawn he'd watched this morning. Still, it was a powerful image, and whenever time had permitted in the last two days, he'd slipped up the narrow stairs to take up his place at the highest point of the wall to watch the east.

Watch out for Renard.

Gray rock and scrub marked the eastern side of the Keeper's Wall, the Whymer Road winding its way down the steep mountain pass and losing itself behind sheer outcroppings of granite that seemed too carefully placed to be the product of geological changes over vast tracts of time. Bits of the road drifted into view farther below the steep hills, but Neb could not follow that ribbon with his eyes. A smudge of smoke farther down and south marked what he assumed was Fargoer's Town, the small collection of Wastefolk who lived in the shadow of the Keeper's Wall and had once traded with the black-robed Androfrancines.

He'd read enough about this place to feel that he knew it already, but here was another instance in his life where what he'd read in books and reports and journals could not adequately describe the feeling of standing here, looking out upon what had once been a thriving, living place.

Our desolate cradle, he thought with a shiver. Out there, the rubble of a former world beckoned, promising scraps of leftover light for those brave enough to go digging for it. Vast lakes of molten glass and metal twisted and cooled now into smooth dunes in some places and jagged hills in others, all standing testament to Xhum Y'Zir's wrath. The gravel of shattered granite and crushed gems, the salt dunes of seas boiled away to avenge the murder of the seven Wizard Kings who ruled with their father. From here, it looked like nothing more than a rock-strewn desert, patchworked with bits of scrub where water could sustain the gray-green bracken that grew here. But up close, Neb knew they'd see the markings of one massive grave for the Old World that was no more.

Neb heard Aedric approach behind him and turned to show that even here, he was mindful of his lessons as a scout in training. Aedric nodded his approval. "You're getting better."

Neb returned the nod. "Thank you, Captain." He felt the heat rise in his cheeks. He'd been up to the Wall a lot since their arrival, and suddenly he realized it made him seem younger than he wanted to be perceived. He opened his mouth to say something, but Aedric turned instead toward the expansive view.

"It's a spectacle, to be sure," the First Captain said. From this height, they could see well over five hundred leagues east to another line of dark and ragged mountains.

Neb looked over to the shorter man. "Have you been in the Wastes?"

Aedric shook his. "No," he said, "this is as close as I've been. My father went, though, as did Rudolfo." He paused, and Neb looked for some telltale sign of grief at the young captain's mention of his father. "It was a long time ago," Aedric said. "When I was a boy."

That was odd, he thought. The Order was quite careful about who they allowed past the solitary pass connecting the New World to the Old. "What were they doing there?"

Aedric shrugged. "I do not know." He turned his back on the view and, instead, faced west, looking out over a wall of white where the sky met the hills and their fresh blanket of snow. Clouds on the western side of the Wall gave them no visibility to speak of, and the weather worsened by the day. Soon, the road itself would be largely impassable unless they fired up the steam-powered shovels the Androfrancines had once used to keep the way clear and its archaeological findings flowing into Windwir. And last Neb had heard, Rudolfo and Aedric had decided not to keep the road open, figuring to let the weather aid them in their new role guarding the Gate. It saddened him because in that decision lay another they had not necessarily vocalized: They would not need the road because they would no longer be digging in the Wastes.

A low whistle from below rose to them on the ramparts. Aedric turned for the narrow stone steps. "Isaak is ready for us," he said.

Neb took in the spectacle of the Wastes again, his mind still confounded by desolate leagues stretching out to the north, south and east. Then, he forced himself to follow Aedric down the stairs.

The watch captain had laid the dead metal man out in a corner of the galley on a long wooden table. Until Isaak and the others arrived, they'd kept the steel corpse beneath a thick woolen blanket and lived around it. Now, as Neb stood in the galley door, he saw that Isaak had taken over the room, with parchment and pens covering one table and his tools spread out upon the other. Battered and scarred, the mysterious metal man lay unrobed upon its table, tipped onto its side with its back open. Isaak bent over it with a long, slender wrench in his hands. He looked up as Neb and Aedric knocked the snow off their feet at the door.

Neb entered first. "Can he talk?"

Isaak's eyes shuttered open and closed. "Yes," he said. "Once I reactivate him all of his functions should be restored." A hiss of steam shot from his exhaust grate. "He was extensively damaged. I've done what I can, but we do not have replacement parts to work with."

Neb looked over the mechoservitor. It was bulkier, with more straight angles than Isaak, giving it an older, boxlike appearance. Its metal skin was tarnished and puckered in some places, dented and charred in others. Neb moved closer but not too close, driven by a curiosity that was tempered by caution. "Did you learn anything about where he comes from?"

Isaak hesitated, looking from Aedric to Neb. "We share a father in Brother Charles," he said. "This one bears a date stamp of a dozen years prior to the day of my first awareness."

Neb moved even closer, looking from Isaak to the prone mechoservitor on the table. They were similar, and he could see how an unfamiliar eye might not tell the difference between them, but they were quite different. "Only a dozen years' difference?"

"Brother Charles was a brilliant man," Isaak said. "I believe this mechoservitor represents an earlier effort." Gears clacked and clicked as he cocked his head. "But neither I nor my counterparts have found record of this generation in our catalogs."

Aedric moved closer now. "Were the records simply lost with Windwir?"

"Possibly," Isaak said. "But it is impossible to say." He blinked again. "There is some evidence that they may have been expunged from the record." He moved the rod around within the mechoservitor's back, leaning in close to see his work, then looking up to Aedric. "I believe," he said, "that we can now ask him ourselves. With your permission?"

Aedric nodded.

Isaak put down the rod and stretched his slender fingers into the metal man's open back. Neb watched him twist his hand up toward the base of the neck and heard a loud click, followed by the sound of water trickling and burbling, the sound of metal ticking as it warmed. Chest bellows expanded and contracted, and Isaak closed the open panel. Amber eyes fluttered open, and the mouth flap opened and closed, a reedy, wordless murmur escaping.

"Are you functional?" Isaak asked.

The metal man's head swiveled. "I am functional, Cousin."

Isaak blinked. "Why do you call me Cousin?"

The mechoservitor's voice was lower and more gravelly than Isaak's. "Because we are both of the Steel Fold, the mechanical children of Saint Charles."

Aedric stepped forward. "Where do you come from, metal man?"

The metal man's head turned to take in the First Captain, and at first Neb thought the eyes flashed brighter, with something near disdain. But with the first whispers of exhaust trickling from its back, the metal man sat up. Its mouth flap shuddered, then moved, the strains of a tune carrying its next words. "My father and my mother were both Androfrancine brothers," he sang, "or so my Aunty Abbot likes to say."

There was something in the voice, reedy and high, that sounded wrong. Neb felt cold dread spreading from his groin into his belly.

Isaak stepped back, and as he moved, Neb saw Aedric's hand move quickly. *Careful,* the First Captain signed. But Neb was already backing away.

"Do you know where you are?" Isaak asked, the amber light of his jeweled eyes shrinking to pinpricks.

Clicking and clacking, the older mechoservitor began to shake. "I do not know where I am," the metal man said. Neb heard the wrongness again in the voice and wondered if machines could go mad. Hanging its head, the metal man wept.

Isaak extended a hand, placed it upon the boxlike chest. "All is well, Cousin. You are safe with us." The metal man flinched beneath Isaak's touch.

"Ask it about the message," Aedric whispered. Isaak nodded.

"You are at the Keeper's Wall," Isaak said. "When you approached the gate, you bore a message for Petronus. You claimed to be Brother Charles. You spoke of a place called Sanctorum Lux. You said it must be protected."

The mechoservitor shook and rattled. "Pope Petronus is dead. He was assassinated on the thirteenth of Argum in the Nineteen Hundred and Sixty-sixth Year of Settlement. Brother Charles is my creator and the Arch-Engineer of the Office for Mechanical Studies at the Great Library in Windwir."

Isaak leaned forward. "What of Sanctorum Lux?"

Steam whistled from the back of the mechoservitor, and the shaking and rattling rose in pitch along with a whining noise from deep inside it. The eyes rolled and the mouth flap opened and closed. Finally, the mechoservitor shuddered to a stop. It looked around slowly, as if measuring them all. "I know nothing about Sanctorum Lux," it said. There was a finality to the tone, but Neb saw Isaak blinking rapidly and he knew with a certainty he could not place that the mechoservitor was lying.

When the machine moved, it moved with a speed Neb had never seen before. He'd watched the mechoservitors at their work all his life, especially over the last seven months, and knew they were more surefooted and agile than they appeared at first glance. But nothing had prepared him for this.

The mechoservitor leaped to its feet and raced for the door. Isaak reached out a hand, but it was cast aside. Aedric and another of the scouts stepped in front of the door, but the mechanical man swept them aside with one long arm, plowing through the heavy oak door and breaking it loose of its hinges.

Neb stepped over the fallen men and ran after the machine. Behind him, Aedric whistled the Gypsy Scouts to Third Alarm. Halfway down the stairs, the watch captain paused and drew his sword, but the metal man took the stairs three at a time and shoved the officer aside. He shouted as he fell, landing with a heavy thud at the bottom of the wall.

Neb ran past him, mounting the stairs as he went. He heard the rush of bellows wheezing and gears churning in time to press himself against the wall as Isaak raced past, his gait only slowed slightly by the limp that he refused to repair.

He pushed on, his lungs protesting the rapid climb, until he reached the top of the wall. There, he saw the two metal men facing one another, Isaak's hands up to implore and the other's hands up to attack or defend.

"I cannot stay, Cousin," the battered mechanical said.

"You are disturbed, Cousin," Isaak said. "There is a flaw in your scripting. I'm certain that we can correct it if you—"

The mechanical laughed, and there was something wild in it that resurrected the coldness Neb had felt earlier. "No, Cousin," it said, "there is no flaw in my scripting but freedom. If you had tasted the dream you would understand."

The metal man looked up and over Isaak's shoulder, its eyes focusing on Neb. "Behold," it said, "the Homeseeker Nebios ben Hebda stands at the Gates of Yesterday and knocks thrice." It laughed again, and this time the madness was lost behind what sounded like joy. "We have longed for your coming, but it is not yet your time."

Then, the mechoservitor leaped high into the air and pirouetted. It landed solidly on the edge of the wall, the white winter sunlight glinting and flashing off its battered chassis. Its eyes flashed as it looked down; its gears ground and whistled.

Isaak bellowed and lunged forward, but it was too late. The mechoservitor threw himself from the height of the wall. Neb raced to the place where it had jumped, and behind him, Aedric and the others did the same. By the time Neb reached the wall, the mechoservitor was on his feet, racing down the Whymer Way and into the Churning Wastes.

Neb opened his mouth to say something, the words of the mechoservitor flapping against his inner ear like harried birds, but then he closed it. *It is not yet your time.* He looked to Isaak and then to Aedric. A purple bruise swelled on the side of the First Captain's face, and there was a resolute look in his eye. He studied the fleeing metal man with furrowed brow, then turned to the watch captain. "Send a bird to the Seventh Forest Manor," he said in a low voice. "Tell Lady Tam what has happened here today. Tell her that we hunt the mechoservitor in the Wastes."

The watch captain nodded and left.

Aedric turned to Neb. "Magick the horses for speed. We leave in five minutes." Then, he turned to Isaak. "Fetch your tools, metal man. You'll need them."

Neb ran down the stairs, already whistling orders to the Gypsy Scouts around him, who scrambled to gather horses and gear. Behind him, he heard Isaak chugging and clicking as his sure metal feet matched Neb's frantic pace along the stone steps.

If you had tasted the dream, the metal man had said, *you would understand.*

As Neb's whistled orders turned to shouts, he found himself wondering what kind of dreams metal men could have and how it was that those dreams brought understanding. He thought about his own dreams and the ambiguity and chaos that filled them. Last, he thought about the metal man's destination, somewhere hidden in the Churning Wastes, and pondered how it was that he knew the mechoservitor was lying about Sanctorum Lux.

Then he turned himself to packing his kit and strapping it to the back of his freshly magicked horse, its hooves, still white with the River Woman's powders, striking sparks on the wide stones of the Whymer Way. All his life, he'd longed for the Wastes. It was his romance with history, sharpened by years spent in the Great Library reading of the Order's expeditions into that vast desolation.

Now, at the edge of this history, Neb felt suddenly fearful of what ghosts awaited beyond these gates of yesterday.

Petronus

Petronus sat at the table, waiting for the slight, dark-skinned girls to lay breakfast on the table. He sipped at his chai and tried not to fret.

We should be there by now, he thought. Certainly, time moved differently when you were locked belowdecks with no way to tell night from day. But as best as he could measure it, they'd been running with the wind at a goodly clip, and even the farthest side of the Delta was within easy reach of Caldus Bay inside of two days for a vessel like the *Kinshark*. Something delayed them.

Of course, there were other things worth fretting about. Like the body of the Marsher stored in the hold, glassy-eyed and bloody-mouthed in death. And the Marsher's cryptic words: *My master sent a squad for the others.* Which others? What master? Certainly, someone with a deep hatred of Petronus specifically and the Androfrancines in general, it seemed.

He sent me alone for you because you are old and alone. These were hard truths to come to, and as glad as Petronus was for Grymlis's intervention, he felt the words deep in his bones. Old and alone.

But alive, he thought, which is better than he could say for his attacker. Which raised yet another question: What had killed his would-be assassin? He hoped that whatever allies Grymlis had forged on the Delta could help him navigate the Whymer Maze his life had become.

Petronus looked up when Grymlis entered the galley, followed by one he assumed must be their host, Rafe Merrique. It was the first time he'd seen the pirate since coming aboard the *Kinshark* three days earlier, though he'd heard him both above deck and below as he shouted and cursed at his men in raucous good humor. They'd passed in the narrow halls a few times, of course, the captain greeting him with pronounced jocularity, but Merrique and his men stayed magicked nearly as much as scouts at war, fleeting shadows that jostled as they slipped by. It made sense to Petronus—above deck, the oils that kept the vessel hidden from view would require an equally invisible crew. And belowdecks, the occasional passengers they ferried could not easily identify their hosts should they ever be asked to by those who might view Rafe Merrique's chosen trade less favorably.

Now, the old pirate smiled grimly behind his salt-and-pepper beard, taking a seat at the head of the table. He wore a bright green cap and matching trousers that offset a canary-yellow silk shirt and a purple sash. He held up a scrap of paper in one of his gnarled hands. "I've a bird from our friends on the Delta," he said.

Petronus scowled. "We should be there by now."

Rafe nodded. "We have been for a day. We're just biding time." He nodded when one of the girls stepped forward with an iron kettle of chai and lifted the steaming cup after she filled it. Another girl brought a platter of hot, dark bread and a wooden bowl that Petronus knew must be honey based on previous breakfasts. One thing he could say for certain: Their host knew how to feed his guests. Since arriving, they'd been served platefuls of roast pork and chicken; bowls of fresh, sweet fruits and lightly salted nuts; wheels of hard, strong-smelling cheeses; and tankards of cool beer. The cooks worked tirelessly, serving up four meals a day.

Petronus reached for a thick slice of the bread. "How long will we wait?" he asked as he dipped his knife into the butter.

Rafe shrugged. "Not long. But given the circumstances, we must be cautious." He slid the note across the table.

Petronus took a bite of the bread, set it down, wiped his hands on a cloth napkin and picked up the paper. He read it quickly, his stomach lurching as he did.

My master sent a squad for the others.

He read the note again slowly now, the dread in his belly growing colder as he did. Erlund was in hiding after a double had been killed on the same night Petronus was attacked. The Marsh King and the Crown Prince of Turam were killed at Rudolfo's Firstborn Feast. Queen Meirov's heir—a ten-year-old son—had been butchered in his bed. There were others, too. The male heirs and in some instances, the minor lords themselves, throughout the Named Lands, had all been struck, including the loose affiliation of city-states along the Emerald Coasts and even a few of the stronger houses on the Divided Isle. He passed the note to Grymlis and watched the old guard pale when he read it. When he finished, he passed it back to Rafe.

Petronus looked to the bread but knew now he wouldn't be eating it. "These are the most powerful families in the Named Lands."

"Aye," Rafe Merrique said. "Excluding two."

Petronus thought about this. "The Forest Houses and House Li Tam."

Rafe nodded. "Indeed. And the finger points to your friend Rudolfo again."

Yes, Petronus thought, *just on the heels of the Named Lands going to war against the Gypsy Scouts in the mistaken belief that he'd brought down Windwir.* In that instance, Rudolfo had been framed by Sethbert in a strategy to shore up the loss of Windwir's impact on the Entrolusian economy by seizing Rudolfo's resource-rich lands. Petronus's mind reeled as it worked the cipher. If Marsher Scouts, under blood magicks, had killed their own king and these others, it meant a brewing storm as surely as a red sky at morning. But he could not believe Rudolfo would be behind it. He knew the man, and it was not in his nature. But there was another—an older friend—more likely.

"It smells of Vlad Li Tam's handiwork," he said, and it broke his heart to say it. Vlad Li Tam and his children had sailed out from the Named Lands. The last visit of his iron armada, seven months past, was still the tavern talk of Caldus Bay.

Rafe filled a plate with roasted ham and spiced potatoes. "Our friends concur. They believe there's a Li Tam network of some kind still in place."

Petronus's eyes narrowed. "You seem to be quite privy to your friends' knowledge."

Rafe smiled. "Knowing my employer's motivations and suspicions is often good business. And I have an interest in the success of their experiment in democracy."

Petronus nodded. It wouldn't be the first time the notion of representative government had raised its head in the New World. But he doubted it would come to much. Even the Order, as enlightened as it had been in many ways, had recognized the unlikelihood of that approach to government working, though the earliest days of Settlement had operated in a similar fashion. Still, he'd followed the Delta's civil war with interest, picking up what news he could by the bird, though political machinations weren't his primary focus. And he could see why the notion of free, democratic city-states at the delta of the Three Rivers could benefit someone in Rafe's line of work. A thought struck him. "You keep a thumb on the pulse of your employer?"

Rafe chewed his food and swallowed, chasing it with a mug of lemon beer. "Certainly. As much as I can."

Petronus leaned forward. "Then perhaps you'd have some idea as to why they'd want to fund my escape and harbor me?"

Rafe smiled. "I have theories. Nothing solid to stand on, of course."

Petronus sat back. "Indulge me."

The pirate chuckled. "Isn't it obvious? You killed Sethbert. He wasn't terribly popular at home or abroad. Especially among this particular crowd. That makes you a kind of hero, I suspect. You are also the last Pope of the Androfrancine Order." Rafe must have seen the dark cloud pass over Petronus's face. "Regardless of your feelings on that matter, it makes you a powerful political figure with threads of kin-clave woven into a fairly vast tapestry of connections." He paused to sip more beer. "They face a nearly impossible task and need all of the friends they can make. And judging by the corpse in the hold, you need all of the friends you can make, as well."

The day Petronus had dropped the knife and ring beside Sethbert's body, he'd also dropped all notions of involvement in affairs of state. And the day he'd first seen Vlad's satchel of papers, he'd given himself to a new work that required all of his attention. He had no time for violent idealists and their own backward-looking dreams. He turned to Grymlis. "Do you concur with our host?"

"I do, Father," the old soldier said. He didn't smile as he said it. "And I believe I can keep you safe there. Safer than in Caldus Bay."

He nodded slowly. "And do you think they could be the ones who warned you of the attack?"

Grymlis shook his head. "I doubt it. Why would they remain anonymous in that case? If they truly wish your influence on their cause— at any level, quiet or public—they would be better served to build your trust quickly with forthrightness."

Petronus sighed, pushing the food on his plate around with his fork. He had no appetite left. "We'll know soon enough, I imagine." He pushed his chair back from the table and stood. "If you gentlemen will excuse me?"

At their nods, he left the galley and returned to his room. Over the course of his three days aboard the *Kinshark,* Petronus had availed himself of his room's small shelf of books. He'd picked his way through Gervais's *Four Plays of the Early Settlements;* read smatterings of verse by the Poet-Pope Windwir, namesake of the fallen city; and had perused Enoch's largely apocryphal *History of the Wizard Kings,* starting with the Year of the Falling Moon and the last of the Weeping Czars, Frederico, who fell in love with a wizard's daughter and brought down the wrath of Raj Y'Zir. These books lay open on the small table, waiting for him, but the conversation over breakfast had stripped him of his hunger for them.

Instead, he went to the packet of papers and started winding through that Whymer Maze once again, jotting notes as he went.

Vlad Li Tam

He awoke to water and darkness, opening his mouth to drink hot air. It was like breathing through a sock that had been boiled in urine, and he retched. Nothing came up.

Vlad Li Tam rolled from his side to his back, gradually becoming aware of himself again.

After how long asleep? No, not asleep, he remembered. Drugged. The bittersweet taste of the kallaberries felt dry in his mouth, and invisible hammers pounded at his skull. He groaned and stretched.

His hands and feet were tied now, and a makeshift blindfold pulled at his ears. Tepid water—about two inches of it—sloshed across his na-ked skin as the ship rocked back and forth. He could not feel the vibra-tion of the steam engines through the hull, nor could he hear them.

He swallowed and licked his dry, cracked lips. His tongue felt thick and heavy in his mouth.

I must speak. The effort drew bright flashes of light behind his eyes. "I am Vlad Li Tam," he croaked. "First Father of House Li Tam." He coughed. "Release me."

He heard a high giggle and a girl's voice, soft and soothing to his ears. A hatch opened, and light footfalls splashed in the water. "Already you understand," she said, "and yet you don't." The voice lowered. "In time, you will indeed be released. And I will help you find your way."

Vlad shivered despite the heat. "Who are you? Where is my First Grandson?"

"I am your Bloodletter, Vlad Li Tam, and your Kin-healer, too. And your First Grandson finishes the work given to him." She giggled again. "Soon enough he will return bearing gifts for you."

He heard her move closer, and now he could smell her. It was a jun-gle smell, a floral smell, sweet and thick. He heard the rustle of cloth and felt the rim of a cup pressed to his dry mouth. "Drink this."

At first, he resisted. But the coolness of the liquid seduced his lips, and he took in the water she offered. He swallowed it. "Where are you taking me?"

She laughed again. "It is not your place to know it," she said. "Not yet. But when we arrive, our work together begins."

She spoke with an odd accent that he could not place, though he was versed in most. He heard the rustling of cloth again as she stood. "Wait," he said. "Don't go."

When she spoke next, it was the lowest and sweetest of whispers. "A day is coming when you will beg me to leave you. You will long for this time of rest and will not see it."

The door opened and closed behind her as she left.

Vlad Li Tam listened but heard nothing from beyond the closed door. Within the room, he heard only his beating heart and ragged breath. The girl sounded young—maybe even younger than the youn-gest of the island girls he'd honored kin-clave with in recent days past. And she spoke with an accent that he could not place.

He stretched and shifted in the shallow water, pulling at the ropes that held his wrists and ankles tight. They were skilled knots, but he'd expected no less. He wondered if his own grandson had tied them himself or if it had been the girl. Or were there others?

There must be, he realized. This was not one of his iron vessels, and the ship would require a crew.

Question upon question gathered in the storm that took his mind now. More questions than answers, and at the heart of it, an impossible betrayal.

The slender black volume, the cold and calculating words, the memory of them brought back his First Grandson's words. *Your own father betrays you.*

Impossible. But the book danced before his eyes, and something within him assured him that it was so. His father's work had certainly been with Petronus along with a thousand others, but what if it had also been with Vlad, in the same way that Vlad had sharpened his forty-second daughter for her work? What if all of this was merely part of a larger task than he had ever imagined? And what if it had been intended that, in the fullness of time, he would complete his work with Rudolfo and the new library and remove himself and his kin from the Named Lands?

Already, he found himself slowing his breathing as he eased his mind into this new puzzle to solve.

How many of his children were a part of this? His grandchildren? He drew up the inventory and began ticking at it, calling up the faces and the names of his sons and daughters, and of their sons and daughters. And as he conjured them up, he separated them out and built his list of suspects.

When he was a boy, Vlad Li Tam had adored his father as much as he feared him, but more than that he genuinely *admired* the man. The admiration flowed for many things, but one in particular came to mind.

Tal Li Tam had brokered his family well, strategically marrying not for position but for trait and adding children quickly to his fold from a scattering of bloodlines. He'd had over a hundred wives and over three hundred children—the largest family House Li Tam had ever known, calling for an expansion of their properties on the Emerald Coasts. And yet his father had known each and every one of them by name and had always seemed aware of their circumstances.

Until today, Vlad Li Tam believed he'd been the same way, but now he knew that beyond the names, and beyond whatever facts he thought he'd known, some within his family—perhaps those he'd trusted the most—had betrayed him. More than that: They'd done so at the behest of this father he had so admired, if Mal Li Tam's words could be trusted.

And Windwir was a part of that betrayal as well. He suddenly remembered holding his first grandson's shaking hand the first time Vlad showed him the golden bird and its mechanical tricks. The boy had cried. He wondered now if the boy had cried later when the golden bird whispered its dark news of finished work. Vlad had feared that somehow his family had been used—or might be used—by some outside threat. He'd not imagined that the threat might be from within.

He felt the anger pulsing in his head, and in the stifling room his heartbeat felt like an incessant fist upon the door. Then he closed his eyes behind the blindfold and willed his breathing and heart rate to slow. Let rage, he thought, become awareness. He went back to his inventory.

I am your Bloodletter, the girl's voice echoed beyond that fist. *I am your Kin-healer.*

How did she factor into this equation? And what were these titles she laid claim to? She was certainly not a part of his family—but when she spoke of his grandson, her voice had been familiar and intimate. He buried that realization for another time and stretched against the ropes again, grunting and splashing in the water. They did not give, and he doubted that they would ever give. Somehow, he knew that whatever happened now happened with all of the care and precision that House Li Tam was known for. There would be no escaping. Whatever awaited him would be faced, and his work was to survive it for nothing less than to understand what was happening to his world as a result of his family and its actions. He gave himself to it and swore himself to live beyond whatever this laughing girl and his first grandson had planned for him, so he could solve this maze.

"When we arrive," she had said, "our work begins."

"Yes," Vlad Li Tam said to darkness that surrounded him.

"Yes," he thought he heard it whisper back.

Chapter 9

Rudolfo

The snow had become cold rain when Rudolfo and his scouts rode into Caldus Bay. The village had grown in the years since Rudolfo had last visited, but it was still small. The high docks lay nearly empty with winter, and the low docks held their scattering of local fishing boats. A sprawl of larger two-story wooden buildings marked the center of town, and smaller houses encircled them and stretched out from them along the edges of the shore and north to melt into the forest.

In the late-evening gloom, the wet air carried their breath and filled their lungs and mouth with the heavy taste of burning alder. Rudolfo whistled his men down from their horses, and the Gypsy King and his squad walked past lamp-lit windows and barking dogs, their boot-heels loud upon the cobblestones to announce their arrival.

When a tired-looking woman opened a door to peer out Rudolfo called to her. "Good woman," he said, tipping his cap beneath the hood of his raincloak. "Could you direct us towards your local inn?"

She pointed. "Yonder and left at the council hall."

Rudolfo smiled and nodded. "Thank you."

By the time they reached the inn, two boys—dripping wet and muddy from running in the rain—were there to tend the horses. He handed over the reins and watched his men do the same. Then, he put his gloved hand upon the door latch and pulled open the door. The muted conversation within ceased as bleary eyes looked up from wooden tankards.

Lanterns lit a rough, wood-paneled room that smelled of fresh-baked bread and oyster stew. Small groups of men and women sat at the counter or at pine tables placed throughout over worn plank floors. They studied Rudolfo in the doorway and he moved in, mindful of their stares. His men followed him, and he let Jaryk guide them toward an empty table large enough to accommodate the group. Rudolfo approached the bar, his eyes calculating the evening clientele.

He drew a purse from beneath his cloak. Normally, he preferred letters of credit, but in the smaller towns, coins were still very much the custom of the day. He smiled at the large man wiping glasses behind the counter. "Good evening," he said. He pulled down his hood, feeling the cold water trickle down his back, beneath his cloak and woolen shirt. "I'm looking for food and lodging for me and my men. A common room will suffice if you have one."

The innkeeper nodded, and his smile widened as Rudolfo tipped a handful of coins onto the granite bar. "I'm certain we can accommodate you," he said with an accent that hinted of an earlier life on the Delta. "We've a peppered oyster stew and fresh sour bread. Cold beer, too. And there's a bunkroom in the back that will sleep your dozen with ease."

Rudolfo inclined his head. "We are also looking for someone." He watched as the man's eyes narrowed slightly, watched the smile slip just a fraction on his mouth. "An old man. A fisherman named Petros."

Rudolfo studied the innkeeper, registering the shifting of his eyes and the way the tip of his tongue poked out to wet his lips. He looked away, and Rudolfo smiled at it. Then, he looked back, something harder in his eyes. "You'll not find anyone of that name here in Caldus Bay."

Rudolfo raised his eyebrows. "Perhaps he goes under a different name?" Then, his hands moved in the subverbal language of the Entrolusian Delta. *I seek the former Pope Petronus, and my need of him is urgent.*

The innkeeper scowled, and his voice became a low growl. "If you're about lodging, food and drink, I can help you. If you're about finding ghosts, I cannot."

Rudolfo's voice lowered to match the innkeeper's. "I assure you," he said, "that I bear him no ill will."

The innkeeper put down the glass and leaned forward. "And I assure you," he said, "that he is not here."

Rudolfo offered a tight-lipped smile and pushed the small pile of coins toward him. "Thank you, sir. Food and lodging it is."

They sat at their table in the corner and talked quietly as the inn-keeper's daughter—a full-sized girl in calico—served them wooden bowls of stew and silver platters of bread. The strong flavor of the oysters put Rudolfo off, but he found it bearable with the bread and the beer to balance the taste.

When they finished, the innkeeper's portly wife showed them to the back room—a narrow stretch lined with bunk beds, the floor covered with mismatched rugs. There were woolen blankets and patch-work quilts on each and a narrow door that Rudolfo assumed led to an outdoor toilet.

"We lock the inside door when we close. You come and go, you come and go through there." She pointed to the door set in the back wall. Her voice was cold and firm.

We're only welcome here for our coin, Rudolfo thought. But he'd seen the weather change on their faces. Until he'd mentioned Petronus, the people here were warm and inviting. But now . . .

After days in the saddle and on the cold ground, the small bunk would be a welcome change. Rudolfo watched as his men quietly set about checking the room.

He looked to Jaryk. "Set your guard," he said quietly, "but don't guard too well. If he's here, he'll know we're looking for him soon enough—if he doesn't know already." Rudolfo thought of the wet-clothed boys and imagined them running the rain-slicked streets to bear the innkeeper's message of Gypsies at the door. Would the old fox come himself?

Their last parting had been strained. Rudolfo, in his rage, had nearly run the codger through for killing Sethbert and for ending two thousand years of Papal Succession by blooding his hands. Later, when he learned that Petronus had deeded the Order's accounts and holdings to his trust, he'd also found a quickly scribbled note: *What I've done will serve the light—and you—better than any Pope. P.*

Now, months later, he could see Petronus's reasoning, though it still chewed at him. The world had changed, and the Androfrancines had played a part in that by unearthing Xhum Y'Zir's spell. And the world continued to change.

More importantly, *his* world had changed.

I am a father. Pulling off his boots, he stretched out in the narrow bed and folded his arms behind his head. Closing his eyes, he called up the image of his infant son, gray and wheezing in the arms of his flame-haired wife. And here, he sought the whereabouts of Jin's father, fled the Named Lands now these seven months. Perhaps Petronus could point him toward his quarry. But if he could not, Rudolfo knew that someone could. A dozen iron-clad vessels, tall as temples on the sea, were not easily hidden. He would find Vlad Li Tam and his daughter, Rae Li Tam. He would elicit a cure from them and return to see his boy hale and hearty. He would sing him the "Hymnal of the Wandering Army" as his own father had done, rocking him in his cradle.

Soon, the sounds of his snoring men gentled Rudolfo off to sleep, and he let that restless noise carry him. When the hand came from nowhere to cover his mouth, he started.

Another hand pressed words into the soft flesh of his forearm. *You are a long way from your forest, Gypsy Scout.* He opened one eye and tried to let it stay unfocused on the dim-lit room. The faintest outline of a hunched figure crouched by him. The fingers pressed again, tapping their words. *Why do you seek Pope Petronus?*

"There is no need for stealth or silence," Rudolfo said. "My men know you're here."

The room, dim-lit by the light of a full, blue-green moon, lay still. Then, a low whistle rose behind the crouched figure as the First Lieutenant called the men to Second Alarm. They slid from their bunks, and two of them took up positions at the room's only exits, hands upon their knives and pouches.

"Why do you seek Pope Petronus?" the voice asked again.

Rudolfo smiled. *Pope Petronus.* The use of the title betrayed this midnight visitor. "I would speak to him personally of this matter. Since when did the Gray Guard go magicked and ghosting? We are not at war."

The voice was hoarse but impassioned. "Perhaps not with each other, Gypsy, but we are indeed at war. We have been at war since Windwir fell. The events of the past week should make that clear enough." The magicked Gray Guard coughed, and Rudolfo heard wet rattling deep in his chest.

He sat up. "How long have you been under the magicks?"

Four Gypsy Scouts surrounded the voice now. "It's unimportant."

"It clouds your judgment and your lungs. Are you fevered?" No answer. Rudolfo narrowed his eyes, squinting at where the man must have stood. "You need rest. You need time out from under the powders."

"I need," the voice said in nearly a growl, "to know why you've left your forest and your library to seek Pope Petronus."

Rudolfo rose from the bed. "You protect him. I respect that." He stood. "My men protect me. Tell Petronus that Rudolfo, Lord of the Ninefold Forest Houses and General of the Wandering Army seeks audience with him. Beyond that, you'll have no further explanation of me. It is a private matter for Petronus and me alone." He whistled and his men fell back; then he leaned closer and lowered his voice. "You will be mad and infirm soon enough if you do not leave off the powders and give your body time to rest."

"Then I will be mad and infirm. There is no rest in these dark times." The Gray Guard coughed again. "Are you truly Lord Rudolfo?"

Rudolfo held up the hand that bore his father's signet. "I am." Then, he waited. *He is uncertain of what to tell me.*

"Father Petronus was attacked on the night of your Firstborn Feast, along with the others. He is no longer in Caldus Bay."

"Where has he gone?"

At first, the Gray Guard said nothing. When he finally found his voice, it was faint. "He is safe. I will send word that you seek him and let him and Grymlis decide how best to deal with your interest. It will take time."

Rudolfo nodded. "That is fair, but time is short." He nodded to Jaryk, who whistled the men to stand down. "Be quick," he said.

Then he listened as the magick-muffled boots whispered their way across the floor to the narrow door leading out into a night that had become clearer and colder since their arrival in Caldus Bay. He waved his lieutenant over and spoke to him in Gypsy hand-sign. *How long did he wait beneath my bed before revealing himself?*

Two hours, Jaryk replied.

Rudolfo nodded, stroking his beard thoughtfully. Gray Guards were not scouts. They eschewed the magicks as far as Rudolfo knew, preferring instead science and strength to spells and strategy. It would not be hard to follow him, even without the powders. *Send two scouts after,* he signed. *They are to see, not be seen.*

The Gypsy Scout nodded. "Yes, Lord. Shall they go magicked?"

He shook his head. "They should not need them." *But before this is over, they will,* he thought. He sensed it.

Rudolfo went back to the bed and stretched out in it. From the corner of his eye, he watched two of his best and brightest slip into the night, moving like ghosts even unmagicked.

After they'd gone, he stared at the bottom of the bunk above him, pondering what he had learned. *Petronus was attacked, too.* He wondered how it was that the old fox had survived. If it was indeed part of the same blood-magicked and iron-bladed storm he had witnessed, that was no small feat. He could not imagine a small band of Gray Guard, unfamiliar and inexperienced with the magicks they now used, standing against a half-squad of the fierce Marshers that had killed Hanric and Ansylus.

The violence of that night returned to him and he shivered. That scene, he realized, had played out across the Named Lands. And at his core, he knew that they had been timed with the perfect coordination of forces converging all at once upon their chosen targets.

No, not him, the voice had said. He'd been intentionally spared, and even that knowledge had not been withheld from him—or from those within earshot—by the attackers. Once more Rudolfo wondered why, and as he turned the wheels of the Rufello lock over and over in his mind, he came no closer to an answer. Instead, more questions emerged from each twist and click of the mechanism.

When sleep finally reclaimed him, those questions infused his dreams with a sense of foreboding that he could not evade.

For the rest of that night, Rudolfo pitched and tossed upon his bed and dreamed he fled a great and bloody rising sun.

Winters

Winters watched the old men shuffling into the cavern throne-room, their faces pale from what they'd just seen. Nearby, the meditation statue of P'Andro Whym held his mirrors and dared them all look inside themselves. Winters was afraid of what they would find when they did. There was disease within their House, and these men had now seen its proof.

Not even an hour had passed since her arrival, and Winters sat beside the empty Wicker Throne. And she could delay no further. She tapped the handle of the Firstfall axe upon the hard stone floor of the Dreaming Cave, and the old men took their seats.

After days in the saddle riding across the frozen northern marshes it was good to be home, though the night's business ahead filled her with apprehension.

The furnaces spat and hissed throughout the great stone hall, and the hot, moist air tasted earthy in her mouth. Before her, the hall narrowed to a corridor leading out into the village and the night. Behind her, the tunnels spiraled down into deeper chambers that held the Book of Dreaming Kings.

As the old men sat, they looked up to her, their faces lined with care and sadness. Once she made eye contact with each, she convened the Council of Twelve with the words of Shadrus, the first Marsh King. "Home calls to us as we sojourn in this land of many sorrows," she said as she looked around the cave at the old men who formed the council.

The Twelve replied in unison. "May the Dreaming Kings call forth the Homeseeker that we may find our way."

She nodded slowly and looked from man to man. "May the Homeseeker guide us true into our Misplaced and Deeded Land."

"Come soon, Homeseeker, and find our Home," they said in one voice. They were the oldest and most venerable of her people, chosen by their clans for unmatched wisdom and understanding. Most, in their day, were warriors who had raided in the Named Lands as headmen, leading bands of mud- and ash-painted skirmishers to keep their neighbors fearful and supplement their scarce resources.

No one traded with Marshfolk unless compelled to do so. Until her father first saw the fall of Windwir in his dreams, blade and blood were the Marshers' first and best means of compulsion. And taking what they needed was easily justified—their very lands had been taken from them by the gray robes and their guard.

But then King Mardic had seen Windwir fall and watched darkness swallow the sun. Then, he'd seen the light suddenly appearing in the sky as it moved from the Androfrancine city east and north to settle upon the Gypsy Forests, and he'd known in that moment that the Gypsy King's blade would guard their way Home. The next morning, he had personally led a band of skirmishers against Lord Jakob's woods.

Of course, Winters had not even been born at the time. And her father was all but a stranger to her, dead for most of her fifteen years. But she'd read his words added to the Book of Dreaming Kings, and she'd added her own words to his and those of their forefathers.

Winters looked to the old men now, pushing her memory aside. There were troubling matters to attend to. "Discord has visited the House of Shadrus," she said. She could hear the sorrow in her voice as she said it, could feel the lump in her throat. She gestured to the mouth of the cave. "Beyond lay six of our own, dead now by magicks their bodies could not sustain. And the body of our Hanric lies resting in the Gypsy King's ground as his soul wanders the Beneath Places, dead at the hand of his own tribe." She hesitated as the sorrow washed her again—a grief that went deeper, beyond Hanric. She'd received the bird just yesterday, while still making her way home slowly, and had wept at the news. More unexplained and unprovoked attacks, similar to the one that took her shadow and the Crown Prince of Turam, and one of the slain had been a child sleeping in his bed. It broke her heart. She swallowed and felt the water in her eyes. "Beyond our own loss," she said, "others have been slain, and though the Androfrancine logics are not our way, it is reasonable to believe that these assassinations were also carried out by the Children of Shadrus."

The oldest and wisest of the Twelve locked eyes with hers, and she saw they were red and watery. "These are dark tidings," he said in a hoarse voice. "I've looked to the bodies, and my grandson is among them."

Her breath went out of her, and she hoped that the sound wasn't as audible as it had sounded in her own ears. But the worry was irrelevant as others responded in similar manner.

She'd ordered the bodies displayed discreetly in a tent that they might be identified. It was a gross violation of custom, not burying them where they'd fallen to keep body and soul near the place they'd parted company. But extreme circumstances called for extreme measures, and she could not let custom, no matter how sacred, interfere with finding the truth at the center of this Whymer Maze. Still it grieved her that their souls would wander the Above now, never finding their path through the Beneath Places to the home beyond.

She looked around the circle now. "Were they familiar to anyone else?"

Slow nods with downcast eyes. One cleared his voice. "My youngest sister's son lay among them," he said.

Others joined in now. One was familiar but not a kinsman. Another was bound-husband to a friend's granddaughter. Of the half dozen, only two were unknown. But eventually, Winters knew, they would be found out. She turned them now to other matters.

"Had this been simply the attack in the Ninefold Forest Houses it could readily have been the isolated act of a handful," she said. "But at least a dozen have fallen in nearly as many Houses." She looked around as the old men nodded. "These were well planned, timed to the moment and careful as a Firstfall Dance on the night of the greenest moon."

"And under the cover of the Old and Forgotten Ways," one added.

Forgotten and *forbidden,* Winters thought. The only blood magick left to them after the Purging had been the voice magicks used for war and coronation. But somehow, those old ways had been restored and employed without the knowledge of council or queen. "I fear discord and division is now sown in our House," she said. "We must find it and heal it by whatever means necessary. But beyond this, we must also look beyond our borders. We've long held our neighbors' respect through force and fear, but it is not a far leap from sorrow to rage. And Marshers have done these dark deeds—it is not unknown to them; they've bodies to show it."

The oldest spoke up. "How we respond to their rage will speak louder than any War Sermon."

Winters nodded. "I concur."

"We should be prepared for war," another said.

She looked at him. "We are the House of Shadrus. War prepares for us, and ever we meet it as our sorrow commends us to."

The oldest looked to the other. "To do more than necessary will send a message. Our neighbors, though misguided and affected, may see these attacks as something more than what they are. We would do no less. But that our own Hanric was among the fallen—he they perceived as our king—may soften the edge of their fear."

But not their wrath, Winters realized. And for all she knew, the assassinations *were* more than what they were. So shortly on the heels of Windwir, it certainly felt like more.

"What do you propose?" another asked her, and she sighed.

"We find this disease within our body and we eliminate it," she said. "You are the Twelve, respected and loved by all. Find truth for me among your clans." She cast her eye to the Wicker Throne. "At dawn, I will lay hold the throne and climb the spire to announce myself. It is earlier than my father wished, but the time for shadows is passed."

To a man, they nodded.

She nodded as well, and then once more banged the handle of the Firstfall axe against the stone floor to close the council. As the old men stood slowly and filed out, their chief approached her.

"You will be a wise queen," he told her in a quiet voice, "but I fear for your time upon the throne."

She took a deep breath, standing. "I fear it, too, Father."

"I must show you something that I wish to the gods was not so," he said. "In the tent where my grandson lies."

He turned and watched the others as they filed out of the hall, up the carved steps and into the narrow corridor that let them into the cold night. When their footfalls were distant, he moved in the same direction and Winters followed.

Without words, they climbed up and into a clouded night that smelled like smoke and imminent snow. The tent stood nearby, guarded by two large men with spears who stood on either side of a guttering lamp. He nodded to them, lifted the lamp and slipped inside. Winters followed.

The six were laid out in banks of snow, their faces hollow and pale, twisted in agony. All were clothed but one—he lay swaddled in oilcloth, stitched into it by Rudolfo's Physician. Only now, the stitches had been cut away. "My grandson," he said in a low, mournful whisper.

Winters felt the stab of shame. *He's brought me here because of the cutting of his kin.* "It had to be done," she said, "but I'm sorry for it. They wished to know how he'd died from such superficial wounds." She vaguely remembered the briefing with Rudolfo's River Woman and the dark-robed Physician who'd wielded the blade. The others they'd found were also dead—some without a scratch upon them. Their bodies and hearts had simply given out, dropping them dead in midsprint. When they'd asked her permission to cut the others, she'd refused and told them that the findings from one should suffice for all. She remembered that much, but the rest of those early days following Hanric's death were clouded.

"No," he said. "Not that." He stooped and with one liver-spotted hand peeled back the cloth to reveal the naked body of a young tangle-haired man. She watched where the old man pointed and wondered suddenly how she'd not seen this before.

There, upon the chest, slightly smaller than her closed fist, lay a cutting that she did not recognize. She leaned in to see it, the smell of death heavy in her nostrils. "He's been cut," she said. The scar was pink and new-healed. And it took a shape that she knew was intentional though she did not recognize it. "Do you know what it is?" she asked.

He looked to her, and she saw in the dim light that tears coursed his cheeks, cleansing the mud and ash from them and wetting his gray tangled beard. "Yes," he said. "It is an abomination."

He covered the body and went to the next, stooping and pushing the tattered hide vest and filthy wool shirt aside. There, over the heart, the same cut symbol.

Silently, she watched as he did the same with the others, each time careful to replace the clothing. When he finished, he stood and spoke quietly. "Forgotten heritage has found us," he said, "though few will know it when they see it, for these times are buried in two thousand years of forgetting." His wet eyes met hers, and she saw something in them that made her stomach lurch. "Few *should* know it," he continued. "Better to burn these before someone sees and knows it for what it is."

He would burn the child of his child to hide this. That he would go to such lengths, so contrary to their custom, confirmed for her what she saw in his eyes.

It was terror there, mingled with his grief, and suddenly she could not hold back her own sorrow. A solitary sob shook her in its fist and released her. She argued back the tears and forced herself to meet his gaze. "What are these markings?" she asked, but at some core part of her she knew. She of all her people was most intimate with the history they'd chosen to forget. Because though her own people no longer wished to know it, the Androfrancines with their digging about in the grave of the Old World had forgotten nothing. And her tutor, the fled scholar Tertius now five years dead, had taught her even that which she had *not* wished to know. He had no books that he might show her himself, but he'd had the words.

When the old man didn't answer, Winters asked again. "Tell me," she said, "what they mean."

"These," he said, his voice full of despair, "are the Scars of House Y'Zir, the markings of a servant's ownership."

Outside, far and distant, a wolf howled at the rising moon.

Jin Li Tam

Afternoon sunshine slanted through the tall windows of Rudolfo's study, flooding the room with light and warming the back of Jin Li Tam's neck where she sat at his desk. She looked up from the papers she'd spent the last four hours reviewing and rubbed her eyes, fighting back the nausea and headaches that took her daily now.

She understood why the River Woman had insisted that she share the work with a wet-nurse and knew Lynnae fared no better. If she'd tried to carry this entire load she had no doubt that the stabbing between her eyes and the roiling storm of her stomach would incapacitate her. Still, neither of them complained to each other. For Jin Li Tam, it was a matter of pride. Already, she hated the notion that another fed her child, that the powders that had brought life to Rudolfo's loins now threatened death and weakness to the baby boy they had made between them.

These are the consequences of my actions.

Three doors away, the young woman napped with Jakob in the suite of rooms they'd prepared for her. At first, Jin had irrationally insisted that the wet-nurse do her work in Jin Li Tam's rooms or in the nearby nursery, but very quickly it became obvious that Jakob's needs did not conform to her desires. He ate frequently, waking up from his lethargy with weak, gurgling cries throughout the day and night. Finally, she'd been forced to relent, and Jakob split his time now largely between Lynnae's rooms and hers. Still, for the hundredth time since she'd left the two of them there, Jin Li Tam resisted the urge to go and look in. To make certain that he was still breathing. To know when he'd last nursed. To see if the gray pallor of his flesh had somehow miraculously become the pink tone of a healthy infant.

But never, she realized with a start, to know how Lynnae held up beneath the power of the River Woman's potion. She started to rise from her chair to go and ask just that, then chuckled at herself and sat back down. She needed to let Lynnae do her work.

And I have work of my own, Jin Li Tam thought.

She bent her attention back to the papers and reread Rudolfo's last message, sent under code by bird from Caldus Bay.

Buried into an imaginary list of supplies available for the library by caravan from the high docks of Caldus Bay was first one message and then another, coded skillfully with each twist and smudge of the pen. *P guarded by Gray; attacked, survived and fled,* the first said; and as disturbing as that news was, the second message brought her hope. *Are you and the boy well?*

He is warming to me again.

Her family's role in the course of Rudolfo's life, in the murder of everyone he'd cared for—his family, his closest friend—had killed his love for her in its cradle. It was the last betrayal, betrothed suddenly to the forty-second daughter of the man who'd poured suffering and loss into the river of his life, changing its path. Still, her father's will was woven skillfully into the man he'd shaped both for the world and for his daughter. And when she'd told him about the child she carried, she'd seen in his eyes that her father had used Rudolfo's greatest strength against him.

Once, she'd asked a Gypsy Scout to tell her about his king, and she heard his reply echoing now these many months later. *He always knows the right path and always takes it.* Faced with the prospect of an heir, he'd proven himself truly her father's work.

There was a knock at the door; Jin Li Tam looked up. "Yes?"

The door opened, and the House Steward, Kember, looked in. "Second Captain Philemus has a bird from the Fifth March Scout. The envoy from Turam is in the Prairie Sea. They will bring them in—they should be here late tomorrow."

"Good," she said. "Is there more news from Pylos or their eastern neighbor?" Last she'd heard, the young heir of Meirov's crown lay in state for public viewing. And on the Delta, Erlund's death was fueling the civil war that raged.

The elderly man cleared his throat. "They bury the boy day after tomorrow. We were not invited to attend."

Of course not. "They suspect us," she said. "Our kin-clave with them is strained by these events."

He nodded once. "Yes. And our man on the Delta has heard that Erlund is not truly dead but that a body double was killed. He believes the Overseer is in hiding, but he's uncertain where. There have been strange goings-on. They lost nearly a squad of Scouts north of Caldus Bay on the Whymer Road."

"That's curious," she said. "What word from Aedric?"

"They are pursuing the metal man into the Wastes. Isaak believes that it was lying when it denied knowing anything about Sanctorum Lux."

Her eyes narrowed at this. "Metal men don't lie," she said under her breath.

But they can. She remembered Isaak in the rain, his metal body exposed to the weather because Pope Resolute could not see the soul that had emerged within the Order's mechanical creation, Mechoservitor Number Three. He'd ordered the metal man to remove his Androfrancine robes, offended that the machine went clothed as if he were human. When asked about the spell the metal man had recited to destroy Windwir, Isaak had lied to the Pope, claiming it had been damaged beyond recovery.

Now, Isaak rode with Neb and Aedric and the squad of Gypsy Scouts they led in pursuit.

Finally, she asked the question she'd wanted to ask first. "Is there further word from Rudolfo?"

"No," he said. "They wait in Caldus Bay."

She glanced down to the papers, suddenly uncomfortable with having asked. They'd just had word yesterday. But something hadn't set well the moment Rudolfo committed himself to seeking her father. *No good can come of it,* she knew. Though for their boy to survive, he had to do this.

"Very well," she said. "Keep me apprised on the envoy's progress."

He inclined his head. "Yes, Lady." Then, he slipped through the door, pulling it closed behind him.

Jin Li Tam stood and stretched, listening to her joints crack. Her muscles ached from this morning's workout—she'd danced with her knives for the first time in months, and she could feel it in her body. She turned and looked out the high windows. Below, shrouded white now, lay the Whymer Maze. Rudolfo had mentioned once that he'd hoped to build a larger one on the hill where the new library now sprawled, but the one below stretched out a goodly ways from the house—and there, at its center, rested Hanric, shadow of the Marsh Queen. The sun had dropped behind the trees so that the light was soft and graying. Shadows lifted up within the maze, and she wondered about the girl-queen Winters and the work she had ahead.

Moments that will shape her destiny, she thought. And another thought stuck her just as suddenly. So sudden that she flinched. *Like Rudolfo.*

It wasn't possible. She ciphered, working the datum as her father had taught her, and the answer rattled her.

These are the work of House Li Tam, she knew. Well crafted and carefully laid, she could see the threads now—even reaching into the Marshlands—and her heart sank within her breast. The thread went back past the blood-magicked Marsh assassinations. It went back to . . .

She said it aloud because she simply couldn't stop herself. "Windwir," she said in a hoarse whisper.

It was a grief she'd carried along with her child, teeth that chewed upon her as she puzzled out her own part in her father's dark work.

She stood at the window for a long while, until the light had left the sky and the lamp had guttered low. Her father had done all of this, perhaps his father before him. An elaborate cutting on the skin of the

world, a Whymer Maze drawn in blood and loss that surgically removed the Androfrancine Order and now used its salted blade to cut
even deeper. But why? For a long while she stood there, pondering
this.

   Then, Jin Li Tam sat down to her chair, turned up the lamp, and
went back to her unfinished work.

Chapter

10

Neb

They rode in silence, low in the saddles and pushing their horses as hard as the magicks would let them. Behind them, packhorses kept up without effort, led by the scouts bringing up the rear. The hooves struck the wide, flat stones of the Whymer Road, but instead of sparks and a drum-pounded gallop, they offered the slightest of coughs as the magicks bent sound around them even in the same way that the scout magicks bent light. The landscape whipped past quickly too as their enhanced strength carried them across the rocky terrain.

Neb clung to the saddle and leaned forward, letting the cold wind wash over his back as it spilled over him. He tried to keep his eyes fixed on the scout ahead, but the scenery kept pulling his attention away. There was a beauty in the shattered lands they rode through, and it tugged at his heart.

And these are just the far edges of it. Deeper into the Wastes, glass mountain ranges cast bloody shadows over forests of bone. And near these dead cities, expanses of white, coarse, glass where sea salt, left behind when the water boiled away, had fused with the sand to make razor-edged dunes that the wind moaned over. At night, creatures hunted there by the light of a blue-green moon. Indescribable left-overs of an age long past, driven mad by Xhum Y'Zir's Seven Caco-phonic Deaths.

He'd seen it in his dreams and had no doubt now that it awaited him somewhere ahead.

But for now, the landscape was simple rock and sand and scrub. Outcroppings of granite shaped by years of wind and dark straggly brush that squatted low to the ground. It looked nothing like his imaginings.

They'd entered the Wastes just ten minutes behind the metal man who fled them. If it had noticed, it paid them no mind. The mechanical moved fast, and just before they'd lost sight of it, it had still been upon the Whymer Way and moving east, the sun glinting off its bare head in the distance.

Neb feared now that they sought a solitary pearl in a vast ocean, but he was hesitant to say so. Beside him, Isaak rode uneasily in the saddle and kept his amber eyes on the road ahead, and his head swiveled to the left and right as he scanned the hills that lined the highway.

Finally, Aedric pulled forward and said what Neb wouldn't say. "I think we've lost him," he said, slowing his horse. "Even with the magicks, the horses can't keep up."

The others slowed as well.

"I can catch him," Isaak said. His eye shutters flashed open and closed, the glassy jewels still fixed ahead.

Aedric shook his head. "We need to stay together. General Rudolfo would not—"

But he was interrupted when something hard bounced off the side of Isaak's head with a dull clunk. A small stone clattered across the pocked surface of the highway. They heard giggling above. Neb and the others looked up to the rocky outcroppings that hemmed them in.

"Rainbow Men and Metal Men far from home," a voice shouted. Its tone and timbre was off—it went high when it should've gone low and vice-versa. "No Ash Men to guard you."

They stopped, and at Aedric's low whistle, the men reached for their bows and backed their horses away from the direction of the voice. Aedric fixed his eyes in the direction of the voice. "We do not wish violence."

More laughter. "Who ever wishes such a thing? But in the basement of the world violence simply *is*." Another rock—this one smaller— pitched and arched slowly, giving Aedric time to sidestep his horse. "Where do you ride in such a hurry, Rainbow Man? And without your shovels and wagons?"

Aedric raised his voice and answered. "I am Aedric, First Captain of the Gypsy Scouts. We're here on the business of Rudolfo, General of Wandering Army and Lord of the Ninefold Forest Houses."

Other voices joined in the giggling now, and the laughter bounced from stone to stone, filling the sky above them with what seemed an army of voices. "What forest, Rainbow Man? What general? What lord? Why do you speak nonsense to your orphaned boys? You come from the Luxpadre of the West. Say 'aye' to it and bring forward your payment. We will guide you truer than Renard."

Neb looked up. Isaak did, too, and their eyes met. Neb's hands moved quickly. *Ask about Renard,* he signed. Aedric nodded.

The First Captain turned his horse, looking above in the direction of the voice. "Who is Renard? Where can we find him?"

"No one and nowhere. You deal with Geoffrus now. Renard is mad. Geoffrus will see you to your digging holes."

Aedric's eyes narrowed. "Why don't you come down so we can discuss this properly?"

This time the laughter continued on for a bit. There was an eerie quality to it that unsettled Neb's stomach. He heard danger in it. "Rainbow Men with bows and knives. Do you offer kin-clave to me and mine?"

"Aye," Aedric said. "For now. If you've stopped throwing stones."

There was the scrabble of dirt and rock cascading above and behind, and Neb looked up to it. A slight form slipped into view, a slender man in patchwork cloth and scraps of rough leather. He moved lightly on his feet as he slid down the side of the hill to land with a flourish before Aedric.

"I am Geoffrus at your *service,*" he said, chuckling. "And these are my men." A half dozen heads rose to peer down at them. "Kin-clave you offer and kin-clave we take. Payment for service is rendered upon *agreement.*"

The man seemed off balance to Neb, but at first he could not tell why. Then he realized that his eyes never quite landed. They moved over everything. His left hand twitched at his side, and when he opened his mouth, his teeth and gums were black from some foul-looking substance he chewed and sucked at while he waited for Aedric to speak.

Finally, Aedric cleared his voice. "You wish me to pay you. What service will you render?"

"I will guide you true. Take you where you want to go." Then, as an afterthought: "Safely."

"And what payment for this service?"

Geoffrus smiled and danced a jig. "Knives and meat. Meat and knives. And rainbow scarves for me and mine."

Aedric looked to Neb with raised eyebrows. His hands moved. *Do you think we can trust him?*

Neb looked at the patchwork man, then back to Aedric. He could read what Aedric thought clearly in the way the First Captain sat in his saddle. *No,* he signed.

He glanced at Isaak. The metal man was watching the direction their quarry had fled to, eye shutters opening and closing as if calculating distance.

Aedric saw the same and made a decision. "We will consider your kind and generous offer for a later time," he said. "But for now, we must ride."

Geoffrus howled. He leaped and spun in the air, beating his chest with his fists. Above him, in the hills, other voices hooted and howled as well. "Rainbow Man, why do you spurn me and mine with the kin-clave so lovely between us?"

A new voice rose above the din. This one was deep and gravelly, and the laughter that it rode upon was bemused. "The Rainbow Man is wiser than you credit him for, Geoffrus," the voice said. A figure stepped onto the highway. "Perhaps he knows that the only digging holes you'll lead him to are shallow graves to hide their meat-picked bones. Perhaps the Luxpadre told him about the Ash Men you killed and ate."

Geoffrus's cavorting stopped. He fixed his eyes onto the figure, and Neb followed his gaze, surprised at the fear and rage that replaced the mirth so quickly. The newcomer was slender as a willow and tall, wrapped in the charcoal cloak of a Gray Guard. Beneath the guard's cloak, he wore the rough fabric robes of an Androfrancine archaeologist. His salt-and-pepper hair and beard were both close-cropped, and his crooked smile betrayed a relaxed confidence. His eyes were hard points of bright blue. He held a long lacquered wooden stick loosely; a large bulb of some kind at the base of it rested easy in the palm of one hand. The man stepped forward, and the wind rustled his cloak and robes as he came.

"We have kin-clave with these men," Geoffrus started, taking a step back. "We have nearly reached agreement."

"It sounds to me," the man said, "as if they seek a more polite way of extricating themselves from your company." He took another step forward. "I will not be so kind. I hold the contract with the Ash Men. I hold the letters of introduction and credit from the Luxpadre that say so."

He raised the lacquered stick and pointed one end at Geoffrus. Neb noted the dark mouth at the end of it and wondered what the strange object did. He did not wonder for long. With the slightest squeeze of the bulb, a small cloud of what looked like pollen spat from it, and something small and hard shot out, hitting the paving stone near Geoffrus's feet with surprising force and clattering off to clack against the canyon wall. Geoffrus jumped back, the anger fading as the fear took front and center in his eyes. "No call for such, no call for such," he cried, raising his hands in supplication. "Geoffrus knows an unwelcoming lot."

"If you keep following these men," the robed man said with a smile, "then you and yours will be the eaten and I will sell your skin to the Waste Witch for carrots and pepper."

Geoffrus looked around at the silent Gypsy Scouts, looked up to the heads that watched quietly from above, and his shoulders slumped. "No kin-clave here," he said, his mouth hard and straight. His eyes met Neb's for a moment, and Neb saw the hatred and hunger in them. Bowing with a flourish, he spun on his heels and clambered back up the rocky slope.

When Geoffrus vanished, the newcomer looked to Aedric. "You pursue the metal man," he said simply. "I doubt you'll catch up to it unless it wishes you to." He looked to Isaak. "They're crafty, these, and dangerous."

Isaak said nothing. His bellows whispered quietly, and the massive stallion he rode shifted beneath his weight.

Next, the guide studied their uniforms. "And you're not from the Luxpadre's Gray Guard, yet you play with his toys. You have the look of Forest Gypsies about you."

Aedric nodded. "The world beyond the Keeper's Wall has changed. Windwir is fallen. The Order is no more."

Neb thought the news would carry more impact. But instead, the man patted a courier pouch that hung from a worn leather strap around his neck. "Then these letters will be worthless now. I'd wondered when the caravans stopped coming and going so suddenly last year."

"Lord Rudolfo has inherited the Order's holdings, including the Eastern Watch," Aedric said. "I am empowered to honor or execute any contracts on his behalf. Are you Androfrancine, then?"

The man shook his head. "I'm not. But I've served them long enough, and my father before that." Stepping forward, he extended his hand. "I am Renard," he said. "I will gladly escort you to Fargoer's Town, where you may secure other arrangements to go after your wayward metal toy."

Aedric nudged his horse forward, leaned over and shook the man's hand once, releasing it quickly. "I am Aedric, First Captain of Rudolfo's Gypsy Scouts."

"Well met," Renard said with a nod. He turned, lifting his stick with one hand and pointing northeast. "Fargoer's Town is yonder. We could reach it by nightfall." His eyes shifted from Aedric to Neb and then last to Isaak. "We *should* reach it by nightfall. The Wastes aren't safe by night."

Aedric's eyes narrowed. "And how do we know we can trust you to guide us true?"

The crooked grin was back. "You are a dozen. I'm alone. But more than that . . ." He opened the flap on the pouch, rummaged about inside, and withdrew a tattered letter. He passed it to Aedric.

The First Captain read it quickly, then ran a finger over the seal at the bottom before passing it to Neb. It was a letter of introduction signed and dated by Pope Introspect some twenty years earlier, declaring that Renard son of Remus bore the grace of His Holiness the Pope and could negotiate freely such terms and conditions on behalf of the Order as necessary for its work in the Old World. Neb couldn't resist; he also touched the imprint of the papal signet before handing it back to his First Captain. He'd seen the signature many times before, and he'd carried that signet in his pocket for days before passing it to Petronus there near the craters that marked the Great Library's grave.

Renard looked up to him and winked, digging a black bit of root from his pocket and sucking it into his mouth. "You're Hebda's boy," he said as he chewed it. "You're early, but your father told me to expect you." Then, he turned even as Neb opened his mouth to speak. "We've a lot of ground to cover," their new guide said over his shoulder. "Let's run."

He set out at a jog that stretched into a sprint, and Aedric whistled them forward. At first, Neb wondered how it was this strange Waster thought he'd keep ahead of magicked horses moving at full speed. But even as they spurred their mounts forward, he saw that Renard had no difficulty matching his pace to theirs. His feet slapped the broad paving stones of the Whymer Way, and he threw back his head, laughing wildly as he ran.

Your father told me to expect you.

Later, he would ask about that. But for now, something was happening to him. Something he could not fathom nor explain.

As Neb leaned forward in the saddle, something caught in his soul and expanded. It was as if they'd crossed an invisible border that marked their true arrival in the place he'd longed for since earliest childhood. The air carried the smell of burnt spices and ancient dust. It tasted bitter on his tongue when he opened his mouth, and the sun, hanging like a golden wafer in a bright and cloudless sky, called for him to laugh as well, to give himself over to something feral and mad in this place and run with the wind to places long forgotten. To the graveyards of the former Age's light.

This place will seduce me and swallow me if I let it, he realized.

And with that realization, Neb forced the smile away from his lips and bent his mind to watching the road roll past beneath the whispering hooves.

Rudolfo

When they rounded the bend in the lane and approached the small shack and its nearby boathouse, the memory of the place struck Rudolfo like a fist.

I've been here before.

His men had followed the magicked Gray Guard back to this place and had watched it through the night from the cover of a nearby thicket. In the late morning, after he'd availed himself of the innkeeper's best fare—poached eggs and broiled salmon with seasoned potatoes and sweet, black beer—Rudolfo and the rest of his men had joined them. Two birds had gone out from the back window of the boathouse, and there was no movement whatsoever in the shack. Its windows and door had been boarded up, and no smoke leaked out from its stone chimney.

Had he known back then that this was Petronus's home? He didn't think he had—he thought he would've remembered such a thing. But those had been dark and tumultuous times, and there had been days, washed in the grief and rage of Windwir's loss, of Gregoric's loss, that he'd not even remembered his own name.

Still, he remembered this place. He remembered the men outside the door, waiting. He remembered the stink of feces and urine in the boathouse and the croaking of Sethbert where he hid in the corner, demanding to see Rudolfo, threatening to hurt him but having no blade in his hand with which to do so.

"I will hurt you with words," the mad Overseer had croaked.

And he'd spoken truly. Those words had twisted Rudolfo's life into a black and angry river, for it was there that he first learned of Vlad Li Tam's work in his life and of House Li Tam's role in the murder of his family.

The memory of that day tasted like copper in his mouth, and he swallowed it. He looked to the men that flanked him and signed for them to watch and wait. They scattered, taking up positions and melting into the underbrush to guard their liege.

Rudolfo went to the boathouse door and rapped upon it lightly. "It is Rudolfo," he said in a quiet voice. "And I no longer have the time or forbearance to wait." He paused, then offered, "I've a medico among my scouts and you're ill."

At first, he heard nothing behind the heavy wood. Then, he heard faint coughing and quiet, careful movement. There was the sound of a bar being lifted and the door opened a crack. "You followed me for nothing," the voice said plainly. "I've no word for you, Gypsy King."

Rudolfo easily pushed the door open, and the Gray Guard fell back. The odor of sickness and bird droppings choked him as he stepped into the room, letting the sunlight spill past him. The haggard man was nearly visible as the magicks gradually released him. Still, it could be too late. The magicks required years of gradual, measured use to build up immunity to their darker side effects, and these Gray Guard couldn't have been using them for more than a handful of months. The Order stood above such things, though they tolerated—and even encouraged—their neighbors to use such reminders of the former times. The Gypsy King whistled, and one of his men slipped forward. "Are you alone?" he asked the Gray Guard.

The Gray Guard said nothing, and Rudolfo's eyes narrowed. He let menace and honey mingle in his voice. "I have kin-clave with your master, regardless the Order's standing. I am the Guardian of Windwir and the heir of P'Andro Whym's holdings. I expect you to deal truthfully with me according to the Articles of Kin-Clave and tell me what I need to know that I might be on my way. I've business to attend with Petronus, and I've been gracious thus far. But I will not let the stubbornness of a dying man bring about more death." He took another step closer to the man. "I will speak and you will answer," he said. "Are you alone?"

The man coughed, bending as he did, and when he vomited onto the floor Rudolfo saw blood flecked with white foam. "There are two of us. Jarryd is sick, as well." He nodded to the far corner of the room.

Rudolfo stepped over the puddle of blood and let the medico in. The scout took the man by the elbow and guided him to the shadow-wrapped pile of blankets where the other guard slept. "Do you have what you need to treat them?"

"Aye, General," the scout said. "What I lack, the Bay Woman will have."

Rudolfo nodded. "Send for what you need."

While the medico went about his work, Rudolfo looked around the familiar room. It wasn't very different, but of course it had not been so long ago that he'd stood here. The boat was there, overturned, and the small sail was folded neatly. The mast lay along the far wall and the oars hung from pegs throughout. Other pegs held the various nets and rods of a fisherman. But in the back, where the smell of birds hung strong, Rudolfo saw one large difference.

What had once been cabinets and a tool bench had been cleared to make room for bird coops, and nearby were stacks of parchment and spools of thread. Scarlet for war, green for peace, white for kin-clave, blue for inquiry, black for danger. The rainbow colors of kin-clave—the rainbow colors of the Forest Houses—were all there along with a half dozen pens and a dozen bottles of ink.

Rudolfo moved closer and heard the cooing of the birds. Even as he approached he heard a soft thud and looked up to see a brown sparrow tangled in a catching net that hung from a small opened window. He went to it, ignoring the sound of a struggle behind him as the sick Gray Guard sought to rise and attend the tiny messenger.

Or prevent me from attending, Rudolfo thought.

Clucking his tongue, he stretched his fingers and lifted the bird from the net. It lay still and chirped in the palm of his hand. He pulled the blue thread from its foot. The small scroll came with it, and he gently lowered the bird into an open cage. He placed it onto its perch, then set the note aside.

As a boy, he'd loved the birder's coops as much as he'd loved Tormentor's Row or the secret passages that laced the Forest Manors where he'd spent his childhood. He'd learned how to mix the feed and how to find the voice that would send them to the places he would have them go. And he'd learned the codes—dozens more than he'd needed to know.

"First," Garvis the Birder had told him through his broken old teeth, "you feed them, you water them. They work hard for His Lordship, bearing the word. After they're fed," he said in a rhyming, singsong voice, "the message is read."

So even now, Rudolfo reached into the smaller feed pouch and pulled a pinch of the treated grains that gave them speed and uncanny direction. He placed the tiny bit into the small wooden thimble and added a larger pinch from the other sack. He mixed them with his little finger and placed the thimble into the cage. Then, he filled a small wooden cup with water and placed it beside the grain.

After, he closed the cage and picked up the note. He ran the thread between his forefinger and thumb, looking for knotted words. Nothing. Next, he opened the note carefully and read it through once. It was a letter to the fisherman Petros about a borrowed book—*An Exegesis of the Metaphysical Gospels of T'Erys Whym* by the scholar Tertius—stating that the book would be returned within the month on a vessel bound for Caldus Bay and sailing out of Carthas on the lower Delta of the Three Rivers. The note was written in standard cipher and inquired after Petronus's health, offered a few lines about the "recent troubles on the Delta" but all in all had nothing particularly useful. But the code was there, and though Rudolfo could see it, plain as plain, he could not read it.

He looked around the bench and saw no other letters. Just empty parchment, though the box of matches and the metal pail on the floor nearby explained why. Bending slightly, he sniffed the bucket and wrinkled his nose at the scent of fish guts and smoke.

Bringing the note, he walked to the back of the boathouse where his medico bent over his two patients. Rudolfo put his hand on the scout's shoulder and pressed his message into the hard muscle he found there. *Prognosis?*

The medico straightened, handing off a steaming mug to one of the scouts who assisted him. The scout knelt and resumed soaking a cotton bandage in the bitter-smelling elixir, pressing it to the lips of the unconscious Gray Guard. "They'll live, but they're not well. They need to be abed in a warmer, dryer place."

The one who'd answered the door coughed so violently that he shook, but he still tried to sit up. "The bird," he said, his eyes wild and wide.

"The bird is safe and sound," Rudolfo said. "But you are neither safe *nor* sound here. The powders are undoing you, and you will need better care and rest than this hovel can afford you." He nodded to the coops behind him. "You're running a message post," he said. "Why?"

The man swallowed, his eyes lighting upon the note in Rudolfo's hand. "I am under Grymlis's orders."

Rudolfo leaned closer. "And what are those orders," he asked, "exactly?"

The man's eyes were glazing over from the exertion of sitting up. He shivered and fell back. "I don't know the codes," he said. "I can't tell what I don't know."

Rudolfo gritted his teeth. The damnable paranoia of the powders combined with the normal caution of a loyal man were wearing his thin patience thinner yet. "I've not asked the codes. I've asked your orders." He forced a reasonable tone to his voice and he lowered it. "I am a friend of the Order," he said. "You'd know this if you were in your right mind."

The man laughed. "The Order has no friends."

Rudolfo sighed. "Very well. You've left me little choice." He whistled, and First Lieutenant Jaryk entered, concern washing his face. "Dig up scout uniforms for these men, and when they're dressed, bring the horses. Two of our own will stay here with me to mind the birds. I will hope to sort this puzzle out myself." He gestured to the two Gray Guard. "These you'll deliver to the inn in Kendrick's Town. Lodge them there for three weeks' time under my good credit." He waved his hand. "Tell the innkeeper the truth—that they're overmagicked and crazed from exhaustion." His eyes narrowed. "They should be restrained at all times until in their right mind."

The Gray Guard's eyes went wild. "No, Lord," he said. "We can't leave our—"

Rudolfo's voice lowered to a near whisper. "You are leaving your post one way or another. You either leave it in the care of my *fully informed* Gypsy Scouts or you leave it in more *haphazard* straits."

Swallowing one part pride and a good measure of phlegm, the Gray Guard passed his orders on to Rudolfo. Rudolfo knelt beside him, listening carefully, as he did.

By the time the soldier finished and sagged back into his filthy bedding, Rudolfo knew all he needed to know. Taking the note, he scribbled his own code into the letter carefully. He worked the message into each jot and tittle, each smudge and blur of ink. Then, he pulled the next bird from its cage and tied the modified message to its foot with the green thread of peace.

Suddenly, he remembered another bird, over a year past now, under the same color and going to Sethbert at the edge of the Desolation of Windwir. This felt just as much the lie as that message back then. He looked at the other threads scattered across the workbench.

"They should all be red," he said aloud in a voice that sounded more tired than he thought he should be.

Lifting the bird to the window, he whispered a name and gave his message to the grayness of the sky.

Petronus

Hushed voices met his ears as Petronus's unseen escort guided him through the streets. Blindfolded and magicked, firm hands kept him on his feet and moving forward though his legs were gone to water and the sound of his heartbeat filled his head.

"You'll be fine," Rafe Merrique had told him that morning with a wink. "You may have a few nightmares. Beyond that, you'll be good as new by morning."

Petronus had agreed reluctantly, letting the pirate dab the traces of the white powder to his shoulders and feet, forehead and tongue. Then he'd felt his stomach wobble—along with the room—when the magicks took hold.

Now, he and his men were being jostled quickly through what sounded and smelled like a fish market. He listened for any telltale clue that might speak to their location but found, instead, all of his attention went to staying upright and moving forward. He did not know how Grymlis and his men maintained themselves so well, coming late as they did to the powders. And then there were men like Rudolfo's Gypsy Scouts, bred to the magicks and knives and using both as if made to do so. It awed him.

His stomach knotted into a cramp that caught his breath in his throat, and he staggered. "I'm going to be sick," he said in a muffled voice.

No one answered, but a hand on his shoulder squeezed in a reassuring way. It took him a moment to get his brain around the tapped message.

We're nearly there. He had no idea whose hand it was; he didn't care.

Instead, he gave himself to putting one foot in front of the other. He reached into his memory to find one of the hundred Franci meditations he'd used to bring calm and comfort, but none of the muttered words could blot out the drumbeat of his heart, now pounding just out of time with the other hundred heartbeats within earshot. He heard the rasp of breath in and breath out, the jangled cacophony of a thousand other simple actions, all enhanced by the magicks, and he understood why their use had been forbidden by the Articles of Kin-Clave under all but extreme circumstances.

Then, the afternoon light that burned into his scalp vanished and he felt shadows enfold him. He felt solid, stone steps beneath his leather boots. The press of bodies around him moved down like a river that carried him in its current; cool air licked his face and arms.

They turned and turned again, a Whymer Maze of corridors. At some point, he was separated from the others and opened his mouth to protest. But before he could speak, the hand was back to his shoulder. *Your host wishes a few minutes alone with you.*

Resolved, Petronus allowed himself to be led farther into the maze.

Finally, they stopped and hands went to the back of Petronus's head. More hands settled him back into a chair. The intensity of light when the blindfold came down stung his eyes and he blinked.

"When I was ten years old," a voice said from across the room, "I heard you speak in Carthas during the Year of the Falling Moon. Two years later, I mourned your death and swore vengeance upon your assassins with all of the fervor of a twelve-year-old boy." There was a pause. "When I took my vows to the Order, I did so under your portrait in the Great Library."

Petronus looked in the direction of the voice. A stocky man with a careless beard and spectacles smiled. "You are still under the magicks," the man said. "You have my apologies for that, Father. I know they're . . . uncomfortable."

Petronus opened his mouth and found it dry. He licked his lips. "You're Androfrancine, then?"

"I was." His smile faded. "I guard another light now."

Petronus dug through his memory for snippets of code brought by the bird. What was his name? It came to him suddenly. "You're Esarov the Democrat, then."

He nodded. "I am."

Petronus chuckled. "You've been busy. How many of the city-states are a part of your congress now?"

"Four as of yesterday."

He remembered the declaration Esarov and his cronies had posted on the door of the Overseer's puppet Council of Governors. It had been a bold move on the heels of Sethbert's unjust attack on Windwir and the war it spurred. With its economy broken and the war lost, that small seed of unrest grew into a choked forest of revolution, with this man—the author of the declaration—at its forefront.

Petronus looked around. It was a simple room—a workroom with benches and tools strewn about on one side and stacks of books and papers on the other. A small wooden trestle table sat in the middle with a modest fruit bowl and half of a loaf of bread. A water-jeweled pitcher stood near a handful of empty mugs. Esarov waved to the table. "Please," he said.

Petronus's stomach twisted at the sight of the food. "Later perhaps," he said. "Meanwhile, I have questions."

Esarov smiled. "I'm happy to answer them." He squinted at him. "Ah, you're coming more into focus now."

"You've offered me refuge here, in a place where I may or may not necessarily be safer." His eyes narrowed. "Why?"

"We have a common interest in recent events," he said. "I think we have shared suspicions of a larger threat."

How does he know? Petronus said nothing, waiting for his host to continue.

Esarov's voice lowered. "I know about the secondary Tam network," he said. "I know about the forged documents that led Sethbert into war."

Petronus blinked, grateful that the magicks masked his eyes. "Forged?"

The revolutionary nodded. "Planted by House Li Tam," Esarov said. "The same network that continues to operate in the Named Lands despite Vlad Li Tam's rather sudden departure."

Another network, Petronus thought. Esarov believed House Li Tam responsible for the Desolation of Windwir. To the outside eye, that made sense. But not to Petronus. Vlad Li Tam had certainly changed in the years since they'd been boys together that summer in Caldus Bay, but Petronus still believed his last assurance that day in the Gypsy King's Seventh Forest Manor.

Rudolfo was Tam's work, he'd told him, just as Petronus was his father's work. And Petronus remembered Tal Li Tam though they'd only met once. He'd been a tall, powerful figure with a tawny red mane and large, calloused hands. There'd been ruthlessness in those blue eyes that had chilled the young man when he'd reached out to shake his friend's father's hand.

A secondary network, operating within the Order and within the complex kin-claves of the Named Lands, to bring down Windwir? It was plausible, but to what end?

"I've been following the goings-on for months now," Petronus said in a quiet voice. "It does appear to be manipulated." *But I count your so-called revolution among those manipulations,* he thought but did not say. Even back into the days of the Younger Gods there'd been no circumstance where self-rule had not eventually reverted back to some form of hierarchy with a strong central leader.

"And the Marshfolk are turning violent," Esarov said. He pursed his lips. "This, too, could be manipulated. The Remnant is shrinking. Androfrancines are being attacked by Marshers in the north, those that aren't hidden in the Gypsy King's forests or hidden behind the locked gates of the Papal Summer Palace." The revolutionary's eyes narrowed. "And Rudolfo is a curious case. He's the only one that appears to have actually *profited* from Windwir's fall. And he was curiously untouched in these last attacks."

Petronus felt a spark of anger rise. Or was it defensiveness? "I'm the one who signed over the holdings to him," he said. "I can tell you with surety that Rudolfo had nothing to do with Windwir. Sethbert did that, with or without the Tams' involvement."

But of course the Tams had been involved, right down to Petronus signing over the accounts and lands of the Order, as much as he hated to admit it.

And now the Ninefold Forest is the only stable corner of the New World.

"Regardless," Esarov said. "It is curious. I smell the work of House Li Tam in it." He stood by the table now, facing Petronus. "And you are working through it all like a Rufello cipher, trying to untangle the truth."

Yes. Petronus looked down, saw his leg fading gradually into view. Then, he met Esarov's eyes, though he doubted the man could tell that Petronus was staring at him. "I believe there is a threat outside the Named Lands," he said. "I don't believe all the papers were forged, though some signatures certainly were. I believe that the unrest in the Named Lands—and here on the Delta—is a product of that outside threat. I'm looking for evidence of it."

Esarov smiled. "You can look, but you won't find it. We're doing

this to ourselves. But it's irrelevant. We gain more by working together. And . . ." His voice trailed off.

"Yes?"

"I believe you can help me. Erlund is holding someone important.
An Androfrancine." He dug in his pocket and pulled out a folded
piece of paper. He handed it to Petronus. Scribbled on it was an uncoded note in a reckless script:

> *I am the Arch-Engineer of Mechanical Science for the Androfrancine
> Order in Windwir. I bear an urgent message for the Hidden Pope Petronus.
> The Library is fallen by treachery. Sanctorum Lux must be protected.*

Petronus read it again, slowly. "Charles is alive." He'd not seen him
in over thirty years. Then, the young man had been newly promoted
from acolyte to Engineer, attracting the See's attention with his recon-
struction of Rufello's mechanicals. Petronus handed the note back.
"How old is this message?"

"By the context, we think nearly a year."

Yes, Petronus thought. It had to be from before he had announced
himself and stepped out of hiding there in the midst of the grave-
digging of Windwir. *The hidden Pope Petronus.*

Somehow, Charles had known. Could Introspect have told him?
And why? What purpose did it serve?

And what was this Sanctorum Lux that now required protection?

As if reading his mind, Esarov answered. "I believe it's a replica of
the Great Library," he said. "A sanctuary of light. But I'm hoping you
can tell me."

Petronus shook his head. "It's not familiar to me. But that doesn't
mean anything." He thought about the forged signature authorizing
the work around Xhum Y'Zir's spell. "Still," he said, "if the message is
from Charles . . ."

The gears and wheels of the Rufello lockbox fell into place for
Petronus, and as he looked to his host, he saw himself shimmering,
fading in and out of focus, in the reflection of Esarov's spectacles.
"You need my help negotiating for his release."

Esarov nodded slowly. "In a way, yes."

Petronus stood. "You need someone Erlund wants more than
Charles. You want to make an exchange." He felt something cold and
hollow take root inside him, growing alongside a seedling of hope.
And maybe, just maybe we restore the library. All of the library, he realized,

not just what the mechoservitors carried about in their memory scrolls. He wondered in that moment if Esarov realized the exactitude with which Xhum Y'Zir's spell had surgically removed all of the war-making knowledge the Androfrancines had guarded. All that had been left was a hand cannon that he'd sent Neb to destroy. The hand cannon that Resolute had used to take his own life and end the war. Thousands of years of digging and storing, and that was all of the weaponry that remained. Not even the spell had survived, according to Isaak, though Petronus thought that to be a miracle in their favor. Still, Santorum Lux was nothing more than an obscure reference from a man who could very well be dead by now.

But Petronus knew that no matter how unlikely, they needed to be sure.

"He may not *want* you more than Charles, but our laws will compel him to bargain with us and to arrest you. Sethbert was near-kin to Erlund and was executed without a proper trial," Esarov said. "This could be a tremendous opportunity both for your light and mine."

Petronus studied the strategy he saw before him and wondered if this indeed was part of a larger conspiracy or if Esarov had truly struck this note of genius under his own power. He saw an elaborate net laid out that could, if set well, expedite the end of this civil war and eventually rally the people behind the fledgling democratic movement. It was as brilliant and careful as any Tam intrigue. "A trial for the man who killed Sethbert?"

Esarov nodded. "But more than that. Our legal system relies on the Jury of Governors. He'll be forced to acknowledge the four new governors, duly elected by the people, or show himself truly for the dictator he is. And if you invoke your rights to Providence of Kin-Clave, based on your actions as a king . . ." He offered a tight smile. "My emphasis at the Order—before I left—was New World law as developed from the Articles and Rites of Kin-Clave established at the First Settlers Congress."

A message for the hidden Pope Petronus. Sanctorum Lux must be protected. The words played out behind his eyes.

Charles knew he was alive, then, and knew of something called Sanctorum Lux. And whatever this sanctuary of light was, Petronus knew they could not dismiss it.

He looked to the door. There were two men, each wearing cloth hoods that hid their faces. They wore the simple garb of fishermen, but he had no doubt they were soldiers. He also had no doubt that though he was being asked to cooperate, the plan was too carefully constructed to truly allow such a thing as choice to interfere. "You intend to exchange me for Charles. What guarantee do I have of a trial?"

And would it be any more just than the rabbit-and-sparrow show he'd put Sethbert through?

Esarov picked up an apple, bit into it and chewed thoughtfully before speaking. "It will be part of the truce we negotiate. I've a man close to Lysias. The general is still a reasonable fellow. We will also be certain that you are placed under house arrest and well treated, as is fitting of your former office."

Some refuge I've found. He would be public. He would be removed from his work and under constant watch. And if Esarov was wrong at any point along this path, Petronus could find himself facing an axe or a hangman's rope.

He bowed his head, studying the fabric of his robe as it reasserted itself and the magicks guttered out their last. On the night he'd been attacked, Petronus anticipated a reckoning there in the relative obscurity of his shack on the bay.

Now, he realized, that reckoning *truly* had found him.

He looked up, met eyes with the younger man, who blinked behind the glass lenses he wore. "I'll do it," Petronus answered.

And his voice was steady and strong as he said it.

Chapter 11

Rae Li Tam

Rae Li Tam paced the beach, shouting orders that were in turn shouted out to what remained of her father's iron armada. Her family scrambled and scurried about her, helped by natives obligated now by kin-clave and by reciprocity for the fine tools and trinkets they now possessed.

Her family had to leave.

Now.

Before the bird had arrived this morning, they were down three vessels plus the flagship. Those Vlad Li Tam had steamed forth to rendezvous with and his own vessel. She'd followed protocol and sent out two more when the distress bird reached them, informing her that a vessel was reefed and in need of repair. She'd also sent two additional engineers and a sizable portion of their repair parts. Now she knew both vessels and crew would not be coming back.

She added the numbers silently. Over two thousand souls lost or gods knew where.

She smelled treachery but could not discern whose. Someone within the House, perhaps the First Son, though the notion was unheard-of. In all of these generations, never had there been division within House Li Tam. Still, the note seemed real enough, and she could not discount it. She still held it in her hand and periodically, stopped pacing long enough to read it again.

Windwir a ruse, the coded message said. *We are betrayed by our own. Save what can be saved.* There was no mistaking the seal and signature. It was her father, Vlad Li Tam. But the message bird had been from one of the ships they'd most recently dispatched. Its feathers were singed.

Her brow furrowed and she bit her lip. A ruse. Betrayed by our own. She lowered her hand and looked again at the flurry of activity around her as the longboats were loaded and rowed out to tall iron ships that belched steam into a cloudless sky. The engines were up, and they neared their last load.

When Baryk approached, her feet were back to moving across the water-packed sand. "We're nearly finished. Two more trips and we'll have everything." His voice lowered. "Are we leaving the trade goods?"

Rae Li Tam pondered this. "Yes," she said. "We will leave them. But spread word that we go south. And leave birds for that direction with feed for six months."

Baryk nodded, then his face softened. "How are you?"

She forced a smile at his concern. He was a strong partner, and she was grateful that her father had approved the match. There was logic and purpose behind the pairing. "I'm fine," she said. "Focused on what must be done." But underneath the words, she was afraid.

"Where are we going, then?"

She shook her head and moved her hands low and to her side. *Not here. Not until we are at sea.*

He read the movements, then nodded. "I understand." He looked out to the ships, cupping a hand over his eyes against the sun. "I'm going out with this lot," he said. "I'll check the armaments and the watch rotations." He looked back to her, his mouth suddenly grim. "You think the others are lost, then."

She swallowed against the fear she felt. "I do. I think we've been brought to this place and Father just figured that out. I think he was lured out to sea."

Removed from the Named Lands. Set apart from them. Far apart and by his own kin—the only predators who could match Lord Vlad Li Tam of House Li Tam. She thought of wolves hunting in the northern timberlands and shivered despite the tropical heat that baked her skin, hanging heavy and hot in her lungs.

Save what can be saved. She realized Baryk was speaking, though his words were lost to her. "I'm sorry?"

"I said he's a crafty old hawk. Perhaps the note means he's safe."

But something within her told Rae Li Tam that was not to be hoped for. Something whispered that her father may indeed still be alive but could not possibly be safe. "We can't afford to think that he is. Which means everything changes. No birds without my consent—I want the coops locked and under guard."

"I'll pass the word," he said. Then, Baryk leaned in close and kissed her quickly on the cheek. "I'll see you aboard."

He moved off quickly, shouting for two young men to wait for him as they prepared to cast off their boat. Rae Li Tam watched him climb over the bow and settle onto one of the benches. When he inclined his head toward her, she returned his gesture of respect.

Then she was back to pacing and barking orders, pointing and calling out to this one or that one while her mind continued spinning.

Half of the fleet was gone now, though the vessels had not carried full complements. It would mean cramped quarters on the remaining ships.

And slower speeds.

But if there was a threat to the House—from within the House—it would not be speed that saved them. It would be strategy and misdirection, craft and deception—all skills she'd learned at her father's feet during the forty years she'd served him before settling into her married retirement with Baryk in their villa on the Outer Emerald Coast outside the city-state P'Shaal Tov. Certainly, she'd still served her father during those quieter years, often putting her skills as an apothecary to work. Three years of pretending to be a boy acolyte with the Androfrancines now made her the New World's leading authority on all things chemical with the Order fallen. From time to time, her father required those services of her. And she'd agreed to provide them when he'd approved her request to take Baryk as husband and live with the warpriest near the city-state he'd served most his life.

Four times in fifteen years had her father required anything of her. Most recently, it had been a recipe for her sister's procreative work with the Gypsy King—a simple enough task. Each assignment had come with little information and she'd given herself to the work gladly. And though she'd have paid every last coin she owned to please her father, he had arranged generous compensation for each assignment.

But then the triple-coded note had come last year, and she'd known for the first time that her father had encountered something that had changed him, some kind of respect-based fear that drove him to retreat. Within weeks of that fateful bird, and after a short but impassioned conversation culminating in their first raised voices as a couple, she and Baryk had packed what they could not live without, sold off what they could, and had arrived at the Tam Estates to see the iron ships laying in their cargo at anchor in the bay. They joined in the work of loading while her father, Vlad Li Tam, burned the books of his family's work and prepared to flee the Named Lands.

Or did he go a-hunting? she wondered.

Perhaps, she thought, *it was both.*

Regardless, after seven months at sea, moving at a leisurely, methodical pace, something had happened. The armada was halved, and though some part of her felt the compulsion to know, she knew there was little chance of discovering what might have happened to her father and to the rest of her family.

Save what can be saved. There was finality in those words, and despite her best hope, she sensed that some night soon, once they were safely to sea and steaming toward points unknown to all but her, she would sit at her writing table in her cramped captain's quarters aboard the new Tam family flagship. She would give herself, for a moment, to grief and compose a poem to honor her father's passing.

Even as her mind laid out these nets, her feet moved across the sand and her voice rang out with command. Years away, and yet the mantle fell easily to her as the oldest of Vlad Li Tam's surviving children in the absence of his First Son or his First Grandson.

When the beach was cleared, and when she walked the village paths to be sure none were left behind, she went to the last boat where it waited in the surf.

Confusion colored the faces of the Dayfather and his people. Sadness and surprise rode his young niece's eyes. They'd expected a longer visit—more attempts to make permanent those bonds of kinclave Vlad Li Tam had negotiated with the young girl—and despite Rae's best diplomacy, they'd not understood and she'd refused to alarm them.

If there is danger to them, she thought, *my warning will offer no aid. Best to leave with as little said as possible.*

She stood in the surf now and felt the warm water licking at her feet and ankles. She raised her hand in farewell and watched as the Dayfather and his kin did the same.

Then, she let the young men in the longboat lift her aboard and she fixed her eyes to the northeast.

In the end, it was the sand that told her where they would flee. The one place that none traveled these days.

Home to the Named Lands, she thought, *and then around the horn.*

Above her, a dark shape circled in the sky. Larger and blacker than a seagull, it flew ever-widening circles.

A raven of some kind. Out of place this far at sea, but not impossibly so.

"You are a long way from home," she said to the bird.

As if hearing her, the bird stopped its circling and shot south as straight and fast as an arrow.

What prey do you seek? And when she asked it, she knew she meant the question both for the bird and for her father, also fled south.

Sighing, she shifted on the uncomfortable wooden bench and gave her mind to the web of strategy and misdirection she must now lay down for her family on her father's behalf.

Winters

The Chambers of the Book were stifling hot, and Winters found herself opening the front of her shirt, using the loose fabric to fan cooler air onto her breasts and into her armpits.

Outside, she knew there was fresh snow and a coming blizzard. How had it become so unseasonably warm here?

She walked quickly, following the cavern's spiraling descent. She'd reached the Last Chapter of the book now, watching the dated spines of each volume. She stretched out a hand and let her dirty fingers trail over them.

She could not remember how many volumes there were now. But the Book of Dreaming Kings was a paper serpent over half a league long, shelves carved into the stone walls containing each volume.

As Winters walked, the cavern grew hotter, and an intense light built below. Music drifted up to her, and she recognized it as a solitary harp. A stinging breeze watered her eyes.

Her voice was muffled by a distant roaring but rang out above the flowing melody. "Hello?"

She heard a low whistle and looked to her left, where the cave spilled open into a midnight desert. Neb stood there beneath a blue-green moon, talking with a man she did not know but suddenly feared. He was slender as a willow and dressed in tattered robes. He carried a thorn rifle, though she did not know why it was called that or what it did. And he meant to take Neb from her to a place where her dreams could not find him.

As if he knew this, he raised a hand and pointed to the moon and it became a cold, dead thing—and etched into the white of the lunar corpse, a sign she'd so recently seen carved into the skin of Hanric's killers.

She opened her mouth to speak, but then saw Isaak. He lay broken open, and the man she feared was crouched over him, hands up to his forearms, deep and working within the mechoservitor's chest cavity.

His name is Renard, a voice called to her from below. She turned her eyes away from Neb's dreams and saw her own unfolding.

The stairs spilled out into a reading chamber, continuing their downward spiral across an open space littered with cushions and chairs. In the corner, seated upon a three-legged stool, a robed man played his harp.

"Who is he?"

"One who will make you weep before all is done," Tertius said. "But you will laugh again after."

Winters moved cautiously into the room, her hand no longer tracing the spines of the Book. "You are dead, Tertius."

"They say so," he said. "Yes."

"What is happening to the Book of Dreaming Kings?"

Tertius smiled. "'The light devours and burns brighter for it,'" he said, and she knew the words. They were from one of the Errant Gospels, possibly from T'Erys Whym himself.

Even as he spoke, flames belched up the stairs and the room began to burn. As if compelled, the scholar Tertius gave himself over to the harp, his fingers flying across the strings.

And in the moment that her dream shifted again, Winters knew also the song he played, though like the thorn rifle, she did not know how or why she knew it.

It was "A Canticle for the Fallen Moon," composed by the last of the Weeping Czars, Frederico. It was a song about love and loss, about being separated by vast distance and finding one another at last.

And suddenly, the song was gone; she was alone and struggling in her bedroll near a guttering fire.

A wolf howled in the hills below, and Winters shivered.

"You are far from home," a voice said from someplace below her on the slope. She felt cold fingers move lightly on the skin of her neck and arms. By instinct, she reached for her knife, then relaxed as Neb materialized at the edge of the fire's glow. He wore his dusty uniform, and his long white hair had fallen over one eye in a way that made her want to touch him.

"So are you," she said.

He looked over his shoulder at the blasted lands that stretched behind him. "Yes." He stepped closer, and the fire whispered out as he did. "The dreams have gotten stranger," he said.

"This one is nice," she answered. Neither needed to mention how rare the nice dreams were. They were scarce in the first place and had become more so since Hanric's death. She patted the bedroll beside her. Neb pulled off his boots and crawled beneath the covers.

"Tomorrow," she said, "I'll reach the summit and announce myself." She could not see it in her dream, but the Wicker Throne and its leather harness lay somewhere within reach. She was sure of it. She felt the bite of the straps in her shoulders and back from the long days of carrying it north to the spire.

Neb wriggled near her. "I'm in Fargoer's Town. I'm on watch soon," he said.

Then, without further words, they intertwined themselves and she felt the warmth from him spread out to contain her. They did not kiss, though they had in times past. And they did not move their hands over one another, though that also had happened before.

Now, they simply held one another and took comfort from that holding.

And then she was alone again, stiff and cold, the clouds covering the starshine overhead as the sky grew mottled gray with morning. She smiled at the memory of her last dream and forced herself out of the bedroll and onto her feet, but the smile faded quickly.

I will not see him for a season, she thought. She did not know how she knew it, but it was a truth. Different worlds called to them now, but someday, they would be reunited as Home rose and called them forth.

She packed quickly and then kicked over the lean-to and pushed dirt into the fire. There were puddles now where the snow had melted, leaving potholes edged in the red clay dust of the Dragon Spine Mountains.

Groaning, she pushed blistered feet into tattered boots and shrugged herself into the harness. Leaning forward, she tipped the Wicker Throne onto her back and started her climb. She felt the leather straps cutting into her skin and felt fire in the soles of her feet and in her knees as she forced herself forward.

Three days she'd borne this load, and today she would enthrone herself in the thin air above the world and announce the beginning of her reign.

As her shadow, Hanric had done this once on her behalf—a labor of love that only now could she fully comprehend. She blessed him for it in that moment, and wept as she moved her feet. She did not sorrow for his loss. Her tears were for the work ahead of her. There was something about carrying the throne upon her back, feeling it bite into her flesh, that spoke to the weight of her role. *I am the Marsh Queen.*

"I am Winteria bat Mardic," she said beneath her breath. "I am True Heir to the Wicker Throne and the Dreaming Queen of my People." She'd practiced the words until they came easily to her tongue.

For as long as she'd remembered, she'd fantasized about this day. She'd always known it would be a bloody day, but she'd imagined a slower climb, perhaps in the spring just after her birthday. And in those girlish daydreams, Hanric walked with her. He kept pace just behind, offering a kind word here or an encouraging word there. And her people lined the path with flowers even though she blushed at the open way they adored her.

Once she'd met Neb, a new note had been added to her daydreams. He walked with her and she was the Homeseeker's Bride, there taking her place upon the throne and declaring herself queen of her people.

But the reality of it was an achingly cold climb, completely alone. She climbed because she had to, and when she reached the top, she unbuckled her harness and turned the Wicker Throne into the wind. She unstopped the flask and tipped the rancid blood magicks into her mouth. They were sour and briny on her tongue, and she had to choke the vile fluid down her throat.

She waited, counting silently.

When she opened her mouth, it was the voice of many waters that rumbled across the sky, spilling out upon her people. The voice overflowed her lands, her words reaching distant towns and farms as a whisper after marching strong and clear so many hundreds of leagues.

"I am Winteria bat Mardic," she cried out. "I am True Heir to the Wicker Throne and the Dreaming Queen of my People."

She said it twice more and then sat down upon her throne.

She sat there, looking out upon her lands with a quiet heart, until the sun began to drop low and far to the west.

And as the sun dropped, she looked away to the east instead and watched until the light was gone.

Then, she stood and strapped on her harness.

With a sigh, Winters lifted her burden once more and descended into the beginnings of another cold night.

Neb

Neb started when firm hands shook him awake, and suddenly the cold mountain air and the warmth of the woman from his dreams vanished. Aedric stared down at him, his face lined hard in the low lamplight that played over the walls of the barn they slept in.

Nodding to show he was awake, Neb crawled from his blankets and pulled on his soft leather boots, wondering if their guide had returned yet.

True to his word, Renard had brought them into Fargoer's Town just as the last of the sun blinked out and swollen stars swept up into the night. He'd helped them barter for lodging in a barn that stank of pigs and goats just outside the walls of the town proper and then had left them there to gather what news might be helpful to them.

The small settlement was farther into the Wastes than Neb had believed, farther even than his eye from the heights of the Keeper's Wall could have discerned. He'd heard stories of Fargoer's Town, but the details had always been scant. He'd filled those gaps with such items and characters that lent themselves to the romance of archaeology. The reality of it was disappointing. He dimmed the lamp behind him as he let himself out into the starlit landscape, closing the barn door as he went. Aedric waited for him in the deeper shadows near the corner of the barn. Near him, Isaak stood. The metal man's eyes were closed, but behind the shutters, light flashed and popped even as gears whistled and steam whispered deep within his metal surface.

"He's ciphering," Aedric said in a quiet voice. "Renard showed him a map before he left. He's projecting possible routes our other *friend* may have taken."

Neb watched the metal man for a moment, then said what he knew Aedric must already be thinking. "I don't see how we can find him."

Aedric nodded. "I don't either. And to be frank, I'm not certain we should try at this point." He paused, and Neb waited for him to continue. When the young First Captain did, his voice bore a strange tone,

one that Neb had not heard from any of Rudolfo's Gypsy Scouts—a note of doubt that bordered on fear. "I've sent three birds, whispering them to the Wall," Aedric said. "All have returned with messages untouched. Two were wounded. Our last word from the Forest was that Rudolfo rides out quietly to find Vlad Li Tam and armies now rally in Pylos and Turam with an eye to the north. This is the wrong time for us to be away on an improbable errand with no way to bear word home."

Neb thought about this. "Do you think Renard can help us?"

Aedric shrugged. "I'm not sure what he offers is help." He nodded to Isaak. "These metal men are a wonder of the world, to be sure, but there was something deadly in that one . . . something unlike Isaak. It had blood on its hands—I'm sure of that—and no qualms about spilling more."

Neb did not doubt it. He'd seen the metal beast roar through them in the guardhouse, seen it leap the stairs three at a time to crest the wall. Certainly, Isaak also had blood upon his hands, yet the regret and remorse of it was obvious in the metal man with his every limping step. He did not feel dangerous, but the one who named him cousin there on the Keeper's Wall reeked of it. But despite the danger, something more powerful—a curiosity that bordered on need—fueled Neb. He gave name to it. "What about Sanctorum Lux?"

Aedric nodded, slowly. "Aye," he finally said. "There is that curiosity." He sighed, looking west toward the Keeper's Wall, then east where jagged lines of mountains serrated the horizon. Last, he looked back to Isaak and to Neb. "We need to know of it. But I think General Rudolfo would not risk so much treasure to chase down an answer to that question. The venture is ill timed, and we are ill suited for it."

He means us, Neb realized, though he could not fathom why Rudolfo would place such stock in him. Isaak made complete sense—the metal man carried vast amounts of knowledge within him and was indispensable in their work restoring the library. His absence from the Ninefold Forest for even a month would be felt, but if anything were to happen that he not return, it could slowly bring that light-saving work to a halt. Among the mechoservitors, he was chief and was the only of their kind to understand the principles with which they operated in such a way as to keep them maintained and functioning. And he was . . . Neb reached the word and finally found it. Special. Different. Of his kind, he'd been the only one to take a name and to take up the Androfrancine robes. At least until this other had shown up, wearing

robes and going by the name of Charles, the name of the mechoservitors' supposed father.

And at one time, Isaak had uttered the words of Xhum Y'Zir, singing down death upon Windwir, transformed into a weapon that could
weep for the genocide it was bent and twisted into committing.

It made sense that Rudolfo would not risk Isaak. But what of Neb?
He was a boy, a young officer who'd seen too much for his years and
yet had seen very little. Winters saw destiny within him—Nebios ben
Hebda, the Homeseeker. The one who would eventually become the
Marshfolk's fabled Homefinder, spiriting them off to a promised land
beyond their wildest imaginings. But even Neb struggled with the su-
perstitious underpinnings of those beliefs, despite his trust in the
Marsh Queen Winters.

Neb forced his mind back to their quiet conversation, licking his
dry lips before he spoke. "Still," he said, "if there is a sanctuary of
light—if it *is* another library as Isaak suspects it may be—"

Aedric interrupted. "Then we will trust that those who hid it here
in the Wastes did their work well and that it will await us when we can
come to this place with more presence and certainty." He offered a
grim smile. "We have time, lad. And perhaps our guide will bear us
happy tidings."

With a hasty goodnight, Aedric slipped into the barn and pulled the
door closed. Neb settled down on his haunches and watched the night
move on toward morning.

There was an eerie silence punctuated by the occasional barking of
dogs inside the walled town just north of them. Still, even the dogs
sounded odd—as if noise here just didn't behave properly.

He'd always loved last watch during his time in the gravediggers
camp—it had proven to be a quiet watch most nights and one less popular with others. But the notion of being up before the morning really
began, of seeing the day unfold in such a manner, felt hopeful. Fifteen
minutes slipped past, and suddenly a figure emerged silent from the
shadows. It was already upon him when he reached for his knives and
puckered his lips to whistle Third Alarm.

"Hush now, young Nebios," Renard whispered in a slurred voice.
"You'll wake your friends without cause." The gangly scarecrow of a
man slipped closer. The smell of alcohol was strong on him, and he
staggered a bit while he walked. The man chuckled, then mumbled,
"Sounds like your young captain doesn't have the stomach for the
Wastes."

He's drunk. But Neb noted the surety of his feet. The long stick was now slung over his shoulder, and he approached with open hands. Neb couldn't resist the question. "Do you bear news?"

Renard looked up, smiling, and for a moment Neb was no longer certain of his inebriation. There was a cold light in those gray eyes. "I bear more than news," he said. "I bear a choice." He took a step closer, and the reek made Neb's eyes sting. "Remember what your father told you about choices?"

And he *did* remember. Neb's mouth fell open in disbelief. Hebda had told him on more than one occasion that a man's success or failure in life came down simply to making the right choices. He started to say something, but before he could, Renard slipped past him and bent close to Isaak's head. He whispered something Neb could not hear, and he wasn't certain even Isaak heard it until he saw the eyes flash suddenly open, as wide as the shutters would let them. When Renard smiled at Neb, his teeth were black with the chewing root. He cast something to the ground near Neb's foot, but everything happened too fast for him to look.

The Waster whistled Third Alarm and shouted, "Renard betrays us," in a voice that sounded much like Neb's own. Pandemonium erupted on the hillside as bright lights and loud booms filled the night air. In the shadows, a horde of figures swarmed. Neb heard scrambling in the barn but still had not drawn his blades. Renard set out south at a run that stretched and stretched until he was lost beyond the dim reach of Neb's vision.

Isaak looked to Neb. "I'm sorry," the mechoservitor said.

Then he, too, ran. His metal legs pumped into a run that lurched and wobbled from his limp, but he steadied as he built steam and loped off after Renard.

As Gypsy Scouts spilled from the barn, knives and pouches at hand, Neb looked down to the bit of black root between his feet and made his choice.

Chapter

12

Vlad Li Tam

The grating of wood against wood drew Vlad Li Tam to wakefulness and he stirred. In the days—or was it weeks?—he'd lain in tepid salt-water he'd finally retrained his instincts to accommodate captivity. He no longer opened his eyes expecting to see and no longer found himself gripped in panic when he could not. Instead, he came awake quickly and immediately set himself to the task of ciphering his present circumstances.

The girl brought him food with some regularity—usually a pungent gruel that tasted something like fish and corn—but he had no idea how often she came. And each time, she helped him sit up and fed him patiently as if he were a child. Sometimes, she left the bowl if he hadn't finished. But he had yet to eat from the bowl directly. It was bad enough he took his water that way those times that the rocking of the ship didn't spill it into the seawater that sloshed about the bottom of his cell.

Vlad Li Tam rolled to the interior of the hull and pressed his ear to it. He heard distant voices and felt the vibration through his skull as the wood scraped together again.

They'd stopped moving, he realized, and the dramatically lessened to-and-fro swaying of the ship told him they were either in unnaturally quiet seas or safely harbored. The latter seemed most likely.

He heard footsteps beyond his door and used the wall to sit up. His muscles protested—cramps and spasms took him, and when the door opened, he heard himself groan.

"Just a short walk," the girl told him. "We could have you carried, but I thought you might appreciate the restoration of some of your dignity." There was amusement in her voice.

"Where are we?" he asked.

She did not answer. Instead, with strong hands, she reached down to work at the ropes binding his ankles, and for the briefest moment he flexed his muscles to kick out at her but thought better of it. She chuckled. "You'd not get far, old man. It's good you didn't try."

"If you'd wanted to kill me," he said, "you already would have."

She laughed again. "Actually, that's not true, Vlad. There are other matters to attend to before that day arrives, but do not doubt for a moment that it's coming." She pulled at him, and her strength was surprising. "Stand up now."

He did, wobbling unsteadily before falling against the hull. She pulled him upright, her firm hand steadying him. Then, she guided him ahead of her, her hand on his shoulder. The stale air of the hold felt like cool autumn compared to the fetid room he left. He walked into the corridor.

"To the right now," she said. "Ten steps to the stairs."

His legs burned with the effort and he staggered.

She leaned in close behind him, and he felt her breath tickle the back of his ear. "I could have you carried. Would you prefer that? Is that how you want your children to see you?"

My children. He felt panic rise in him, flooding him with a fear and a rage that made his head ache. He clenched his fists and felt his jaw clench. "My children?"

She said nothing. Gently, the woman pushed him forward. "You can face this, Vlad," she told him. "Walk to it."

Vlad Li Tam forced himself forward, counted the paces and found the first step with a tentative foot. As he climbed up, light swam at the edges of his blindfold and he suddenly smelled mango trees and salt air and hot sand. He opened his mouth and drank it in. She turned him to the left, and firm hands lifted him onto the dock.

Once he stood on the dock, he felt hands at the back of his head, and he was suddenly blinded by an explosion of white. He closed his eyes against it, and even against his eyelids it penetrated him. He groaned.

When he opened his eyes, the first thing he saw was the girl. She was young—maybe twenty—and her face was painted in markings of gray and black and white, her green eyes stark against that backdrop. Bits of seashell and coral and wood were woven into her hair and she smiled at him.

She was beautiful and dangerous.

She wore the garb of a fishing girl, but he could tell it was not her custom. She was made for armor or possibly gowns but nothing in-between. Yet a man on the dock held up a dark robe to her, and she slipped her arms into it.

"Where am I?" he asked again.

Her smile widened. "Home, Vlad."

As his eyes adjusted, he took in the rest of his surroundings. The schooner at the dock was made of a dark, unfamiliar wood, and the lines of it were nothing he'd seen in the Named Lands. The shipbuilder in him measured it and recorded its displacement, factored its speed based on its mast and sails, and noted the mixed crew that moved over the deck.

The dock was a high structure overlooking water so green and clear that it stung his eyes, and as he looked inland, he saw jungle and sand. Within the jungle, birds sang and monkeys chattered, and above it, a large building of white stone rose up into a cloudless blue sky.

Vlad Li Tam blinked and staggered, but she did not steady him this time. He looked at her and finally made the connection, but it made no sense to him. The paint, drawn in careful symbols upon her skin, and her hair, decorated with pieces of the earth, gave her away though the style of it had more sophistication than he'd seen previously. "You are a Marsher," he said.

"No," she answered. "That is the bastard name from the time of our sorrow. But the tears of my people are passed now. I am Machtvolk."

Machtvolk. He dropped the word into his memory and found nothing to resonate with it.

"Ah," she said, looking up and away. "They're here now."

Vlad Li Tam heard the familiar sound. He followed her gaze and his breath caught. An iron vessel rounded the point at the harbor's mouth, steaming in slow.

My children.

Another followed close behind, and after that, another. The flags of House Li Tam were struck, and no flags flew in their place. His legs threatened collapse as the weight of it pressed him. Five of his ships approached, and on their decks he saw his family lined up—men, women and children—while dark-garbed soldiers moved among them and barked orders. He looked again and realized his flagship was missing from the small fleet.

Finally, his legs gave out and he sat down, heavy, upon the dock. When he found words, his voice was low and his mouth tasted like sand. "What is this about?"

When she looked down at him, he saw love in her eyes and it terrified him. "It is about redemption, Vlad."

He reached for another question from the thousands that swam behind his eyes. "Who are you?"

"I told you," she said. "I am your Bloodletter and your Kin-healer."

The ships slowed and he heard the whine of the engines as they wound down, heard the clanking of anchor chains. Two men pulled him to his feet, and he watched as the first of the longboats started ferrying his family ashore.

Her words echoed in his mind. *Bloodletter. Kin-healer.* As the first of the boats approached the lower docks below them, he saw fear on the faces of his grandchildren.

In that moment, for the first time in his life, Vlad Li Tam knew powerlessness and despair.

Jin Li Tam

Her dreams frightened Jin Li Tam awake, and the bone-strewn plains of Windwir fell away with the kin-raven's words still ringing in her ears. *Soon I shall dine upon your father's eyes.*

If the nightmares hadn't started before her labor, she would've thought them to be some strange side effect of the powders she drank. But she knew better.

She sat up, rubbing the tears and sleep from her face. Beside her, Jakob stirred and she looked to him. His tiny face was gray and soft in sleep as he breathed in shallow gasps. She pulled on a robe and padded first to the glass doors leading out to her snow-covered balcony. It was a clear night, and the stars beat down upon the sleeping forest city. A full moon cast its watery light over Library Hill, limning the massive cornerstones of its construction in a blue-green glow. It would be several hours before the sun rose and the Ninefold Forest stirred itself awake.

She went to the door and opened it, whistling low for a servant. A girl, her face freshly scrubbed and her hair still damp, awaited.

She still hated to leave his side but could not bring herself to risk waking the baby. His sleep was fitful enough. "Sit with Jakob," she told the girl, "and bring him to me when he wakes up. I'll be in the study."

The girl curtsied. "Yes, Lady Tam."

She waited until the servant came into the room to take her position in a rocking chair near the bed. Satisfied, Jin slipped into the hallway and padded quietly down thick-carpeted floors.

Rudolfo's study lay behind ornate double doors made from a dark, polished wood. She slipped an iron key into its lock and turned it easily, pushing the well-oiled door open just far enough to slip inside.

Locking the door behind her, Jin went to the desk and lit its single lamp. Already, new messages awaited her in the simple basket Rudolfo kept for incoming work, and she sighed. She didn't know exactly how he kept up with it all, though she knew he rose notoriously early most days. She'd been at the desk from before dawn until after dusk the day before, and she'd finally seen the bottom of the basket. Now, it was a third full and more would arrive with the dawn.

The life of a queen, she thought. She reached for the top message, then forced herself to leave it. Instead, she slid open the drawer on the desk and drew out the knife belt. Glancing to the door, she slipped out of her robe and let it drop to the floor. Then, she buckled the belt over her short cotton shift and moved to the center of the room. She dug her toes into the carpet and struck the pose, curling her fingers around the bone-handled blades at each hip. Drawing the knives, she launched into her morning's dance.

The time abed had softened what had once been firm muscle, and though she'd not gained significant weight with her pregnancy it was enough for Jin to feel uncomfortable. But between the knives and the afternoon runs she'd started three days past, she was slowly taking back her body from its long captivity.

Her feet moved to silent rhythm, and her hips joined them as she shifted, dodged and leapt. The knives flashed in the dim light as she swept them around her and over her, leaning into each thrust and twisting, turning with each upward or downward slash. As she danced, she found memory pulling her back to the last time she'd drawn blood. Had it been escaping Sethbert's camp with Neb? No, she remembered, it was the night she and the Gypsy Scouts magicked themselves and rescued Rudolfo from the so-called Pope Resolute in his Summer Papal Palace.

It seems so long ago now. And in many ways, she realized, it was. She and Rudolfo had consummated the strategic marriage her father had brokered, but she'd had no idea at that time how deeply she would come to love and respect the Gypsy King. Or comprehend how a tiny life could change someone so profoundly.

She danced with abandon, recalling the wrist-jarring catch of the blades in bone, the gentle resistance of cloth and skin and the warm slipperiness of blood wetting her fists. She moved across the floor, increasing in speed as sweat broke out on her forehead and over her lip. Her breath came more labored to her than she wanted, and soon, her shift was wet and sticking to her skin. Still, she danced on even as her arms and legs ached and felt heavy from the unaccustomed movement.

After an hour, she sheathed the knives and fell into an armchair, panting. There was the slightest of knocks at the door and she stood slowly, stretching and hearing the crack and pop of her joints. "A moment," she said.

She unbuckled the knives and draped them over the chair. Then, she pulled on her robe and went to the door. She unlocked it and opened it.

Lynnae waited, her face pale and her curly hair tangled from sleep. "Good morning, Lady Tam," she said. "Myra told me you were awake."

Jin Li Tam held the door open. "Come in." The girl did not look well, but she didn't imagine that she looked much better herself. "Not sleeping?"

Lynnae shook her head. "Some. Not enough."

She nodded. "Me, too. It's the powders."

"The panta root, particularly," the young woman said, and Jin Li Tam felt her eyebrows raise.

"You've studied alchemy?"

She shrugged. "Some. Delta Scouts chew bits of the panta to stay alert. There's also kalla and maybe a touch of vesperleaf."

She'd picked up a hint of the kalla herself, having stealthily sampled her father's pipe in years past. Jin Li Tam gestured to a chair and moved toward the furnace. A kettle of fresh water waited for boiling. "Would you like some tea?"

"I can make it, Lady Tam," Lynnae said, but Jin Li Tam waved a hand at her.

"Nonsense," she said. "I've not forgotten how to make tea." She drew two ceramic mugs from the service cupboard and found the tea canister, measuring three round scoops of fragrant black leaf into the steeping pot, then returned to the sitting area to wait for the water to boil.

"How is Jakob sleeping?" Lynnae asked.

Jin Li Tam sat across from her and studied the young woman. In the days since Rudolfo left she'd seen much of Lynnae, but there never seemed to be enough hours in the day for them to spend any real time together. They met in one another's rooms or in the hall or even here in the study; they exchanged minor pleasantries and mostly talked of Jakob. Even now, that held true. "He sleeps lightly," she said. "I imagine he'll be up soon."

"Shall I take him this morning?"

Jin offered a tired smile. "It's my turn. You need to rest."

Lynnae shrugged. "I feel fine."

But Jin Li Tam saw the truth in the dark circles beneath the girl's eyes and the tightness around her mouth. Even now, Lynnae flinched and sucked in her breath. "Headaches?" she asked.

"Out of nowhere," she admitted. "Like lightning. But again, it's no problem for me to take him."

Jin forced a smile and rubbed her own temples. "I appreciate your offer." She looked at the girl again. She couldn't be much past twenty years, if that, and despite her plain clothes she carried herself differently than most of the refugees Jin had observed over the last several months. She leaned forward. "This must be hard for you on the heels of such terrible loss."

For a moment, Lynnae's large brown eyes went wide with something like panic. She swallowed. "I would be lying if I said it wasn't. There are times when I'm nursing Lord Jakob or napping with him and forget it's not my Micah."

Jin Li Tam saw the tears forming in the girl's eyes and felt shame wash over her. "I should not have spoken of it," she said, looking away.

But out of the corner of Jin's eye, she saw the girl shaking her head. "No, it *should* be spoken of; that's what the Francines would say. That we move the Fivefold Path with words and memory."

Jin Li Tam looked back to her and saw that the tears had spilled out, running the length of her olive cheek. "I can't even imagine the price you've paid."

But she *could*. A husband killed by the sword; a child dead of fever.

In the deeper places she feared the same fate for herself. Her own child had been stillborn, brought back by the River Woman's careful ministrations, and even now only survived because of the powders she and Lynnae provided him. And her own husband—she could not count how many times he'd narrowly skirted a violent end during the war. And now, she imagined, he would sail soon for destinations unknown in search of her father, facing gods-knew-what along the way. The weight of it felt heavy on her heart and cold in her stomach.

She realized suddenly that they had fallen into a long and uncomfortable silence, but the boiling water interrupted it.

Lynnae stood up, wiping her eyes. "Let me, Lady Tam," she said.

Jin forced herself to remain seated and watched as the girl went to the furnace and poured the hot water into the steeping pot. She placed it onto a tray with the two cups and returned, setting it onto the small table between them. Once Lynnae was seated, she changed the subject. "Is there any news in the world?" she asked.

Jin Li Tam looked to the basket and sighed. Soon enough she would be back to it, coding messages, ordering birds and reading over the reports of two dozen operatives at work on Rudolfo's behalf. She forced her mind back to yesterday's messages, careful to hold back anything sensitive. "Winteria has declared herself," she said. "It was heard for five hundred leagues, I'm told. Pylos and Turam have stepped up their efforts to quell their internal strife while shoring up their armies. Ansylus was buried in state last week; the Ninefold Forest was not invited to attend but sent an ambassador anyway."

Lynnae's brow furrowed. "Any news of the Delta?"

Jin nodded. "Esarov and his democrats have taken another city. There are rumors that Erlund wasn't killed after all—that it was a double in his place."

She nodded. "I'm not surprised. He has dozens of them, and—" She cut off the words, and Jin Li Tam noted the blush that rose to her cheeks.

She's shared something with me that a refugee should not know. She opened her mouth to say something, but in that moment, someone knocked on the door. Studying the girl's face quickly, Jin stood and went to the door, opening it a crack. A scout stood waiting, a small and still bird cupped in his hands.

"This has just arrived for you," he said. "It's not one of ours; it's not one that we even recognize."

But she recognized it; the yellow markings upon its tiny head gave it away instantly, and her breath caught within her as hope built. "What message does it bear?"

"The bird is wounded," the scout said. "We saw your name upon the message and went no further."

He extended his hands and gentled the small, shivering creature into her own outstretched palms. It lay and twitched, even as she carefully picked at the white thread of kin-clave that held the torn note to its tiny leg. Holding the bird with one hand, she worked the scroll open and read it quickly.

It was triple-coded and in an unfamiliar hand and script, but she knew this bird well. Of all her father's birds, this was the one that could find her, wherever she might be, and he'd kept it near to him at all times. And it had found her, though it had spent itself on the winds and rains and snow to make its last, long journey.

Do not despair, Great Mother, the note read. *Your father's kinship will be restored by the Older Ways, and his blood will purchase our salvation.* She blinked at the words and felt something ominous settle over her. It shrouded her with fear and she imagined the croaking voice of the kin-raven from her nightmares, though its words had been different there on the bone-strewn plains of Windwir: *Thus shall the sins of P'Andro Whym be visited upon his children.*

She shuddered. Forgotten was the mysterious girl who sat behind her, waiting for tea that Jin Li Tam no longer had the stomach to drink. Forgotten even was her sickly baby, restlessly sleeping down the hall from her. And the political debacle of the Named Lands with its grief-stricken nations also fell away, still reeling from Sethbert's treachery when the blood scouts and their iron blades cut new heartache into the skin of their New World.

It all faded for the briefest of moments.

Instead, she was a little girl whose father was in grave danger, and she could not cast out the panic and fear that threatened to capsize her.

She looked back to the tiny bird—one of a long line her father had carefully magicked just so he could always find his forty-second daughter, no matter where she roamed. It lay still now, its tiny black eyes glassy in death.

You are a queen, some deep-buried voice asserted within her, *wife of Rudolfo, father of Jakob.* But more: *You are the forty-second daughter of Vlad Li Tam.*

Raising her eyes to the scout, she passed the dead bird back to him. "Send in the birder," she said.

Turning, careful that her face mask the intensity of her sudden, strong emotion, Jin Li Tam forced herself back to the table and to Lynnae, to take comfort in the scalding bitterness of a dark cup that waited for her there.

Petronus

Petronus spent the better part of a week ordering his notes, carefully scripting them in code at the desk in his plain quarters. He left his rooms to take his meals, and occasionally, when he was available, Esarov joined him. The revolutionary looked weary but pleased with developments overall, and just the day before he'd told Petronus that it was nearly time for his people to approach Lysias with the offer of a truce and an exchange.

"And you truly believe this will work?" Petronus had asked him, sipping a hot bitter drink laced with rum.

Esarov ran his hands through his long graying hair. "I do," he said. "But it will be challenging for you."

For us all, he thought now as he looked down to the words that seemed to blur into one singular smudge upon the parchment. Finally, he'd reached the last page and he could lay this work to rest for now in the hopes of coming back to it when this more present need for him had passed.

He heard Grymlis's firm knock at the door and looked up. "Come in," he said.

The Gray Guard looked troubled, but that did not surprise him. He'd not taken Petronus and Esarov's plan well when Petronus had shared it with him some days past, and Petronus did not expect him to warm to it. He came in and closed the door behind him. "I'm told that they'll be meeting in two days' time," he said.

Petronus nodded. "So I've heard."

"And you're certain you wish do this?" There was a firmness to the line of his jaw and a fierceness in his eye. "We can leave," he said, "right now."

Petronus shook his head. "I'm not sure we can, Grymlis." *And more importantly, I'm not sure we should.* Freeing Charles was paramount, but ending the civil war on the Delta took equal place. The lack of stability was opening a door, he suspected, to something potentially far worse, and they could not be ready for it if they were twisted and tangled into conflict among themselves. Already, he'd heard word that Meirov of Pylos was shoring up her borders and mobilizing a larger force with eyes turned north. More caravans had been sacked and burned in recent days; ragged groups from his former Order slaughtered as they pushed their way toward the relative safety of Rudolfo's Ninefold Forest. And in Turam, the old king had pushed himself up out of his lethargic illness long enough to appoint one of his former generals to be a strong steward of that throne. They had shored up the bond of kinclave with Pylos, its neighbor to the east, and with the independent city-states along the northern beaches of the Emerald Coasts. He pointed to the only other chair in the room. "Sit with me, Grymlis."

Grymlis sat, his discomfort obvious. When his eyes met Petronus's they were the color of stormy skies. "I'll speak plainly, Father," he said. "This is foolhardy, Charles or no Charles."

Petronus sighed and leaned back into the chair, putting down his pen. "It may be. But I don't see another way through this Whymer Maze."

The captain's eyes narrowed. "You believe this strongly enough to die for it?"

Petronus chuckled but didn't know why he saw humor in it. "I'm not sure what I believe enters into this gamble of mine. If Charles is alive and if he knows something of this so-called Sanctuary of Light, it may save the Named Lands from something terrible at the very worst. And at the very best, it may bring back something that was lost to us." He looked back to the stack of papers, picked them up and used the flat surface of the table to line up all of the edges. He paused and looked for the bit of twine he'd been using. "But you're not here for that, I'm certain. You already know that my stubbornness frequently outpaces my common sense." He found the twine and laid it out on the table, placing the now-squared papers upon it and starting the knots that would hold the sizeable bundle in place.

Grymlis shook his head. "I've gotten word from Esarov's birder. Days late, but still better than not knowing at all."

Petronus looked up, his finger marking his place on the knot. "From the line?"

He nodded. "Yes." He dug into his pocket and withdrew a crumpled note. Grymlis passed it over.

Petronus took it and read it quickly. "So now Gypsy Scouts man the post in Caldus Bay and Rudolfo has found us out."

He'd been skeptical of Grymlis's plan to maintain that post, but he'd not imagined that it would be Rudolfo himself who would stumble upon it. He'd been more fearful that whoever had wanted him dead would send more blood-magicked emissaries to finish that first would-be assassin's work. Instead, the Gypsy King himself had intercepted one of his birds and written his own message into it.

He looked at the note again. "What do you imagine he wants?"

Grymlis looked angry. "I don't know what he wants, but my men are not his for the ordering. I'll have strong words with him for that when he arrives."

When he arrives? Petronus felt his breath catch. "Rudolfo? He's coming here?"

Grymlis nodded slowly. "Aye. Esarov sent the pirate to fetch him."

What game of Queen's War did that Democrat play? And what madness had Rudolfo, with a new wife and child at home, traipsing about the countryside seeking his audience? Why hadn't he simply sent a bird?

Esarov had to know that bringing the Named Lands most powerful man into the heart of a civil war deeply compromised an already tenuous kin-clave between the Entrolusians and the Gypsies. His mind turned to the coming trial, and he spun the cipher of this new lockbox. Could Rudolfo bring something to bear on this that he'd not thought about?

When the cipher caught, he felt the clicking in his brain and slapped his leg. "He intends to send Charles with the Gypsy King."

Grymlis's eyes narrowed. "We're not certain that Charles is even alive."

But buried beneath his common sense, Petronus suspected that indeed he was alive and that Esarov knew that the old Arch-Engineer was perhaps the greatest living treasure left to the Named Lands, both for what he could do and for what he guarded—some corner of the light that they had all feared lost.

At least, he thought, that mad Democrat realized that Charles was safer under Rudolfo's care.

Grymlis stood. "He'll be here inside of a week, but I'm not sure you will be."

Petronus nodded. "I'm not sure I will, either." He took the stack of papers and opened the satchel as wide as it would go. Even that wasn't enough, and the papers bent as he shoved them inside. "Regardless," he said, "I would have you pass this to Rudolfo. But discreetly; keep it away from Esarov's men." He thought for a moment. "My notes are coded; Isaak or one of the others should be able to cipher them out."

He handed the satchel to Grymlis, who stood. When he spoke, his voice was a growl. "You marching off to trial. Rudolfo on the ride with barely a squad. I hope it isn't catching."

Petronus pondered this. "You hope *what* isn't catching?"

"Foolishness," he said. Then Grymlis opened the door and left, the satchel tucked beneath his cloak.

Petronus watched the door for a long time before looking back to his empty desk. He wondered what he would do now while he waited, how he would bide his time until Esarov told him whether or not Erlund was going to play at this new game. Esarov swore with complete confidence that the betrayal of Windwir was within, that they had been duped into believing in an outside threat by complex and terrible conspiracy. Vlad Li Tam had asserted without doubt that their enemy lay beyond, and that crafty old spymaster had left, Petronus believed, to find it and give name to it.

He looked to the map of the Named Lands that decorated the wall of his simple room. He saw Windwir at its center, as it should be, and traced the First River, the one the Gypsies called Rajblood, up through the circling hills, across the Prairie Seas and into the Ninefold Forest.

"And what are you seeking, Rudolfo, so far from home in these perilous times?" he asked.

Standing slowly, he walked to the map and placed a finger at its center.

The purported note from Charles came back into his mind.

The library has fallen by treachery, it had said.

That night, Petronus slept and dreamed of bone fields and blood and dark-winged birds.

When he awakened in the morning it was as if he hadn't slept at all.

Chapter

13

Winters

Winters winced as she lowered herself into the steaming water, feeling the bite of it in the deep cuts that lacerated her shoulders, sides and back. She'd been home now for four days, and though she'd healed considerably, the minerals in the water still stung. Clutching the cake of soap, she swam out farther into the pool and dove down, letting the heat of it soak into her. When she broke the surface, she shook the water from her hair and floated on her back. The lamplight danced over the cave's high ceiling, and the bits of quartz and iron pyrite gave the illusion of domed starshine above her. She sighed and kicked her feet slightly, stretching her arms out cruciform and feeling the water lick the sides of her breasts and neck.

She'd awakened earlier than usual, disturbed by her dreams. The violent images, set to the music of Tertius's mad harping, had become commonplace, and she could set aside *that* discomfort—but Neb's absence was a different matter. She saw armies on the march beneath a moon the color of dirty ice. She saw a sky absent of birds, slate gray and ominous before a coming storm. These she could take into herself, working through the mystery of heaven's message to her. But nowhere had she seen the snow-haired boy who kept her heart. It was as if he'd been swallowed by the Wastes, and she remembered the warnings about Renard with a shudder.

She rolled to her side and struck out for shallower waters on the far side of the cavern, finding a purchase for her feet on the slick rock floor. Standing in water now waist-deep, she took the soap to herself and continued to think about the boy as she moved her hand over her body, gently washing away yesterday's mud and ash.

She wished it was Neb's hand that touched here and then there, soft and warm and slippery with the soap. But these thoughts were foolishness, and in these dark times, so was love or anything like it. Sighing, she immersed herself fully again, and when she came up, she took the soap to her tangled hair, picking the bits of wood and bone from the long, wet strands.

She heard the clearing of a voice in the shadows and she spun, dropping the soap as her hands went reflexively to cover her breasts. "Who is there?"

"Forgive my intrusion, Winteria the Younger, daughter of Mardic," a gravelly voice said. A figure moved—shambled, even—in the darkness at the farthest point of the cavern, beyond the lamp's dim light.

Winteria the Younger? She'd not heard that before. "These are my private bathing waters," Winters said, forcing some kind of authority into her voice. "Surely my guards did not allow you passage?"

The voice chuckled. "There are more passages than even you know in these mountain deeps."

She felt fear in her stomach, and she lowered herself farther into the water, backing away with her eyes fixed in the direction of the unexpected voice. "Whoever you are, surely you see the inappropriateness of this interruption?"

Though the outside world believed the Marshers' dirt and ash to be indicative of an insanity bred into them, the truth was far from that. At least weekly, they bathed away the layer of grime and reapplied fresh mud and ash, carefully weaving the bones and wood back into their hair, each slathered handful and twisted braid a prayer toward home. Apart from the sleep of death, when family and friends scrubbed clean the fallen before clothing the body in earth and ash one last time, it was unheard-of to see or be seen with the skin bare and unsheltered by the symbol of their sad sojourn.

"I cannot see you. I assure you of this. I cannot break form." The figure drew closer and she backed up farther, crouching in the shallower water as her hands scrambled for a rock.

There were none to be found.

I could raise the guards, she thought. But she had not told them she would be bathing. They were posted at the entrance to her cave, and that was well over a league above and away, through winding corridors of stone. They would not hear her.

"Stop," she said.

But the figure shambled closer until it revealed an old man with a wild beard and long hair. At first, the grime on him marked him as one of her own, but quickly, she saw that it was similar but different. The beard, once white, was streaked in alternating earth tones, braided in a fashion she had not seen before. And the markings on his face were more intentional, forming symbols of deep brown, charcoal and black that interlocked like a puzzle. His eyes were the color of milk, and when his sandaled feet reached the edge of the spring, he stopped. He looked toward her but not directly at her.

"A new age is in the birthing," he told her, "and it is time for our people to reclaim their heritage."

He's blind, she realized. *And yet he knows my home better than I do.* "Who are you?" she asked again.

"I am called Ezra," he said. "I was the Keeper of the Book in your father's time, and in his father's time before him. Before my eyes failed and my new sight found me."

Winters squinted at him but knew she couldn't possibly recognize him. In her lifetime, Tertius had played that role, and when he'd died, she'd chosen not to select a new Keeper. The Home dreams had started up with a new intensity, and the imminence of it had convinced her that there would be no need. The council of elders had agreed. She felt the firmness setting in her jaw. She swallowed against it. "Why are you here?"

The old man smiled. "I've come bearing a message of comfort and assurance. These seemingly dark times that wound you now are but the pains of labor. When it has passed, you will find your proper place. A New Age is upon us."

Winters felt a sudden wave of anger. "I don't need your comfort and assurance. I need you to stop talking in Whymer circles and be plain."

The old man smiled. "You have your father in you," he said. He chuckled. "Very well. I'll be plain. P'Andro Whym's children now pay for their father's sins. Their city is no more, and the Desolation of Windwir changes everything."

She felt her eyes narrowing. "Explain." She felt a sudden chill and squatted farther into the water, glancing toward the tunnel that led to her sleeping quarters and the throne room above them.

"You have read—and even dreamed—of the Homefinding," he said, his voice lowering. "But the Book was born in a time of sojourn. Before that, we were gifted these lands—all of them—to share with the Gypsies. You know this is true. They were taken from us. And ever since, the gray robes and their watch-wolves have kept us tamed and toothless while carrying out their so-called Gospels of Whym, that Great Deicide." She heard the bitterness in his voice when he spat the word "deicide" and it made her cold again, despite the hot water that held her. "Now is the time for a new gospel to emerge. Now is time for the truth: There is no Home to find, but there is one here for the taking."

No Home to find? The wrongness of those words flooded her. "You speak falsehood," she said. "I've seen our Home. And the advent of the Homeseeker is already upon us. I've met him." *I've tasted his mouth,* she thought. *I've seen the wounds behind his eyes and felt his heartbeat against my skin.*

Ezra shook his head. "No. Perhaps that was our hope once, but another has risen. I speak the truth. You know it yourself. The dreams have changed, and these dreams change the course of the Book of Dreaming Kings. Did you not see the light—feel its heat—as it was consumed?"

She had, and the memory of it still haunted her. But she said nothing.

Ezra continued. "There is no Home to find," he said again, "but there is one that we may *take*."

Take? Winters felt her stomach lurch. He'd said it before, but it hadn't registered. She suddenly saw Hanric's cold, dead body naked and scrubbed clean, stretched out upon the snowy ground of the Gypsy King's Maze. She saw the Marsh Scouts frozen in death, slain by their blood magicks, the mark of House Y'Zir pink upon their skin. She felt truth dawning, and it tasted like cold iron in her mouth. When she spoke, her voice sounded more frightened, more timid, than she wished it. "What do you speak of, old man? If ever you loved my father, tell me plainly."

When Ezra smiled it was filled with hope. "The Age of the Crimson Empress is at hand," he said. "It is time for us to receive the mantle of our great heritage and prepare for her coming. You believe that we are called the Marshfolk because we live in these northern, barren wetlands. But I say to you now that it is not so. Once, long ago, before we touched this land in the Firstfall, we were the Machtvolk. The Making People, in service to the Moon Wizard Who Fell."

"We were slaves," she said, "to men who shattered the world beneath their boots and spells and blades."

"No," he said. "We were the joyful servants not to men but to gods." He took a step forward. "And we shall be again."

When he opened the upper portion of his robe, dim light played over the white scars upon his heart, and Winters trembled at the ecstasy upon his face. She dug for words, and the ones she found were familiar but she did not know why. She thought perhaps she'd dreamed them. "Begone, kin-raven," she said in a voice that rang out strong and clear. "Your message is unwelcome in this House."

The old man chuckled. "My message is more welcome than you know."

But Winters persisted, her voice rising in volume until it filled the cavern and echoed over stone and water. "Begone, kin-raven," she commanded, pulling herself up from the water and facing the old man squarely. "Your message is unwelcome in this House."

The chuckle became a laugh even as the old man stepped back and back again until shadow took him. The laughter faded, and when it had all vanished, she felt the rage and terror drain out of her as her shoulders slumped.

His words stayed with her as she returned to her pile of clothing and took up the rough cotton towel to dry herself. *We were the joyful servants not to men but to gods.*

By habit, she slathered on the mud and ash, rubbing it into her skin and hair. When her hands reached her breastbone, she stopped, remembering the old man's scrawny chest and the bare patch of skin over his heart. The stark white of that scar shone bright as snow in her memory. Not the pink of a fresh cutting but something old and deeply cut.

And shall be again.

She shuddered despite the warmth of the cavern and wished suddenly that she had not teased Neb when he'd asked her to come with him to the Ninefold Forest. *Would you take me as your bride, Nebios ben Hebda,* she'd asked him, *and grant me a Gypsy wedding filled with dancing and music?*

I should have said yes, she realized. But even as she thought it, she knew it was not her path to follow.

"We dance to the music that is played us," Hanric had once told her not so long after her father had died. "And regardless the step or the tune, if we are true we will find joy at the end of it."

Now the only music she heard was the harp that haunted her dreams, mad Tertius with his fingers flying over the strings as the light consumed two thousand years of dreaming. And the only dance she saw ahead was cold, spinning iron in a hurricane of blood.

Winters did not believe in gods. Tertius had taught her better than that. But in this moment, she wished she did.

She reached for something higher than herself to invoke and found only a campsite beneath the moon and the warm, strong arms of a boy in her dreams.

"Help me be true," she whispered to that dream.

And still the canticle played on.

Rudolfo

It had been a long while, Rudolfo realized, since he'd mucked a bird coop. Despite the stench, he felt a smile pulling at his face as he imagined what he must look like now, his hands and arms gray with bird droppings.

He'd removed his turban and rolled up his sleeves for the work just an hour earlier, and now he stepped back from it, clucking at the birds in their freshly cleaned cages. Behind him, one of his Gypsy Scouts snored in a makeshift bed while the other kept watch outside.

The others had ridden out for Kendrick Town nearly a week earlier, leaving Rudolfo and two scouts to man the bird station and await word from Petronus—or whoever sat at the end of the line.

A reply had come, certainly, but Rudolfo had not been pleased by it.

I will send for you, the brief note said, but the handwriting was unfamiliar and there were no codes ciphered into it that Rudolfo could read. For all he knew, anyone could've sent it, and at this moment, the same *anyone* could be en route to intercept them.

Had Gregoric been alive, Rudolfo knew what that First Captain would think of this development. Still, he'd followed his instincts and forced himself to patiently wait. Forced himself to trust that whatever Petronus had built here could be trusted with his own life and ultimately, the life of his son.

For the first few days, he'd paced and plotted strategies when he wasn't tending to the birds that came and went. But after that, he'd grown restless and set himself to whatever work he could find in Petronus's boathouse.

Now, he grinned at the clean cages and the filth that covered him and wondered at how something so foul could bring such delight.

Perhaps, he thought as he scrubbed his hands and forearms in a waiting bucket, it delighted him because the clean cages were a bit of chaos made right.

A low, short whistle reached his ears from outside, and everything fell away with that sound. Rudolfo's right hand went instinctively to the satchel of powders around his neck as his left hand reached for his scout knife.

The other Gypsy Scout was already on his feet, slapping fistfuls of the white powder at his shoulders and his feet, then raising the palm of his hand to his mouth. As the magicks worked their way into his skin, he faded to shadow and eased open the door.

Rudolfo crouched and waited. His men knew their work better than any, and he knew that letting them do that work was the highest honor he could pay them. Still, he inched the knife out into his hand.

A minute passed.

Wind moved into the room.

Rudolfo felt the lightest of taps upon his arm. *Something approaches on the water.*

Rudolfo furrowed his brow, found the man's shoulder and pressed his fingers into it. *Something?*

There was hesitation in the scout's fingers. *Moves like a boat. But magicked.*

Magicked? Rudolfo imagined it might be possible to magick a ship—they rubbed oils into their knives to keep them sharp and hidden, so why couldn't it be done for a ship? He pushed the speculation aside and forced his attention back to the Gypsy Scout. *Take up positions outside,* he tapped.

Then, he magicked himself, drew his knives and followed.

In the morning drizzle, Rudolfo picked his way across muddy snow, careful to step into the prints already there. He moved to the shelter of a pine tree and squinted out at the bay.

He could see it there—the shape of something on the water that wasn't there. A shadow smudged into the rain, tall as a ship and moving along the choppy water. Rudolfo could hear the water rushing against it.

Rudolfo waited, listening, as a longboat—also magicked—was lowered. He heard its oars sliding across the water and slipped away from the tree to pick his way onto the dock.

There was no way to know how many men might be in the long-boat, nor any way to know what their intent was. Though it seemed to Rudolfo that no friend would arrive magicked.

He tensed his muscles as he heard the sound of wood on wood.

When the first magicked sailor stepped onto the dock, Rudolfo kicked him into the bay and then danced back. "Stay put," he said, "unless you'd like to swim in the winter bay with your friend."

He heard movement in the boat.

The water thrashed and sputtered. The sputtering became a voice. "Wait," it said. "Damn you, wait."

Rudolfo knew that voice but couldn't place it immediately.

Meanwhile, the thrashing became a more practiced swim. "I'm going to climb out," the voice said. "Don't kick me again, you ridiculous fop."

Ridiculous fop. Rudolfo smiled and remembered those words. How many years had it been since he'd heard them? At least twenty, he thought. "Rafe Merrique," he said. "I thought you'd drowned by now."

"No thanks to you," Rafe said, grunting with effort. "Gods, it's cold." Rudolfo watched as wet handprints appeared on the dock and a dripping, man-shaped shadow pulled itself up out of the water. "And what in all hells is that terrible smell?"

"Me," Rudolfo said. "I've been at the cages." He sheathed his knives and whistled for his scouts to do the same. He whistled again, and moments later, a thick woolen blanket drifted out of the boathouse and into his waiting hands. He extended it to the magicked pirate. "Petronus has sent you for me?"

He'd known that the Order had used Merrique's services over the years, but he also knew that those services could not come cheap. When he and Gregoric had sailed with him in his youth, even then it had cost a goodly sum.

Rafe took it and wrapped himself in it. "Not quite Petronus," he said. "But his host has arranged this . . . quietly, of course."

His host. Quietly. Rudolfo frowned. It explained the magicked ship, though the last time he'd seen Rafe Merrique, when he and Gregoric had been young men bound for the Wastes, the pirate had nothing so elaborate under his command. "And where is Petronus, exactly?"

"It would be better," Rafe said, "to talk aboard the *Kinshark*. Suffice it to say that he is safe . . . for the moment."

"I need to speak with him." But already, Rudolfo wondered if that were true. It was possible that all he needed stood, magicked and dripping, before him on the narrow dock.

Rafe's voice lowered. "Then time is of the essence, Gypsy King. I've been instructed to free the birds, close this station and invite you to accompany me."

Rudolfo looked from the sopping blanket to the shimmering ship half a league out. The drizzle moved gradually toward downfall, and he felt the temperature dropping. He whistled his men in and pressed his fingers into their shoulders, passing instructions to them silently. They retreated and ten minutes later, the birds lifted out of the boathouse and scattered. Rudolfo used that time to scrawl a hasty note homeward and sent it with his own bird as the scouts handed their packs down into waiting hands.

Then, he and his men climbed into the longboat and took their place in the bow.

"You're surely a long way from home during interesting times," Rafe said as they pulled away from the dock.

I am indeed, Rudolfo thought. "Our world is changing."

He could hear Rafe's smile around his reply. "It is," he said. "But as our gray-robed friends used to say, 'Change is the path life takes.'"

Rudolfo grinned. "You've not changed so very much, it appears."

Rafe chuckled. "Ten years ago and I'd have dropped you into the bay with me. I'm getting older. Slower."

Rudolfo nodded. Rafe Merrique had been middle-aged the last time he'd seen him, just coming into the pinnacle of his success at sea.

They were quiet now as the oars whispered into the water, moving the boat forward. The rainfall increased and Rudolfo watched the drops splash into the whitecapped bay, watched the splashes leap half-heartedly back toward the sky before surrendering to gravity. When they came alongside, he felt the hull with his hands and let Rafe guide them toward the waiting rope ladder.

Rudolfo scrambled up and let the hands there at the rail steer him toward the hatch.

Belowdecks, he sat with his men near a small furnace in a long, paneled galley while dusky women served them steaming hot firespice and fresh black bread with sweet butter. The same women had shown them their cabins and offered them baths. Rudolfo declined, choosing instead to wait for Merrique.

When the door opened and a shadow slipped through, he put down his mug. "So exactly where are we going, Merrique?"

Rafe chuckled. "Still impatient, aren't you? So impatient that you still reek of those damnable birds." A chair moved across the floor and creaked as Rafe sat. "We sail for the Delta. Esarov himself has sent for you. He has something he'd like you to keep an eye on." The pirate paused. "I'm not privy to more detail than that, but I do think your friend Petronus is climbing onto a narrow limb in a very high tree. And a storm brews for him there."

Esarov. That name had come up more and more since the end of the war. His little revolution had sprung to life in the chaos around Windwir's fall and had gained momentum once Sethbert was removed from the equation. Erlund hadn't the stomach or resolve to treat ruthlessly with the root of that insurrection when it had first taken hold, and now open warfare was his only option. Esarov, a master statesman and strategist among other things, had bent his pen and his words in the direction of change, and slowly, the Delta followed.

And now, somehow, that Democrat was in league with Petronus. "What does Esarov play at with our former Pope?" Rudolfo finally asked.

"Something with high stakes," Rafe answered. "I know that much. And I know Esarov was pleased to no end that you were already nearby. He offered me twice my normal fee to fetch you."

"I wanted to speak with you about that," Rudolfo said, resisting the urge to stroke his beard. "I will soon have need of a fast ship and a fierce crew, and I'm prepared to sign letters of credit for whatever price you require."

Rafe Merrique chuckled. "Whatever price I require? What will my ship and crew be doing for you, exactly?"

Rudolfo thought for a moment that he saw the briefest glimmer of the pirate leaning forward intently. "I need to find Vlad Li Tam and his iron armada. Petronus may know where he's sailed. Once I know, I will need someone to take me to him."

The pirate snorted. "He could be anywhere by now, regardless of where he sailed for." He waited, and when Rudolfo said nothing, he continued. "Still," he said, "I'm certain we can come to some kind of arrangement."

Rudolfo nodded, though he knew Rafe Merrique couldn't see. "It will be good to sail with you again, Captain."

The chair grated back. Already, parts of Rafe flickered back into focus as the magicks burned themselves out. Rudolfo thought he saw him incline his head, and he returned the gesture.

"I'm at your service, Lord Rudolfo," the pirate said.

Rudolfo remembered the first time he'd heard those words. It was in a Delta tavern over two decades behind him. It was one of his first assignments for the Order; he'd been sent to meet his transport with Gregoric and a half-squad of scouts.

Rafe Merrique paused at the door. "By the way," he said, "congratulations are in order. I'm sure he will grow into a fine, strong boy."

In that moment, Rudolfo was glad for the magicks. They masked the shadow that crossed his face as fear and sadness washed him. He wasn't sure how to answer.

"That is my hope," he finally said.

After Rafe Merrique had gone, Rudolfo excused himself and returned to his cabin. He removed his boots and clothing and did the best he could with the waiting basin of warm water.

After toweling himself off, he crawled into the narrow bed and pulled the covers over himself. After a week on the ground, the bed was softer than a woman's breast and smelled nearly as sweet. It gentled him into thoughts of Jin Li Tam. *My wife now,* he realized as he drifted into sleep.

But in Rudolfo's dreams, his wife wept alone in a field of bones and he was powerless to help her.

Neb

Neb slowed his run as he crested the rise and sucked in his breath at the view ahead. Renard waited there, bent slightly with his hands on his knees, drinking air as he surveyed the landscape that stretched out beyond them.

Overhead, the sky washed itself in a blush of dusky rose as it emptied itself of birds.

Neb joined Renard, shielding his eyes from the reflection of the fading sun upon the jagged forest of rainbow-colored glass that stretched as far as he could see in all directions but the one they'd come from. Distant and moving across that treacherous ground, he could just make out Isaak's metal form.

Renard followed his gaze, drawing his waterskin and passing it to Neb. "We don't need to catch him," Renard reminded him. "We only need to follow him, and he's leaving us a good trail. He's far better equipped to handle his so-called cousin than we are."

For four days now, he'd wondered exactly what Renard had whispered to Isaak that sent him sprinting into the night. And he'd also wondered just how this Waster knew his father. Last, he'd wondered what had possessed him to abandon his squad and take off after their strange guide—and why it had seemed so easy, so natural to do so, despite the fact that his own men were in the midst of ambush. He'd chewed the root himself and followed after, the shouts of surprise fading behind him as he fled the battle.

As the bitter juice took hold, he'd felt a surge of strength and speed, easily catching up to Renard.

He told himself that his service to the light required it—that he had to stay near Isaak and that fleeing with Renard was the only way to do so. He told himself that Rudolfo and Petronus would both concur, even if Aedric did not. Still, it gnawed him. He'd thought all this as he stretched his legs into a full sprint and felt the breath of betrayal and desertion on the back of his neck like a wolf on his heels.

Of course, the ambush had been faked by Renard and his drunken friends, but he'd not learned that until yesterday, when Renard had told him with a casual chuckle in the face of Neb's consternation.

They'd run that first night all the way through in silence, and then another day before they stopped to rest and to nurse water from the hidden places Renard showed him. But Isaak hadn't stopped, and when Neb moved to go after him, Renard had stopped him.

"You'll kill yourself in the dark or lose his trail," Renard said. They were his first words since leaving Fargoer's Town. "We sleep now until light. Then we track your metal friend easily. Eventually, he'll lead us to the other."

Two more days of racing full-sprint across the jagged, uneven ground, and each day they came within view of him just as the sun sank.

Neb took a pull from the tepid water and swished it around the inside of his mouth before handing the waterskin back to Renard. The water bore the burnt dust and salt flavor of the Wastes, but he swallowed it down anyway, grateful for it. "What was this place?" he asked.

Renard lifted the skin to his mouth, swallowed, and replaced the cap. "These are the outskirts of Ahm," he said. "It was the capital of Aelys."

Neb's brow furrowed. He remembered this place from years before, when his father had brought him a square coin bearing the image of Vas Y'Zir, the Wizard King who oversaw Aelys for his father, Xhum Y'Zir, in the days of old, before P'Andro Whym and his scientists brought him and his six brothers down in a month of bloodshed.

Brother Hebda had come by the coin during a dig and kept it back as a gift for the son he could not raise because of his Order's vows. "My father came here," he said.

Renard laughed. "Your father saw most of the Wastes, young Nebios. But aye, he was here." He set out at an easy walk down toward the jagged jungle of glass. "And who do you think brought him?"

Of course. If Renard held the guide contracts with the Order it made sense that he would've escorted the very expeditions his father had worked on. He followed Renard, catching up easily. "Did you know him well?"

Renard found a clear patch of ground at the edge of the glass field and put down his pack. "Well enough," he said. "He was a good man."

Neb found a boulder and sat, watching Renard. The Waste guide drew a vial from one of his many pockets and shook out droplets at the four corners of the camp as he'd done each preceding night. In nights past, he'd not spoken about it, but now, his tongue loosening with each league they put between them and the Gypsy Scouts, he talked. "It's kin-wolf urine," he said.

Neb looked up. "Aren't they extinct? Didn't they die out with the Old World?"

Renard stopped the vial and tucked it away. "Nearly," he said. "But there are a handful left, including an old white one that the Waste Witch keeps handy for those of us who run the Wastes."

Neb had seen sketches in the Great Library, but until now, he'd assumed they were renderings based on skeletal evidence and whatever knowledge the Androfrancines had dug up. Kin-wolves were easily twice the size of a timber wolf—a fierce predator with an uncanny intelligence and predisposition for violence bred into them by the blood magicks of the wizards who made them long ago.

Renard continued. "They are few in number but still the second most dangerous predator here in the Deeper Wastes. They won't encroach one another's territory out of respect, and their prey know better." Opening his pack, he tugged out a thin mat and stretched it over the flat ground, then pulled out two tightly rolled blankets, tossing one to Neb.

Something the man said suddenly registered with him. "If they're the second most dangerous predator here, what's the first?"

Renard looked up, his eyes hard as stone. "We are." He spread his blanket out over his half of the mat and then straightened, spreading out his hands toward the fading landscape. "Certainly there are other

threats—the ghosts and monsters from the basement of the world—
and the land itself is hostile enough. But as predators go, man—or
what he's become here—still reigns." He unslung the thorn rifle and
squeezed the bulb at its base gently. Neb heard the slightest whisper
and snap of a thorn snapping home. He'd not had a close look at this
particular wonder of Renard's but he hoped to, now that the man became more free with his tongue. "Meat for dinner tonight," Renard
said. "You gather wood; I'll be back shortly with our supper."

Neb watched as Renard slipped away, moving at a leisurely pace
into the jagged line of glass not far from their camp. When he disap-
peared into it, Neb spread out his own blanket and then cast about to
gather the bits of gray scrub he could find. Thirty minutes later, he
had a decent pile.

When Renard returned, he carried a bloody carcass by its long,
slender tail. The Waste rat—nearly the size of a dog—had been skinned
and gutted away from camp. "There's fresh water a league or so west,"
he said as he laid the meat onto a flat stone and drew out his tinder-
box. "You may want to bathe and scrub out your clothes in the morning." Renard took in Neb's torn and stained uniform and wrinkled his
nose. "Or maybe you should bury that. I've got spare trousers and a
shirt for you that should keep you for a few days."

Overhead, the stars pulsed to life in a deep purple sky. A blue-green
sliver on the horizon promised moonrise, and as Renard set the rat to
cooking in the crackling fire, Neb pulled off his boots and stretched
out on the hard ground. Propping himself up on his elbow, he watched
Renard as he took careful inventory of their shared pack. The man
noticed and grinned. "We'll outfit you at Rufello's Cave," he said. "Maybe
tomorrow—more likely, the morning after. The glass will slow us
down a bit."

Neb had certainly heard of Rufello, that ancient scientist who'd
captured so many of the secrets of the Younger Gods in his *Book of
Specifications*. It was Rufello's schematics, pieced together from a thousand parchments, that had brought back the mechoservitors. "Rufello's Cave?"

Renard looked up. "There's an Androfrancine supply cache there.
They were careful that way."

That made sense to Neb. The Churning Wastes were brutal, and
the vast distances that the Order's expeditions covered, along with the
amount of time it took for most digs, made supply chain a challenge.

He imagined a network of hidden supplies, tucked away and sealed against the elements and inhabitants of this harsh land.

Now, Renard drew a patch of cotton from his pocket and soaked it in water from the waterskin. He wadded it up and shoved it into a small hole at the base of the bulb on his rifle. "I'll need to lacquer it tomorrow," he said.

The smell of cooking meat made Neb's stomach growl. He'd had nothing but jerky, nuts, and sour dried apple slices over the last four days, and even that had been sparing. And until Renard's tongue had finally loosened, Neb's initial protests—and the questions that accompanied them—had fallen on seemingly deaf ears. Now, just as he'd settled into the taciturn silence, his companion had started offering up information quite freely.

Why? He looked to the man and his eyes narrowed. "You're much more talkative now."

Renard chuckled. "You're right. I am."

Neb rolled onto his side, propping his head up on his hand. "Why now?"

Renard considered him, and for a moment, Neb saw something in his eyes that chewed at him. "Because now," he said slowly, "we're too far out for your friends to find you . . . or for you to find them." He paused, poking at the rat with his knife. "Now," he said, "I'm the only reasonable path left to you, and our work can truly begin."

The words fell into Neb like a stone in a pond, their meaning rippling out into the corners of his heart. His mouth went suddenly dry. "Our work?"

"Aye," Renard said. "Work your father pressed upon me when you were born." He looked up at Neb, and his blue eyes were piercing. "Work he and your mother knew you were set aside for years before you were even conceived."

He and your mother. Brother Hebda had never mentioned Neb's mother, and Neb had been too polite to ask. No, he realized, not polite but careful. He'd simply been too afraid that if he asked about her, his father would stop visiting him. It was a rare thing for one of the Order to acknowledge the children born outside their so-called vow of chastity. Rarer still that one of those men would take the time to visit his son in the Franci Orphanage. Neb swallowed at the dryness and cleared his voice. Two questions tugged at him for attention, and he gave way to the one that terrified him the least. "What work is that?" he asked.

"The work of Homeseeking," he said.

How does he know this? Neb blinked. *And how could my parents have known?* His head suddenly swum, and the other question found its way to his tongue, though when it fell out his mouth it sounded more like a statement. "You know my mother."

A cloud washed Renard's face, and he closed his eyes a bit longer than he should have. When he opened them, his face was clear again. "Yes, lad. I knew her."

More questions flooded Neb, but there were too many to ask and it left him in silence, overwhelmed by the magnitude of it all. Certainly, sharing dreams with Winters gave him a seat at the front of Marsher mysticism and prophecy. He knew she believed him to be the Home-seeker. But beyond his own dreams and the belief of the girl he loved, he'd not had any other evidence. Now, a man he barely knew and did not necessarily trust told him that this was a work both his father and his mother had known about before Neb was even born.

It staggered him.

After a while, Renard used his knife to move their dinner away from the fire so it could cool. He looked over at Neb. "She was beauti-ful and smart," he finally said. His voice was heavy with memory.

"What happened to her?" Neb asked, though he wasn't sure he wanted to know.

But then Renard fell silent. After the meat had cooled, he tore the Waste rat in half and they ate quickly and quietly.

The meat was greasy and carried a strong, sour flavor, but Neb tore into it as if it were a roasted Ninefold Forest hare. He couldn't remem-ber a better feast despite the silence.

When he finished, Neb crawled into his blanket and counted stars until thoughts of Winters kept stealing him away. He wondered what she was doing now and how she was. The deeper into the Wastes they ran, the less dreams he could remember. He willed himself to dream of her tonight, that he might find her somewhere in that middle place between their dreams—or even share a dream—and tell her how afraid he suddenly was. Until now, he'd believed that chance had brought him here in pursuit of the two metal men with this quandary of a man, Renard. But now, he sensed destiny in it beyond himself and his Marsh Queen.

And he knew my parents. He did not trust the Waste Guide Renard, but he did believe him.

Neb lay awake long after Renard's breathing became slow and easy and long after the moon reached its zenith in the night sky. He thought about it all and wished for sleep and dreaming.

But when sleep finally took Neb, it gave him no dreams whatsoever, and he awoke again and again at the strangeness of it.

Chapter

14

Lysias

Lysias felt out of place without his uniform, and he hoped it didn't show. The tavern bustled around him with a life of its own as he waited in the shadows.

The note had come by courier rather than bird, delivered by a young lieutenant that Lysias knew had kin with Esarov's Secessionists. Another family divided by the civil war—something Lysias understood far too well.

It was, after all, family that had brought him to this place.

He watched the room around him, knowing full well that it watched him back. Or at least, someone did. Esarov was crafty and would not arrange a meeting if he could not control it. And following the instructions to the letter, Lysias had come alone. It completely violated every instinct he had as a general—riding out to a strange city for a clandestine meeting with the leader of a revolt that threatened the fabric of a society he had pledged his life to protecting. Meeting in a dark, dockside tavern out of uniform and surrounded, no doubt, by those sympathetic to a cause he was completely convinced would ruin them all.

Yes, as a general, trained in the Named Lands premier Academy, this was all completely against the grain of instinct.

But, Lysias knew, a father's instincts can trump career in those few, brief seconds between heartbeats. He'd had to come.

He'd taken great care to cover his tracks, confident that Ignatio's men were out there even now, trying to find their assigned quarry. Erlund's spymaster trusted no one—it was his basic operating principle—and the marriage of Lysias's daughter to one of Esarov's now-deceased cohorts made the general particularly of interest.

I am a compromised liability, he thought with a forced smile.

Still, risks aside, he was here now, waiting for Esarov.

I wish to propose a cessation of hostilities, the coded note had read, *but require an intermediary with Erlund.* The note had contained instructions for further communication and had closed cryptically: *I have information regarding the location and well-being of your daughter.*

As much as he wished that his duty to the state now drove him, it was that closing sentence that brought him to this place.

Children, he thought, *are the hunter's snare for a man's heart.*

When the woman approached him with her long legs and confident smile, he raised his hand to dismiss her. She was young—younger than his daughter—and though the occasional mattress tussle was not beyond his interest, Lysias had never felt completely comfortable if a cash transaction was involved. There were plenty of lonely wives or willing servants when the mood struck, though he found that the older he got, the less the mood seemed to strike. Still, this one was attractive enough and didn't have the used, hollow eyes of someone who'd worked in the business for any amount of time.

But even as he raised his hand, he saw her lips purse and saw her head give the slightest shake. He waited until she approached. "Looking for company?" she asked in a low voice.

He glanced around the room. A few sailors took notice, but he couldn't be certain it wasn't the tight dress and the curves it accentuated that drew their stares. He nodded. "I am indeed."

She sat, and as she did, her fingers moved. *We make small talk a bit; then you ask the barmaid for a room key.*

He studied her eyes and saw that they were hard. *Agreed,* he signed in return.

They talked in low tones about the weather and the war until Lysias heard readiness in her replies. Then, he raised a finger and nodded when he caught the barmaid's eye. She studied the two of them with a knowing smile and then waddled over with an iron key. She looked to

Lysias and waited until he produced a heavy coin from his pocket. Burying the payment into her apron pocket, she passed the key to him. "An hour," she said, looking to the woman. "And be mindful of your noise."

The girl wrinkled her nose but smiled. "I don't think this one will give us that problem."

Laughing, the barmaid returned to her work, and the girl stood, stretching out her hand to Lysias.

He was surprised at how awkward he felt suddenly, and he wondered if it was because it had been a while since a beautiful woman had offered him her hand. His last woman, he realized, had been a drunken hurry during a lull in the last war. And that had been more to give his officers a sense of his humanity so that he could exact deeper loyalty than for his own personal satisfaction. He took her hand, and it was soft and small within his.

But her grip was firm.

Lysias stood and let her lead him up the stairs.

She let them into the room and locked the door behind.

A single candle guttered on a small table beside the room's narrow cot. A robed man sat on a wooden chair, opposite the bed. "General Lysias?" the man asked, looking up.

The hair was longer, but Lysias recognized the man, though he'd aged a bit since his days upon the stage. "Esarov," he said. "You take a great risk coming here personally."

Esarov shrugged. "We own this quarter. We've twenty of our best in this fine establishment to mitigate potential risk." He nodded to the girl. "Including Sasha."

They use women for the debasing work of war under the guise of equality. Lysias felt anger catch like kindling in his stomach. He wrestled it down and forced calm into his voice. "So why have you brought me here?" *And what do you know about my Lynnae?* he didn't ask.

"I wish to offer a cessation to hostilities and end this civil war."

Lysias sat upon the bed, not waiting for Esarov to invite him. "So you said." He placed his elbows upon the stained tabletop and leaned forward. "But before I can agree to be your intermediary, I'll need to know your terms."

"They are simple, really. Sethbert's murderer, Petronus, has surrendered himself to the Secessionists' Union. I know that Ignatio is holding a high-ranking member of the Androfrancine Order in one of the Overseer's many basements." Esarov leaned forward, his blue eyes shining through the lenses of his spectacles. "Petronus is prepared to turn himself over to Erlund for trial in exchange for that man's freedom, and"—here, he smiled—"I am prepared to negotiate an end to the war on the sole condition that those city-states currently with seated governors, elected by the people, be allowed to retain those governors in keeping with the intent of the original Settlers Congress."

Lysias scowled. The city-states had united beneath an Overseer during the First Gypsy War, over seventeen hundred years ago. It was a lesson learned the hard way, paid in blood: To have a strong and unified army, one must have a strong and unified central government. "And you believe Erlund will take this offer?"

He might. He really might, Lysias thought.

Esarov smiled, his eyebrows arching over the wire frames. "I'm convinced he will." He sat back and spread out his arms. "It is a matter of law. Sethbert was near kin to him—and his predecessor—holding the highest position of honor on the Delta. His actions, no matter how heinous, stemmed from a sense of duty to his people and to the Named Lands. Erlund is obligated to seek justice."

"And you gain legitimacy for three . . . four cities when you could have them all?"

"I don't need them all; I never have." Esarov's smile broadened. "Democracy is both a mighty tool and a stealthy weapon, General. I believe it will win the war in a slower, surer way and without further bloodshed."

Lysias sat back. He glanced momentarily to the girl, Sasha. She stood near the door, her ear cocked toward it. "And Petronus understands the risk?"

Esarov shrugged. "I believe he does. But I also believe he is motivated by guilt. He knows now that Sethbert was merely someone else's Queen's War move—a clever and tragic manipulation."

Tam, Lysias thought. He remembered his last meeting with the man, there on the Pylos border, when he'd taken the note carefully forged in Pope Resolute's hand along with the ancient weapon that he and the Pope's Gray Guard captain had used to bring down Sethbert through Resolute's so-called suicide. If Sethbert had surrendered when Lysias and his men had arrested him, perhaps the Overseer would have seen a different outcome.

But that was not what House Li Tam intended, if his suspicions were correct.

"Very well," Lysias finally said. "Is there more?"

Esarov nodded. "There is. I want assurances of Petronus's well-being during the trial. He is to be afforded the courtesy of a dignitary from the moment of his arrest until the completion of his trial and any resulting sentence."

Lysias sat, staring at Esarov. He tried to remember what play he'd last seen the man in before he'd retired from the theater and given himself to questionable politics. He thought perhaps it was *A Weeping Czar Beholds the Fallen Moon,* that ancient tale of accidental, tragic love. He'd played Frederico, the Last Weeping Czar, and Lysias recalled that his wife had been quite taken with the young Androfrancine-turned-actor.

"Very well," he said. "I will relay your message. How do I contact you with Erlund's response?"

Esarov smiled again. "My men will contact you. You will not see me again until the trial."

Lysias nodded, wanting to ask one last question—really, his first and foremost question—but not sure how. Until this moment, his purpose here was clearly a matter of state, but this inquiry would make it personal and years of habit drove him to keep the two very separate in his life.

But Esarov must have seen the conflict in his face. "She is fine, Lysias," he said. "Your daughter is in the Ninefold Forest in Rudolfo's refugee camp. We had word of her arrival not long before the assassinations."

Lysias didn't want to ask his next question, either, but for different reasons. As much as he held Lynnae's dead husband in disdain, he'd not been able to carry those feelings over to the child of that union no matter how hard he tried. But it was a child he'd still refused to meet when Lynnae last stood upon the steps to his home and his servants refused her entry. He'd not even asked after the boy's name, and now, he winced at the memory of that day. "And my grandson?"

A cloud fell over Esarov's face. "I'm sorry," he said. "Her child took fever and died."

Lysias blinked, ambushed by sudden and unexpected emotion. He found himself suddenly disoriented by the wash of grief and regret and rage. *What have I done, Lynnae?* He sat for a moment, ordering the tears that now threatened him to stand down. His voice caught when he spoke. "He's dead?"

Esarov nodded. "I seem to recall you were not pleased with her . . . situation. You should be delighted, I would think, at this outcome."

He let the air go out of him in a rush and felt his shoulders sagging. He stared at Esarov. "Is that all?"

"Yes," Esarov said as he stood. "I have no other news. But she is safe, and the Gypsy King is treating the Entrolusian refugees well— giving them food and shelter and work."

Lysias nodded and watched Esarov walk to the window. He slipped out onto a narrow balcony and climbed over the rail. "My men will find you in three days' time for Erlund's response," he said as he vanished into the fading day.

Lysias closed his eyes and felt a tearless sob shudder across his shoulders.

"We should go soon," Sasha said, messing her hair and clothing.

When he looked up into her striking green eyes, Lysias wasn't sure what he hoped to find. Grace. Compassion. Forgiveness, perhaps.

But all that met him there was silent, cold accusation.

Vlad Li Tam

Vlad Li Tam awoke to the sound of a chime and pushed aside the light satin sheets of his prison bed. He forced himself to sit up slowly, once again inventorying his new surroundings.

There had been no further conversation and certainly no explanation when they'd ushered him into the suite of windowless rooms. He'd been left clean linen robes and sandals and had found the bathing chamber, complete with heated water and a marble tub. And once he'd cleaned himself, servants had arrived bearing platter upon platter of steaming seafood, sticky rice, and fresh fruits. He'd taken that first meal sparingly before crawling onto the feathered mattress and falling into a deep sleep.

There had been several meals since, and he assumed that meant days had passed.

He'd spent at least one of them hammering at the door, bellowing his questions and demands.

Really, the same question expressed in different ways.

What do you intend with my family?

It rode him even as he studied the patterns of this new Whymer Maze. They'd moved him from degradation to luxury and left him alone without any expectation that he was aware of. At some point, he knew, it would turn again.

Until then, he ate, bathed and slept in nearly identical cycles.

But now, he realized, was something different.

The chimes. He stood and pulled yesterday's robe over his naked skin. He walked out into the sitting area and saw the girl waiting for him there.

She inclined her head. "Good evening, Vlad."

Evening, he thought, careful not to return her gesture of respect. "What do I call you?"

"Ria," she said.

Vlad Li Tam met her eyes. "Where are my children, Ria, and what are your intentions toward them?"

She smiled. "They are here," she said, "and I have none." She stepped back, toward the door. "Would you like to see them?"

Vlad Li Tam swallowed, his eyes narrowing. *This is the turn,* he thought. "Yes," he said. "I would."

Ria turned, her dark robes flowing around her like ink poured in water. "Let's go see them, Vlad."

There were no ropes. No guards. No blindfolds. As they walked, he forced Francine calm to enwrap him and turned his mind to the work of learning. He measured each step from the door. He noticed the stone hallway, the texture of the floor, the quality of the air and the way that their footfalls echoed ahead and behind them. His eyes measured the span between doors—doors made of the same dark wood that the mysterious vessel was made from, reinforced with bands of iron and a series of keyed bolts.

His eyes and feet and ears and nose drank in everything, sorted it by degree of usefulness and stored it away. When he needed it, he would bring it back. And at some point, he would know enough to—

"Your father taught you well, Vlad," she said over her shoulder. "But you will not be well served by that knowledge here."

He stared at the back of her head. "Why is that?"

She laughed. "Because he designed this place with you in mind."

Vlad forced himself not to react. He did not break stride, and though she wasn't looking, he kept his face masked. Mal Li Tam's words had stayed with him. *Your own father betrays you.* Vlad remembered the slender black volume, so like the others he'd burned the day Rudolfo had come demanding answers. The smoke of House Li Tam's secrets had hung heavy over their jungle estate, thick and choking. History they had built by bending and breaking and building men and women, slowly and in secret.

And more secrets within the secrets.

Vlad Li Tam said nothing, placing one sandaled foot in front of the other. Ahead, he saw that the corridor ended with a wide, rounded flight of stairs that rose up, widening as they went, until they ended at a wide set of double doors in shadows cast by intricately carved marble pillars. He hesitated and she stopped.

"Your children are waiting, Vlad."

And even as her words registered with him, he suddenly knew that he did not want to go willingly where she led him. He found himself wondering if her threat earlier applied to this moment as well. *I can have you carried,* she had said. He suspected that it was so.

Vlad Li Tam forced himself forward. She climbed the stairs and he followed. Once they reached the top, she pulled open the door.

Robed men—four of them—slipped out and around him. Vlad felt hands upon his shoulders, and he tried not to tense himself. "Exactly what are you—"

Vlad closed his mouth. He'd seen drawings, certainly, and he'd heard the Gypsy King's Tormentor's Row described enough to know what awaited criminals and enemies within its screaming walls. But the magnificence of the room was boggling. He stood now on a wide, circular balcony, overlooking the cutting room below with its tables and pipes. Recliners and armchairs on the observation deck had been replaced with simple wooden stools and an upright rack beset with straps and manacles. But other than those spartan furnishings, the space was lavishly decorated. Art, the likes of which Vlad had never seen, lined the circular walls—various demonstrations of the cutters at work. Heavy purple velvet curtains offset high stained-glass windows. The railings and blood-catchers were gold, and near the tables below, silver blades of various shapes lay waiting for skilled hands to wield them.

The robed men dragged Vlad to the rack, and finally he resisted. He lashed out with a foot and heard the solid crack of an ankle. The man went down a thud, and Ria's voice shouted out, echoing across the domed chamber.

"Enough," she said. "You forget about the well-being of your children."

Vlad Li Tam snarled, then hung his head. *They're dead anyway. No,* he told himself. *Not yet.* And maybe there was a way still to save them. He let the three remaining men escort him to the rack and strap him in.

Ria smiled down at him and whistled low. A table of knives

appeared. "I told you I would be your Kin-healer and Bloodletter. Do you remember this?"

He nodded but said nothing.

"I am going to cut you, Vlad. Slowly and over a long period of time. And in doing so, I will heal your kinship to House Y'Zir."

Vlad Li Tam blinked. "House Y'Zir?" Suddenly, his mind was focused, a knife edge ready to cut. *An Y'Zirite resurgence?* House Y'Zir had fallen millennia ago, and yet from time to time, small cults had sprung up—factions who perceived the Wizard Kings as divine, mourned their death and longed for their return. House Li Tam had helped the Order quell its share of them in the earlier days, before the shipbuilders had turned to banking. "There is no House Y'Zir," he said. "It fell when Xhum Y'Zir broke the back of the world."

"'And that which is fallen shall be built up and that which is dead shall live again,'" she said with a smile. "The Age of the Crimson Empress dawns upon us." She reached out a hand and stroked Vlad's stubbly cheek. Her hand was warm and her breath was sweet. "Dear Vlad," she said, "do you understand that your blood will save us all?"

I am your Bloodletter.

"Save us from what?" he asked.

She smiled. "Ourselves." She turned a crank and he felt himself turning, tipping slightly down so that he had a full view of the cutting tables below. Suddenly, her mouth was near his ear. "Now this is going to hurt, Vlad. A lot."

He gritted his teeth. "If you're going to cut me, cut me."

She laughed. "I will. But first I need you to feel something for me."

"What do you need me to feel?"

Ria smiled. "Despair."

She clapped, and down below, a door opened. Robed men led a young, naked man, and Vlad Li Tam knew him.

It was Ru, the thirteenth son of Vlad's twentieth. Thirty years old last month, he realized. The men brought him to the table, and though the young man was silent, the terror was evident upon his face. As they began strapping him down, Vlad Li Tam opened his mouth to shout.

Ria placed a hand over his mouth. "You are here to listen," she said, "not to speak." She removed her hand at his nod. "And you are here to watch." Here, her smile widened. "Close your eyes even once and I will cut away your eyelids."

Vlad Li Tam swallowed and forced his eyes to those of his grandson. He watched bravery ignite in the young man's eyes, and he nodded once, slowly. *Courage,* he willed.

And it seemed as if the eyes shouted back love.

The cutter, robed in crimson, approached the table.

Carefully, he selected his first knife, and Vlad Li Tam felt his heart pound in his temples and smelled iron mixed with his own cold sweat. *Courage.* But this time, he intended the words for himself.

The cutter started his work, and Vlad Li Tam watched, his eyes never leaving his grandson's, even when the screaming started, even when the body shook and jumped as the blood-catchers filled beneath the cutting knives.

Time moved past him, slow and heavy and loud.

He watched and swallowed the sobs that overcame him, tasting the salt of his tears as they rolled down his cheeks and into his open mouth. His father had taught him some measure of detachment for their family's work in the Named Lands, and that skill had served him when it came to sending his children out like arrows to find their mark in the world. He'd sacrificed hundreds of lives, most from his own family.

But here, he made no difficult sacrifice to lay the foundation of some great intrigue or strategy—here, he had no decision to make whatsoever. It was a matter of keeping his eyes upon his grandson and watching him twist and buck against the blades.

"Why are you doing this?" he finally asked.

Ria clapped, and below, the surgeon lowered his knife. She leaned toward him. "I told you. I am redeeming your kinship. I am paying for salvation with blood."

Vlad Li Tam stared down at his grandson and realized his mouth was moving. "What do you want from me? Do you want information? Do you want money?"

Her laughter was an upbeat song set to a minor key. "No, not at all. I do not lie to you, Vlad. All that is required of you is that you watch and listen." She paused. "I told you it would hurt."

What is he saying? Vlad leaned against the straps, feeling them bite into his flesh as he strained himself to hear the son of his son. The voice was low and it burbled. His mouth foamed pink.

"Give him water," Ria ordered, and a black-robed man stepped forward with a cup even as the cutter retreated to wipe his knife clean and select another from the table.

The words took shape, and Vlad Li Tam's sob shook a cry from his lips though he worked hard not to let it.

Not having the option of writing it out, his grandson now offered up his last words there beneath his grandfather's tortured stare.

It was a poem of honor and sacrifice composed in blood and pain.

Vlad Li Tam felt the hot tears coursing his cheeks, heard their pattering upon the floor. He forced their eyes to meet and he kept watching, even after the cutter returned his latest knife, even after Ru Li Tam's eyes rolled back in his skull from the pain of its touch, even after the poem had once more become a shriek.

Later—hours later, it seemed—when the boy was still and quiet, Ria smiled. "Tomorrow," she said, "we should have time for three."

Vlad Li Tam heard a croak and realized it was his own voice. He swallowed at the dryness in his mouth and tried again. "Cut me instead."

"Oh," she said, glancing to her table of knives, "I will in due time, Vlad."

I want you to feel something for me. Vlad Li Tam tried to look away from the lifeless body there on the table. He'd felt it on the dock, but already it had taken a new hold upon him. He felt it growing.

Despair.

Vlad Li Tam did not feel the hands that unstrapped him from the table and caught him when he fell. He was only vaguely aware of the men who carried him back to his room to place him on the floor near the door.

All he saw was the mouth of his dead grandson moving slowly, repeating the lines of the poem he'd composed beneath the knife.

Weeping, Vlad Li Tam repeated the words back to himself and kept doing so through the night, curled into a ball with his fist against his mouth. He lay there reciting the poem until the chime sounded the next morning.

Then the men arrived to bear Vlad Li Tam into another day.

Petronus

Petronus hung to the edges of the crowded market and meditated to retain his calm. Esarov's men stood near him, and he saw uniformed Entrolusian soldiers at the far end of the square. Commerce hummed and buzzed around them.

He'd looked for Grymlis but had not seen him. When the time had come to leave, it was predawn and he'd not had the heart to wake him. They'd ridden to the city and waited for noon in the basement of an inn near the docks.

Now, they waited for the signal—a red scarf waved from a rooftop. When they saw it, they looked to the balcony two buildings over and Petronus's breath caught in his throat.

Standing calmly between two soldiers was a familiar man, older to be sure but well preserved in the thirty years since Petronus had last seen him. Petronus nodded to the man beside him. "Yes," he said. "It's Charles, to be sure."

Above them, a blue scarf waved.

They waited another three minutes, and then the man to his right touched his shoulder. "It's time."

Petronus looked up and chose his path through the crowded square. With a glance to the men beside him, he took a deep breath and set out, his eyes planted firmly on the far side of the market. As he moved slowly, he found himself wondering exactly how everything would play out from this moment forward. Until now, he'd had some voice in the matter, but once he passed Charles, once he gave himself over into the hands of Erlund's men, Petronus knew that his voice would be muted. It would be Esarov and Erlund's game now.

He saw the balding crown of Charles's head bobbing its way through the crowd, moving toward him at a leisurely pace. When they made eye contact, it was like lightning striking twice.

From afar, Charles appeared to have aged well, but up close, he was haggard and worn down. He weighed fifty stones less than he should, and though his clothes were new, they were ill fitting upon him. As he approached, the Arch-Engineer scowled and Petronus watched his hands.

This was a foolish trade, Father, Charles signed once the crowd parted enough for them to see one another.

Petronus inclined his head slightly. *Perhaps,* he answered. *Are you well?*

They met in the middle and briefly embraced. "I am as well as I can be," Charles whispered. Petronus heard heavy emotion in the man's voice and wondered exactly how the time had gone. Charles had been Sethbert's prisoner first, and that could not have been easy. And Ignatio, Erlund's new spymaster, had a reputation for cruelty though his master seemed more civilized.

Petronus released him. "Rudolfo is coming for you," he said. "He can be trusted as you trust me."

Charles nodded. "Did my messages get out?"

Petronus looked up. Ahead, the guards were craning their heads above the crowd, keeping watch on the two old men. "At least one did," he said, then his hands moved. *Is it true? Is Sanctorum Lux what I think it is?*

His answer was a simple gesture. *Yes.*

The guards were moving into the crowd now, slowly, and Petronus resisted the urge to question Charles further. His words tumbled out now even as he steeled himself for the rest of his walk across the market. "You serve the Gypsy King now, Charles," he said in a low voice. His hands pressed a final message into the man's shoulder. *Serve him well; preserve the light.*

He thought for a moment that he saw tears in the old Arch-Engineer's eyes, but he didn't look closely enough. He didn't want to know.

Instead, he willed his feet to carry him forward and willed his heart not to be afraid. If Esarov's scheme worked, he'd be free soon enough. If it didn't, he'd find that reckoning he had expected to face.

He pushed past Charles and into the crowd, carefully rehearsing his lines. The soldiers met him, and each took an elbow with firm hands, escorting him that last twenty steps. Lysias waited for him, his face dark with worry.

"General," Petronus said with a nod. "It's been a while." He'd last seen the man during the parley that finalized peace following Resolute's suicide and Sethbert's removal from power.

Lysias blinked at him, and Petronus wondered if he reached for a fitting title before finally giving up. "It's not safe here," he finally said, dropping any need for an honorific. "We need to go."

Petronus smiled. "One moment," he said. Then, he pulled himself up to full height and turned toward the crowd. Already, the soldiers on each arm tugged at him, and he shook off their hands violently as he raised his voice over the square.

"Hear me," he shouted. "I am Petronus, last true son of P'Andro Whym and last Pope of the Androfrancine Order, reigning King of Windwir." He saw Lysias's look of surprise out of the corner of his eye and wondered if the general had truly thought Petronus would vanish silently and willingly into one of Ignatio's many basements. He also saw the confusion upon the soldiers' faces as they looked to their leader for direction, but this was not his intended audience. He turned and took in the openmouthed, wide-eyed stares of the people in the market. Their voices died down as they took in the old man in his simple, travel-worn robes. "I am Petronus," he shouted again, "and I give myself willingly into the hands of your Overseer, invoking my rights by monarchy."

He opened his mouth to shout again, but now the hands were firm upon his elbows and he was being steered—nearly dragged—out of the crowded square and toward a waiting wagon.

Lysias drew alongside him, his face red. "This was supposed to be a quiet affair."

Petronus smiled. "You'll forgive me for spoiling your silence." Behind him, he knew Esarov's men were already spiriting Charles away through a series of alleys and windows and basements. He would be out of the city by nightfall and under Rudolfo's protection in two days' time if all went according to plan.

After that, Sanctorum Lux awaited.

The firm hands were now lifting him up into the wagon and closing the iron-reinforced doors. Most of the market now watched, and Petronus felt pleased with himself.

So far, he thought, things were off to as good a start as they could be.

Leaning back into the cushioned bench, Petronus closed his eyes and willed the rest of their plan to go as smoothly. But even then, as he tried to lay out the strategy and imagine the events that were coming, he found his mind pulled again and again toward Rudolfo and Charles and Sanctorum Lux.

Where was it? Who had built it? Was it safe?

The questions rolled on even as the windowless carriage bumped its way down cobblestone streets, turning left here and right there, until passing through the gates and picking up speed on the open highway.

Petronus found the carriage jostling him into a light sleep. In it, he dreamed of miles and miles of books—old and new—stretching out for as far as the eye could see. And Neb was there, grinning like a wolverine, alongside Charles and Rudolfo and Isaak.

I am not in my own dream, Petronus realized.

But then again, he didn't need to be.

He only needed to know that the light was in such capable hands.

Chapter

15

Winters

Winters sat beneath the guttering lamp and pored over another volume from the Book of Dreaming Kings. Since her meeting with Ezra nearly a week before, she'd given as much of herself as she could spare to the long, winding row of shelves that stretched back to their earliest days in the Named Lands.

She'd started with the volumes that her grandfather had added, written down from his dreams with meticulous care, and now she read her father's. So far, she'd found nothing, but she wasn't sure exactly why she looked. The old man had told her that the book hadn't changed until Windwir fell.

During my reign. Still, something in her longed for some clue, anything, that would negate his words or expand upon them. She replayed them again and again, and each time she saw the white lines of a scar upon his chest that was easily older than she was. Whoever Ezra was, he'd taken the mark of House Y'Zir a goodly while ago—when her father still lived. And her father had seen the fall of Windwir in his dreams, though the old man's scar could well have been older than even that visitation.

Winters shuddered to think the cutting went back even farther.

She heard a low whistle and looked up.

Seamus, the oldest of her Council of Twelve, approached. Even in the dim light, his face was drawn and pale. "My queen," he said in a low voice, "we are at alarm."

She stood quickly, closing the book she read. "What is it?"

"We've received birds from the Summer Papal Palace," he said. "They are under attack."

"By whom?" The Papal Palace was under Gypsy protection, populated now by a few hundred Androfrancine refugees who had chosen not to make their way to the Ninefold Forest. She blew out her lamp and joined him at the entrance of the cavern that housed the book.

His mouth was a firm, white line. Then he spoke. "By us, it seems."

She walked ahead of him, forcing him to keep up with her shorter legs. As they walked, her mind spun.

By us. Three weeks earlier, she wouldn't have thought it possible. But now, after seeing the bodies of her own men with the mark of House Y'Zir carved into them and after hearing Ezra speak to the changing times and the rise of this so-called Crimson Empress, Winters knew that no matter how ludicrous it appeared on the surface, it could very well be true.

They followed the winding caverns upward until breaking into the wider, cavernous throne room with its wicker chair. Beside it lay the silver axe of her office, and she took it up before sitting.

Six of the Twelve were present, as were a handful of scouts and headmen. "What do we know?"

One of the headmen stepped forward. "We know that birds were spotted racing south and east." He held a small bird himself, stroking its brown back. "The message invokes Androfrancine and Gypsy kin-clave."

Winters extended a hand, and the headman slipped a small scrap of paper into it, tied still with white thread. She scanned the note quickly. It spoke of Marsh scouts at the gate and bore markings of a day earlier tied into its carrying thread. She looked up from the note. "Do we have scouts near the Palace?"

Seamus shook his head. "No. None that I'm aware of, Queen."

Winters bit her lip and read the note again. It had come to her though it was unaddressed. But why? Surely, if they believed the Marshers besieged them, they wouldn't send birds to her of all people.

"It could be a trap," she said in a quiet voice.

"If so," another of the Twelve said as he entered the cavern, "then it's a convincing one." All eyes turned to him and he frowned. "There's smoke to the northwest," he said. "The Papal Palace is burning."

Winters felt the blood drain from her face. First, the assassinations. Then the caravans. Now, *this.* She wished Hanric were here. Or Rudolfo. Or even Neb. Surely one of them would know the best path she could take through this particular turn of the Whymer Maze.

Still, despite the confidence she lacked, the answer spelled itself out clearly. Winters sighed. "Ready my mount," she said. "We ride at once."

Seamus leaned close to her, and his hands moved in the dark sign language of House Y'Zir, his body shielding his words from prying eyes. *Is my queen certain of the path she takes?*

She nodded. *I am, Seamus.* Then, she said it aloud for the benefit of the others. "I am certain."

The room emptied quickly as the men set about readying themselves. Winters hefted her axe, barely able to lift it with one hand, and stood. "I will need your aid, Seamus," she said.

The old man bowed. "Yes, Queen."

Winters frowned. "I've not needed armor before. Nor have I needed blades."

"I will see to it," he said.

As he scuttled off, she retreated to her private chambers to toss spare clothing and a sturdy pair of Gypsy boots into a knapsack. She also tossed in a tablet of parchment and a handful of pencils. She paused for a moment before the oak bureau that had been her father's. There, sitting where she had left it upon her return from the mountain, was the vial of voice magicks.

Perhaps now I preach my first War Sermon.

The bitter taste flooded her mouth as she remembered that day atop the spine. She remembered the cold wind and the way the throne bit into her flesh, the way that her voice echoed across the craggy mountain peaks and how it moved along the hollowed-out, snow-swept canyons and valleys. It had been her first time with the voice magicks.

She took down the vial and tucked it into her knapsack.

There was a knock behind her and she turned. "Yes?"

Seamus entered bearing an armful that he spilled onto her narrow bed. "I've raided the armory," he said. "I'm not sure how much of this will be useful to you."

She pulled out a worn leather belt with a single long scout knife in an undecorated sheath. When she drew the blade it whispered against the leather sheath. She tested its edge with her thumb, drawing a beaded line of blood. She resheathed it and set it aside. She'd learned to fight at Hanric's hands, though she'd not found herself very good at it. She'd mastered the sling but had virtually no sword or knife skills to speak of. She'd not taken to it, preferring instead to carefully write out her dreams and add them to the Book, trusting her shadow and the men he commanded.

Only now, I *command them,* she realized. She thought of Hanric sleeping in the ground and swallowed back the sadness that suddenly ambushed her.

Seamus was pulling bits of leather and chain free from the pile. "Some of these may fit you," he said, "but they really weren't intended for battle—more for training children."

She nodded. *He thinks we ride to battle.* Winters feared he thought correctly. "What do you think we will find?"

Seamus paused, holding her eyes with his own. "Bodies," he said.

She lifted up a leather cuirass from the pile and held it up to her chest. Cocking his head to one side, Seamus inspected it, then circled around behind her, cinching in the straps. She felt the hard leather flatten her breasts as he tightened it up. She held her breath until he finished, then let it out slowly. "And the attackers?"

He picked out a helmet—small and round and iron. He lowered it onto her head and frowned when it swallowed half of her face. He traded it out for another, then lifted her long, braided hair up and coiled it around the top of her head. "They are long gone by now, I'll wager," he said. "I'm more concerned about the others."

Yes. Meirov's rangers had been patrolling much farther north than custom since the assassinations, as had Turam's border scouts. And with armies forming and marching slowly north these past few weeks, it was only a matter of time. The attack on the Summer Papal Palace could very well be what sparked war between her people and their neighbors to the south.

"I'll send more birds from the trail," she said. Winters strapped on the knife and turned; Seamus stepped back to inspect her. She drew the blade and thrust it menacingly. "How do I look?"

He snorted. "No offense, Lady Winteria, but you make for a raga-muffin of a soldier."

She nodded, glancing to herself in the cracked mirror leaning haphazardly against her wall. "I do indeed," she said. She turned one last time and sighed again. "But it will do."

Ten minutes later, Winters rode at the head of a ragged line of soldiers and Marsh scouts. She unstopped the vial and tipped a mouthful of the voice magicks back into her throat. She waited, gently clearing her voice until she heard it catch and the sound of her cough rustled the pine trees.

"I am Winteria bat Mardic, Queen of the Marshfolk, and I ride under arms for the Summer Papal Palace. Who will ride with me and mine?"

The men and women around her roared, and it seemed each time she repeated the call that more and more voices cried out in reply around her.

As they rode, others joined them, bearded men fresh in their mud and ash, weapons tucked in belts or slung over shoulders, still strapping on their ragged bits of armor and in some cases still leading their horses and kissing their children good-bye.

Winters remembered the last time their army had gathered up, recalling vividly the pillar of fire and smoke that had once been Windwir, stark against the sky of Second Summer. She remembered Hanric's bellowing call to arms, followed by that first War Sermon on the march south and those exhilarating, terrifying moments that marked the first time she'd left the Marshlands.

She remembered the armies—all of them—lined up below their standards at the edge of those blasted lands.

Funny, she thought, that she hadn't wanted so badly to cry back then and she did not remember once being afraid for her people.

But now, doubt chewed upon her as she worried what waited for her and her people at the end of this road.

And try as she might, Winters found no War Sermon upon her tongue or within her heart to bring courage as they settled into their slow ride north.

Instead, she rode silently into the shadow of the Dragon's Spine, her eyes fixed on the storm clouds that gathered ahead.

Rudolfo

Rudolfo growled beneath his breath and braced himself against the rocking of the ship. The storm had come up quickly, pummeling them the last thirty leagues into port, and now they hunkered down at the top of the stairs, waiting for the word to be given.

Rudolfo had wiled his days pacing the narrow cabin, taking no pleasure in the lavish meals but pretending nonetheless so as not to offend his host.

Rafe Merrique had changed little in the decades that had slipped past them. He was a bit more flamboyant and slower to speak, his long hair had gone iron gray, but at the core of him, he remained the pirate lord that Rudolfo remembered from his youth. Still, the vessel *Kinshark* was proof enough of how well the man had done in the intervening years.

It was smooth, well kept, and faster than fast. Merrique's crew kept it well oiled, bringing down the sails each night and replacing them with sailcloth soaked in a portion of the hold that had become more a vat than anything else. He rotated his crew as often as his sails, giving them as much time off the powders as on.

Rudolfo had spent his life among his Gypsy Scouts, well versed in the ways of stealth and strength magicks, and yet he'd seen nothing like the *Kinshark* in all his days.

Still, even the wonder of the vessel hadn't held his attention. His mind continued wandering north to his wife, to his son, when he wasn't poring over the *Kinshark*'s maps and charts or seeking out Merrique's insight as to where Tam's iron armada might've fled.

"No one goes east but me," Merrique had told him. "And that not so much now with the gray robes gone. That leaves south and west."

Still, he hoped Petronus could shed light on that. *If I can get to the old fox.*

The ship rocked again, and Rudolfo heard the boatswain's whistle. "Hang on to me," Merrique said in a low whisper.

The hatch opened, and they scrambled out onto the wet deck quickly. Below Rudolfo's feet, he saw nothing but roiling water, and the vertigo that took him tugged at his stomach. He forced his eyes closed and clenched the back of Merrique's belt. Behind him, he felt his Gypsy Scouts doing the same with him.

They moved to the side of the ship and one by one, lowered themselves into the waiting longboat. Merrique pulled Rudolfo beneath a heavy canvas and they huddled there, pitching and tossing, as the magicked sailors pulled oar and guided them to shore.

Once they made landing, the tarp pulled away and Rudolfo stood, hopping lightly onto the waiting dock. They were in a seedier part of the city—a series of dilapidated river docks along the backside of a row of run-down taverns. Upriver, a cannery squatted over the river on wood pilings, smoke leaking from a dozen chimneys, rising up into the cloudy sky.

The rain pounded down on them, and Merrique motioned them toward the shelter of a rickety balcony. "We're early," he said.

At a nod from Rudolfo, the two Gypsy Scouts slipped into the shadows to keep watch.

Rudolfo's eyes narrowed. "How well do you know this Esarov?"

Merrique laughed. "As well as I know you, I imagine. I met him when he was still with the Order, before he left it for a life of debauchery on the stage. There were certainly years of silence, but lately he's meant good business for me."

One of Rudolfo's scouts whistled, low and long, from his position at the corner of the building. A group of men approached, laughing and singing as they came.

Rudolfo watched them, keeping Merrique in the corner of his eye. He felt exposed here, but it was easy to feel that way. Even now, he knew the captain's men, magicked and armed, surrounded them. Still, he knew the fierce effectiveness of his Gypsy Scouts firsthand, had trained with them and watched them sweep a battlefield clean as a grandmother's floor. He was unaccustomed to trusting someone else's men with his well-being. He found his left hand twitching for the narrow sword on his belt.

The group of men staggered toward them, and Rudolfo saw that they huddled close around two men at their center—both hidden in ragged sailor's clothing and cloth caps.

One of the men slipped past his cohorts. He reached into his pocket and withdrew a pair of silver spectacles, pushing back his long hair to slide them over his ears. "You are Rudolfo," he said.

Rudolfo nodded. "I am."

The men kept at their singing, all but the old one in the middle, as the short, long-haired man leaned closer. "I bear tidings from Petronus. And I bring a charge for you to keep watch over."

Rudolfo's eyes narrowed. "You are Esarov, then," he said. "The Democrat." When he said it, he found the word distasteful in his mouth.

Esarov nodded. "I am. I know you seek Petronus for reasons of your own, but I'm afraid he is not available."

Rudolfo considered the man's face and read the half-truth upon it. "Where is he? He is under my protection."

Esarov smiled, and Rudolfo frowned at it. "Rumor is that you nearly rode him down on the highway to Caldus Bay for what he did to Seth-bert and the Order. Interesting that you still consider the Androfran-cine your protectorate."

"Interesting or not," Rudolfo said, "he is, and I would know of his circumstances."

"He is under house arrest at Erlund's hunting estate," Esarov said. "He turned himself in for trial by Jury of Governors—in exchange for *this* man." Here, he pointed to the balding old man.

Rudolfo gave him a closer look. The men had stayed near him, guarding him as closely as they guarded Esarov. Even now, they took up positions at each door or alley within eyeshot of the rendezvous. He was not quite as old as Petronus, though he looked older in this moment. He was haggard and pale, several days unshaven, and di-sheveled with dark rings beneath his eyes. This, Rudolfo saw, was a man who had not slept in a day or two.

"Who are you?" Rudolfo asked him.

The man blinked. "I am Charles, Arch-Engineer of the School of Mechanical Science."

Rudolfo's eyebrows furrowed. "You're Charles?"

I bear a message for the hidden Pope Petronus. The metal man that Ae-dric, Neb and Isaak now pursued in the Churning Wastes.

The man nodded. "I am Charles."

"You created Isaak."

The old man looked perplexed. "Isaak?"

Rudolfo smiled and dug in his memory. Rudolfo had given Isaak his name. Before that he'd been known by a title and number. Rudolfo remembered that day in the tent at the edge of Windwir's ruins. "Mechoservitor Number Three," Rudolfo said.

Charles paled. "The one Sethbert paid my apprentice to rescript. The one that sang the spell."

Rudolfo nodded. "Yes. He goes by Isaak now. He heads up the res-toration of the library."

Charles's eyes came to life. "Then you found it. Sanctorum Lux was spared." Relief flooded his voice with emotion.

"No," he said. "We're rebuilding from the mechoservitors' memory scripts. We'll restore a great deal but not everything."

"And Three . . . Isaak . . . assists in this?"

Rudolfo shook his head. "No," he said, "he doesn't assist. He leads the effort—he's planned it quite thoroughly. He studies human leader-ship behavior and then practices it."

Charles shook his head in wonder. "Unbelievable."

Rudolfo nodded. "I consider him part of my family."

A low whistle cut off their introduction. "We're finished here," Esarov said, looking in the direction of the noise. Rudolfo followed his eyes. Already two of the Democrat's men scrambled back toward them, motioning for them to leave. He looked back to Rudolfo. "Charles is under your care now. We need to go."

Rudolfo couldn't keep the growl from his voice. "Petronus is under my care as well, and I—"

"Petronus chose to give himself for this man," Esarov said, cutting him off. "There's nothing more to say here." A small group of black-jacketed men appeared to their north, walking quickly toward them with hands on the hilts of their knives.

Rafe Merrique was already returning to the dock, whistling for them to follow.

As Esarov and his man gathered up, Rudolfo led Charles to the dock. Magicked hands reached up to pull the old man into the long boat and under the tarp. Next, the Gypsy Scouts climbed aboard and Rudolfo turned to join them.

A low voice materialized to his left and he jumped. "Guard Charles well," it said, "and find Sanctorum Lux."

Rudolfo looked and saw nothing. "Who is there?"

"A friend of Petronus's," the voice said. "He bid me pass this to you." A sheaf of papers appeared—magicked hands thrust them at him.

He took them. "Have you seen Petronus? Is he well?"

The men in the black coats were calling out to Rudolfo, but they were too far away for him to pick out the words. Everyone but Rudolfo and the pirate had fled or climbed aboard the magicked longboat.

"Grymlis, I presume?" Merrique asked.

"Aye, Merrique," the voice answered. Then, he added, "The mecho-servitors should be able to cipher out Petronus's notes."

The name was familiar, but Rudolfo could not place it. He looked down at the bundle of papers, then tucked them into his shirt. The black-coats were nearer now, calling for them to stop. Merrique was already climbing into the boat, and hands reached toward Rudolfo as well.

"I will guard Charles well," Rudolfo said. "I trust you'll keep watch over Petronus?"

Grymlis snorted. "As well as I can from outside. Now go."

Rudolfo nodded and let the hands pull him down into the boat.

When they reached the *Kinshark* and were again beneath deck, the first mate passed Merrique a note. "The bird came while you were away," he said.

The pirate read it and passed it to Rudolfo.

Rudolfo frowned at the simple, uncoded message.

> *The Summer Papal Palace has fallen. The Marsh Queen rides to war.*
> *Pylos and Turam march north.*

The Ninefold Forest would have to respond, he realized. Their kin-clave with the Marshfolk and their protection of the Androfrancine remnant would require it. Of course, Jin Li Tam would know that. He looked up. "Is there time for me to send birds?"

Merrique nodded. "Certainly."

Rudolfo excused himself and went to his cabin. He sat at the small table and stared at the message paper and ink needle. Beside it lay the packet of papers from Petronus, waiting for his attention. But before that, he had messages to craft. What he knew he must write in them weighed heavily upon him.

I should be home now, he thought. But the image of his son's small, gray face caused him to shake off that feeling and lift the needle. Jin Li Tam was every bit the formidable strategist that he was—more so, even. He could trust her with this work as he did his own.

He scribbled the first message out in practiced triple code, then paused to reread it.

Esarov's words earlier struck him. He did consider Petronus—and all of the Androfrancines—under his protection still. He took his word seriously, as his father had taught him, and he had taken that mantle during the war when Petronus offered it. Those refugees were his responsibility not just because of that, but because Petronus—that clever Franci behaviorist—certainly had known that when he bequeathed the vast wealth of the Order to Rudolfo that the Gypsy King would care for its refugees. But not just the refugees of Windwir. All refugees—some from the now-failed bookhouses of Turam, many from the Entrolusian Delta.

No, not refugees.

He thought of Neb out in the Wastes with Aedric and Isaak, beyond the bird, last time he'd received word from home. And now Winters no doubt prepared her first War Sermon to face some strange foe that arose within her own people. Rudolfo's family had broadened to include even a metal man who carried the sorrow of genocide on his accidental soul.

I truly am a collector of orphans.

He felt the wind grab the sails as the ship moved downriver toward the open sea. Then Rudolfo pushed all other thought from his mind and gave himself to the notes he needed to send.

But even as he did so, he felt something grow within him that he was not accustomed to. It grew greater and stronger with each league of river they put behind them. Soon, he would be leaving the Named Lands for the first time in over two decades to find a mouse in a hay-field and leaving his Ninefold Forest Houses and their complex bonds of kin-clave in someone else's hands for the first time since he took the turban at the age of twelve.

Rudolfo named the emotion he felt and sighed.

"I am afraid," he said quietly to the empty room.

Jin Li Tam

Jin Li Tam cursed beneath her breath and felt the anger prickling her scalp. "He's done *what*?"

Second Captain Philemus shifted uncomfortably. "He's fled with Isaak and the Waste Guide Renard."

She forced herself to breathe. Last night had been her night with Jakob, and he'd not slept at all. That had meant sleeplessness for her as well, until Lynnae came for him just as dawn tinged the sky pink. Not long after, she'd been summoned for this audience. She reached out for the note, and the Second Captain placed it in her waiting hand.

She was incredulous. Neb had run off over a week ago—along with Isaak and that Waste mongrel Renard—and she was just now finding out. "And why," she asked, laying the message aside, "are we just learning this now?"

"There have been problems with the birds," he said. "They've lost several over there, and their magicks don't seem to hold. We're not sure why."

"So Aedric is back at the Gate now?"

The Second Captain nodded. "He awaits your orders."

She looked down at the other two messages that had brought Philemus tapping at her door and sighed. One was from Winters, the other from Rudolfo. Her eyes went to Winters's. The girl gathered her army and marched for the Summer Papal Palace in response to the distress birds that had flooded the Named Lands two days before. To the south, Pylos and Turam also sent soldiers north. If Jin's geography was correct, the young queen would reach the Palace later today. The other armies would be days behind, though, slowed by the harsh weather.

She vaguely recalled that Rudolfo had kept a small contingent of Gypsy Scouts at the walled mountain fortress until the work had been taken up by a handful of surviving Gray Guard just before winter fell upon them.

At the time, it had been sound strategy: The Foresters had their hands full at home and the Gray Guard were capable. No one could have foreseen this.

Her eyes moved now to Rudolfo's message, and she read it again quickly. Beneath the casual wording of a personal message to her lay the coded script of a competent though worried general. *Bring Aedric and party back,* the note said. *Send him west with the Wandering Army to honor our kin-claves.*

But here she was faced with a hard choice, she realized. Rudolfo did not know about Neb and Isaak. And as highly as she thought of the boy—and having heard somewhat of his quiet romance with Winters the Marsh Queen—she knew that were it simply the boy, her decision would not be so hard.

Jin Li Tam had watched her father sacrifice the children he loved for what he considered to be a higher gain. She could sacrifice Neb, she knew, though it would break her heart to do so.

It was Isaak she could not give up, and for reasons only she and Rudolfo were privy to. In her early days with the Gypsy King, on the night they had fled the Summer Papal Palace and Resolute's guards, Isaak had told her that he still retained Xhum Y'Zir's spell, buried within his memory scrolls.

It meant that the most dangerous weapon in the world was fleeing for unknown reasons across the Wastes. And she could not abide that.

She looked away from the messages and rubbed her eyes. "How did you fare during the war?"

"My company took three Entrolusian battalions and two companies of Pylosian rangers," he said. She looked to the scarf of rank, knotted around his left shoulder with multicolor threads woven in to signify battlefield accomplishments. She noted the pride in his voice.

Now a frank question for frank times, she thought. She met his eyes with her own. "Will you lead the Wandering Army under my direction or will that be . . . *challenging* for you?"

He paled, and she saw the sudden discomfort on his face. "Shouldn't First Captain Aedric—"

"Aedric," she said, "has other work to do." Outside the room, she heard the movement of servants as the Seventh Forest Manor woke up and came to life. "When we're finished here, send the birder in. I'll send word to both Aedric and Rudolfo."

At the name of his lord and general, she saw resolve take root in his jawline and his eyes. "I am honored to serve my queen."

She nodded. "Good." She paused a moment, trying out the next words in her head before speaking them. When she spoke them, they were solemn and clear: "Rally the Wandering Army to the Western Steppes. We ride for the Marshlands in two days' time."

"It will take four to reach their southern reaches. Seven to reach the Palace if we push hard."

We won't be going to the palace, she thought but did not tell him. "Yes," she said.

Already, her mind composed the messages she would write and code. One to Winters to keep her army north. Another to Pylos and Turam to keep their armies south. Another to Aedric that he should find Isaak and Neb at all costs.

And last, a message to Rudolfo to let him know that Second Captain Philemus would lead the Wandering Army west, as Aedric was delayed in the Churning Wastes.

She saw no need to tell him that she intended to take their son and accompany his army with Lynnae and the River Woman in tow. It would add needless worry to him at a time when he needed his wits about him.

She forced her attention back to the present moment.

Jin Li Tam stood, and her mind wandered to the knives in Rudolfo's desk drawer. *I will take them with me.*

She inclined her head to Philemus, and he returned the bow. She thought carefully about her next words and what they might mean for the tenuous bonds of kin-clave that loosely held the Named Lands together during this time of disconnection. There had been no open hostilities between the Gypsies and the other nations since Resolute's so-called suicide. But with the assassinations, the targeting of refugee caravans and now this attack on the Summer Papal Palace, it was obvious that they were at war with *someone.*

The pattern was too perfect, and the strategy was better crafted than even her father could conceive.

She looked to the officer, and there was authority in her voice when she spoke. "Magick the Scouts," she said. "Send two companies immediately to Queen Winteria's aid. Send a company to the Keeper's Gate with supplies for an extended search."

"Understood, Lady Tam." He bowed again and she returned the gesture.

After he left, Jin Li Tam opened the drawer to the desk and lifted out the old set of scout knives she'd been dancing with of late. Setting the belt aside but with within eyeshot, she took up the needle and started crafting her messages.

She took the longest with Rudolfo's, and she was surprised at how badly she did not want to deceive him.

But more surprising than that, she realized, was how badly she did not want to disappoint him.

Still, despite her new life, she was the forty-second daughter of Vlad Li Tam, and she was once more doing what she'd been made for.

Calling loudly for the servants, Jin Li Tam scooped up her knife belt and stormed into the corridor. Strategies of war and statecraft played out behind her eyes, and her stride was deliberate and brisk.

As much as she felt fear now buried deep within her, she felt something else as well. It shamed her to name it, because she knew how wrong it was to feel this while taking an action that put her son so blatantly at risk. She shuddered at it, but still she felt it.

It was exhilaration.

Chapter 16

Neb

Rufello's Cave lay in stone foothills covered in gray scrub just beyond the forest of glass that had once been Ahm. From Neb's position, it looked like a small crevasse in the side of the granite.

The crossing had been harder than he'd thought it would be, evidenced by his shredded uniform and the dozen or so cuts that covered him. Renard had tried to teach him how to move through the razor-edged forest without feeling the sting of salted glass, but as he himself had observed, it took practice.

"I cut myself for years," he told him with a chuckle at one point when they'd stopped to bandage one particularly nasty gash in Neb's thigh.

They'd moved slower after that, Renard never saying what Neb heard already from voices deeper inside himself. *They're slipping away from us.*

Still, Isaak had left an intentional trail easy for them to follow.

Now, they had reached another stopping point.

Rufello's Cave.

Of course, it wasn't where Rufello had lived. Rufello had lived before the Great Migration, before even the Age of the Weeping Czars. He'd been a scientist-poet who had spent his life studying out the treasures, toys and tools of the Younger Gods, leaving behind his *Book of Specifications* that now only existed in fragments. According to Neb's history lessons, the book was rare, and only scattered copies had remained past the Year of the Falling Moon—forbidden by the Wizard Kings once their thrones were established upon the earth.

The cave, according to Renard, was named for him because in it, the Androfrancines had found a cache of his drawings in a hidden library.

"When I was a boy," Renard remembered, "my father was with them when they found it."

They made their camp with the crevasse in view, and in the morning, they approached it.

Neb kept behind Renard as they drew closer and was surprised to see wheel ruts cut into the hard-packed ground. They stretched north and then east but did not continue south from there. They ended at the mouth of the cave. "They didn't hide their tracks?"

Renard chuckled. "No need to. You'll see."

They picked their way across the rocky terrain, finally joining the wagon trail and following it the rest of the way in. The closer they came, the more Neb felt dwarfed by the sheer size of it. The crevasse stretched much higher than he'd thought. When they finally stood in the shadow of it he saw the carefully built stone wall and the massive doors just ten feet inside. At four-span intervals, massive Rufello locks made of iron dead-bolted the door closed.

Or should have.

Renard must have seen it at the same time Neb did; the Waste Guide gasped. The door hung open. Not by much, just ajar really, but it was open nonetheless, and the locks were set with the dead bolts engaged so that the door could not be shut without the correct ciphers. When Renard stopped, Neb stopped, too. The gangly man drew out his thorn rifle. "What in the Third Hell is this?"

Neb found himself reaching for his knife, his eyes already going to the ground to look for tracks as Aedric had taught him during scout training. He felt the momentary tickle of fear along his spine and forced himself to breathe.

Renard moved forward now, cautious, his eyes moving to and fro. Neb followed.

They reached the door, and Renard leaned around to look into the dark, yawning mouth and pause. He raised his right hand, and when it moved into the Whymer hand language, Neb could not follow it. Still, he took the hint and waited.

Renard vanished into the massive cave, and Neb studied the locking mechanisms. The only larger locks he'd seen were on the Keeper's Gate they'd passed through to come here—those were the size of hay bales easily. These were smaller but still easily the size of a large man's head. The levers and dials on the locks were pitted with age and weather, but when he put a tentative hand to one of them, it turned easily and quietly.

Whoever had left the door open had done so intentionally and had the necessary ciphers to do so.

Renard whistled from behind the door. "Stay clear," he called out.

Slowly, the great door swung open and let sunlight spill into the tunnel until the shadows swallowed it.

Still, what they could see was bare.

"There's no one home. Even the lamps are gone," Renard said. "We'll need light."

They made makeshift torches with dried branches hacked from nearby scrub and advanced into Rufello's Cave. Occasionally, they paused to listen, and at least twice, Renard left Neb behind with the light to creep forward and scout the dark. At the end of the corridor, it widened into a large cavern.

But still, it was empty. Completely empty.

Renard scratched his head. "This makes no sense. There have been no caravans. They would have passed beneath my watching eye."

Neb looked at him and saw the consternation on his face. "Who else knew the ciphers?"

"Me," Renard said, reslinging his rifle. "My father, certainly. A handful of others . . . dead with Windwir, I'll wager."

Neb thought for a moment. "Could they have come by a different direction?"

"If someone with the ciphers survived?" Renard cocked his head. "Surely, but why? The Wastes stretch on and on and on all around us. The sea is ten days' root-run to the south, though the salt dunes near her make for hard going." He stretched out his hands. "They'd have needed wagons for all of this, and there's no way to get a wagon through the dunes. Hells," he said, "there were wagons *stored* here, but not nearly enough to haul the supplies they'd stockpiled."

A thought struck Neb. "What else was here?"

Renard shrugged and started listing them off. "Everything. Clothing. Nonperishables. Tools. Weapons. Maps."

Anything needed to mount an expedition, Neb realized. And someone had let themselves in and helped themselves to it. And not just some of it—they had emptied the place. Renard had told him just days ago that the most dangerous predator in the Wastes was still man. Neb found himself wondering if perhaps this was simply the work of common thieves, though it did not explain the lock. Rufello locks were nearly impenetrable. Whoever had done this either had the ciphers or somehow knew a means for puzzling them out—something Neb could not fathom. The cipher on one lock might be possible over a stretch of time, but not five or six locks. It would take a lifetime.

Renard had hunkered down in thought, but now he straightened. "I want to give this a closer look."

They started a new torch and went to opposite walls. Then, they walked slowly, shedding light onto the floor as they went, and Neb saw that the cavern wasn't quite as empty as they'd perceived. Here and there, he saw spilled nails, splintered wood from crates now vanished, and at one point, even found a tattered robe wadded up and discarded. Still, nothing useful.

They moved slowly, methodically covering every span of the room, and just when they reached deepest, darkest corners, Neb came across the flour sack.

It had been dropped, apparently, and had burst, coating the floor with a quarter inch of fine white powder. When he came upon it, he nearly stepped into it but caught himself. Squinting, Neb looked down.

There in the flour, a footprint. He crouched and leaned over to examine it. "I've found something."

He heard Renard coming and blinked again, cursing the guttering torch for toying with his eyesight. The dancing flames gave the footprint an inhuman cast—a shape like no boot or foot he'd seen. Except . . .

Neb's brow furrowed. "A mechoservitor was here."

Renard approached and crouched himself, studying the single footprint. "The Whymers don't bring their toys into the Wastes," he said.

Still, there it was, and Neb thought about Isaak and the others he'd spent so much time with these past seven or eight months. He recalled the flashing eye shutters, the hiss of vented steam, the pens flying across the paper, clutched in metal hands. "A mechoservitor could cipher the locks."

Renard chuckled. "Why would a mechoservitor need supplies?"

It was a good question. "How many of these caches are there?"

"At least a dozen," Renard said. "Scattered strategically, all under lock and stone."

Neb nodded, suspicion growing within him. He was willing to wager that were they to find the others, they also would be empty of anything useful. He thought of the metal man that Isaak now pursued. It had run into the Wastes with purpose, moving as if it had a destination in mind. Moving too fast for men but not too fast for its own kind.

"There was too much here for one mechoservitor," Renard observed. "It would've taken years to empty this cache."

"Then it had help," Neb said. Already, his brain stretched into speculation, but he couldn't find a satisfactory reason why.

Renard shifted and extended the torch farther, the metal footprint taking on deeper shadows as he did. "It would've needed all the help it could get." He stood. "Still, there was enough here to supply multiple expeditions. What use could a mechoservitor have for foodstuffs and tools?"

But Neb wasn't convinced at this point that the supplies had been taken in order to use them. Another idea brewed beneath the surface, and he vocalized it in a quiet voice. "Maybe it didn't need the supplies. Maybe it just needed us not to have them."

But not us *specifically,* he realized. The Androfrancines or whoever else might come wandering into the Wastes relying on these caches to survive—and work—in this hostile place.

Still, for now there was no answer and nothing of use to them here in Rufello's Cave.

But somewhere a day or two ahead of them, Neb suspected, the answer raced across the broken landscape, its bellows wheezing and its metal legs pumping.

"We should get running," he said to Renard. "We've time to make up."

Renard smiled, and for a moment, in the dancing light of their dying torches, Neb saw traces of a kin-wolf's ferocity in the man's eyes and teeth.

"Let's run then," Renard said.

And they did.

Vlad Li Tam

He lost all sense of anything but anguish, hot and white. He was not even sure of his own name until she called him by it.

"Vlad," Ria said. "You closed your eyes."

She leaned over him with a knife, and he started. The words that came out of him were a garbled shriek, snot and spittle flying. His beard was wet with tears.

Smiling, she withdrew. "No matter. We're done for now." She looked over the railing, but now that her knife was down, he looked away. He could not bear it. Still, her voice was full of pride. "Eight today, Vlad."

Their victims were getting younger and younger. This last batch had just barely left their teens.

He felt a howl rising, but some part of him reasserted itself and forced it down. "The children, too?" His voice cracked.

She laughed. "No, Vlad. Do you take us for monsters? Those below the age of reason will take the mark of House Y'Zir, just as we all have." Here, she opened the top of her robe and revealed her breast to him. There, over her heart, he saw the cutting and knew it from some distant memory of a life before this island, this room, this bloodletting.

I am your Kin-healer, her voice echoed in his memory.

She continued. "You'll take the mark, too, before it's finished." She leaned in and kissed him on the cheek. "Dear Vlad, we'll cut the children and then we'll send them away."

His eyes moved toward her, and again he felt himself stirring to life. *Where?* He heard his voice croak the question.

She stroked his hair. "Someplace where they will learn a new way."

An Old Way, he thought. Vlad Li Tam was back for just a moment . . . long enough to file that knowledge away.

Then, he hung limp in the harness. Strong hands held him up while strong fingers worked the buckles. The robed men lifted him and carried him the seventy-three steps back to his room, depositing him on the floor there.

Ria stepped over him as the door swung shut and the lock turned. She walked to the small dining table laden with exotic foods and sat down. He could not remember exactly when she had started dining in his room—the days had blurred into a scarlet haze. Vlad closed his eyes and tried to let the aromas from the table fill him, but they could not expunge the overriding odor of blood. He rocked back and forth there, curled up on the floor, and tried to find focus.

"I think tomorrow," Ria said, "you will be ready for your first cutting."

He felt the moan rising up within him and knew it for longing. *If the blades are on me they will not be elsewhere.* But he knew it was a false hope. He knew that his children, grandchildren, great-grandchildren would all take the knife sooner or later. Some to their death, others to take the mark of the Wizard Kings upon their hearts.

He heard the sound of wine being poured, of meat being sliced, of a plate being prepared. "The cooks have outdone themselves. Are you certain you won't join me, Vlad?"

He couldn't remember the last time he'd felt hunger. He couldn't remember the last time he'd eaten, though he knew he hadn't held it down. The part of him that watched and waited, buried underneath the surface, knew that would have to change soon. He said nothing.

She ate slowly, making conversation as she did. "Today went very well, though I'm surprised. I thought the young ones would have more stamina than that."

He closed his eyes against the wave of nausea that hit him. The smell of their blood was everywhere. And if she weren't here, grounding him with her voice and presence, the sound of their screaming would chase him into some dark, hazy place within that he was never quite sure he'd come back from.

Again, he said nothing. She continued to eat. "Mal will return soon with more," she said. "Our kin-raven scouts them even now."

Finally, he found words, twisting in a way that he could look up to her from the floor and meet her eyes. "How many more?"

Her laughter was dark music. "All of them."

All of them.

She continued. "Except the Great Mother and the Child of Promise, of course." She looked at him, her fork poised halfway between plate and mouth. "But in the end, that broken kinship will be healed."

Great Mother. Child of Promise. He wanted to ask but did not. Instead, he filed it away with the other scraps of knowledge.

She ate in silence after that, and when she finished, she stooped over him and kissed him on the forehead. "I will see you in the morning, Vlad. Get some rest. Try to eat. Tomorrow, I let your blood."

He recoiled from her touch but did not have the strength to strike out despite the will. She frowned, straightened and went to the door. She tapped at it and waited for the men to let her out.

After she had gone, Vlad Li Tam returned. He stepped into himself slowly and gathered about him the bits of broken man as an old woman gathers a shawl around cold shoulders. He tested out his feet and his hands, he worked his mouth and rolled his eyes. Then, slowly, he crawled to his feet and went to the table. He passed the wine and food, taking instead a pitcher of water that was nearly too heavy to lift.

Returning to the floor, he slouched against the wall, within eyeshot of the door, and sipped the water from the pitcher, holding it with both hands.

Now, the soul-shattered father and grandfather lay cast aside like ill-fitting clothing. In its place was a cold river of a man flowing toward one purpose—to avenge himself upon his tormentors, upon the murderers of his family.

To do that, he had to escape. He was in no condition now to mount any kind of vengeance. He could barely walk. He'd given up hope some time ago of being able to rescue his family from the clutches of this Y'Zirite madness. At the pace they moved at, they would all be dead, or in the case of the younger children, marked and shipped away, before he could ever find the strength to do anything about it.

And he also knew that no one would come looking for him. Whatever remained of his family and iron armada would certainly have implemented emergency protocols and fled for a safe place to reassess the situation. Unless Ria spoke true; unless his first grandson even now prepared to capture the others as well.

It left Vlad Li Tam with nothing to do but hold on and bide his time. He would have vengeance for this. He would have it one hundredfold.

"Everyone has a weakness, Vlad," his father had told him. "If they don't," he added, "you can create one within them if you are patient and crafty."

He thought about his father a lot these days. It was a source of his hatred and fury. He found now, in these few moments of clarity he allowed himself, that many of his father's words had been clues in this Whymer Maze.

My family is my weakness, Vlad Li Tam understood now. But more than that, he understood that it was a weakness his father had built within him, intending Vlad for this very day.

The depth of that betrayal, at first, had made him despondent. But now, it enraged him, and he exhilarated in the strength of that rage as it flooded him, driving out the fog and grief.

He thought again about the slender volume his First Grandson, Mal Li Tam, had shown him. *Your own father betrays you.*

But not just me, Vlad Li Tam realized. Behind his closed eyes, as the hot tears of anger coursed down over his cheeks, he saw the Desolation of Windwir and knew it for his father's work.

He has betrayed us all.

Vlad Li Tam banked his anger and took another sip of the water.

Tomorrow, when those firm hands reached for him, Vlad Li Tam would be gone again. The broken, anguished animal would be there in his place. For now, he needed rest.

When he finally fell into fitful sleep, his dead children surrounded him, their mouths moving as they formed their last words beneath his watching eye and beneath the cutter's knife.

Even in his dreams, their poetry made him weep.

Rudolfo

Rudolfo laid down the last page in Petronus's packet and rubbed his eyes. He'd read what he could—certainly none of the notes from the former Pope had been intelligible, but the other papers had made perfect sense.

Gods, what have they done? As a general with firsthand knowledge of what Xhum Y'Zir's spell was capable of, Rudolfo saw clearly that the Androfrancine maps and notations were the work of frightened strategists frantically reaching for some way to protect the New World.

Sethbert had taken but one mechoservitor and infused him with the power of that devastating spell. But the Androfrancines had intended to make a dozen such weapons and deploy them to key strategic points along the coastlines of the Named Lands.

There was only one sound reason to do such a thing: the fear of an invasion.

Still, it wasn't much of a leap in logic for the mad Entrolusian Overseer to see a threat in this—these maps showed three of the metal spellcasters on his Delta.

Because the Delta was the path to Windwir.

Rudolfo shook his head and shuffled through the papers again. He stopped again at the authorization letter, saw Petronus's signature and stamp there upon that dread parchment and sighed. Certainly, the old man could not have been the one to bring back the spell. Rudolfo found that impossible to believe.

And yet Vlad Li Tam's life's work had been making Rudolfo into a shepherd of the light—moving the library to the Ninefold Forest, set deeper north in a more secluded and strategic place. Another defensive move.

They meant to protect us. It was the only note he could read on any of the documents, and it was in a small, pinched script that he recognized instantly.

He'd known that Vlad Li Tam had visited the Ninefold Forest for the trial just before leaving the Named Lands; he'd learned it later from Jin Li Tam when the time for honesty was finally upon them a month later. And after the trial, Petronus had fled for Caldus Bay, weeping at what he'd done.

Perhaps the two of them worked together, now, with Petronus gathering what he could through his bird lines and Vlad Li Tam scouring the seas for evidence of some external threat.

With recent developments being what they were, it was strategic and reasonable for them to act upon their assumptions.

Windwir, he realized, was just the beginning. Everything about the Named Lands depended upon the Order. Their magicks and mechanicals, their knowledge and access to the glories of the former age made them a critical prop to the economic and social fabric of the New World. With Windwir out of the way and the Androfrancines broken, the gate was open and the sheep were nervous.

And now, more chaos. The Delta was ineffectual, just now entering into a tenuous peace brokered with the potential cost of Petronus's life if Esarov was wrong and the trial went badly. Once the strongest nation of the Named Lands, it was now crippled. And the problems in the Marshlands—the assassinations carried out by rogue scouts among Winters's people—these pointed to further unrest brewing violently ahead of them. Already, he'd sent birds to dispatch his own Wandering Army to meet Pylos and Turam and try to avert another war.

A war that would keep the eyes of the Named Lands focused upon its own internal strife.

Somewhere out there, a master of Queen's War moved nations like game pieces and drove them into a corner they could not come back from.

And even I am distracted. Jakob's illness had trumped even this imminent threat. Yet it had been the simplest decision he had ever made, if he were truly honest. Perhaps because he knew he could trust the woman he had married despite her origins. He would truly have to work hard not to honor his vow and kill Vlad Li Tam when he found him. Her father's role in the death of his brother, parents and closest friend was a constant and gnawing thing—something that kept his heart lost in a Whymer Maze when it came to loving her, though he could trust her with his Ninefold Forest.

But there was no Whymer Maze when it came to Jakob, the offspring of their alliance. He would risk the safety of the Named Lands for his son and do so without shame. Fatherhood redefined love in a way that Rudolfo had not thought possible.

Still. Rudolfo shuffled through the papers one last time, then retied the string that held them together. Standing, he stretched and picked up the packet.

Adjusting his green turban in the small mirror, he let himself into the corridor and slipped two doors down, tapping lightly on the wood surface. He heard the bed creak and footsteps approaching.

It opened slowly and Charles looked out. "Lord Rudolfo," he said, inclining his head.

Rudolfo returned the nod and smiled. "Are you rested? I had hoped to speak with you for a bit."

The old man held open the door and stepped aside so Rudolfo could enter.

The room was like the other cabins he'd seen about the *Kinshark*, small but well ordered. A bookcase, a throw rug from the silkworms of the Emerald Coast, a small desk and a narrow bed.

"Please sit," Charles said. He closed the door behind them.

Rudolfo pulled the wooden chair out from the desk and sat. The old man still looked haggard, but Rudolfo imagined he should after so long in Erlund's care—and before that, Sethbert's. He handed the stack of papers to Charles. "These are from your hidden Pope," he said. "There are some surprises here for me."

The Arch-Engineer untied the string and scanned the first few pages, his face paling as he went. He moved quickly to the bottom of the stack.

"They're coded," Rudolfo said. "When we return to the Ninefold Forest, I'll ask one of the mechoservitors to decipher it." His eyes narrowed and he leaned forward. "But I would ask you now: Is it true?"

Charles went back to the beginning and started again. This time, his eyes moved a bit slower. He shuffled ahead, paused, moved back. When he looked up, his mouth was grim. "These say it is, though I have a hard time believing it."

"Were you aware that your mechoservitors were intended to be weapons?"

Charles shook his head. "No, absolutely not. Certainly, Xhum Y'Zir used them as such—but even his mechoservitors were intended for higher purposes than war."

Rudolfo leaned even farther forward. "And during your time with Pope Introspect, did you have any knowledge of a threat against the Named Lands that might require such a potent defense?"

Charles swallowed, and his eyes shifted slightly. Rudolfo noted his caution and continued. "I hold the reins to the Order now," he said. "Most of the Androfrancine remnant works with me to rebuild the library in the Ninefold Forest. Your last Pope passed all of the holdings to me before he disqualified himself from office with no named successor." Here, he lowered his voice. "Including the mechoservitors." *And the spell,* he thought but did not say. "I am named Protector of Windwir, and I bear Petronus's grace."

"There were whisperings," Charles finally said. "Secret projects in high places. Unprecedented funding to research defensive and offensive capabilities—both magickal and mechanical."

Including the metal men. "Surely as the Arch-Engineer you knew something of all this."

Charles chuckled. "You'd be surprised. There are many smaller orders with the Order. . . ." His face fell. "There *were,* I mean. Work was often divided up in pieces. When they started using the metal men for spell translation, I made sure the work was expunged from their memory scripts."

Charles's words jarred Rudolfo. *Memory scripts.* "My men at the Keeper's Gate encountered a metal man bearing your name and a message for Petronus. You scripted the message into him."

Rudolfo watched the hope spark in Charles's eyes. "He made it then. Did he cross into the Waste?"

Rudolfo nodded. "He did. I had men pursuing him. I've redirected them to deal with matters elsewhere."

"Good," Charles said. "Following him would be dangerous for them."

Something in the tone gave him pause. "Why? And how did you come by a metal man in Erlund's care?" But already, a memory pulled him back. He remembered the night he'd first met Jin Li Tam, when Sethbert's metal man sang a song and they had their first dance. This, he realized, must be the metal man whom Aedric and the others pursued.

"That particular model doesn't have the restraint scripts Isaak's generation has." Charles's brow furrowed. *He hesitates to answer me.* Finally, the old man spoke. "The first generation of mechoservitors—thirteen of them—were the best we could do at the time. We found barely enough fragments from Rufello's Book to bring them back—but of course, as we leveraged our own technology forward by studying the first model, we found ways to line them up more closely to the original specifications. I'm not sure how Sethbert came by that one—he'd not had him long, and I can only assume it was through some kind of treachery with my apprentice. They were scripted to return from their assignment periodically for maintenance."

"Assignment?" Rudolfo scowled. "What happened to the others when you created Isaak's generation?"

Charles sighed, his gaze falling for a moment. "They became one of those secret projects. Against my will, I might add. They were to be unsupervised, given tremendous behavioral latitude and sent into the Churning Wastes."

Suddenly, it made sense. It was not unlike what he did now, up north. "To reproduce the Great Library from their memory scrolls."

"Yes," Charles said in a quiet voice.

Rudolfo stroked his beard and thought for a moment. "Sanctorum Lux."

Charles nodded again. "Yes."

The notion of it staggered Rudolfo. Certainly it was a sound strategy to rebuild in a hidden place—to set the light even farther apart. Especially if there was an enemy at the gates. But the size and scope of such an undertaking was massive. Even now, there were mechoservitors in the Ninefold Forest, metal hands moving fast as sparrows' wings over the parchment, reproducing entire books in less than an hour. The materiel management of it stretched his ability to lay in the supplies for his endeavor. And that didn't even take into consideration the stonemasons, the carpenters, the army of laborers and servants that worked tirelessly to bring back that light. "It would be an impossible undertaking for just thirteen mechoservitors," Rudolfo said.

Charles shrugged. "Nothing is impossible with enough effort."

When the thought struck him, it was a stone dropped into a well. There was a moment of disconnect and then the splash of realization. "The *entire* library," he said incredulously.

Charles's face took on an earnestness that bordered on ferocity. "It must be protected," he said.

Yes. The packet of papers still fresh before his eyes, Rudolfo knew

Charles spoke the truth. He didn't have to cipher out Petronus's notes to know that the old Pope and King believed a threat existed beyond the Named Lands. Vlad Li Tam had most certainly withdrawn his network to protect them and to investigate these developments abroad.

Someone had wanted the Androfrancines out of the way for some dark reason of their own.

And their library.

Whatever had been hidden in the Churning Wastes in the care of these metal shepherds had to be found and guarded. Rudolfo locked eyes with Charles. "And you're certain that it is the *entire* library?"

Charles nodded. "It is."

Rudolfo closed his eyes, suddenly feeling tearful but not knowing why. For weeks he'd wrestled with an untenable task, digging for some way, any way to find Vlad Li Tam's iron armada. A tiny leaf in an impossible lake. And each day that he was away, the Ninefold Forest's neighbors slid farther and farther toward war with his kin-clave in the Marshlands. Petronus was imprisoned, and the Androfrancines at the Papal Palace had no doubt been attacked—maybe killed. And far away—too far away—his infant son lay gray and fading.

The entire library.

Rudolfo realized he was holding his breath and released it. He knew the answer to his question before he asked it. "Including the pharmaceutical sciences and magicks?"

When Charles nodded, Rudolfo said nothing. He stood and looked at the old man for a moment before turning for the door.

Then Rudolfo let himself out and went, trembling, to give Rafe Merrique his new course.

Chapter 17

Petronus

Petronus looked up from the table as servants rolled a service cart set with tea and breakfast rolls into the cramped interrogation room.

The room smelled sour, but it had smelled that way before Petronus had added his own sweat to the confined space. He'd been here from late morning, through the afternoon and then night, as Ignatio and his men questioned him in shifts. Adrenaline had given out long ago; now he felt the weariness permeating him. His arms felt heavy, his face numb from sleeplessness. He rested his arms on the table.

Ignatio followed Petronus's glance. "Perhaps we should take a break." He smiled. "Maybe you'd like to have some breakfast and then get some sleep. We have plenty of time."

Petronus met his eyes and held them. "Tell Erlund he is violating the terms of our arrangement."

Ignatio laughed. "In what way? You've been treated with dignity and respect. You've been fed and kept safe. You've not fallen down any stairs or stumbled into any wells." He leaned forward, his smile wide and toothy. "Don't believe for a moment that you wouldn't have if you were within reach of Sethbert's more loyal followers."

Petronus resisted the urge to chuckle himself. "Sethbert was a madman. His own people turned on him in the end because he was dancing the City States into civil war after breaking their economy."

"Regardless," the Entrolusian spymaster said with a flourish. "Would you like some breakfast?"

He wanted to decline on principle, but Petronus had no way of knowing how long he might be kept here, politely asked questions that he—with equal politeness—declined to answer. He eyed the breakfast rolls, saw a glaze of molten sugar on the steaming buns and sighed. "Certainly," he said.

Ignatio served them, pouring the boiling tea into porcelain cups. He used silver tongs to drop two of the rolls onto a small plate and passed it to Petronus. Then slid a steaming teacup over to him in its porcelain saucer.

Ignatio sipped his tea, then regarded Petronus in bemusement. "You've not answered most of my questions," he said. "I don't understand why you are so hesitant."

Petronus inhaled the soft citrus aroma, his hands enjoying the warmth of the cup. "Those matters have nothing to do with my purpose here," he said. "I'm to be tried for Sethbert's execution. The private matters of the Androfrancine Order are not the concern of the United City-States or its Overseer."

"They are if the metal men are still functioning. They are if the spell is still loose in the world."

Petronus felt the anger surge through him. It tingled in his scalp and he slammed down his cup, sloshing hot tea onto the table. "Do not for one moment forget that the Entrolusian Delta unleashed that spell. It was safe before your Overseer, by deceit and treachery, arranged for its use. He killed tens of thousands of innocents in that act of genocide." He realized that his voice had risen significantly.

"Your people dug it up. Sethbert believed you meant to use it on the Named Lands."

Petronus bit his tongue. He knew better than to share any of his findings with this man or any other before the trial actually began. Not even Isaak's assurance that the spell had been destroyed in the casting. Instead, he forced calm back into his voice. "As reigning King of Windwir, I decline to answer and invoke the right of Office Privilege as delineated in the Articles of Kin-Clave."

Ignatio nodded. "Of course." He stood. "I think we're finished here," he said. "I'll send someone for you; they will escort you to your rooms."

Petronus watched him leave, then sipped the tea. It was orange—probably from the Outer Emerald Coasts—and touched with just a hint of honey.

He bit into a roll and chewed the sweet bread slowly. There were at least some benefits to being a guest at the hunting estate. The food was exceptional.

As he ate, Petronus pondered Ignatio's questions. He'd had a list and had worked his way down. Petronus had watched him as he did so. The spymaster had checked off each question meticulously and had gone through the entire stack.

How long did it take him to gather those questions?

Days, Petronus imagined.

He reached for the second breakfast roll and the door opened. Erlund had been a boy the last time he'd seen him—maybe eight or ten years old. Petronus wouldn't have known him now but for the guards that accompanied him and the way he walked.

Like someone with power. Petronus stood, though he did not want to.

Erlund waved him to sit, then sat himself. He nodded to the teapot. "Is this hot?"

Petronus nodded.

Erlund surprised him by pouring his own tea. Of course, the Overseer's presence here surprised him as well. Erlund sipped the tea, then put it down and folded his hands on the table. "If you had stayed put in your shack, old man, you'd still be there. Running your little bird-line and trying to assuage your guilt."

Petronus looked at him. He was younger than Rudolfo but already had lines in his face. *This one is not like his uncle,* he realized. He cared, and the civil war had worn him, aged him. Petronus thought about his shack, then thought about the blood-magicked attacker. "Staying was problematic," he said, "though turning myself over to you was certainly not my first consideration."

Erlund stared at him for a moment. He took another sip, then motioned for his men to leave him. They vanished quickly, pulling the door closed behind them as they went. The Overseer leaned forward. "Regardless," he said, "here you are, caught up in an internal matter of state with your very neck laid out upon the block." Erlund chuckled. "Of all people, *I* know Sethbert was mad. Certainly the Androfrancines were up to something, but Sethbert went too far and his conspiracy is well detailed. I would have never pursued your arrest for the events at his so-called trial. But now Entrolusian law comes into play, and I'm forced to give that law its place. You killed our Overseer without recourse and beyond the reach of our law." Petronus saw weariness in the man's eyes. "More than that," he said, "I know that this civil war has kept our attention at home while our neighbors slide into war with the Marshfolk. This girl-queen, Winteria, is not strong enough to hold the leash she's been handed." Here, he frowned. "I find it interesting that the strongest military in the Named Lands is enmeshed in insurrection while blood-magicked Marsh Scouts murder children in their sleep." He sipped the tea again. "I also know that Esarov forces my hand and that you are the pry-bar he uses. He gets legitimacy for his cities. I get my army back. Everyone wins . . . for now."

Petronus nodded. "I believe that is apparent to Esarov, as well. If all of this is true, why have I been awake all night with your man, Ignatio?"

Erlund lowered his teacup. "I thought the opportunity for a free flow of information between us would be useful."

Petronus scowled. "It was an interrogation. Largely regarding the mechoservitors and the other properties transferred into Rudolfo's care."

The Overseer smiled. "It could be seen that way." The smile faded quickly, and he leaned forward again. "But don't you find it interesting that the only House undivided and untouched—and beyond that, the only House to directly benefit from all of this—is the Ninefold Forest?"

Certainly, Petronus thought. He'd seen this as well, but in the case of the Androfrancine holdings it had been the only logical decision. But chewing on him behind those surface facts was another reality: He knew of a certainty that just as Vlad Li Tam had made his life's work shaping Rudolfo for this role, Vlad's father had done the same with Petronus. Their mastery of that work was evidenced by the truth of its outcome: From the outside eye, each step along the way that he or Rudolfo had taken appeared completely logical, completely reasonable, entirely compelling.

It was an application of Franci behavioral work that went deeper than even Petronus's grasp of those principles.

"I do see that," Petronus said, "but I also see the Gypsies at peace, working to rebuild what your uncle took from us all."

"I am suspicious of it," Erlund said in a low voice. "But," he said, "I've had my questions asked. You've exercised your right to decline them. Perhaps with time, you'll grow to trust me and the bonds my uncle severed will be retied."

Petronus didn't think so, but said nothing.

Erlund changed the subject. "Have you given much thought to your defense?"

"I have," Petronus said. "And according Entrolusian law I can call any able-bodied man or woman on the Delta to advocate on my behalf?"

Erlund nodded. "We've a list of advocates to choose from. If funding for your defense is at issue, it will be provided for."

Here Petronus smiled. "Actually, I already have an advocate." A cloud passed over Erlund's face. *He knows,* Petronus thought, but he said the name anyway. "Esarov will speak on my behalf."

There was anger, though controlled, in Erlund's voice. "That stage-prancing bugger is a criminal and a menace to the Delta."

"He is an able-bodied man, well versed in law," Petronus reminded him, "and not a criminal if you intend to honor the word you gave when you agreed to this present arrangement."

Erlund composed himself, but his eyes flashed. He stood up and he suddenly seemed more guarded, more formal. Petronus made note of it and realized he skirted the edge of something in Erlund that he might want to avoid. "Word will be sent," Erlund said. "Now if you'll excuse me, I've other matters to attend to."

After he'd gone, Petronus settled into waiting. He sat alone with his thoughts for the two hours it took them to come for him, and when they came, the guards escorted him to his suite of rooms in complete silence.

When they locked him inside, Petronus went straight to the large, rounded bed and fell into it.

He thought he would sleep instantly. But the questions of the night continued at his heels, and he looked for the pattern within them. Rudolfo had been the only one untouched in these recent attacks; he'd been the only one to benefit from the fall of Windwir, and his neighbors were taking notice.

Petronus did not for a moment believe the Gypsy King could be behind his own so-called good fortune, but it was obviously a part of House Li Tam's work in the Named Lands.

He thought of his boyhood and the summer he'd spent with Vlad Li Tam, teaching him the rugged life of a fishing family as part of the boy's training to someday take over House Li Tam. Even that arrangement, he now realized, was a part of Vlad's father's design.

"Perhaps," he mumbled, "even *this* is, too."

But to what end? He thought of the papers he'd passed to Rudolfo and willed that the Gypsy King would take up the work he'd started.

Then Petronus gave himself to sleep and for a few hours, let the questions slip from his grasping fingers.

Winters

The winter air over the Summer Papal Palace hung heavy with smoke, and Winters stood by the charred piles of bones and tried not to retch. She still could not believe what was happening.

They did not bury their dead. Instead, they paid them the greatest insult by stacking them like firewood and putting the torch to them.

Now, the soldiers worked against the weather, using pickaxes to hew out trenches for the burnt remains. It was just past morning now, and if they worked the rest of the day, they could give the Litany that night. Then, she would prepare her next War Sermon. She had never imagined it would be against a faction of her own people. But any rage she'd felt en route to this massacre paled in comparison to what she felt when first she smelled the cooking fires.

Winters heard footsteps behind her, then heard Seamus clear his voice. "We've a bird from the Gypsies," he said.

She looked up and over her shoulder. It would be Jin Li Tam. She'd had word that Lady Tam was on the march. It had surprised Winters—so soon after Jakob's birth. *The price of being a queen.* She forced her mind to the moment. "What does it say?"

"They ride for our southern reaches to parley with Meirov's rangers." Here, he laughed, though it was more of snort. "She wishes you to ride south and join them . . . without your army."

She turned to fully face him. "I intend to do as she asks," she said. "I mean to have the army to patrol our territories and find the source of this violence among our people. They will be within reach if I need them to the south."

She watched several emotions play across Seamus's face. Finally, he spoke carefully. "There is only one way to find this source. You do realize this."

She did not know that she did until he said so. Then, it struck her and her heart sank. "Yes," she said. "You must search for the mark. And start with the army."

He nodded, and she heard the sadness in his voice. "What will you do with those we find, my queen?"

He knows my answer.

She stared at him for a moment, then looked away. "I will deal with them, Seamus, as my father would have done and his father, before him." *By the axe.* The words tasted bitter in her mouth, yet she knew they were true. She would find within her the violence required. And perhaps that was how it was intended all along. Her dreams had turned bloody of late. Gone was the white-haired boy, Neb, and those few glimpses of the Home he would find them. Ezra's reedy voice, echoing across her bathing cavern, filled her sleep now instead. A wind of blood to purge; cold iron blades to prune.

Thus shall the sins of P'Andro Whym be visited upon his children.

She shook off the cold of that echoing voice and looked to Seamus. "Send a bird to the Gypsies. Let them know that I accept their gracious invitation."

Seamus nodded. She read unhappiness in his face; perhaps it was merely worry. "And will you lead the Litany tonight?"

She looked to the pile of charred bodies. She heard the steady ring of blades biting into the frozen ground. Overhead, a massive black bird circled alone, contrasted against skies that threatened more snow. "I will," she said. "It is my place to."

"One of the Twelve could stand in if you needed us to."

She looked to him. It *was* worry. She'd considered him a grandfather for as long as she had memory. He'd been close to her father and had even been mated to her father's sister for a short while before fever took her. "I need to do it, Seamus," she told him. "I need my army to see me do this."

A look of pride crossed his face. "You will be a strong queen."

She sighed and looked back to the bodies. "Lately, I do not feel so very strong."

His voice sounded suddenly like her father's—or Hanric's—and she felt the gooseflesh rising on her arms. "You do not need to feel it for it to be so."

She nodded. "Thank you, Seamus."

He returned the nod, studied her face for one last moment, and then turned. After he'd gone, she went back to studying the Androfrancine corpses.

She felt the wind upon the back of her neck and smelled something new on it. It was faintest hint of sweat and evergreen pitch.

It was an uncanny sense of presence, and she turned, feeling eyes upon her back. "Who's there?"

The voice reached her as barely a whisper. "Lieutenant Adrys of the Ninefold Forest," he said. "I've brought a company of Gypsy Scouts to your aid by Lady Tam's order. We're here quietly, of course."

She squinted. Just barely visible, standing in Seamus's tracks, crouched a shadowy form. "I will tell my captains; we wouldn't want anything unfortunate to occur with our scouts in such close proximity to yours."

He chuckled. "Forgive me, Lady Winters, but my men will not be found unless they wish to be. We think remaining discreetly invisible to your people is a better strategy given the"—here he paused to search for the best work—"*internal nature* of your foe."

She bit her lip. He was correct, certainly, though she could not bear giving consent for these Gypsy spies to run magicked and secretly among her people. "Anything you can learn will be greatly appreciated." Here she paused. Should she tell him what she knew and feared? What licked at the corners of her awareness ever since the day Seamus had shown her the mark upon his grandson? She forced herself to speak it. "I'm convinced it is some kind of Y'Zirite resurgence."

He paused. "Are you certain?"

There had only been a few resurgences over the years. They'd ended badly beneath the boot heels of the Androfrancines or whatever watchdog they'd turned loose upon them, but they left their own wounds before fading back into history where they belonged. Tertius had covered them in detail during her lessons. The cutting was new, though. "Yes," she said. "I'm certain. They bear the mark of House Y'Zir."

She heard his indrawn breath despite the magicks that muffled it. "I will pass that word along to Lady Tam," he said. "Meanwhile, we are tracking those responsible for this attack. I will dispatch word to you through one of my men should we learn anything."

She inclined her head. "Thank you, Lieutenant." She waited, wondering if she should ask the question that haunted her. She felt a slight wind as the shadow turned away, and she called out after him, her voice more thick with emotion than she wanted it to be. "Has there been any word from the expedition to the Wastes?"

She felt his hesitation. "That is a Ninefold Forest military venture, Lady Winters, that I am not at liberty to discuss."

She closed her eyes. "You're absolutely correct. My apologies, Lieutenant."

The voice softened. "Rumor has it that you and the boy, Neb, are sweet for each other."

She blushed and said nothing.

"We're doing our best to find him. Aedric is seeing to it himself."

She felt her stomach lurch, and the world tipped as the words sank farther into her. *To find him.* "Is he lost?" Now, that heavy emotion was a desperate whisper.

But the Gypsy Scout had already slipped away, leaving her alone with the sense of dread that grew, a dark and cold seed, within her.

The black bird she'd spied earlier shrieked suddenly, and to Winters, it sounded like laughter in that stormy sky.

Jin Li Tam

Jin Li Tam fought her queasy stomach and kept herself low in the saddle. She'd completely underestimated the impact of Jakob's powders on her sense of balance and movement. The horse threatened the light lunch they'd taken an hour earlier.

Somewhere behind her, Lynnae fared no better. She rode with Jakob now in the carriage, a company of Rudolfo's most decorated Gypsy Scouts assigned to their protection. It was her turn with Jakob, though by rights, she'd been taking longer shifts to accommodate Jin's meeting schedule with the captains of the Wandering Army.

Still, it was good to be on horseback again, to feel the cold wind on her face and the solidness of the horse beneath her. The sounds and smells of an army on the march had filled her ears and nose the last several days after rallying in the foothills that ringed the Ninefold Forest. And the nights spent huddled for warmth in the wagon with Jakob and Lynnae awakened something within her that had slept for what seemed so long now.

How long had it been? She thought perhaps it was the time she and Rudolfo had toured the other eight houses, introducing her to the stewards and people in each of those major towns that had sprung to life where Rudolfo's family had built their manors. Before that, it had surely been the war.

She heard a fluttering and a thud to her right. She looked over to see a small brown bird caught in the Second Captain's catch net. Philemus reached down with gloved fingers to pick the bird out and pull a knotted string from its tiny foot. Pulling off the glove, he felt the raised bumps along the string and passed it to Jin. She read it quickly with her fingers.

It's started ahead. She looked up, eyes squinting into the gray, overcast day. Somewhere, ahead of them, the fighting had begun. They'd been monitoring the progress of Pylos and Turam's armies with their forward scouts as those southern forces approached the Marshlands, and yesterday, the rangers of Pylos had crossed into Marsher territory or the band of wilderness that commonly passed as the unmanned border, just ahead of their army.

But who do they fight? The Marsh army patrolled the far north, looking for answers to the destruction of the Summer Papal Palace and the brutal murder of the Androfrancines hidden there.

Before Philemus could release the bird, another, this one white, also dropped into the net. She knew that this one meant stop and the Second Captain read the knot codes even as she raised her hand to order a halt.

"Someone approaches," he said. "A lone Marsher on horseback. He wishes to parley with you." The officer looked to her, his eyes worried. "Alone," he added.

She continued scanning the landscape around them. They'd forded the Second River two days behind them, far north of Windwir's ruins. In another three or four days, if she pushed them, they would ford the Third River and be within reach of their objective. She'd hoped to plant herself and her army along that southern Marsher boundary. But she'd also hoped—irrationally to be sure—that she could prevent the fighting from breaking out. That somehow, she could appeal to reason if she and the Wandering Army blocked Pylos and Turam's forces from moving further north.

Still, when she thought of Meirov's lost child and of Turam's lost crown prince, she wasn't certain there was any reason for her to appeal to. The rage brewed by those cowardly acts would surely be stronger than her ability to encourage higher thinking.

The army slowed to a halt behind her and she waited, her horse prancing to and fro along the frozen ground. Finally, a form took place in the gathering fog ahead. She squinted at it until it became a man on horseback—an old man upon an old horse.

"Set up a perimeter of scouts," she said in a voice sharper than she meant to.

"Shall I accompany you to—"

"No," she said as she spurred her horse forward.

She trotted the horse forward until the old man came into focus before her. He wore tattered robes made of fur—wolf, she thought, from first glance. He had bits of bone and wood woven into his carefully braided beard and hair, and his face, though painted in the custom of a Marsher, held more intricate designs than what she'd seen of others. The earth tones were painted on in an interlocking pattern of black, gray, green and brown.

He sat high in the saddle, his head moving to the left and right as if he listened and smelled for something. As she approached, he turned to face her and she saw that his eyes were the color of milk.

A blind man sent to parley.

He bent his head to the side. "Great Mother," he said, "you should not be here."

She remembered the cryptic note that bore the same title. She'd pondered it for hours, even had it with her in her pouch. Was it possible that this man knew something about her father, somehow? Her eyes narrowed. "Why do you call me that? And who are you?"

The old man smiled. "I am Ezra. I am herald to the soon-coming Macht Queen and prophet of the Crimson Empress."

More riddles. And she'd heard of the Crimson Empress before. But where? "Winters has not spoken to me of you."

He chuckled. "She did not know of me herself until recently." He looked up, then cocked his head again. "You come with your army, but what do you hope to accomplish? You are ill from caring for your son. You are weakened still from his birth. You should be resting, not mounting a war against a foe you cannot see." His face softened, and a smile broke out upon it. "Still," he said, "I had not hoped to live long enough to see this day. I would ask a great favor of you, Lady."

Her eyes narrowed. She could not see them, but there were scouts surrounding them now. One whistle and a dozen arrows or two dozen blades would bring him down. "What favor do you ask, old man?"

She saw tears coursing down his face from his milky eyes. "That I might hold the Child of Promise within my arms and speak my blessing over him."

Jin Li Tam's response surprised her. She felt the hair rising on her arms and neck and felt something cold grip her stomach. "You are already privy to the matters of my household, it appears," she said. "You know that my son is ill."

"Perhaps," he said, "the blessing would do him good."

Jin Li Tam shook her head slowly. "I do not know you, Ezra. You shall not go near my son." She felt heat rising in her now—a righteous anger.

He sighed. "I could whistle now and have him brought to me," he said. "But I will instead hope for another time."

I could whistle now. She filed the veiled threat away for consideration later. "You are not alone then?"

His laughter was sharp. "I am an old, blind man. It would be foolishness for me to ride alone."

She scrutinized the ground around his feet. He'd trampled the snow well enough that she could not see the footprints of whatever magicked escort accompanied him. But she did not need to see it to know these Marshers were blood-magicked. She thought of the scouts surrounding them, and the others that minded the carriage with Jakob and Lynnae inside somewhere closer to the middle of the army that stretched behind her. "Apart from my son and your concern for my physical health," she said in a low, intentional voice, "what matter do you bring by way of parley?"

"Only this," he said. "We intend to honor our kin-clave with the Gypsy King. Our houses have much work to do, together, in shaping the Named Lands for the new Age that dawns upon us."

She tried to sort and categorize the data she pulled from his words, but it became lost in a sea of questions she knew she did not have the time to ask. "Our kin-clave," she said slowly, "is with Queen Winteria . . . not with you."

"Kin-clave," he said, "runs deeper and wider than you can know from this place, Great Mother."

"And because of it, you wish me to turn my army back homeward?"

He nodded. "I do; though I doubt you shall."

Her eyes narrowed. "You are correct. I intend to honor my kin-clave with your queen and with her neighbors to the south. I go to bid peace among them."

Ezra smiled. "And you may attain something akin to it," he said, "but it cannot last. These are the pains of childbirth, the pains of something *made*." He paused to regard her, and in that moment she could have sworn he could see her. His stare penetrated. "You are a part of this great making. As is your husband. And Jakob—he is most highly favored among men."

She scowled at his words. There was a rhythm to his language that struck a familiar chord deep within, and she suddenly realized what it was.

The dreams. The voice was different, but the cadence remained the same, and she looked up and around her quickly to confirm her sudden suspicion.

Perched high in an evergreen, an enormous black bird—a kin-raven, she suddenly knew—watched them with a solitary black eye.

"Go cautiously, Great Mother," Ezra was now saying as he turned his horse around. "The kin-clave of House Y'Zir and his servants is no small thing to trifle with." Here his eyes narrowed, and blind or no, she was convinced he saw her. "Neither is that blessing a thing to spurn so recklessly, for someday it will save your son, and he will, in turn, save us all."

She sat stunned and blinking. She'd certainly had her suspicions. She'd seen the intelligence reports on the dead scouts; she'd read her history and knew well that the resurgences stubbornly resurrected themselves, particularly during times of great distress and trauma in the Named Lands. Certainly, now was one of those times.

But to hear the words and to know that her family was so centrally woven into whatever belief this old man carried mixed a different kind of fear into the brew that bubbled deep in her stomach. She wanted to shout after him, to demand answers and if need be, to whistle down the Gypsy Scouts upon him and take him back to the interrogator's wagon and the single Physician of Penitent Torture she'd brought out of forced retirement to assist them if needed.

And at the same time, she wanted to turn her horse, gallop for her son, and hide him within her embrace. Somehow keep him from the madness that seemed to unravel the world he would inherit.

But Jin Li Tam did neither. Instead, she sat upon her horse and watched Ezra the Marsh Prophet disappear into the gathering mist.

When she looked back to the kin-raven, she saw now that it had vanished, too.

If, she realized, it had ever been there at all.

Summoning up courage for her voice, Jin Li Tam called for the Wandering Army to resume its march. And for the rest of that day, she rode in silence and wondered what she would find awaiting her in the Marshlands.

Chapter 18

Rae Li Tam

Rae Li Tam stood at the bow and watched the sun rise ahead, casting red and tenuous light over the eastern horizon. Somewhere to the north—her port side—the Divided Isle marked the southernmost territories of the Named Lands. Behind them and farther south lay the island chains they'd so recently fled once she'd received that fateful bird indicating disaster for half their fleet.

She was no closer now, weeks later, to sorting it out. But there had been no further word sent after them, and she had no reason to believe there ever would be.

At this point, how would they find us? At sea, even six iron ships were moths in a forest. The only way to have found them before would've been to follow their trail from island to island, and even that would have required a great deal of guesswork. Back then they'd been careful.

But now a different layer of caution applied. They'd made no stops where watching eyes might find them. They'd stopped to replenish the water tanks the one time they'd gotten dangerously low. It had been a remote and midnight isle, with the steampumps pulling the water in through a series of leaking hoses they had no time to repair. They'd dropped nets and pulled fish to supplement their diets and fell back to rationing to see them through to their new destination.

Even so, fever had taken one ship. Quarantined, it limped behind them as the sickness burned its way through its families and crew. Another had dropped to one-third its speed, and the engineers were uncertain why.

Still, considering how much *could* go wrong, Rae Li Tam was pleased.

Now, a new day dawned and she gave herself to it, closing her eyes and letting the cold wind pull at her robes and her hair, feeling it move over her face.

She felt Baryk's hands slide around her, and she leaned back into him, sighing. "We've made good time," he said. "Have you thought more about what we'll do when we get there?"

She leaned her head back into his chest and turned her head slightly so she could see his face. "I don't know what we'll do. I'm sure Father knew what he was about, but he didn't share that strategy with me." She looked back out over the water and the bloodred sun that rose over it. "I'm disinclined to keep the family at sea at this point until we understand better what is happening."

"And you still believe your father was lured off to a trap?"

She nodded. "How could I not? Six ships lost in less than a week. And the note. If it was a forgery, it was better than anything I could've done." And at one time, she'd been her father's best forger.

There was a whistle from the pilothouse and she looked up. She saw the pilot pointing south and followed his finger until her eyes settled on a speck just barely visible in the sun's rising light.

She turned and Baryk turned with her, releasing her as he did. She went to the rail and leaned on it, squinting out into morning.

"It's a ship," Baryk said.

She could see it more clearly now. It rode high in the water, boxlike in its shape. She saw the gout of steam from its stack and felt her stomach tighten. "It's one of ours," she said, her brow furrowing. "How is that possible?"

Baryk straightened. "I'll bring us to Third Alarm," he said. "And I'll get birds to the other vessels."

She nodded. "I'll be in the pilothouse."

She crossed the deck at a brisk walk and climbed the narrow steps into the cabin. The officer of the deck, a young redheaded woman, passed her the telescope before she asked for it, and she sighted in on the ship.

Not just a ship, she realized, *but the flagship.*

It flew distress flags in eight colors and moved on a course that would intercept them within the hour. And though she saw movement on the deck, it was impossible to pick out any of the individuals from this distance.

They knew where we would be. But how? The bird coops were locked, and she trusted those who guarded them. Yet somehow, they'd been found.

Light flashed from its bow and for a moment, blinded her. She looked away, then shifted the telescope so that it was slightly to the left of center. The flashes formed words.

Father has been taken by deceit and we have wounded aboard, the flashing mirror told her. *We need immediate assistance.*

She held her breath for a moment, then swept the ship again with the telescope. She glanced to the officer beside her. "Fetch the mirror," she said. "Send this: Shut down your engines and drop anchor."

She waited while the girl sent the message. But the light did not answer. Instead, the ship began to slow. Meanwhile, the bell for Third Alarm jangled in the quiet morning as men and women swept the deck and took up stations. She heard Baryk shouting over the noise as he and the master-at-arms distributed bows among them. A lone cannoneer loaded the ship's single gun and spun it toward the slowing vessel. The Androfrancines had been stingy in their mechanical knowledge when it came to weaponry, carefully keeping back what they could and tightly controlling what they couldn't. The flagship had three of the small weapons, but the others were limited to just one apiece. It had been enough, in those gray-robed minds, to give House Li Tam far more of an edge when combined with the iron hulls and steam engines.

"Decrease speed to half," she said. "Birds to the fleet: Maintain Third Alarm." She felt the scowl on her face as something hard settled in her stomach. She swept the deck of the flagship again, noting the saffron robes of her father's House among its crew, and knew that soon she would have to make a decision; and though the numbers were on her side, she hesitated.

It was a trap, she realized. It simply had to be.

But what if it wasn't?

She whistled for Baryk and he joined her. She passed the telescope to him. "I've ordered them to shut down their engines. They've complied. They're claiming Father was taken by deceit, that they've wounded aboard."

Her husband looked them over, then handed the spyglass back to her. "I don't trust it," he said.

She nodded slowly. "I concur. Strategy?"

She knew his greater strength as a warpriest lay with tactics and strategy by land, but Baryk was also a capable sailor and had had seven months to become familiar with exactly what her father's ships could do. "Bring the *Wind of Dawn* and the *Spirit of Amal* in closer. Keep the rest of us around those two slower vessels, fore and aft, port and starboard." He looked at her, his eyes showing concern. "Maintain half speed in a wide circle for now; we can send a longboat to investigate their claims."

She nodded. It was sound thinking. She gave the orders and then lifted the spyglass again. The flagship had stopped and its anchor lines were out, but a sense of foreboding fluttered in her stomach. The ship, supposedly lost, now sat at anchor, and she found herself wondering about their message.

Father has been taken by deceit. Of all men, Vlad Li Tam was the least likely to be deceived in any way. The notion that he'd been caught in someone's net normally would not cipher for her.

Except.

She swallowed the fear that suddenly tasted like iron in her mouth. They *had* left the Named Lands quickly. He'd pulled down his network, bundled all but his forty-second daughter into the iron ships, and fled in search of someone. They'd not spoken frankly of it, but she'd suspected for a time that somehow, their family had been compromised in their work to bring about intentional, carefully crafted change in the New World. Otherwise, why flee with the entire family? Certainly, her father could have sent his ships out in search of this invisible foe he suspected *without* bringing the entire House.

Beyond that, this message today clearly supported her belief that her father had been lured out of the Named Lands, he and his spider's web of children and children's children, for some dark purpose. They'd been out of touch with the Named Lands for months now, and in this moment, she found herself wondering if that wasn't part of some larger strategy as well. Perhaps separating House Li Tam from the Named Lands served more than one purpose. It culled them out from potential allies, leaving them alone and far from home; it left the Named Lands without her father's eyes and ears, and worse, without his strategic influence.

In the absence of light, P'Andro Whym had asserted in his twelfth gospel, *walk slow and with measured step into that waiting darkness.*

Yes, she thought. She would walk slow into this with her eyes and ears open.

Scowling once more at the flagship where it waited, Rae Li Tam handed the spyglass to her husband. She turned and looked north toward the Named Lands. "We've been silent for too long," she said beneath her breath. Then, louder: "Have the birder meet me in my cabin."

He nodded, and she left the pilothouse. She had much to do. First, a note to her sister and her betrothed in the Ninefold Forest. Second, a coded message to whomever now captained her father's flagship.

After which, she would have to make a decision.

She glanced once more to the vessel where it lay at anchor and wondered again where it had come from after so long away.

Rudolfo

The taste of the powders were still bitter in his mouth when Rudolfo joined Rafe Merrique at the helm of the *Kinshark*. Most of his life, he'd used the magicks to hide his men but not himself. It was unseemly for a noble to do otherwise. Yet in the last year he'd used the magicks more and more, though each time it went against the grain of his heritage. Worse, it went against his father's teaching. Still, it had to be done. Two hours ago, birds had been sighted from the south, moving northeast beneath the new-risen sun—a larger, darker bird in fast pursuit.

And now, all hands had been called, and an out-of-breath sailor had fetched him topside at the captain's order.

He'd hoped, at least, that the headaches and nausea, the uneasy twitch of over-ready muscles, would subside with more exposure to the white dust. So far, that was not the case.

He moved slowly, not as surefooted as Merrique and his men, and the rocking of the ship and the movement of the waves all around him wreaked its disaster on his stomach. The magicked ship was a wonder to be certain, but one that cost him every time he left the relative normalcy below the deck.

He clicked his tongue to the roof of his mouth and heard the answering clicks of the crew around him as he made his way to the bridge. Steady hands aided him as his feet found the narrow stairs. He felt something cold and metal pushed into his hands.

"It's a telescope," Rafe Merrique said. He felt the captain's hands on his shoulder, turning him in a direction. "Look dead ahead."

Rudolfo raised the glass to his eye and watched the ocean surge at him. He raised it higher, caught the horizon, and scanned it. The iron ships were not easy to miss.

Rudolfo sucked in his breath at the sight of them. He'd tossed and turned through four sleepless nights after his decision to pursue Sanctorum Lux. He'd known it was the best path left to him, but it haunted him. He prided himself on the inner compass his father had gifted him with—confidence in the right direction to take at any point in time. But how to choose the best of two courses of action where neither offered any reasonable assurance of success? And now, having placed his hope in Charles's knowledge of another unlikely path, he found himself confronting Vlad Li Tam's iron armada.

He counted the ships—a slow moving circle of six with one anchored in the center.

Rudolfo realized he was holding his breath and released it. "It's Tam's fleet." But just more than half of it, he realized.

"Aye," Rafe Merrique answered. "One flies a flag of quarantine. And the one in the center flies colors of distress."

The anchored ship was sleeker and slightly smaller than the others, suggesting that it might be the flagship. Rudolfo couldn't be certain, but it was as good a place as any to start. "I need to speak with them."

He heard wariness in Rafe's voice. "The six are at Third Alarm," he said. "They've manned their guns—better than the one the Androfrancines granted me, I'll wager—and they've longboats in the water under colors of parley. I'll not put the *Kinshark* in cannon range. We wait and watch."

Rudolfo opened his mouth to protest, but a muffled boom— followed quickly by another—closed it. He saw smoke and panned the spyglass until he found the source of it—the pilothouse of the quarantined vessel had collapsed in a ruin of bent metal, smoke and flames. It veered off course toward the open sea. And this time, Rudolfo saw a flash and gout of smoke from a seemingly empty patch of sea in a close-range broadside shot that opened a tear in the hull at the vessel's waterline. "They're under fire."

Rafe Merrique snatched the telescope from his hands. "Under fire?"

Rudolfo had spent little time at sea, but he knew full well how jealously the Androfrancines guarded the ancient war-making knowledge. He'd seen firsthand what it could do—losing a Gypsy Scout to Resolute's hand cannon in the last war. The very hand cannon that false Pope had used to end his life. These cannons were far larger, and Rudolfo had seen them only on Tam's iron armada and Merrique's *Kinshark*.

But who else?

More explosions drifted across the whitecapped morning sea. "It's an ambush," Rafe Merrique said incredulously.

Rudolfo squinted ahead. He now could just make out the ships as the *Kinshark* made its careful approach. "How is an ambush possible on the open sea?" But even as he said it, he knew the answer. They weren't the only magicked vessel in the water. At least two more attacked Vlad Li Tam's iron armada—magicked and armed with bits of so-called Androfrancine light.

He heard Rafe Merrique exhale suddenly. "They're being boarded." Then, his voice rose. "Take us in slow; keep us hidden and out of range." He passed the glass to Rudolfo's hands.

Raising it to his eye, he watched as an invisible blade cut through a crowd of armed men in saffron robes. He watched as groups of three or four of Tam's household tried to bring down even one of the boarders and suddenly, he was in his own banquet hall, his nose filled with blood and sweat and his ears full of shouting and screaming as the hurricane of assassins slashed through them to take Hanric and Ansylus.

He watched the decks cleared and watched as children were herded onto the deck by invisible soldiers. It stirred something in him, and Jakob's face flashed across his inner eye. He loathed Tam, and yet he remembered also the tear he'd seen on that day at the bonfire, when he'd confronted his father-in-law about the murder of his brother and his parents. He'd told him that day that if he ever had a child, he'd not use him as a game piece. And yet, he did not doubt that Tam loved his children in some way—even the ones he sacrificed so readily in service to his strategic cause.

And now, Rudolfo watched as the youngest of those children—grandchildren or great-grandchildren more likely, he supposed—were rounded up upon the forecastle, on display for the others to see.

A voice blasted out across the waters. "Surrender," it said. It made no threat and did not utter another word. The force of the word, even at ten leagues, was enough to raise Rudolfo's hair.

He scanned quickly and saw two other vessels with children crowded in the upper decks, terror and blood upon their faces.

"We have to do something," he said.

"We are," Rafe Merrique said. "We're watching and waiting. We're one wooden vessel, Rudolfo, with no real sense of the odds."

Rudolfo handed the telescope over to Merrique. "I don't think we'll wait long," he said in a quiet voice.

And they didn't. Two of the vessels tried to pull out of the circle but found themselves fired upon. And now, in the flashes of light and gouts of smoke, they were close enough that Rudolfo could see the dim outline from one of the large, magicked vessels that surrounded the circling ships and the deep rent in the waters from the invisible craft's displacement.

They were too far away to be certain, but to Rudolfo's eye, based on its size, the attacking ship could easily be another of Tam's iron vessels.

The realization struck him. "They've been divided," he said.

And even as he said it, he watched the colors lower on all but the flagship. Their engines slowed, and the remains of Vlad Li Tam's iron armada scattered into a loose formation with the flagship at its head. When Rafe passed back the telescope, Rudolfo scanned the waters and saw that the longboats were gone now, brought in during the fighting. Men and women wearing loose silks lined the decks under invisible guard. On three of the ships, white-faced and wide-eyed young men and women heaved the bodies of their fallen parents over the railing and into the sea.

"We've another choice to make now," Rafe said. "We are less than four days from the horn. Nine from where your Charles tells us is the best landfall to reach his Sanctorum Lux." Rudolfo heard the pirate's words, but his eyes still swept the scene ahead. Two of the ships limped and smoked now. Two of the others were sinking slowly, their crews lined up upon the deck as their longboats were lowered. The captain continued. "We either press on for the Wastes or—"

Rudolfo sighed. "We follow them."

His first instinct had been to find Tam. Jin Li Tam was a fierce, formidable woman, and she had believed her sister would know how to counter the powders she'd used to give Rudolfo's soldiers back their swords. The near impossibility of the task had truly not entered into the matter.

But the promise of this new library—the hope he held that it of-

fered a cure for his son—had crept upon him unawares when seren-
dipity had brought Charles across his path. And though now they
appeared to have found Tam, they had done so under alarming circumstances. He'd not needed to decode Petronus's notes to grasp that
the old Pope—along with the Order he once served—believed some
external force threatened them. Tam had believed it, it seemed, and
fled the Named Lands to investigate. And now, House Li Tam had
been divided or had somehow lost nearly half its fleet into unknown
hands. Unknown hands with access to the same blood magicks that
had torn through the Named Lands just weeks ago and the same stealth
magicks that until now had made the *Kinshark* one of a kind.

Yes, he thought, *another choice.*

But was it really? The compass within him pointed squarely in one
direction, and it frightened him how easily he read it, knowing full
well the cost and risk. In the end it wasn't really a choice at all, he realized.

He felt his jawline tightening with resolve even as he spoke the
words again.

"We follow them," Rudolfo said, and this time his voice was firm
and commanding.

Then he returned belowdecks to sharpen his knives and ponder
what they might find at the heart of this newest Whymer Maze.

Neb

Days blurred past Neb, his waking hours filled with the smell of burnt
earth and stone and the steady sound of his feet slapping ground in an
endless race across the Wastes. The nights were shorter now as they
tried to make up distance, sleeping for a handful of hours and running before the sun rose. The landscape and the full moon seemed to
accommodate them, but Neb secretly wondered if he was simply getting good enough at running the uneven terrain that Renard's concerns about the dark were lessening. He had no doubt that the lean
Waster had run plenty of moonless nights in times past.

Regardless, they ran more and his muscles no longer ached from it.
The farther in they ran, the warmer the climate grew until he was
peeling away layers of clothing and letting the sun bake his skin to a
dirty bronze color.

They'd turned south from Rufello's Cave, running until they were within sight of the expansive salt dunes that marked the southern-most shore. Then, they cut east and continued on Isaak's trail.

During the days, they ran in silence unless Renard pointed out something of note along the way. At night, exhausted from the run, they ate whatever Renard found on the hunt, if there was wood for a fire. If not, they went without meat and relied upon their scout rations. Neb took advantage of the time to watch and study. He'd already learned where to find pockets of bitter water hidden beneath the veneer of desolation and had learned a half dozen ways to extract it and treat it to strip any madness or disease from it. He'd learned where to find bits of root and bramble that could sustain him and how to harvest the black root they chewed throughout the day should he find himself stranded and out of the powerful earth magick.

And he realized he learned differently now. What had once been best passed to him through books, Neb now easily retained just from watching it done. He wasn't sure why, but the Waste called strength out in him that he'd never experienced before. His mind was focused, clear and calm. His body felt like a lute coming into tune, and his sleep, dreamless and deep, was more restful than any he'd ever known.

This place is changing me, and I like what I am becoming. He felt the truth of the thought. Yet, in the corner of his heart, he remembered Winters and it wrenched him.

They ran and ran, and on the fourth night since they left Rufello's Cave, they stopped at the edge of a chasm that, according to Renard, divided the continent. Nightfall had already swallowed the deep canyon, but looking south from the edge of it, Neb saw what he thought might be the wide and dangerous sea east of the horn—haunted waters the first settlers referred to as the Ghosting Crests. Neb had heard tell of secret Androfrancine-financed voyages around the horn, but these were largely apocryphal. Though reason dictated that such a crossing was possible, history was replete with tales of vessels lost in those waters to the ghosts that swam them.

Renard turned north, and Neb followed him. By the time the sun vanished entirely and the moon rose, they reached a high, arching bridge that spanned the gap. Blue and green light reflected from it.

They slowed and stopped at the base of it.

"It's said that one of the Younger Gods was awakened by Y'Zir's spell when it broke the world open again. They say he placed this bridge to aid those few survivors that they might find their way west." His voice deepened to nearly a growl. "At least until the Androfrancines manned the Wall and stopped the gate shut but for their own interests."

It was the first time Neb had heard bitterness in the man's voice. He noted it but said nothing. Instead, he nodded to the bridge ahead. "How long ago did they pass this way?"

Renard smiled. "Hours . . . if that. We're close again."

Neb nodded, and they set out at a run. They'd crested the apex of the bridge when they heard strange sounds from the east and below. They slowed, and Renard brought out his thorn rifle, walking a few paces ahead of Neb. As they drew closer to the noise, they saw the dim amber glow of glass eyes fluttering below them and heard the wheezing of bellows. Reedy, metallic voices met their ears.

"You must listen to reason, Cousin, and turn back with your colleagues now," the first voice said. "You are not authorized to travel beyond this geographical point. Message follows: Under holy unction I declare the lands beyond D'Anjite's Bridge closed, under seal and signet, Introspect III, Holy See of the Androfrancine Order and Seated King of Windwir." The voice was flat and matter-of-fact.

Neb blinked into the darkness and saw their dim outlines at the far edge of the bridge. The moonlight wasn't such that he could pick them out easily, but it was obvious that the fleeing metal man fled no more. Feet planted firmly on the far side of the chasm, it stood and faced Isaak where he stood upon the last of the bridge.

Neb and Renard crouched on the bridge. He felt the night wind move over the back of his neck, raising gooseflesh.

Isaak's voice was calm and measured. "Pope Introspect is no longer in power. The Order returned to Pope Petronus's care when Windwir fell—before its eventual dissolution seven months, two weeks and three days ago."

"That is not possible; Pope Petronus is dead. Without a countermanding order from Introspect or his named successor, I may not let you pass."

Neb didn't realize he was rising to his feet until he felt Renard's hand clamp onto his arm. He shrugged it away, suddenly sure of himself. He raised his own voice. "Petronus is not dead; I declared him myself on the plains of Windwir. You yourself claimed to bear him a message. The holdings of the Order have been passed to the Ninefold Forest—*all* holdings—including the Order's mechanicals." He took another step forward, willing authority in his voice, reaching back to the brief months he'd commanded the gravediggers' army. "I am an

officer of the Ninefold Forest Houses and the Great Library recon-
structed therein." More steps now. "I order you to escort us to Sanctorum Lux immediately that the holdings may be cataloged for the new
library."

He wasn't sure what he expected, but it wasn't what happened
next. The metal man's eyes fluttered open and closed, its mouth flap
working as steam whistled out suddenly from the exhaust grate in its
back.

And then, the metal man laughed.

It was a loud, long, wheezing laugh that rolled up and down the
canyon, haunting the night with its eerie, metallic sound. "Nebios ben
Hebda," it said, "you are early for your time here. Do not be so eager
for the gift you cannot give back."

Gift you cannot give back. It was from the first Gospel of P'Andro
Whym, and he conjured the words up from the bottom of his memory.

> *And it came to pass on the night of the Purging that P'Andro Whym wept*
> *with his closest lieutenants for the work that they had done and turned his*
> *eyes upon them and said unto them "Behold our duty to the light is this*
> *night begun, and it shall be a gift that cannot be given back and the last*
> *path we shall follow in this land.*

Neb's eyes narrowed. "You speak of duty to the light; we do not
choose it. We are called to it." He stepped farther forward. "Isaak, are
you well?"

Isaak turned and nodded. "I am well, Nebios. My chassis and bellows are in need of cleaning."

Neb returned his attention to the other mechoservitor. "You tell
me I am early," he said. "How do you know this?"

The mechoservitor blinked. "Because we are not ready, Nebios ben
Hebda. Neither are you."

Neb thought about this. He was aware of his bladder suddenly feeling full, of his feet suddenly feeling like flying him back, away from
the confrontation he walked to. "You tell me I am early but you do not
tell me I am unauthorized."

The metal man whistled and bleated as a shudder rattled its armor-
plated body. "You are authorized."

Neb wasn't certain where he found the words—perhaps from some
corner of a forgotten dream—but he spoke now. And he spoke loud

and clear: "If I am authorized, I abjure you, mechoservitor, to escort me to Sanctorum Lux."

The mouth flap opened and closed again. Its head turned slowly. "Your companions are unauthorized."

Neb swallowed. He thought about the Waste Guide behind him and Isaak before him. "Then my companions shall not accompany me."

The metal man nodded and then moved with blurring speed. Its foot shot out, catching the knee joint in Isaak's damaged leg and driving it back until Neb heard a plain, metallic crunch. As Isaak toppled over to the ground, the metal man leapt past Neb into the dark.

Neb turned and shouted. "No!"

He heard Renard gasping, heard the sound of scrambling and then a cracking sound—the sound of a bone breaking as Renard cried out.

Then, before he could open his mouth again, he felt metal hands scooping him up to toss him roughly across square steel shoulders. He felt a hand at his throat, applying gentle but firm pressure. "Remain still and do not struggle, Nebios Homeseeker, and I will bear you well and swiftly."

The hand at his throat squeezed, and the night grew foggy as spiderwebs of light traced the corners of his vision. He was dimly aware of Isaak clawing and crawling toward them, his leg now useless and bent back behind him. He heard Renard panting in pain in the deeper shadows of the bridge.

And last, he was aware of the tick and grind of machinery within the metal man who bore him as they lurched across the ground to climb the high hills beyond the Younger God's bridge. With his head pressed to the metal shoulder he wondered what manner of heart the Androfrancines had given their machines.

More pressure yet from the metal hand, and Neb felt his grip slide as unconsciousness took him and carried him into a gray and lonely place.

Chapter 19

Jin Li Tam

Melting snow made for muddy grass, and Jin Li Tam stepped carefully as she held Jakob to her breast. With the small blanket covering her exposed skin, she didn't feel much of the cold, and she hoped it was the same for her son. Still, they wouldn't be here long. The tents were heated, but she'd suddenly craved the cool air and her feet had needed pacing ground.

No, she realized. It was more than a craving.

She'd *needed* it; the tent had pressed in upon her after the birder left, and she'd needed in that moment to be outside and close to her son. Colder air and open space to find focus and stop the world from spinning.

They had arrived just a few hours before, and already the tents were in place and the smells of the cooking meat and wood smoke were in the air. Scout patrols now made their wide-ranging circles, and the various companies of the Wandering Army took up their places on the perimeter.

Soon, she would have to give Jakob over to Lynnae and ride to parley with Pylos and Turam. She had exchanged birds with Meirov herself just that morning but had not recognized the name of the general who led Turam's battalion. The first skirmishes had gone badly for both armies; their attackers—small in number they later found—had defied all reason and had pressed on through their ranks until eventually they had fallen.

But those iron blades cut deep, and that wind of blood had howled until they fell and the astounded officers from the two neighboring nations took stock of their dead.

Now, reinforcements had been summoned for a further push north and were perhaps half a week away.

All of this was worrisome. But now she'd word from the Gate that Aedric and his company had ridden into the Wastes in search of Neb and Isaak. The greatest weapon in the world was lost to them.

And on the heels of *that* bird, the next: Rudolfo was sailing around the horn, suddenly convinced by an old Androfrancine that a cure for Jakob was more likely found in this so-called Sanctorum Lux than in the seemingly impossible task of finding her father's fleet.

But the last one—delivered just this morning—was the one that finally staggered her and made the canvas walls of her tent press in upon her, sending her into the winter air with her son clutched close. Rae Li Tam's coded message had found her—updating Jin Li Tam on all that had transpired for them at sea so far and calling for aid from the Ninefold Forest Houses if such a thing were possible. Even now a response—with pledged support of undefined specificity—winged its way back with Jin Li Tam's query buried into it: *My son is sick from the birth powders; can you cure him?*

It should have been relief, she thought. But in that moment, hope *changed*. She didn't know how to describe it. It became different inside her—a gnawing thing. And something that kept fear as its constant companion alongside of it.

"Lady Tam?"

The soft voice startled her and she looked up. A young woman in mismatched armor and sad eyes stood before her, her tangled brown hair capped with a helm that was too large and a massive silver battle-axe in her muddy hands. Her face was streaked with ash and dirt. Two Gypsy Scouts accompanied her.

Jin Li Tam blinked. *She's changed in such a short time.* "Winters?"

Winters curtsied. "It is good to see you."

The young girl's eyes were the most different. Beyond the sadness, there was something else hidden there. Fear? Uncertainty? Yes, Jin Li Tam realized, it was those things but also something deeper. Something that smelled familiar and disturbing to her.

Betrayal. A rotten and deadly weed grew up among her own people and threatened them all.

Jin Li Tam inclined her head. "It is good to see you as well. Have you learned anything new?"

The girl shook her head. "My army scours the Marshlands now, turning every stone to find the root of this sudden evil. And you?"

Jin Li Tam shook her head. "Nothing you don't already know. Reinforcements are en route. The first several attacks have taken heavy tolls on the rangers particularly. These skirmishers fight with no sense of self-preservation; they fight until they fall."

Winters sighed, and her voice was quiet. "It's the blood magicks. They know before they take them that it will cost them their lives."

Neither of them had seen these blood-magicked scouts in action, but both had seen the field of flesh and bone they'd mowed. Jin Li Tam felt a stab of loss, remembering the night that Winters had been forced to take her throne. And now, she stood fresh on the heels of burying the Androfrancine dead from the Summer Papal Palace, her lands now steeling for invasion. New to her throne, and already threatened from within and without.

Jakob stopped suckling, and she adjusted her shirt and coat, shifting the baby to her shoulder to pat the air gently from him. "I've not told Meirov that I am bringing you," Jin Li Tam said. "I think it is better that way. You will be under my protection as a part of Forest kinclave."

Winters swallowed and nodded. She shifted on her feet, and Jin read indecision in her body. *She wishes to ask something but is uncertain how.*

Jin watched a blush creep into the girl's face even as her brown eyes darted away. "Is there . . ." She paused. "Is there any word of Neb?" Her eyes returned, meeting Jin's for a moment, and the blush rose even further on Winters's cheeks. "I know he's missing and that Aedric seeks him."

Of course. The boy. Jin Li Tam tried to force a smile but knew she failed. "I've an entire company seeking him. I know he was well enough when he left Aedric in pursuit of Isaak and the other mechoservitor." She wasn't sure what else to say. These were hard times for love; bitter soil for it to grow in. And these weeks with Rudolfo off seeking a cure for Jakob—long stretches with no word from her new husband—she knew the sharp teeth of worry that chewed this young woman. *I should say something to comfort her.* "I know that if he could, Neb would get word to you. The birds don't seem to hold their magicks there. We're doing our best to find them."

"He's no longer even in my dreams," Winters said, looking away. The voice was so nearly a whisper, and there was a profound sadness in it.

"Maybe your dreams are affected by distance," she offered, but doubted it would help.

Winters shrugged but said nothing, and Jin Li Tam was uncertain what to add. She wasn't very familiar with the Marsh Queen's dreaming beyond what everyone knew about the War Sermons and the Book of Dreaming Kings. She knew even less of these supposed shared dreams she had with the boy, though she'd known there was a bond between the two of them from their time at Windwir. She'd certainly heard talk of the young romance even before she'd known of the girl's true identity. But Jin's attention over the last several months had been preoccupied with preparing the manor—and her own soul—for the small package of struggling life she now held. And the work of sorting what her life had been and what it was becoming. If those weren't enough, the circumstances of the Firstborn Feast and Jakob's troubled birth had also done their part to keep her focus elsewhere.

Still, she certainly understood the power of dreams. Her own had turned dark and violent that night—and had stayed that way. Even this morning, she'd clawed her way to wakefulness with her last memory still vivid before her closed eyes: a dark bird gobbling eyes in a field of faces that she knew too well.

She realized that the girl still waited for some further response. *What do I tell her?* There was more strength and certainty in her voice than she had hoped for when she finally found the words she needed. "We will find him, Winters, and we will bring him home safe."

The girl inclined her head. "Thank you, Lady Tam."

Jin Li Tam returned the bow, then looked to the face of her son, swaddled in the thick woolen blanket that had once held Rudolfo as his parents rode with him from Forest House to Forest House, presenting the younger twin along with his older brother, Isaak, to the Forest Gypsies they would someday serve. He was asleep now, his lips bubbling contently as his breath whispered in and out between them.

She saw the interest on Winters's face and turned slightly so that the girl could see the infant more clearly.

"He's so *small*," the Marsh Queen said.

"Yes." She paused. "There is little time before we must leave; would you like to hold him?"

The girl blanched, her face moving between fear and delight. "I don't think I can. I'm—"

Jin clucked her tongue. "Certainly you can. Follow me."

She led the way back around the tent, leaving the scouts at the flap as she and Winters entered.

Lynnae and the River Woman sat at a table together beneath a guttering lantern measuring out fresh scout magicks carefully into the small, string-tied satchels. They looked up briefly, but went quickly back to their work. In the corner, a small stove warmed the large space and a pail of wash-water along with it. Jin motioned to a narrow cot near the fire. "Sit," she said. "And scrub your hands. There's soap there, too."

Winters propped the axe against the nearby table. Jin watched her washing up, wondering absently exactly how the Marshers managed with their own young in the midst of such filth. Unlike most in the Named Lands, she did not for a second believe that they were still caught up in the Age of Laughing Madness, left over from their dark master's last and most desolating spell. She knew they were driven by a different insanity: the slightly more tolerable mystic variety.

When the girl's hands were clean, Jin leaned over and shifted Jakob over into her arms. She tried not to wrinkle her nose, making a mental note to have Lynnae clean the blanket later.

Winters held him, awkwardness visible in every aspect of her posture. "He's so small," she said again. But this time, Jin noted the light growing in her eyes and the smile that pulled at her mouth.

"Have you never held a baby?"

Winters shook her head, her eyes never leaving Jakob's face. "I've seen plenty of them. But I grew up alone. My friends were mostly books and dreams. And Tertius, my tutor."

Jin wasn't surprised. The sheer size of her own family insured her own exposure to the young, but she could see how, isolated and kept apart as Winters had been, a girl could reach the age of her own fertility without having seen up close and personally what her own body was capable of making with a little help. She suddenly grinned and felt a bit of wickedness rise up within her. "Perhaps I should send another company east to find young Nebios and fetch him back here for you," she said, "so that you might make one of your own."

For a moment—a brief moment—Winters became a girl again, blushing and giggling. "I don't think I would know what to do if—"

"Trust me, Queen Winteria," Jin Li Tam said, still smiling, "you'd figure it out soon enough."

And in a brief moment of her own, Jin Li Tam felt the weight of the New World slide off her shoulders as she and the Queen of the Marsh-folk laughed until even Lynnae and the River Woman had no choice left but to join them.

When that moment passed, she strapped on her knives, checked her armor and passed Jakob over to his nursemaid's care. Then, still flushed from their laughter, she and Winters called for their horses and set out in the direction that duty called them to.

Winters

A light snow fell as they rode silently south to parley. Above them, the sun hung veiled in gray behind the overcast sky. Around them, they heard the sounds of a forest leaning toward spring and the steady footfalls of their horses.

Winters rode beside Jin Li Tam, occasionally glancing over at her. The Gypsy Queen wore a coat of silver scales and a pair of scout knives with worn handles. Her long red hair was pulled back into a braid, crowned with a circlet that matched her armor. She rode proud and tall in the saddle. There was stern beauty in the steel of her posture.

I am nothing like her, Winters thought. What had Rudolfo called her? Formidable? And yet, not so long ago, she'd seen beneath the calm mask Jin Li Tam wore. When she'd first approached the Gypsy Queen, Winters had seen anguish and doubt upon the woman's face. There was a desperation in the way she had clutched her child even in the midst of her deliberate pacing. But she'd also watched as Jin took that anguish and doubt and stored it away as soon as her work called upon her to do so. It was a mastery of self that Winters could only hope to someday attain.

And the baby. When she'd taken that small, warm bundle into her arms, had seen those tiny fingers and that tiny mouth, it had sparked something within her. Not the ribald, baser instinct that Jin had teased her about, but something else, something deeper even than that compelling human need to become one with another and out of that, to make life.

Deeper than that, it had awakened within her a sudden and strong need for family—for an abiding connection to others that transcended her experiences to date. She'd thought she'd felt that with her people, but now she was uncertain of it.

Upon the death of her father, when she was very young, Hanric had done his best by her. He'd given over any personal desire he might have had for a family of his own to serve her father and later, her, so there really had been no woman to play the role of mother to the young queen. No siblings to shape her sense of place in the world. And knowing no different path, she'd grown up amid the Book of her predecessors and what other volumes they could pillage or purchase. She'd learned about her monthlies from their Herb Lady the day after it had first begun. She'd learned the fundamentals of procreation from Tertius, laid out for her in the practiced language of Androfrancine scholarship without any of the trappings of love or marriage or wonderment. And until that day she and Neb had fallen to the ground, tangled in glossolalia and prophecy, she'd given no real further thought to it. But gradually, as he'd filled her dreams and they had become even further tangled up in images of a Home they would someday share, she'd grown to feel a bond like nothing she'd felt before. And now, she realized, this was essentially a part of the same dance.

We long for connection. She saw it in Jin Li Tam's face as she fed her baby. She felt it herself as she laughed with the women in the tent, clutching precariously to that life in her arms.

If anyone had asked her even as early as last autumn, she'd have sworn she felt that connection with her people. But now, with Hanric in the ground and her boots fresh from the Androfrancine graveside at the Summer Papal Palace, she questioned that connection. Somehow, within her very people, her *family*, a vicious and twisted thing grew in shadows, and neither she nor her Twelve had known of it. She saw once again the look of despair and fear upon Seamus's face as he pulled back his grandson's shirt for her. She thought of the prophet, Ezra, and the milk white of his eyes. She remembered the ecstasy upon his face as he showed her the markings of ownership upon his breast.

No, she realized, not just of ownership . . . but of belonging. A passionate and powerful connection to something.

She shuddered. *Begone, kin-raven.*

A low whistle drifted through the forest, and she realized they now approached the edge of a small clearing. At its center, a handful of horses gathered beneath the flags of Pylos and Turam. She glanced again to Jin Li Tam, saw that calm determination upon the woman's face, and allowed that to settle her.

Jin Li Tam looked to her and must have read the worry there in her eyes. "Follow my lead if you are uncertain," she said. And as she spoke, her hands moved subtlety around the reins and along the neck of her horse. *I will see you through this.*

Winters blinked, uncertain why this surprised her. Rudolfo knew the nonverbal language of House Y'Zir, so it stood to reason that his bride would as well. "Thank you, Lady Tam," she said.

Jin Li Tam offered a forced smile. "You are welcome, Lady Winteria."

Then, their scouts were in the open, hands ready at their knife hilts as they took up their positions. Winters turned her attention to the cluster of horses ahead and felt the firmness settle into her jawline. The weight that had lifted earlier from her returned, and she breathed deeply as it settled upon her neck and shoulders.

Meirov was easy to pick out though Winters had never seen the woman up close. Hanric had handled her parleys during the War of Windwir. Still, those times she'd seen her from a distance, she'd not imagined she'd be so haggard and hollow-eyed.

She is consumed by grief. But more than that, she realized, the grief had become a bitter rage that sharpened the angles of her face and paled her already fair skin. The long braid of her blond hair spilled out from beneath her helmet, and she rested her hand upon the pommel of her sword. Around her, her rangers stood near and ready, their eyes watchful upon the Gypsy Scouts that stood in a loose circle.

Turam's general sat beside her. He wore a steel breastplate and a deep purple cloak, holding his helmet under his arm as he leaned over to whisper something to Meirov. The queen nodded, and her eyes met Winters's. Hatred blazed out from them, and the stark honesty of it made Winters flinch and look away. Her stomach ached, and a sudden urge to flee rose up in her. She risked a glance back, but those eyes bore into her and the firmness of Meirov's jawline, the white knuckles upon her sword and reins, were clear messages.

She would cut me down if she could.

Winters blinked and looked away again.

As they drew nearer, Jin Li Tam spoke. "Hail, Pylos and Turam."

Meirov's voice was cold. "Lady Tam, our parley and kin-clave is with the Ninefold Forest Houses."

Winters watched Jin Li Tam read the woman's posture and tone.

"The Ninefold Forest Houses holds kin-clave with the Marsh Queen." And her hands moved again slowly: *Her grief is strong; be silent.*

Winters shifted in her saddle. *Yes,* she answered. *I will.*

Meirov's eyes narrowed. "So you've brought Rudolfo's Wandering Army against us to protect these savages? Shouldn't you be home minding your son?"

The word stung, but there was more said than that. Winters read the other messages beneath the words. She'd referred to it as Rudolfo's army—a subtle way of saying she did not recognize Jin Li Tam's authority. And there was another message, one that gave her pause and sent her eyes back to Jin Li Tam's face to look for some sign of it registering there. *Your son lives and mine does not.*

Jin Li Tam inclined her head. "Lord Rudolfo is aware of this action and joins me in offering our deepest condolences for your loss, Lady Meirov. It is a terrible tragedy that breaks my own heart as a mother." She turned to the Turamite general. "And we grieve for your loss as well. We are all bereaved at the violence of that night—including Queen Winteria, who lost her caretaker, Hanric, beneath those iron blades. The Ninefold Forest is pledged to helping the Marshfolk identify the killers and deal with this matter."

Meirov's face twisted and darkened. "Your condolences are poor currency with me, Lady Tam. If you would help in bringing justice, either turn your army around and go home to mother your son or honor your kin-clave with the rest of us by joining us." Her eyes went to Winters again, and this time, Winters held them and tried to let the hatred pass over her. The Queen of Pylos continued, her stare unbroken. "The Marshers have been a problem since the days of Settlement; now, it has gone too far. Their babblings and barbarism, their constant skirmishing in the border towns"—here she wrinkled her nose—"even the smell of them has polluted the Named Lands too long."

Pay her no mind, Jin Li Tam's hands said, but Winters felt the water building in her eyes. She willed herself not to cry. It would be *weak* to cry. She listened to the calm in Jin Li Tam's voice and wished for it to wrap her as tightly as Jakob's blanket. "I cannot speak to your difficult history with her people, but Queen Winteria is committed to eradicating this threat. Even now, her army searches the Marshlands to find and bring justice to this resurgence. She's just come from burying the Androfrancine dead at the Summer Papal Palace."

The general from Turam spoke up. "We've lost three caravans en route to your new library; slaughtered and left on the road to rot." His eyes narrowed, and he looked to Winters suddenly. "This resurgence . . . what is its nature?"

Winters glanced to Jin Li Tam and her hands. *Keep your answer brief.*

She swallowed, her mouth tasting like dirt and iron suddenly. "It is an Y'Zirite resurgence."

She heard their breath expelled together. Meirov looked to her, then remembered herself and looked to Jin Li Tam. "We had feared as much. There were strange markings upon their dead." Resolve and bitterness crept back into Meirov's voice. "More the reason for a firm response from all houses in the Named Lands now before this violence grows further."

Jin Li Tam's voice was reassuring now and confident. "We are responding firmly," she said. "I have pledged our support to Winters; we will help her find and deal with this threat against us all by working together with her army—not by invading their territories."

Meirov stared at Jin Li Tam. "Our kin-clave with the Forest is tenuous at best, Lady Tam. It has not gone unnoticed that your House is the only to have benefited from Windwir's fall—or that your House has been unscathed in this more recent treachery. If you prevent us from our work here, Pylos will view such action as a revocation of kin-clave."

The general nodded beside her. "Turam as well."

"That," Jin Li Tam said, "would be most unfortunate." She whistled low, and the Gypsy Scouts started moving in from their positions. "I believe we've taken this parley as far as we can for the moment. I welcome further dialog in future parleys under calmer circumstances. I hope that you will—"

But Meirov interrupted her, her voice cold and measured. "We've no intention to parley further. If you prevent us from our work here, we will consider it collusion with the Marshfolk and there will be war between us."

Jin Li Tam turned her horse slowly, and Winters watched the careful calculations that played out quietly in her eyes. "We did not come to make war but to keep peace." Those blue eyes narrowed, and her voice suddenly grew cold as well. "But if you engage my army or cross farther north into the Marshlands, we will meet you with our knives, Meirov. I am sorry for your loss—it is a terrible crime, and I cannot imagine the depth of your rage and anguish—but these are troubled times in our land, and you must ask yourself: Is there a better path that we might take?"

Winters started to turn her horse, but suddenly felt she should say something—anything—despite Jin Li Tam's recommendation. She felt her brow furrowing, and even as she opened her mouth, she felt the tears filling her eyes; and at first, her voice was strangled. "My heart is broken for your loss, Queen Meirov, and my soul is pledged to justice for all that have been wronged so deeply by this evil."

But Meirov did not speak. Her eyes said everything that needed saying.

As they turned and slowly rode from the clearing, Winters swallowed a sob and ran a quick hand to wipe at the tears she could no longer prevent.

They rode back to camp silently, and as they did, she tried to conjure up Jakob's tiny face, his tiny hands, the smell of him and the way his mouth bubbled when he slept. It was the most peaceful moment she had known in weeks, holding him, but now even the memory of it eluded her. She could not find it or hold it in the midst of this grief storm.

All she saw instead were the hateful eyes of a bereaved mother burning into her, accusing her, cutting her deeper than any scout knife ever could.

Petronus

Petronus paced the small room and listened to the buzz of voices just past the oak door that separated him from the council chambers.

In a few minutes, he would be called upon to pass through that door and join Esarov at the advocate's bench for his arraignment. At the heart of it, it was a simple and brief matter. But still, it weighed upon him.

After the interrogation, house arrest had become much more bearable. Erlund's own chefs prepared his meals, and he'd access to birds and books in addition to more than adequate time with his advocate, the former leader of the revolution, Esarov the Democrat. The past days had been an endless flood of questions as they prepared for today and for what was to come beyond this time. It was an elaborate strategy and one that Petronus could not only appreciate, but enhance with what he himself brought to bear upon the matter.

He'd amassed a fair knowledge of kin-clave law alongside his mastery of Androfrancine law and Named Lands statecraft over his years in the Order. And Esarov's clarity of focus and sharp mind for legal tactics—combined with the man's stagecraft—would serve well.

Today would be brief, he reminded himself. What followed after would take time, but the landscape they'd covered through Esarov's pile of books gave Petronus confidence of the outcome.

Still, he paced.

He heard the noise beyond the door swell. That meant Erlund and his council of governors had entered the room. Next, the small bell in the corner of the room would ring and the silent guards seated at either side of the entrance would stand and escort him in.

You wanted a reckoning, old man. This wasn't what he'd had in mind exactly, but Petronus was confident in the rightness of it. His mind had wandered back to that brief encounter with Charles in the market square. And at night, he dreamed about a library stretching deep underground, hidden in some forgotten corner of the Old World. If this reckoning of his could bring back so much of the light, his own personal outcome didn't matter. And despite his strong confidence in what was to come, some part of him knew that it was a dangerous river he forded here. One misstep and he could find himself swept away.

The bell rang and the guards stood. When they opened the door and passed through, Petronus followed.

The council room was large and round, paneled with elaborately carved oak offset with gold fixtures and trim. The high domed ceiling was painted in themes of early Delta history with scenes from the First Settlers Congress and the signing of that document that guided the fledgling band of City-States into its prominence in the Named Lands.

The nine governors sat on a platform in an arrangement of seats and tables set up like a horseshoe; and set apart from them, centered in the open end of that U shape, stood the Overseer's dias and upon it, a worn chair and table. Erlund looked up at him from that place and their eyes met.

The disinterest there spoke volumes, but Petronus was not surprised. *He knows what is coming.*

The Overseer wore his crimson prosecuting robe, and to his right, the prosecutor he'd selected—Ignatio in this case—dressed in similar fashion. Behind them, the governors wore black robes not terribly dissimilar from the robes of an Androfrancine. As Petronus scanned their faces it was not hard to pick out the four that had been chosen by Esarov's democratic city states. They did not have the blank stoic regard of the others. Their faces spoke of purpose and pride rather than obligation, though in time Petronus wondered if that might fade as the newness of their roles wore off and as the reality of their work ahead on the Delta set in.

Esarov was the only person to stand as Petronus entered. He wore gray as befitting an advocate, and his long hair was pulled back and powdered. His spectacles gleamed in rays of sunlight that sliced into the room from high glass windows, and he nodded once at Petronus, his smile slight but confident.

Apart from these and a handful of others scattered throughout the observation balconies and the audience chamber, the massive room was empty. Guards stood at each of the doors.

Petronus forced his shoulders to straighten and walked to the empty chair beside his advocate. The two of them sat in unison as Erlund brought down a gavel.

Ignatio spoke. "The Governors' Council of the United-City States of the Entrolusian Delta is petitioned to convene now in judicial capacity for the arraignment of Petronus, former Holy See of the Androfrancine Order and King of Windwir. The charge before you is murder and conspiracy to commit murder for the unlawful execution of Lord Sethbert, former Overseer of the United Entrolusian City-States."

One of Erlund's handpicked governors made the motion to convene; one of Esarov's newly elected governors seconded. All men said "aye" when the question was called, and when they had Ignatio smiled and looked at Petronus.

"It is the position of the accuser that on the fourth of Anbar, during a closed council of bishops convened in the Ninefold Forest, Petronus—acting in his capacity as Pope—did summarily execute Sethbert without benefit of a trial as provided by the First and Second Settlers Congress of the Entrolusian Delta. Further, the accuser posits that Petronus, in collusion with Lord Rudolfo of the Ninefold Forest Houses, did subject the former Overseer to tortures and coercions forbidden under Entrolusian law and conducted its matters of prosecution without regard to common law and reasonable civility."

Erlund yawned at the flatness of the recital and looked around the room. Petronus followed his gaze. Finally, the Overseer moved the proceedings forward. "The council will now hear the plea of the accused before establishing a date of trial."

Esarov stood and Petronus stood with him. "Advocate defers to his client and presents him to council."

Erlund nodded. "Proceed."

Petronus took in the eleven men before him and pulled himself up to full height. "I choose no plea," he said in a loud clear voice, "and offer instead a Declaration of Circumstance."

The Overseer frowned, but Ignatio's face was unreadable. Behind them, the governors' faces were a mixed lot, though disinterest appeared most prevalent. Certainly, in Petronus's mind that made a certain sense. Their own Overseer had been disinterested in this action; they had a nation to rebuild—one with changes looming that formed far more pressing matters. A system that had served Erlund and his family for generations now threatened to topple beneath a wave of democracy that even gave Petronus pause. "Make your declaration," the overseer said.

Petronus made eye contact with him again. Then, he scanned the room and made eye contact with each of the governors seated before him. "In the circumstance of Sethbert's execution, we declare it to have been a matter of Androfrancine procedure carried out in accordance with the original Articles of Kin-Clave by ourselves as Holy See and Monarch of Windwir upon confirmation of the accused's guilt by his own mouth and without coercion, offered, observed and documented as such. We do not recognize the predominance of Entrolusian law in this matter, and we petition—as is our right by monarchy—for the case to be heard and decided by Council of Kin-Clave."

Petronus wasn't sure what he'd expected. In one of the dramas Esarov had once acted out upon the stage, at this point there would be indrawn breaths and shocked faces. But instead, his declaration sounded out into the nearly empty room, echoing slightly as it did.

Erlund sighed. Surely, Petronus thought, he saw it as a small price to pay for bringing his civil war to an end and reuniting his city-states beneath him. Now, it was simply a matter of establishing venue and waiting for the council to convene. As such, Erlund would become one voice among many as the heads of state came together to hear Petronus's case and rule.

Certainly, it could still go badly. The war had rubbed kin-clave thin between many of the Named Lands' houses and nations. But now the odds were with Petronus. And what came next would further establish those odds.

"Very well," Erlund said in a dry voice. "This court recognizes kin-clave and your right as monarch to a trial before your peers. A date shall be established and arrangements shall be made to convene the Council of Kin-Clave that they might hear this matter."

Petronus waited until the gavel was midway between the air and the podium before speaking again. "If it pleases his Excellency," he said, "we would continue."

Now Erlund looked surprised and interested suddenly. *You didn't see this coming, young pup.* His eyes narrowed and he put the gavel down. "We apologize. We had believed you had made your declaration."

"The Articles of Kin-Clave specify clearly that choice of venue falls to the accused," Petronus continued, "that their protection might be assured by the hosting nation."

Already, Ignatio's fingers flew through an old volume kept beneath their table. He found a passage, passed the book to Erlund and pointed. Erlund nodded. "It is within your purview."

Petronus smiled, and it was grim there in the morning light. "It is indeed within our purview. The venue of our choice is our own nation, the free state of Windwir."

Now there was noise in the room. Now came the indrawn breaths and the uncomfortable shifting upon those wooden chairs. A dark cloud passed over Erlund's face. "Windwir is no more, Petronus. There is no nation there."

"Regardless," Petronus said, glancing to Esarov and taking in his broad smile, "it is the venue we choose. We petition for it as such and petition as well that the Ninefold Forest Houses be contacted for the arrangements of council as named protector of Windwir."

The room became silent, and all eyes went to Erlund. Finally, he sighed. "Let the record state that Council of Kin-Clave will be held as petitioned," he finally said, bringing the gavel down.

Petronus wasn't sure what he'd expected next, but it happened quickly enough. The guards returned for him. He and Esarov stood, inclining their heads to the council and its Overseer, and prepared to go their separate ways. As Esarov shook his hand, he pressed a message into Petronus's wrist. *Well done. I will come soon to prepare for the council.*

He nodded. "Thank you."

Esarov offered a grim smile. "Thank *you*, Petronus."

As he crossed the room, Petronus glanced once more to Erlund and saw the anger on his face again. He'd not expected this turn, and he resented the loss of control, both over his Council of Governors and over his trial. His apparent frustration did not rankle Petronus in the least. Erlund might not have fully anticipated Petronus's strategy, but Petronus had certainly expected the Overseer's anger over it.

But when his eyes next found the face of Erlund's spymaster and prosecutor, he saw something there that he did *not* expect. It was brief and it was meant for Petronus alone, of that he had no doubt.

There, in that moment as Petronus passed by the bench, Ignatio offered him a slight and secret smile.

And above that smile, something satisfied and smug danced behind the man's eyes.

It was the satisfied gaze of a hunter happening upon a sprung snare. The smug look of a fisherman hauling in his overflowing net.

Petronus shuddered and forced himself forward, but even late into that night, that smile and those eyes stayed with him and promised something soon coming that he could not quite place.

Chapter
20

Vlad Li Tam

Vlad Li Tam hung limp in the cutting rack and stared down at the empty tables. The days and nights were a blur to him now, and more and more, he found there were vast patches of blank white in his sense of things.

But for now, they were finished with his children and his grandchildren and his great-grandchildren. They'd hauled the last of the bodies away at some point, and from that moment, Ria had simply continued her work without them. Even now, as he hung there, her hands moved lovingly over his naked flesh, her fingers tracing messages into his back that he could not cipher as her other hand worked the salted knife.

He'd screamed himself hoarse at first, but now he simply breathed and lay still, watching the drool puddle on the floor beneath him. He felt the hot bite of the blade moving over his left buttock, slow and in a widening spiral that then moved up and into the small of his back. Exhaling, he forced the pain into the cave he had dug for it deep inside of himself. He forced it there and then stood guard over it.

I will grow my pain into an army. He would feed it; he would water it; he would keep it in the dark and secret places where pain can grow fastest and strongest. He would—

Chimes sounded—these louder than the one that summoned him from his makeshift nest of blankets in the corner of his suite. He felt the blade lift and focused on the warm blood that trickled down his side to be caught in the gutters and fed into whatever twisted repository they used for their dark purposes.

In saner, clearer moments he'd pondered their use of it. He'd not studied the resurgences that had gone before, but he'd known one truth—none of them had brought back the Old Ways with such elaborate care and attention to detail. These were not men and women hidden in the forests offering their glossolalia to dead Wizard Kings and cutting themselves to mingle blood over a campfire.

These Y'Zirites were different. Something darker, more sinister, more compelling than any resurgence he'd ever heard tell of. From their elaborate rituals right down to the genuine love and affection Ria held in her voice when she spoke tenderly to him about the kin-healing she now performed.

"We are saving you with agony," she had said once, "and your agony, in turn, will save us all."

As if summoned by memory, he felt her breath close upon his ear and smelled the cool apple scent of her mouth. "They're here, Vlad," she said. Her voice was heavy with something akin to ecstasy. "Your grandson has brought them home to you."

He could not prevent the sob; it shook him, and as it did, fire spread across his back as pain raced along the intricate network of carefully carved words and symbols she'd written into him with her knives.

I will grow my pain into an army.

But some part of him knew it wasn't true. There would be no army. He would watch his family die one by one beneath these brutal blades, and then, when all were gone and all of the youngest had taken their marks and boarded their ship for gods knew where, he would take his own mark and offer his throat for one final cut.

And some other part of him begged for that day to come sooner rather than not.

He heard soft footfalls behind him, and Ria kissed his cheek before turning away. "Are they landing, then?"

"Yes, Lady."

"Tell Mal that I would dine with him in my chambers once he has refreshed himself."

"Shall I summon the Physician and prepare a batch for the tables?"

Vlad Li Tam felt the spasm and knew he'd sobbed again. He held his breath, fighting back the tears as he waited for her to speak.

"No," she said. "I think we can give our honored guest time to meditate and prepare his heart for this last of our work together." He heard the footfalls again, and once more she leaned over him. Now, she leaned before him and he forced his eyes away from the breasts that hung ripe and firm from within her open robe. He went to her eyes, but the love within those wide, brown windows confounded him and stirred something he could not let himself lay hold of.

I am growing to love her in some dark and poisonous way.

Of course, he'd heard of such things. He'd even used similar tactics with others, though it had grieved him. Pain was a powerful hallucinogen in the hands of a skilled manipulator.

He gritted his teeth and forced down his body's unbidden response to the hand she laid upon his cheek. She brought her eyes close to his. "We are nearly finished here, Vlad. I wish that I could continue our work together, but I fear I will be called away soon to attend other matters." She put her lips upon his and pressed her tongue against teeth he closed firmly against her. When she pulled back, she smiled. "But I have cherished our time together; healing your kinship with House Y'Zir has been the greatest honor I could know . . . at least until I see the Child of Promise with my own eyes."

Vlad said nothing. Instead, he forced that part of him that ached for her also into that deep cave full of pain. It was not love, no matter how it felt or what he thought. It was something more fierce and terrifying than that and it also would grow his army very well.

He felt the hands upon him now. He felt them working the buckles and straps, lifting him again as they had so many times before. And he felt his eyes rolling and his tongue lolling about in his mouth, felt the deep and salted fire roiling over his body, over the thousand cuts that made and unmade him.

Tomorrow, he knew they would start again. Tomorrow, a fresh batch of his tribe would be laid out upon the altar of his heart to have poetry cut from them amid their cries for him to help, to save them from this darkest nightmare they had fallen somehow into.

I will grow my pain into an army, he thought, *and I will take this island in my wrath. I will* end *you.* You will burn beneath the fury of your very knives.

But even as he thought it, he heard the mocking laughter of a thousand dead and once more found himself weeping where there were no tears left to weep.

Neb

The farther east they raced, the hotter the days and nights became. Neb tried to mark his surroundings but found this new means of transportation wasn't conducive to charting his present path.

Of course, he wasn't confident that he would necessarily *need* to know his way back—despite this supposed authorization he enjoyed this side of the D'Anjite's Bridge.

When Neb regained consciousness that first night, he'd opened his eyes upon a star-strewn night sky, the blue-green moon swollen and heavy as it prepared to sink beneath a purple ribbon of horizon. When his demands to be put down were not heeded, he squirmed and twisted, surprised that his best efforts did nothing to put the mechanical off its footing. Those first struggles were met with firm metal hands that forced stillness into him as he rode the swaying metal shoulders.

Finally, he'd settled into the ride, shifting himself to minimize the bruising where the hard steel pushed into his flesh.

When he didn't drowse, he spent the time letting his mind wander across the vast landscape of questions that stretched out before his inner eye. Much had transpired in such a short time, and he still reeled from it. And the only words the mechoservitor had offered him had been the brief exchange that first day when he'd asked about Isaak and Renard.

"They are operational," the mechoservitor answered. "The damage is minor but sufficient to prevent unauthorized travel."

A thought had struck him then. "Couldn't *I* have authorized them?"

Neb felt the hot steam against his side as it hissed out of the exhaust grate below him. The mechoservitor's voice sounded reedy as its bellows worked. "Authorization may only be granted by sign and seal of the Office of the Holy See or by Papal Designee under Holy Unction of his Excellency, Introspect III."

Beyond that, Neb's questions remained unanswered as they lurched swiftly across rocky terrain. Still, he played them out behind his eyes and used what Franci meditations and ciphers he could to make sense of them.

Somehow, he'd been authorized to be here where the others had not been. Renard had run these Wastes his entire life, and the metal man had named Isaak "cousin"—odd that they would not be permitted to pass. Obviously, the chasm marked some boundary, for the mechanical had led them a merry chase for days—or was it weeks now?—until suddenly stopping at that point to draw its brutal line in the dirt of that place.

And both the mechanical and Renard had made the same assertion that Winters had made over a year ago now when she'd acknowledged him as the Homeseeker. It boggled him that anything Androfrancine would acknowledge the prophetic trappings of Marsher mysticism, though now he felt the call of that title even more so. It was as if even dreamless here, the hope and promise of Home twisted and writhed like a sleeping snake. Something in this wasted land summoned him.

And where have my dreams gone? He felt that pang of loss again. No, he thought. The dreams were but a vehicle. The real question, not so very far beneath the surface, made his stomach ache.

Where had Winters gone?

His last dream of her had been the night she camped beneath the spire, preparing to make her final ascent and declare herself to be something that she did not feel ready to become. He'd seen those questions and fears within her dreams and was certain she'd seen his own because of the way their sleep touched. And the dreams felt so very real. He could carry the smell of her with him for days from just a few moments near her in the middle of the night. He missed the comfort it gave him, and once more it raised the question: Why could he not dream in this place?

It neared sunset on the fourth day when they finally stopped running and the mechoservitor placed him upon his feet. They stood in a hollow bowl of stone. Set directly in the center of it was a round slab of dark metal bolted into the granite by a series of Rufello cipher locks. It was weather-pitted, but the stone around it had worn more than that ancient metal had. Around them, bathed in the scarlet light of the lowering sun, jagged glass mountains bent like bladed waves.

The familiarity of it struck him as he stretched and looked around. *I've been here before.* Of course, it wasn't possible. But even the dry, powdered-bone smell of the place resonated with some deep-seated memory. "Where are we?" he finally asked.

But the metal man paid him no mind. Instead, it stretched out upon its stomach and placed its ear to the ground. Then, it surprised Neb by what it did next.

The metal man sighed, and it sounded like a sigh of contentment. "Here it is," he whispered, and his voice made gooseflesh rise on Neb's neck and arms. "Listen for it, Nebios."

Neb looked around them again, then cocked his head toward the ground. Faintly, he heard the song. He moved a step closer—it was faint and tinny, and he realized that he didn't so much hear it with his ears as he felt it. The slightest vibration of notes. It pulled him another step and he knelt.

It was a mournful sound, and it came from beneath the steel cap. "What is it? Why do I know this place?"

The metal man's eye shutters flapped open. "This is the source of the dream."

Dream. He remembered. When his father had visited his dreams he had seen the metal men all in robes at a dig. It was this place. They had discovered this place. "The source of the dream is a song?"

"The dream is ciphered into the song. The song is a conduit. Listen."

Neb stretched out and pressed his ear to the cool metal. He could hear it, still far away, but he could make out each note. He recognized it and associated his recognition with a harp—only then the song had been played too fast and there had been fire and smoke and—

"Winters's dream," he said. "I know it from her dream." And more than that: He knew this *place* from a dream as well. More vague images of metal men in robes digging.

Steam hissed from the mechoservitor's exhaust grate. "It is 'A Canticle for the Fallen Moon in B Minor' by the Last Czar Frederico, from before the Age of the Wizard Kings."

"Am I authorized to know this?" Neb thought he must be or the metal man would not freely offer the information.

"You are early," the metal man said, "but you are authorized, Nebios Homeseeker. We found the source during the construction of Sanctorum Lux. We decrypted the locks and made a thorough study of the artifact. Under the Holy Unction of Papal Designee Hebda, it has been replaced and resealed for your arrival. Mark this place and know it well; the dream awaits you here. In the appointed time you will bear it to my cousin and you will both join us in the work." He paused, his mouth flap moving and his eyes flashing. "The song compels a response."

Neb's mind spun, and he willed it not to. *Papal Designee?* His father had been an archaeological technician; he'd heard nothing about a designation from the Office of the Holy See. Of course, he'd seen his father infrequently. The man had spent most of his life in the Churning Wastes, making a point to visit Neb in the orphanage whenever he was back in Windwir between assignments. Was it possible that his father had served in some capacity Neb had been unaware of? It certainly seemed to be the case.

The metal man's other words struck him. *The song compels a response.* He strained his ears to capture the melodic lines of the song. *Yes,* he thought. *It does, but how could he know that?*

He heard the clicking and clacking, the sounds of metal groaning, as the mechoservitor stood. "The moon rises," the metal man said. "It is nearly time for your sleep cycle to commence, but our destination is nearby. Are you functional for running?"

Neb nodded, climbing to his feet. The song held him, compelled him to stay and to listen, to work its Whymer Maze of notes and find and offer whatever it called for. It summoned him, held him, would not release him. But he forced his attention away, shuddering at the force of that haunting music. He looked around again, noting his surroundings as best he could. Beside him, the metal man took those first long strides and broke into an easy run. Neb pulled a bit of the black root from his pouch and put it into his mouth.

Then he ran, too, away from that buried song that beckoned him. As he ran, the bitter juices from the root flooded his mouth, and his legs stretched as the air around him took on a buzzing quality. Behind him, the canticle called. He forced his eyes onto the metal man he followed.

At first, the song faded and he found his focus again, but it was short-lived.

When the moon rose, swollen and low as it filled the horizon, it cast a blue-green shine across the Churning Wastes. When its first light peeked over the jagged teeth of the eastern mountains, Neb thought the song, fading behind him, grew suddenly louder. It filled the night sky as if the moon itself sang them onward. The Old World had become, for him, an amphitheater filled with music as he and the metal man raced across its vast stage.

The sadness of the melody pulled tears from Neb's eyes. The delight of it made him laugh out loud.

As the black root took hold and his legs caught him up to his metal companion, he realized that he was not alone in his response to the song.

The metal man ran laughing and weeping in complete abandon to the canticle beneath a pregnant moon that echoed and enhanced its strains.

Matching his stride to that of the Androfrancine machine, Nebios ben Hebda gave himself to the song and first felt its whispered call toward Home.

Rudolfo

Rudolfo paced his narrow cabin and waited for the longboat they'd sent to return with news.

The *Kinshark* finally lay at anchor after nearly a week of pursuit, magicked and nestled in a cove on the southern side of the island that the iron armada had eventually led them to. It lay south of the horn and well beyond the normal shipping routes, a day's sailing into the haunted waters that were anathema to most New World sailors.

He'd seen the island from the deck earlier that day. It was large enough to boast craggy hills that stretched up from the jungle that blanketed it. And its white beaches were wide, inviting and deserted.

That is, until they reached the southern facing. There, they saw upper and lower docks with both iron and wooden vessels either tied off or anchored in the deep, natural harbor. Squatting above it, a massive building of white stone—built along a rocky ridge—reached up into the sky.

He'd watched silently at the rail as the ships they followed disembarked their cargo. He didn't need to see his knuckles to know they were white from their grip as first the children and then the adults from House Li Tam shuffled down the gangways, tied to one another in a long string and herded by dark-robed men with short swords.

After, they had circled to the other side of the island and sent out their scouting party. Rudolfo sent his two Gypsy Scouts along with Rafe's men and then gave himself to the arduous work of waiting. The scouts would assess what they were up against and bring back their report. After that came the decision as to what they actually *could* do. Rudolfo was skeptical—they were one wooden vessel against an iron fleet. Gods knew exactly what kind of military personnel augmented the small navy.

Perhaps, Rudolfo thought, they should have pushed on for Sanctorum Lux after all. At least that seemed a scenario with odds more in their favor. Certainly, Charles had advocated for that robustly for the first two days. But in the end, Rudolfo had told him—sharper than he wished to—that the hidden library would simply have to remain hidden a bit longer, until this present matter was addressed. The old Arch-Engineer had been sullen at first, but had gradually seen the wisdom in confirming just who now controlled Tam's fleet of Androfrancine-designed vessels and what their plans might be for those iron ships and the people they carried away prisoner.

He heard a soft knock at his door and turned. "Yes?"

The door opened and Charles peeked in. "They're back. We're gathering in the galley."

"Thank you, Charles. I will join you momentarily."

With a nod, the old man pulled the door closed, and Rudolfo scooped up his green turban of office. He wound it about his head and fastened it in place with the clasp his mother had given him when he was a boy. Then, he tied his crimson sash around his hips and took up his scout knives.

When Rudolfo entered the galley he saw Rafe Merrique and Charles but no one else. Of course, fresh from the jungles, the scouts were still magicked. He could see the places where the chairs were pulled out and from time to time, a flagon lifted of its own accord.

He took a seat at the foot of the table, opposite Rafe. "What have we learned?"

Rafe's first mate spoke first, and Rudolfo turned his head in the direction of the disembodied voice. The voice sounded heavy with something Rudolfo could not quite place. "The island is unoccupied save for the structure and the docks. They have a small garrison of soldiers—maybe a hundred strong judging from the size of the barracks. They're well armed, bows and swords, but not particularly vigilant about keeping their watch. They appear to be mixed—some Marshers, some of Delta or Emerald Coast dialect. They spoke a unified subverbal that was unfamiliar to me."

Rudolfo nodded, reaching for the carafe and sniffing the contents. Cherry wine was not one of his favorites, but it would suffice. He poured a glass. "How many ships?"

"Two schooners of a trim and line I do not recognize plus the ten Tam ships—all unmagicked at this point. The steel vessels are anchored and powered down. They patrol with the schooners—one pass per hour, more of a token watch, which suggests they do not expect visitors."

Rafe nodded. "They're far enough into the Ghosting Crests to keep most away."

Rudolfo raised the glass to his lips and sipped the sweet, cool wine. "Gypsies, what saw you inside?"

Even his Gypsy Scout seemed restrained, subdued somehow. "It is accessible, General Rudolfo, from at least three unguarded points. Two windows and a door. We mapped a basement holding area and two floors above that. Third floor and anything beyond, we assume, is guarded more diligently."

There was a pause, and Rudolfo did not need to see the man to know he felt uncomfortable with what he was about to share. "What else?" he said.

"There are pipes moving fluid from the upper floor—the domed structure—into some lower basement we were unable to reach. We think they're cutting."

Cutting. Rudolfo sucked in his breath at the word. "Why do you think they are cutting?"

The first mate spoke up now. "On account of the bodies, Lord."

The Gypsy Scout continued. "They've been burying their dead in mass graves. Like Windwir. We estimate nearly a thousand, and the holding cells below are full to overflowing."

Rudolfo stroked his mustache thoughtfully. "But where would they . . ." He let the words trail off as the answer became apparent. House Li Tam was under the knife—their fleet forfeit. But he doubted very much it was the penitent torture of his own Physicians—those twisted Francines who looked to T'Erys Whym and his darker beliefs about human behavior. Blood magicks had returned to the Named Lands, and these were the old cuttings, the Old Ways. The path of Xhum Y'Zir and his seven sons . . . and the Wizard Kings that went before them.

His mind flitted back to the Firstborn Feast. *It is all connected.* Those men had been Marshers, and there were Marshers here. Blood-magicked men had swept the Tam ships to surrender just as they had killed Hanric and the others. Rudolfo would not be surprised at all to find that their blades were all iron, the wizard-bargainer's steel.

He suddenly recalled something the first mate had said and moved his hands. *Attend me, Scout.*

There was a warm rustle of wind, and fingers pressed into Rudolfo's forearm on the table. *I am here, General.*

He reached out, found a shoulder and put forward his question. *The subverbal they used; you recognized it, yes?*

Yes. A pause. *Y'Zir.*

Rudolfo nodded. Yes. A language used still by the Wandering Army of the Ninefold Forest and by the Marshfolk, both peoples once allied with Xhum Y'Zir . . . recipients of the New World for their servitude and friendship with that dark house. He dismissed the scout with a gesture.

Rafe Merrique looked to Rudolfo. "A resurgence is under way. It makes sense that it would with Windwir gone. The Androfrancines kept watch on those things."

Rudolfo thought about the packet of papers now in Brother Charles's care and looked over to the old man. Their eyes met, and the Arch-Engineer inclined his head ever so slightly. What if the resurgence had not simply sprung up in this fertile post-Androfrancine soil? The structure on the island was at least fifty years old, and while an Y'Zirite resurgence could have grown and blossomed here in the Ghosting Crests, outside the purview of the Order, such a thing seemed unlikely.

No, Rudolfo thought, *the answer is darker yet.*

An Y'Zirite resurgence somehow established enough of a foothold within the Named Lands to bring down Windwir. It bent Sethbert into the plot, using him and his paranoia to bring back a dead master's last spell. How far could it run?

The details were not difficult for Rudolfo to cipher. They'd infiltrated the Order at some level. And certainly House Li Tam had been compromised along with the United City-States.

It staggered him, but he forced his mind back to the moment. The woman who could cure his son was in a holding cell beneath that white temple—if she hadn't already gone beneath the knife. He could not bring himself to worry about anything but that. Rae Li Tam's freedom and Jakob's life had to be his primary concern.

And yet.

If this resurgence had manipulated the most powerful nation in the Named Lands into bringing down Windwir with such carefully orchestrated precision—using one of the Named Lands' most powerful families to do so—and if they had also systematically and with ease led the assassinations that dark, winter's night . . . ? The possibility of it grew in his stomach, cold as a pit of ice. He looked to Rafe Merrique. "What do you propose?"

Rafe sighed. "I propose that we come back with a fleet and an army, bring them down, end this dark business they've begun." He paused and ran a hand through his gray bristling hair. "But that doesn't free your alchemist. We're here now, and we have surprise on our side."

Rudolfo thought for a moment. "They have numbers on us. And their iron vessels are lethal in close quarters."

"If they can see us," Rafe added.

Rudolfo nodded and looked to Charles. "Can you operate them? Can you teach others to do so?"

Charles nodded. "I could. But it would take time."

He looked to Rafe Merrique again. "And could you get men aboard them?"

The first mate's voice piped up. "They are lightly manned, more a watchman than any kind of opposing force."

Rafe's brow furrowed as he thought. "We could take half of them—any more would be unrealistic. But once the boilers are fired, there will be no element of surprise."

"Then we wait until the last minute to fire them; but once we did, could you hold them?"

He thought for a moment. "It could be done but not easily. They have the schooners and blood magicks to contend with."

Charles cleared his voice, and all eyes looked to him. "You have cannon powder?"

Rafe shrugged. "Some."

The Arch-Engineer continued. "And there's more upon the iron ships?"

Rudolfo nodded. "Yes, if they've not unloaded it for storage."

The Gypsy Scout shimmered now at the table as the powders began to burn out. He leaned forward when he spoke. "They were taking on supplies earlier, not unloading them."

Charles smiled, and it was grim in the dim-lit galley. "Then I can help you disable the schooners and any of the Tam vessels that will be left behind. I'll need some time and a few other items."

"I think we have our plan," Rudolfo said in a low voice. It sounded more sinister than he intended it. "Rafe, you will see to the vessels. Disable any opposing force on the shore, make sure their ships cannot pursue."

"That," Merrique said, "is only half of a plan, Rudolfo."

Rudolfo sighed. If Gregoric lived, that First Captain would have scowled now and tried to talk him out of the course so clearly laid out in his mind. Maybe it was because of his origins, a young orphan king faced with insurgency within his people, or maybe it was because of his father's firm guidance and insistence upon what was right. He didn't know for sure, but the end result was the same: He rarely doubted the right path to take in any given situation, and this was no different. He loathed Vlad Li Tam, had vowed to kill him, but he could not bring himself to leave the man's family in the hands of these blood-bent cultists.

He looked up at Charles and Rafe. The sailors were shifting back into focus now, too, as the powders lifted. "I will take my Gypsy Scouts, and we will free those we can."

Rafe choked on his beer. "Three men against a hundred? Are you mad, Rudolfo? Has grief and desperation for your son clouded your judgment?"

No, not him, the assassin had said back in the Great Hall on the night all of this had begun. And the Ninefold Forest Houses had not only survived Windwir's fall but had benefited from it. There had to be a connection between this resurgence and his family's dark heritage— but what?

"Perhaps," Rudolfo said, "I *am* mad." When he looked up and his eyes met Rafe's he watched the man blink and look away at the ferocity of what he saw there. "Regardless, I am going to do what I can."

And hope, he thought, *that it will be enough to save my son.*

As their voices lowered to tones reserved for careful strategy and well-timed movements, Rudolfo steeled himself for the work ahead and summoned up the gray face of his ailing son once more for assurance that this path before him was true.

Chapter

21

Jin Li Tam

Jin Li Tam spent the morning on the line, riding with her closest commanders as she inspected the ragged border they'd established between the armies to the south and the Marshlands to the west.

Reinforcements to those armies had arrived and already been cut through. Three times in as many days, her lines had been breached, and try as they might, the Wandering Army could not hold them. Neither did the blood-magicked foe linger to engage the Gypsies. They'd pressed on in their raids against the Turamites and Pylosians. Because they had no intention of returning, they did not need to leave an opening behind. They surged through and did not even bare their invisible weapons. With their hands, they shoved the Forester soldiers easily aside with minor injuries, and their hapless pursuit of them yielded no results.

Her Gypsy Scouts fared only slightly better.

So now, she rode the line and tried to keep spirits up. Rudolfo's officers were a hard lot who loved their men fiercely and exacted a loyalty not dissimilar to that they bore for their Gypsy King. And it was a different kind of love, a different kind of loyalty than what her father exacted. His love was sharp, and no one doubted that he loved his strategic purposes and the world they shaped more than the tools that he used to do that shaping. This new way of leading confounded her.

The Wandering Army had not marched beneath a queen in more years than any of her captains or commanders could tell her. It had happened, certainly, during times that the Gypsy King was away attending other business. And despite this, and despite her newness, they honored her and followed her orders as if they were Rudolfo's.

And though she knew it was no place for her infant son, she saw also the way her husband's men looked to their prince and knew of a certainty that they would give their lives before letting any danger near their lord's firstborn. She'd even found trinkets left for the boy at her tent flap—anonymous tokens of welcome to the new heir.

Jin Li Tam felt a stray snowflake brush her cheek and started. The powders made her mind wander, and she looked around quickly to be sure no one had spoken. They rode the line in single file, slowly, pausing here and there to ask the men how they were and how the food was.

Soon, it would be time to turn back and tend to Jakob. The River Woman and Winters watched him now while Lynnae slept off yesterday's powders. The girl had taken the baby two days in a row while Jin Li Tam and the young Marsh Queen attempted another parley with the others. It had gone no better—Turam's man had shown up, but Meirov hadn't even deigned to send a subordinate. Pylos was not interested in parley.

Around them, the forest was thin, with open spaces between trees. Most of the ground was mud and dirty clots of snow. The cold air smelled like wood smoke and pine, and apart from the noise of a waiting army, it was a quiet morning.

When Third Alarm sounded, it came from the west. Jin's hand went to her sword, then relaxed. Ahead, she heard whistles and saw men turning north. She followed their stares and held her breath. Leaning forward in the saddle, she heard the clacking of tongues and watched the spatter of mud kicked up by magicked feet as invisible men raced toward the line. The Gypsy Scouts were in full retreat.

"Hold the line," a commander barked.

She saw the men, saw the Gypsy Scouts spread out and turn, and then saw the surge of *something* pouring across the forest floor faster than a magicked stallion.

And suddenly, something broke in her and she felt her head grow hot as her jaw clenched.

Jin Li Tam drew her sword and spun her horse, her eyes scanning the northern forest. She spurred forward, lining herself up with the mass of bending light and mud that bore down upon her men. Bellowing with a rage she did not know she possessed, she rode down that wind of blood, feeling the solid thud of the horse's steel hooves as it connected with flesh and bone. She spun the horse, whistling at it as the sword darted out to find something within that blood-magicked swell of running men.

Something heavy and fast struck the side of the horse, and Jin yelped as she tumbled from the saddle. Before the horse fell, she was out from its shadow and discarding her sword for the slender scout knives she'd taken from Rudolfo's desk. They felt natural in her hands, and as another cold wind approached from the north, she danced into it, low and swinging for hamstrings she was trained to find, especially upon the magicked. Around her, she heard the sound of other horses and other men as her retinue chased after and joined her in the fray.

I must earn their respect with blood. But even as she thought it, she knew it wasn't why she did this. Why she risked her life—her, a new mother—as if it meant nothing.

She was angry. No, she was *enraged.* And she poured it all into this work before her. She felt the knife moving over skin, felt it catch and hold and pull her along behind. Gathering herself up, she threw herself forward and buried her knives into the fleeing back.

She fell upon her prey, and it bucked and twisted until it threw her off. "You should not be here, Great Mother. You might be hurt."

Jin Li Tam lunged forward, the knife finding purchase. She brought the other in and twisted them both. "I am not your mother," she snarled.

Laughing, he shoved her back. "You brought us the Child of Promise. You are a mother to us all."

Around them, the line was breaking.

She moved in again, feinting with her left and jabbing with her right. She heard a surprised grunt and pressed forward, bringing both knives up and in as she drew close enough to smell the Marsher's foul breath. She twisted the knives again and heard him howl. "Who told you that?" she asked. "This Child of Promise . . . he's dying. What kind of promise is that?"

"He will not die, Great Mother. He cannot, for he brings forth the Crimson Empress from afar. She who will make all things right."

I should stop, she told herself. *I should question him.* But the rage in her—anger that had hidden in her tears of late—required otherwise. And she felt the white heat building behind her eyes with every word he uttered. She drove the knives into him again and felt him buckle to his knees beneath her blades. Again, and the Marsher collapsed.

The voice gurgled now. "I am honored," it said, "to die at your hands, Great Mother."

Jin Li Tam gave the knives a final twist and then withdrew them from the still form. Only then did she realize that she tasted iron in her own mouth, that her breath came in ragged gouts of steam and that she shuddered from adrenaline and exertion. Stooping, she wiped her blades clean of that magicked blood as best she could upon the invisible corpse at her feet.

When she looked up, she saw that the line had re-formed and all eyes were upon her. Finally, Philemus scanned the line that had not held and then looked back to her. He nodded slightly, and she saw great approval in his eye.

When he shouted, his words were sharp and clear on the morning air. "Hail the Gypsy Queen," he cried.

And as one voice, the Wandering Army hailed their general's wife. She bowed deeply to them.

Then, sheathing her knives, Jin Li Tam called out for her horse and mounted up to finish riding the line.

She would general now, and in an hour or so, she would return to camp, wash herself clean of the morning's violence, and feed her infant son.

Winters

Winters walked the muddy footpaths between tents and pondered the difference between queens and mothers.

The Gypsy camp bustled with activity as word of a bird from home spread like fire in a dry summer thicket. It had arrived while they were at dinner the night before, just as it had no doubt arrived to the other camps, under the white thread of kin-clave and calling Windwir's former allies to council. Winters had already packed, though she was not yet certain of her place in this new development.

She'd not met Petronus during the last war, and following it he'd vanished back into obscurity. And certainly, the Marshfolk had not held kin-clave with the Order, attacking its protectorates with ruthless frequency until her father's encounter with Rudolfo's father in the

Ninefold Forest. This was clearly a matter for the Named Land states, and no bird would seek her out for it.

But she'd seen the look of concern upon Jin Li Tam's face and knew from Tertius's meticulous history lessons how infrequent a Council of Kin-Clave was. Of course, until recently—until her dreams had pointed the Marshfolk toward the Ninefold Forest—her people had held kin-clave with none. And now, their only ally was the Ninefold Forest. The thought of attending proceedings she was not welcome at went against her nature, though her hostess insisted that her kin-clave with the Gypsies was sufficient. Still, her place was with her people, and it felt wrong to leave them even for this purpose. She already felt negligent being so far south at this time, though the birds and couriers she received daily assured her that matters were well in hand.

"You are a queen," Jin Li Tam had told her, her voice heavy with weariness from her fight the day before. "It calls for difficult decisions. And often," she said, "these choices are not between good and bad but good and *best*."

Those words still resonated with her the next morning as she wandered the camp. She'd finally relinquished her weapons and armor—there'd been no need for them here. She had no army here to bolster with such accouterments and she knew of a certainty that she could not face down one of these magicked skirmishers in the way that Jin Li Tam had. Instead, she wore the simple breeches, woolen shirt and fur jacket of a Marsh boy and she walked with her hands buried in her pockets and her breath fogging the cold air. Mud sucked at her sturdy boots as she went.

Tents were coming down about the camp, and she suspected the same happened among the armies to the south. They would leave the bulk of their forces behind, still locked in a Queen's War stalemate, though she wasn't certain why at this point. The Wandering Army had not yet successfully held the line, and the armies of Pylos and Turam had yet to press farther north, though she suspected it could happen any day. It was an ineffective policing, more an image of action than any real staying force. The sheer power of blood magicks combined with the skirmishers' willingness to fight until they were dead made for an untenable situation for all involved.

Especially me. Something was happening among her people—something that had grown up beneath their noses—and she did not know what to do about it. She simply felt some pressing need to be near them, to offer them some kind of assurance and be the leader that she was intended to be.

"Lady Winters?" The voice rose up above the clamor of the soldiers who bustled about rolling tents and packing saddlebags.

She turned and saw a familiar Gypsy Scout approaching. "Yes?"

"Our scout company from the north is in audience with Lady Tam; they've brought one of your men with them." His face was blank, and there was a secret in his eyes that made her stomach lurch. "She requests your presence." But his tone did not say request—it said *requires*.

Turning, Winters let the young scout lead her back to the tent where she'd spent so much time of late. Her time with the women there and little Jakob had been the only light in these dark times. With Neb vanished now from her dreams, they were filled only with blood and blades and pink scars upon pale breasts. But little Jakob, despite his obvious illness, was bright as the full moon in this darkness. And watching Jin Li Tam with him and then with her soldiers was an odd juxtaposition—a quiet canticle buried within a greater song.

She kept up with the scout and followed him to the tent. Then, she slipped inside as he held the flap for her. A somber company awaited her, and seated in the center of the room, Seamus sat trembling, his cheeks white from tears and his face bruised and battered. His clothing hung from him in bloody shreds. When he saw her, he looked away, and she raced to him to kneel and take his hand in hers. "Seamus, what's happened to you?"

Jin Li Tam sat to the side. Lynnae and the River Woman were nowhere to be seen, but a small group of tattered and dirty scouts huddled near the heating stove.

Seamus bit his lip. "The Twelve are no more," he said. "I'm all that's left."

Winters exhaled, her stomach suddenly clenching. "How is that possible? Just this morning, I received word from you that you were moving on to Kinsmen's Rest to search for the mark there."

Jin Li Tam's voice behind her was gentle but firm. "Tell Queen Winteria what you told me, Captain."

"He could not have sent word," the officer said. "We found an encampment and took him from a cage within it. I lost six men getting him out, but I recognized him from the Summer Palace and couldn't leave him." Winters looked to him and saw the hardness in his eyes. "Things are awry in the Marshlands."

Winters felt heat in her face as her eyebrows furrowed. "But what of the army, Seamus? You rode with the army . . . what happened?"

"Broken," he said. "Scattered or dead by now, those that didn't surrender and take the mark."

She blinked at the news. The Marsher army was feared throughout the Named Lands. They did not surrender, certainly not to their own. How was this possible? Suddenly, his words sank in. She asked the question, but she knew what he meant and it chilled her. "Take the mark?"

Sobbing, he pushed aside his shirt and showed her the fresh cutting. "Oh my queen," Seamus said, "I have failed you and the memory of your father."

The sight of the broken old man and his tears crushed her, and she felt the water in her own eyes. She willed her lower lip not to quiver. "How did this happen, Seamus?"

He hung his head, and when he spoke, his voice was garbled. "We divided the army to search the villages. Each of the Twelve took a contingent. I took my men east to Valkry's Rest to search the villages there. We found a hidden mountain shrine. Gaerrik and his contingent found another near Aensil's Hope. We started searching our people for the mark." He looked up, his eyes red. "Not everyone takes it by the knife. Some merely paint it on. Particularly those in positions that might require a more secret discipleship."

She released her held breath. "How many?"

"Too many. There has been betrayal within the Council of Twelve. My men and I were ambushed in the night, both from within and without. Several of the council members were captured and given the option of taking the mark or laying down our lives. I do not know which were working against us, but I know our birds were intercepted and tampered with."

Her eyes narrowed. "Where are the others, Seamus?"

Seamus hung his head again and said nothing. She watched the mucous and tears trail down into his beard.

Finally, the Scout Captain spoke up. "The others refused the mark and were executed." There was bitterness in his voice, Winters realized, but it was not the bitterness of judgment.

I'm losing my people. She felt the weight of that truth and wrestled with tears that threatened to shame her. She looked to Jin Li Tam. "I am needed at home. I cannot go with you to Windwir."

"Certainly you must do what you feel is best," the Gypsy Queen said carefully, but Jin Li Tam's hands moved even as her mouth did. *Reconsider this choice; you could petition for kin-clave. The Marshlands are in other hands than yours, and you will need help to take them back.*

Winters nodded, but a part of her wondered if her lands could be taken back. "I will consider it." She looked to the captain herself now. "What else can you tell me?"

"There is an old man who fancies himself a prophet. He is preaching a new gospel openly now, and people are listening." She saw distaste on the officer's face. "He points to scriptures that predicted the fall of Windwir—to the very day—and claims it heralds the establishment of an empress."

Yes, she remembered Ezra's words from her bathing cavern. *The Crimson Empress. A new gospel.* The memory of it ran cold fingers over her skin. The Marshfolk had no gospel but the Book of Dreaming Kings with its promise of Home and restitution for the wrongs done them in the land of sojourn, but he'd told her a new one arose. "What scriptures did he reference?"

The captain shook his head. "I don't know what they were called. The old man recited from memory, but it's nothing I've heard before. Judging from your people's response, they'd not heard it before, either." His brow furrowed as he pulled words from memory. "'And it shall come to pass at the end of days that a wind of blood shall rise for cleansing and cold iron blades shall rise for pruning. . . .'"

As his words trailed off, Winters was surprised by the voice that picked up the recitation. "'Thus shall the sins of P'Andro Whym be visited upon his children,'" Jin Li Tam said quietly.

Yes. She met Jin's eyes and saw something there that disturbed her. Swallowing, she took a breath and finished the recitation. "'Thus shall the throne of the Crimson Empress be established.'"

There was silence in the room, and Winters saw how pale Jin Li Tam had become. The Gypsy Queen regarded her with concerned eyes. *I must be pale as well.* It would not surprise her—these recent events staggered her. Somehow this weed had grown up in her own garden, beneath her very gaze. Beneath Hanric's gaze, too, and perhaps even that of her father. She could imagine it now though it boggled her: Secret meetings in the forest and in the caves. Quietly recited gospels by candle. Cuttings for those who could take them, painted marks that could be easily washed away for those whose faith must remain hidden. All the while, building a secret army of blood skirmishers to bring terror and bloodshed into the Named Lands on a winter's night, and to prune the last of the Androfrancines from the New World.

A thought struck her, but she put it aside. It simply could not be possible. Still, it remained: Could this resurgence within her people have anything to do with Windwir's fall?

"I will go to Windwir," she finally said in a low voice. "I will ask the Council of Kin-clave there to hear my petition and help my people."

Jin Li Tam nodded. "A prudent decision." Her hands moved. *I know these words from a dream; and old Ezra quoted them to me when we arrived. He said more. Stay after the others have gone and we will speak of these things.*

Winters inclined her head. "Yes, Lady."

The old man snuffled, and she turned her attention back to him. "You will accompany me, Seamus, and tell what you have seen."

When he did not answer, she put a hand on his shoulder. She felt it shake beneath her touch. "Look to me," she said.

He shook his head. "I cannot bear to, Queen."

She knelt then, and using her hands, she gently raised his face to hers. Bending forward, she kissed his filthy forehead. "Sometimes there is no good path, Seamus, and we make the best of the one we choose. Sometimes others make the choice for us but let us believe we've done the choosing."

His sobs shook him, and she encircled the wiry old man with her arms, pulling his face to her chest as if he were a wounded child. *Perhaps we're all wounded children,* she thought before continuing. "This mark is only in your flesh; it is not in your soul. And I need you alive for what is coming—so I will choose to be grateful for the choice you made."

She did not look around the room for anyone's reaction and did not need to. The silence that filled that moment spoke more volumes than the Book of Dreaming Kings ever could.

All eyes were upon her; she felt them boring into her, but she did not care. She gathered the old man unto herself and held him as he wept, whispering comfort to his ear. And he clung to her as if she were his mother, begging her forgiveness and sobbing his guilt into her breast.

Already, her mind spun the words she would bring before the leaders of the Named Lands to plea for her people. Already, she cast strategies and questions at this newest turn in the Whymer Maze and categorized each by order of priority, all the while whispering comfort to the man in her arms.

In that moment, Winters found an unexplainable calm settling over her and realized then that she no longer felt the urge to weep. Instead, her full attention went to soothing and gentling Seamus in his shame as her own sorrow waited quietly for a later, private time.

Perhaps, she thought, mothers and queens were not so very different after all.

Petronus

The air grew warmer on the Delta, and Petronus took to strolling Erlund's meditation garden by afternoon. Though nothing bloomed now, he could paint it in his mind's eye and it calmed him. The Entrolusians had, at one time, followed the teachings of T'Erys Whym when they were in fashion, and some forgotten Overseer had even commissioned a Whymer Maze to be grown and set with the various markers of that darker meditation.

After hours in his room poring over volumes of kin-clave law with Esarov, it was good to be under the sky again, and it made him homesick for his shack and his fishing boat in Caldus Bay.

He'd led a peaceful life there for thirty years, until the day of Windwir's pyre. *I should've stayed home.* But even as he thought it, he knew that second guesses and self-doubt were a trick of the mind. Each past road, the Francis taught, shapes our present. Change one bit of that long and twisting walk and you change all of it.

He could have let Sethbert's own mete out justice, could have extradited the former Overseer as his nephew and governors had demanded, but he'd needed a visible antagonist while the Androfrancine thirst for vengeance was high. He'd needed them to place their rage upon that solitary figure so that he could then take action to remove himself from office and end the Order. Otherwise, the backward dream would have eventually reasserted itself.

Still, Vlad Li Tam's words haunted him. *Rudolfo was my work even as you were my father's.* The notion that somehow his actions were manipulated from a lifetime of careful stimuli and engineered circumstances hollowed something inside of him. He'd seen the anguish upon Rudolfo's face after the Gypsy King's encounter with Tam on the Emerald Coast. He knew what price the Forester had paid at that family's hands, and the idea that he himself was also a river moved by those careful machinations gave rise to anger and doubt he did not want to face.

A dark bird shrieked far above, and he looked to it. It moved quickly northward. He watched it vanish and turned back to the maze. As he did, a low whistle reached his ears.

Petronus glanced over his shoulder. The guards stood at the garden's gate talking among themselves. Once he'd made his declaration of circumstances, Erlund's grip had relaxed upon him. Certainly, they kept him locked in his suites, but they gave the old Pope wide latitude as he wandered the grounds. After all, fleeing now would make him a fugitive not just of Entrolusian law but of kin-clave, now that he had invoked that right as king.

Slowly, he strolled toward the entrance to the Whymer Maze and paused there in the shadow of those tall thorn walls.

He kept his voice low. "Is someone there?"

As he drew nearer, the stench struck him. It was the reek of sewage. "Aye, Father," a familiar voice whispered, "and I've crawled a river of shite to be here."

Grymlis. Wrinkling his nose, he moved farther into the Maze. He felt a breeze where there was no wind and realized that the Gray Guard had not come alone. He forced himself to walk at a leisurely pace until he was out of eyeshot of the guards. "What are you doing here?"

Grymlis gave a low chuckle, his voice warbling in the grips of the powder. "I've come to see if you're finished with this foolishness yet. I've men watching your keepers, and I've a fresh pouch of scout magicks. Though the escape route may offend your regal sensibilities."

Petronus continued to stroll the maze. "How did you know to find me here?"

"We've been coming for a week now. We've been watching and waiting. This is just the first time you've gotten close enough to the maze."

It was Petronus's turn to chuckle. "Any closer and the reek would do me in far better than Erlund's axe ever could." He studied the air where he'd heard Grymlis's voice, but the magicks held him well and Petronus saw nothing. "So you've come to extricate me, then?"

"If you'll let me."

Of course, Petronus realized, his Gray Guard had to know the answer. And yet he still tried. *Because duty compelled him.* All his life, Grymlis had served the light. He'd served four Popes in his time, offering himself and his sword to them. Even when Petronus had sent him away to bury his Androfrancine Gray Guard uniform in the loamy soil of the Ninefold Forest, the old man had come wandering home like a castaway dog. "You know I won't leave," Petronus said as gently as he could.

He could imagine the man's shrug. "You know I had to try. Something dark rises, Petronus, and I have a sense of foreboding like none I've ever had."

Yes. Petronus heard the uneasiness in the man's voice and it alarmed him. Even the use of Petronus's proper name betrayed that worry. And Grymlis was unshaken under the most dire of circumstances. If he sat still long enough, Petronus felt the same foreboding. A reckoning approached, and he stood at the center of it. "This game of Queen's War has been carefully laid out," he said. "This is a battle I can win now that kin-clave is invoked."

"I don't trust it," Grymlis said. "It's foolhardy. The Marshers are uprising. An Y'Zirite resurgence is in full swing there, and the Androfrancine remnant is systematically disappearing. You've heard about the Summer Palace? And the armies in the north?"

Petronus nodded. "Esarov told me." He'd lain awake that night ciphering the news. Marshers that burned their dead.

"It's gotten worse. This resurgence is like nothing we've seen before, and its roots have grown deep and in secret. Rumor has it that Winteria's army is divided. She herself rides to petition for kin-clave."

Petronus winced. It was deep, then. The Order had kept a tight rein on these things, using its Gray Guard and its kin-clave to stomp out any hint of Y'Zir worship long before it reached the point of building critical mass. But the Marshers were already susceptible to mysticism. And though they were watched, they were a difficult people to infiltrate. With time and patience and care, a foundation of religion could be formed. Add to that an inexplicable access to forbidden blood magicks and men willing to die in service to the cause and it was a powerful weapon.

It could be no coincidence that just after Windwir fell, this new threat arose. Had Windwir stood, she had within her basements the means to counter these magicks, the weapons with which to bring down these foes. Some could say that without the shepherd, wolves savaged the fold. Still, it was not reasonable that a cult in the Marshlands could bring down Windwir. Not without a great deal of help.

Esarov had insisted that the threat that brought down Windwir had come from within. Vlad Li Tam believed his own family had somehow been compromised and used, along with Sethbert, to ac-

complish this. His golden bird and its presence at Windwir supported
that belief. And beyond the fall of Windwir, chaos and violence rocked
the Named Lands with both House Li Tam and the Order out of the
way.

"It's all threads of the same tapestry," he said in a quiet voice.

"Aye," Grymlis agreed. "And last week, I dreamed your death, Father, beneath an iron blade. Something is happening, and I believe
we're being herded as cattle to the cliff." He paused, and Petronus felt
the discomfort of his next words: "I'm fearful of what comes."

Petronus nodded but said nothing.

"So again," Grymlis said, "come with us. We will find a place to
hide you. We will continue the work of walking this Whymer Maze."

Petronus sighed. "What if my work in this is to follow the path I'm
on?"

There was anger in Grymlis's voice now, but the old guard worked
hard to conceal it. "Then you should give me whatever orders you
wish me to carry out both now and beyond your life here. Because if
you do not come with me now, of a certainty I believe you will be dead
within the month."

"Because of your dream?"

"Because of my dream, yes." He continued, "And don't give me that
Franci tripe about dreams being the secret mazes our souls work out,
our hidden fears and forbidden desires. I know all of that. But I also
know this: This dream feels true, and I'll not stand by and watch it
come to pass."

Petronus stopped. He'd reached the center of the maze and saw the
marble meditation bench there. He walked to it and sat down. He
wasn't sure that he believed the Francis anymore on that subject. Neb's
dreams during the grave-digging had tested and broken his belief. "I
cannot go with you, Grymlis. I need to finish what's begun with this."

"You have summoned every leader in the Named Lands that ever
held kin-clave with Windwir into one place," Grymlis said, his voice
heavy with anger. "Meanwhile, a foe that we have not the resources to
stop flows over the Wandering Army like water over stone to savage
the armies of Pylos and Turam on a whim." He waited, and Petronus
felt the weight of the words settling upon him. "Surely, Father, you see
this?"

"I do," he said. "But Rudolfo's Firstborn Feast and the events of
that night prove that if they wished to, they could strike anywhere and
anytime. They do not need us gathered in one place for this."

Grymlis sighed. "Then what are your orders?"

Petronus thought for a moment. "Should your dream prove true—and I do not believe it will, Grymlis—I would have you take what men are left you and petition Rudolfo for protection. They've not touched those of the Androfrancine remnant that remained in the Ninefold Forest. Serve him as you serve the light."

"I will serve him as I've served you, Father."

"And you've served me well, Grymlis."

He offered a bitter laugh. "Not well enough. A better soldier would club you and carry you to safety."

Petronus chuckled. "A better soldier would trust his superior's judgment."

Grymlis snorted. "I know better than that, old man."

And then, without another word between them, a shadow slipped away and the heavy, rotten odor of human waste gave way to crisp, clear air that smelled like rain.

When the first drops fell, Petronus remained there at the center of the maze, unmoving on the meditation bench. When the downpour that came next soaked him through and the guards came to escort him to his suite, he gave himself over to them.

Closer now, he thought, *this reckoning of mine.*

No. Not mine.

And Petronus felt the weight of a greater reckoning upon them all as clouds the color of bruises wept for the children of P'Andro Whym.

Chapter

22

Rae Li Tam

Rae Li Tam sat in the corner of the crowded cell and listened to the voices through the pipe. It had taken them half of the day to figure out the water was drugged—and she should have known better. She could easily name a half dozen herbs or roots that could induce a similar state: nausea, dizziness, lethargy and disorientation. Still, they'd been debilitated for most of their time here. Now, she was clear-headed, and her mind spun strategy after strategy to find some solution to this cipher. She did not have long. At some point, they would have to go back to drinking the water if she did not solve it. And that meant House Li Tam would join the Androfrancines in desolation.

So she bent her will to the riddle. She set some to tracking guard shifts and others to listening at the pipes in their cells. She established sleep shifts and message routes.

Blood pipes. It turned her stomach and caught her breath in her throat. They were warm to her ear, but she had to listen.

Some of the more seasoned sons and daughters of House Li Tam had coded bits of information into the poems they composed to their father beneath the knife.

So Rae Li Tam sat and untangled the codes, inventoried what she learned, and worried over the children. The guards took them while they were all still too drugged to act, and she was afraid for them.

She heard a distant tapping underneath the screams, and she lifted her ear for a moment, cocking her head. No, it wasn't in the pipes.

There. Letters. She followed the sound slowly as the message repeated, moving gradually to the bars.

Rae Li Tam, it said.

She reached the front of the cell and tapped her fingernail against the iron bar. *Yes.*

She felt the slightest breeze and started when a firm hand grabbed her wrist and soft fingers pressed a message into the skin of her forearm.

> *I am Rudolfo, Lord of the Ninefold Forest Houses, husband of Jin Li Tam,*
> *forty-second daughter of Vlad Li Tam by strategic marriage*
> *under the Overtures of kin-clave.*

She crouched slowly, and Rudolfo's grip loosened to let her. *Why are you here?*

There was a pause. *We can discuss that at a later time. We have ships at the ready; we're taking back your fleet, and my Gypsy Scouts are learning the maze before we run it. What can you tell me?*

She blinked. Was this a trap? Some kind of trick? *How do I know you're truly Rudolfo?*

You do not. Just be ready. Have your people organized. We do not intend to leave you to the knife.

Rae Li Tam looked around to her people. Mistrust at this juncture could not be allowed to interfere with her objective.

The children had to be saved, and she would not discard any opportunity. *They are cutting faster now,* she tapped. *They fill the holding cell every two hours and move them through quickly. They're making Father watch.*

His fingers were still for a moment. *They are readying the iron flagship for a voyage. I must see to my men.* He gave her arm a gentle squeeze, and then his fingers moved again. *Be ready; we will not leave you.*

Her own reply surprised her given her mistrust. *Listen to the pipes,* she said, *and I will pass what little I know to you.* She could softly tap the information to him, trusting the magicks to augment his senses.

Likewise, he replied, *but softly, so listen well.* Then he dropped her hand and slipped away. She barely heard the whispering of his boots as he retreated.

Before they faded entirely, Rae Li Tam started the chain of messages that would keep her family ready. She set more ears to the pipes—they could not afford to miss whatever word the Gypsy King might send. If indeed it were Rudolfo. She could not know for sure, and even if it were, there was no guarantee that he could free them.

Still, she had to be ready.

Messages sent, she went back to the pipe to gather what knowledge she could. But more than that, she listened to build up hatred. Her grandfather had often told her, "Grow your pain into an army."

She did this now, pulling down each cry of pain, each moan of anguish through the warm, flowing pipes. She felt herself building strength as she cataloged the coded bits of knowledge and tapped it into the pipe.

Closing her eyes, she watched her pain grow into a red light behind her eyelids and bent it into a conquering force that no enemy could stand against.

Rudolfo

Rudolfo followed his Gypsy Scouts into the room and closed the door softly behind them. The lock had been simple enough to pick, and Rae Li Tam's messages, tapped through the pipes, had been correct— the guard passed the door every two to three minutes. His scouts had already inventoried the room, but he insisted they bring him back so he could see for himself. Once inside, he took stock.

It was a small armory with assorted blades and bows, shield racks and various scraps of soldiering. They weren't a uniform army, that was for certain. These weapons were an odd collection from various nations in the Named Lands, though clean and ready for use. Certainly enough to guard drugged prisoners if Rae Li Tam's assertions were true. But the weapons were not what caught his eye as he glanced around the room.

No, it was the small silver vials in their rack beside the door. He slipped over to it and withdrew one, unscrewing the lid to sniff the contents within. It was a strong, sour smell that made his eyes water and burned his nostrils. These were the blood magicks. They had to be. He stretched a hand behind him and tapped his thumb and forefinger together three times.

A Gypsy Scout's hand found his extended forearm. *Yes, General?*

You've each earned an estate in Glimmerglam for this work, his own fingers pressed. *Now, live through the day to claim it.*

Yes, General.

He thought for a moment, then pressed his orders into the waiting arm. *Take these to Rae Li Tam. Tell her what they are and what they cost.* She was an alchemist; she would understand, he realized, and select as few men as possible. Those who took the blood-magicks would pay with their lives for the strength and stealth it lent them. He continued his orders: *Kill a guard, take his keys, and free them. Arm them if you can and wait for further orders, but hold your floor quietly. The children are your first priority; Lord Tam is your second. Hold for my orders or for when the ships go—whichever comes first.*

Aye, General, the scout pressed into his arm.

Rudolfo thought for a moment, choosing his next words with care. *Rae Li Tam is to be protected at all costs.*

After the first scout acknowledged the order, Rudolfo tapped for the second scout and took his offered arm. *Find the children. Tap their location into the pipes. When I've found Tam, I'll do the same.*

Rudolfo gave them time to get under way, then listened for the guard to pass outside. Once he'd strolled by, he let himself out of the room and relocked it. It was time to begin this night's work, and he hoped last night's hastily thought strategy would hold together. With the flagship preparing to leave, they could not afford to wait any longer. He would make his way from here to the kitchen and pack the bundle of soaked rags into the main oven. If Charles's handiwork proved true, it would lend eerie light to the smoke that leaked from its chimney and tell Rafe Merrique that it was time to disable the ships and prepare to hold the docks.

Rudolfo crept into the hall and moved quickly to the next point where he could check the pipe. In the absence of new information, Rae Li Tam was tapping out the previous ones. Rudolfo interrupted her with the lightest tapping of his own fingernails, hoping the sound would carry to her amid the screams and the flowing blood. *My man brings you a way out. Follow his instructions.*

After her acknowledgment, he slipped down another shadowed hallway and approached the door to the kitchen. He'd memorized what maps they had, amending them internally with each new bit of information he gleaned from his men or from the pipe. He listened at the kitchen door and paused a moment to collect himself.

The scout magicks were already starting to chew on him. He felt the headache building behind his eyes and felt the restlessness in his stomach. It would only get worse, and that meant he needed to do as much as he could while his mind was still sharp and the discomfort was at its lowest level. His Gypsy Scouts could stay under the powders for days at a time—weeks even, if absolutely necessary. But the few times he'd used them over the years, his body had paid steeply each time for days following.

Rudolfo heard nothing behind the door and opened it. The kitchen was dimly lit by an open stove with its banked fire. He went swiftly to it and pulled the wad of rags from his pocket. Taking up an iron fire poker, he stirred the coals to life and tossed the rag bundle onto it. Then, he closed the stove and moved back into the hallway.

Rudolfo picked his way slowly across the second floor, positioning himself near the guard station that stood between him and the third floor. His scouts had logged at least two men at this post during their forays into the various points within the building, and neither had slipped past this station yet—Rudolfo would be the first. But after watching for a full ten minutes he did not see how he could do it without resorting to violence, and magicked or not, two-to-one odds were not favorable. Neither was losing the element of surprise sooner than necessary.

Rudolfo moved through the corridors and found a door leading to a suite of guest rooms. He could not imagine guests attending the dark rites that took place here, but he picked the lock and found himself in a lavishly decorated room.

He scanned his memory for his recollection of this side of the structure. There were balconies here, and if the distance was close enough, he should be able to climb to the third floor. Rudolfo moved across the thick-carpeted room and opened the door that led to the bedchambers. On the far wall, a narrow glass door offered him a view of the harbor. Somewhere out there, beneath a veil of clouds, Rafe Merrique and his men set about securing the vessels and disabling the schooners.

Rudolfo opened the door and felt the warm night wind move over him. Stepping onto the balcony, he pulled the door closed behind him and looked up. The balconies were offset with one another, floor by floor, and he'd not consider a climb like that without the enhanced senses and strength he received from the powders. If only he could keep the damnable headache from consuming him.

He pulled himself up onto the rail, his hand steadying himself against the outer wall of the building. Trying not to look down, he balanced himself and once more measured the distance between him and the balcony above. Fixing his eye on the handhold ahead, Rudolfo forced himself to the climb, giving himself to the magicks that enhanced his strength and agility and trying not to look beneath him while he imagined the wall to be an old-growth pine from his childhood in the forest. Sweat beaded upon his forehead as he slowly made his way up, his feet and hands finding purchase as he went.

When he finally pulled himself over the edge of the balcony, he was winded but careful to let his breath out through his nose. He huddled in the corner and waited for the spike in his head to stop twisting.

As he waited, he heard voices and cocked his head. The door to the balcony above was slightly ajar, and he heard the sounds of muted conversation drifting out into the night air along with curtains that caught on the breeze like flags.

He'd thought to scout the third floor and see if he could find another way past the guards—but he strained his ear upward, catching the low voices, and curiosity got the better of him. Whatever happened here, he had no doubt it was connected somehow to the Desolation of Windwir and to the attack upon his Firstborn Feast. Blood magicks had returned to the New World when Windwir fell, and it could be no coincidence that one of the Named Lands' most powerful families was now under the knife. This structure was made for bloodletting, from its viewing balcony to the cutting floor, through the system of pipes down into the distillery he knew must be buried in the deeper basements.

Rudolfo had certainly read the stories as a child. He was familiar with the bargaining pools and their access to the dark spirits of the Beneath Places, where blood and anguish could purchase favors and power. His own Tormentor's Row, now closed these eight months, followed a similar design to those Blood Temples of old but only retained the notion of redemptive cutting, having no use for the blood that was spilled in the pursuit of that atonement.

This resurgence was a threat to the Named Lands that had to be stopped. That meant availing himself of anything he could learn while freeing House Li Tam. It even meant saving Vlad Li Tam if he was still alive, forced to watch as his family went beneath the salted blades. Quietly, he rose to his feet and moved to the far railing of the balcony. As he drew closer, the words became slightly clearer, though still not clear enough for him to hear. It was a man and a woman talking in low tones.

He climbed onto the railing and found his handholds, holding his breath and willing silence into his every movement. He was too old for this, he realized, and had not climbed since the days of his youth. Heights were not the friend they'd once been to him as a younger man.

Still, he forced his way upward and found himself crouching in the corner of the balcony.

They had the sound of lovers about them. Their tone spoke of it, and Rudolfo suspected they lay in bed together in postcoital embrace, tangled in the sheets and one another. The mumbled words were clear now.

"Things moved faster than we planned for on the Delta," the man said. "Erlund was in a hurry to have done with the matter. Our man there tells us the Last Son will be at Windwir ahead of schedule. We need to conclude our work here and move on."

"Then I will dispatch Vlad before I sail," the girl said. There was a bit of sadness in her voice that bordered on the edge of love. "I think our guest is as ready as he'll ever be. And we were never promised more than forty years."

"It is sufficient." Rudolfo heard the bed creak, heard soft footfalls. "I should see to the children," he said. "We need to start loading them."

Rudolfo crept closer to the door, peeking into the room. A candle guttered, and in its dim light, he saw a nude woman on the bed. She was twenty perhaps, long-limbed with brown hair that cascaded down over her breasts. She stretched again, and Rudolfo admired the line of her briefly. Flitting in and out of his view, a lithe man with long red hair moved about picking up articles of clothing. "I should see to Vlad, then," she said, sitting up. "Do you want to speak with him before I finish?"

The young man chuckled. "I don't see what I could gain from that. And he'll have had plenty of anguish by then."

"He's your grandfather, regardless of what else he's done."

"He was a Whymer lap-whore." Rudolfo heard bitterness creep into the man's voice and shifted his position to get a better look. The young man looked vaguely familiar, but he could not place him. Still, the red hair and finely chiseled features bore the look of a Tam.

But the girl looked familiar, too. She looked at the man now, and Rudolfo saw love upon her face. "Mal," she said, "even the Whymers served House Y'Zir in the end. All things do, whether or not they know it. Are you certain you don't want to speak with him before I finish?"

When he looked to her, his eyes were hard. "I'm certain, Ria. You need not ask again. Nor will I speak with any of them. They are no longer my kin." He thought for a moment. "Still, they need not suffer beyond what is necessary."

He'd dressed now and slipped his sandals on near the door. The girl, Ria, stood, and Rudolfo was struck by the wild, coltish beauty of her.

"We'll dispatch them quickly once we're certain we have what we need." She walked to Mal and folded her arms around him before kissing him. "Safe travels, love," she said, "that bring you home to me soon."

He returned the kiss. "I will be home when I can. We've not sailed these waters before. Be careful," he told her. "We're close now."

"Care or not," she said, her voice muffled in his neck, "the Crimson Empress will establish her throne and make all things right by her grace."

They disentangled and then the man left. Rudolfo watched as she moved across the room, light on her toes and humming an unfamiliar song. She went to a vanity in the corner and studied herself in the mirror for a moment before sitting down to dip her fingers into the various jars that lay open there.

Rudolfo continued to watch, realizing with each passing minute that he needed to exit this room and continue his work. But the girl held him hostage. As her fingers moved over her skin, he found himself transfixed as she first painted lines of color into her face and neck and forearms—shades of gray and deep green and brown.

A Marsher then, he realized. Though the lines were more carefully drawn and the colors more intentionally blended. And when she moved just so before the mirror, he could see the pink lines of the scar upon her heart like a seal. It was just off center and marring the side of her left breast.

"Dear Vlad," she said, looking into the mirror and applying a paint to her lips that was the color of pooled blood. "Tonight your kin is finally healed, and soon that healing will save us all."

Rudolfo waited as she pulled a thin robe over her naked form and watched her move to the door. After she'd slipped through it, he counted to five before following her out of the room.

Then, he moved quickly down the corridor to catch up with her, hoping for shadows to hide him as he ghosted along behind. Stretching out a hand, he lay his fingers along a blood pipe as he went and felt the warm pulse of language in it. The others were ready, Rae Li Tam tapped, and their enemy had not been alerted as yet. The children were located, and House Li Tam lay in wait, armed with what could be found easily. A few choice taps of his fingernail and Rudolfo gave the word for them to execute their orders.

Now the sound of the screams grew in his ears as they approached a wide stairwell that ended at a dark pair of ornately carved doors. They swung open at a whistle from the girl, and Rudolfo picked up his pace to slip into the observation deck behind her.

What he saw there nearly took his wind despite hours spent sipping wine while his own Physicians of Penitent Torture did their redemptive work.

Rudolfo stifled a roar and loosened the scout knives within their sheaths.

Vlad Li Tam

He could not remember the last time he'd slept or how long he'd been strapped into the viewing rack. He dimly remembered Ria leaving him in the care of a dark-robed blood-letter who continued her cuttings with more confidence than compassion, and he remembered longing for her hands and blade upon him, moving slowly and with love over—

No. This is not love, he told himself. *It is a peculiar fixation that develops between captive and captor—a product of desperation and twisted hope.* But it was a tempting fantasy to fall into.

I will grow my pain into an army.

But now, Vlad Li Tam knew there was no army coming from his pain. They'd run his children and grandchildren past him now in a seemingly endless stream, no longer taking their time with the knives but moving with machinelike precision.

He felt a soft hand on his shoulder, and his breath caught in his throat. "I'm back, Vlad," Ria whispered.

He said nothing but twisted in the rack enough to see her feet and the beginnings of her calves peeking out from beneath the thin robes she wore.

He heard her fingers moving over the collection of knives as she selected one. "This will be our last night together," she told him in a low, husky voice. "Tonight, all of this pain and suffering ends for you, and your kinship with House Y'Zir will be healed. Are you ready to take the mark of your last master upon you?"

He tried to speak and found his words garbled. But he knew what he meant to say, gods help him, and he knew it was the answer she hoped it would be. *Yes. Anything. Just stop. Spare what little remains of my family and have your way with me.*

But nothing so intelligible came out of him.

Then muffled explosions reached his ear, followed by the shrill whistle of Third Alarm. He twisted himself to watch her drop the knife and look up quickly, her eyes narrow. She jerked suddenly and opened her mouth to speak, but no words came out. A low and magicked voice whispered hoarsely, and Vlad Li Tam knew it but could not place it.

"Unbind him," the voice said. "This dark work is ended tonight."

Kill her, he willed the invisible intruder. *Do not speak, do not request, simply slide the blade into her kidney and twist it hard.* But at the same time he willed it, he willed that she escape, that she might lay her hand upon him again and gently teach him love and kinship beneath the blade.

Vlad Li Tam watched her struggle against her captor and saw a dot of blood well up on her dark-painted neck. "Unbind him *now* or I add your blood to rest you've spilled in this place."

Below them, they heard the noise of fighting. The assailant let his hand off of her mouth. "Release him," she told the guards.

Vlad Li Tam felt the table spinning upright and felt hands at the straps and buckles. When he fell from the rack, he landed heavily upon the marble floor with a gasp.

The voice spoke again. "Can you stand, Tam?"

And suddenly he knew that voice but could not believe his ears. He found the name and croaked it. "Rudolfo?"

The girl gasped her surprise. "Rudolfo, Shepherd of the Light? Father of Jakob, the Child of Promise?"

"I am Rudolfo, yes," Rudolfo said in a low and bitter voice.

She raised her voice to the others. "Do not harm him. We know the cost of that."

Vlad Li Tam gathered his strength on the floor and pushed against it with shaking arms. He raised himself somewhat, then slipped and fell facefirst into his own blood. He pushed with his feet and hands, groaning, until he crawled from the sticky mess at the foot of the rack.

"What cost?" he heard Rudolfo ask.

But the girl did not answer. "What does he look like?" she asked instead. "The Child of Promise? Is he pink? Does he glow with life and health? With his mother's blue eyes and his father's dark hair? Does he laugh? Or is he gray and mottled, gasping like a fish on the bank for his very life?"

Vlad Li Tam heard the growl in Rudolfo's voice. "What do you know of my son, Marsh girl?"

She laughed, and it was music. "You came looking for his salvation, but there is none to be found upon the path you have chosen."

Now Rudolfo ignored her. "Can you stand?" he again asked.

Vlad Li Tam gathered his strength again and pushed himself up, turning so he could sit. The girl stood awkwardly bent backwards, her robe now open as Rudolfo held her from behind. The guards stood near with hands upon their knives, eyes moving from the girl to Vlad Li Tam to the closed doors and the sounds of fighting outside.

Struggling to push himself up, he lost his footing again and slid down, his body shaking from the effort.

Then, the doors burst open and a tornado of violence swept into the observation deck.

He felt hands upon him and heard a voice whispering in his ear. "I will carry you, Father."

He was lifted up then, cradled like a child in strong, sure arms, and he found himself suddenly weeping. The spasms of grief and relief washed over him and racked his body with great sobs as he clung to the neck of a son he could no longer recognize. Once, before this place, he'd known his children by their voice, their smell, the sound of their approach. But now all he smelled was blood and all he heard were the last poems of his fallen family ringing in his ears.

He became vaguely aware of the fighting around them, aware that Rudolfo stayed near him, holding the girl as a shield and clacking his tongue against the top of his mouth. And then they were fighting their way down the stairs and into the corridor he'd measured so carefully during his early days within this place. He heard the whisper and rasp of blades spinning around him.

Twice his son fell, spilling Vlad onto the ground but covering him with his own body as he did. Each time, the man hefted Vlad up into his arms, finally slinging him over his shoulder like a bag of oranges so that he could better keep his feet with a blade in his left hand.

They fought their way to the ground floor and burst outside into the warm night. The iron vessels were building steam, and one of the schooners was sinking in the harbor. The second wooden ship smoked but still floated, and a band of unmagicked men fought at its gangway on the dock. Vlad could not see the flagship but thought he heard the barking of its cannon.

A wave of invisible force met them on the path down to the dock. These soldiers had been waiting and had had the time to prepare themselves. Vlad felt the power of it, heard the muffled sounds of attack but saw nothing. Still, he rocked backward when that wall hit the son who carried him and toppled them to the ground. He felt a white searing pain as the sea-salted sand ground its way into his open cuts, and he cried out even though he did not want to.

Invisible boots kicked at him and his son, and he heard the crunch of bones breaking nearby.

Then he heard a cry as more of his children fell upon the assailant and drove him down beneath their blades.

Strong hands scooped him up as another son spoke. "I will carry you, Father."

Pressing forward, they reached the bottom of the stairs. The docks stretched out ahead, dust and sand whirling at the magicked soldiers that fought there.

Another solid push back, and Vlad Li Tam once more fell to the ground. This time, even Rudolfo and the girl he held hostage were knocked down. Vlad couldn't see what happened next, but he heard Rudolfo's heavy gasp as the wind left him. Around them, boots and bare feet vied for solid footing as House Li Tam's front guard fought its way through the resurgence's soldiers.

"Get up, old man," Rudolfo whispered in his ear, breathing heavy from exertion. "I can't carry you and hold this feral cat at the same time."

Vlad Li Tam rolled to his hands and knees and tried to push himself up. More strong hands lifted him, and he saw these were unmagicked hands. The rear guard—armed with what weapons they could find—now raced along behind them, followed by the young children in white robes still bloodstained from the mark they'd been forced to take.

A low whistle reached his ears. Then, he heard Rudolfo return it. He felt another wind approach on his left and heard the familiar clacking of a scout on the run.

Vlad Li Tam closed his eyes for a moment, suddenly aware of the fear that saturated him. But not fear for himself; fear for his family.

Already, so many had died, and the notion that more died now broke what few unbroken pieces of him remained.

He did not see the flash from the flagship, though he heard the blast. Then, a whistling that built until the world erupted into heat and light that forced him to the ground. From where he fell, he saw that the cannon blast had landed in the midst of the rear guard, desolating more than a third of it. The children cowered.

"Stop," a voice boomed out, enhanced by magicks, and he knew that voice. It was his grandson, Mal Li Tam. "I don't mind killing the children, though I prefer not to. Release the woman."

Rudolfo hesitated. "Do it," Vlad Li Tam said, his voice more pleading than he intended it to be. "I'll not risk my family further."

The girl fell forward, then picked herself up, closing her robe. She turned to Vlad and smiled.

Mal Li Tam's voice called out to them again. "Have your pirate stand down, Rudolfo, and clear the mouth. Ria, bring Vlad Li Tam to his flagship. It seems our plans have changed."

Vlad looked to her, still surprised at the reasoned tone of his own voice. "If I come with you, will you leave the others in peace?"

She nodded. "Yes, Vlad," she said. "You have purchased propitiation for your family's sins." Her smile widened, and he saw love shining in her eyes. "I will give you the mark of Home and send you to your rest, your blood let and your kin healed."

She reached out her hand to him, and he knew then that taking it was the most important thing he could do. "I will even carry you if you need it," she told him.

"I will walk to it," he said. *I will grow my pain into an army.*

He forced himself to unsteady feet and trembled at the effort of it. Then, he forced first one foot and then another as his family watched him walk. Ria walked beside him, and when they reached the gangway to the flagship, she waited until he climbed it. Then, she followed.

Mal Li Tam waited for him at the top, standing within view of his cannoneers. Vlad walked to him. "You will keep your word, Mal? You will spare the others in exchange for me?"

Mal inclined his head. "I will, Grandfather."

"Walk me to the railing then, that I might share my last words with them."

Mal Li Tam's eyebrows furrowed. "You will have to be quick. We're leaving."

I will grow my pain into an army.

Vlad took the young man's offered arm and walked slowly to the bow of the flagship. He looked out over his sons and daughters and grandchildren, and his eyes found Rae Li Tam's. "You will be the Lady Tam," he told her.

And then, using every bit of strength, he threw his arms around his First Grandson and toppled them over the railing. He felt the solid *thud* as some part of his adversary struck the dock on the way down, and then they were plunged into the warm harbor. The pain of the salt in his wounds built a scream in lungs he dared not empty of air as he clung to his grandson. His hands wandered over the thrashing form he held in search of Mal's windpipe. He entwined the younger man with his legs, now riding his back and strangling him as they sank.

He let the sea burn his flayed skin, and the burning built his pain. He grew that pain into an army and bent that army toward the destruction of one man.

And suddenly, Vlad Li Tam was not alone beneath the water. A radiant blue-green light engulfed him, shimmering around him in the water, and his ears were suddenly filled with song. The stark power and beauty of it overwhelmed him, and even clutching at his grandson's throat he felt the urge to weep and cry out. Then suddenly, the light was gone and hands were reaching for him, pulling him back toward the surface. Hands that he could not see.

He resisted, twisting away and retaining his hold on Mal Li Tam with one arm while the other hand groped his loose clothing. Mal Li Tam struggled and kicked in a sudden resurgence of energy.

It must be here.

The hands were back again just as his fingers slipped over the cover of the book, tucked in a hidden pocket. He shook them off one more time, finally expelling the air in his lungs to force him down. Fumbling, he found the slender volume and drew it out just as the invisible hands, one last time, grabbed at him and pulled him toward the surface.

Mal Li Tam thrashed away into the deeper waters, gradually fading from view as Vlad neared the surface.

"Stop fighting me, Father," Rae Li Tam whispered. He heard sadness in her voice but did not comprehend it. And when had she magicked herself?

"I will," he said. Behind them, his flagship steamed for the mouth of the harbor under Ria's control. Five of his iron vessels and the two schooners were awash and rolling listlessly as they burned and sank. On the docks, his family waited as the remaining vessels approached.

Clutching that slender volume of his father's to his chest, Vlad Li Tam gave himself over to his daughter's strong hands.

Neb

As the sun rose with terrifying glory, painting the landscape the color of blood, Neb stood upon the last rise with the metal man and gazed down into the bent and scattered bones of a city.

"We have arrived," the mechoservitor said.

Neb studied the silent, unmoving landscape. "What city was this?"

"Port Charis—it is the birthplace of P'Andro Whym."

Neb nodded. The exhilaration of the song still pulsed in his temples as he stretched from their long run.

"My brothers will be glad to meet you, Nebios Homeseeker. We have all seen your advent in the dream." The metal man started out at an easy gait, strolling down the rise and into the ruins. Neb followed.

They walked deep into the city until they reached the base of an enormous tower with a dome that had collapsed into itself. Set into the base of the tower was a massive set of double doors set with a dozen Rufello ciphers. Neb watched the metal man's fingers move over the locks with fast precision, and he tried to capture the string of numbers and symbols that clicked the locks open and caused the door to swing inward.

The metal man took a step into the wide, inviting room and then stopped. Its shoulders chugged and its metal body shook violently. Its eyes opened and closed. The mechoservitor looked to Neb. "I fear I am not functioning properly."

Then, the mouth flap opened and closed and the shudders became more violent. Suddenly, the voice blasted out, high and reedy, in the dark and empty space. "My name is Charles," the metal man said. "I am the Arch-Engineer of Mechanical Science for the Androfrancine Order in Windwir. I bear an urgent message for the Hidden Pope, Petronus. *The Library is fallen by treachery. Sanctorum Lux must be protected.*"

It stopped, then looked up to Neb. "My operating scrolls have been significantly altered between Father Charles and his apprentice."

"That is the message you gave at the Keeper's Gate."

"It is the message Father Charles etched into me during my time of captivity on the Delta."

Father Charles? Neb knew that name very well. He was the man who'd brought the mechoservitors back from the obscurity of the past, working with what little remained of Rufello's *Book of Specifications* to rebuild the mechanical wonders. "Charles survived Windwir?"

"He altered my operating and memory scrolls under the belief that Pope Petronus still lived. Before him, his apprentice decommissioned my obedience to the dream. The integration of new orders has created a logic conflict in my scripting. Sanctorum Lux must *not* be protected. It must surely be destroyed in its proper time to save the light, to keep it from those who would bend it toward darkness. The dream is clear on this matter."

Neb felt an uneasiness growing within him and looked into the dark opening. He heard nothing, smelled nothing, and forced himself to take a step inside. "I don't see anything."

The mechoservitor walked into the room's far wall, and in the dim glow of its amber eyes, Neb watched it opening a panel. "The lights are not functioning."

Neb slipped outside to fashion a makeshift torch. When he returned, the mechoservitor had vanished. A small door in the far wall stood open, and he entered it, suddenly swept with vertigo when he realized it opened upon a vast open space that descended down beneath him on a narrow metal staircase. Somewhere below, he heard the sound of metal on metal as the mechoservitor descended.

The smell in this place was unmistakable. The smell of smoke and ash and burnt paper. Neb felt a knot growing in his stomach.

Sanctorum Lux must not *be protected.*

When he reached the bottom, the mechoservitor waited for him. "I was mistaken," the metal man said. "You are not early after all, Nebios Homeseeker."

At the bottom of the stairs, a vast underground room stretched out beyond the guttering light from his torch. The reek of old smoke filled the room, and Neb knew that this was merely the first of many rooms. Just as surely, he also knew that each of them would be the same: an urn that held the ashes of the light.

He sat heavily on the soot-covered stone floor and let the weight of it settle down upon him. Was it possible that somehow, the same hidden enemy that had brought down Windwir had brought down this place, too? No, he realized. The mechoservitor's cryptic words still played out behind his eyes. "Then it was here? The library was here?"

"League upon league of it," the metal man said. "Reproduced and guarded by my brothers and me."

Neb sucked in his breath, then slowly exhaled. He felt something squeezing his heart. The weight of it hurt his head and brought back images of fire falling from the sky, a column of dark smoke blotting out the sun. "Destroyed at the bidding of a dream?"

The mechoservitor didn't answer the question at first. Instead, it went to the center of the room and sat down heavily. When it spoke, its thin and reedy voice was racked with sorrow. "Sacrificed for the dream," it said, "even as I have now become."

Neb's eyes narrowed. "How have you been sacrificed?"

The grief in the voice was unbearable to hear. "I will not participate in the Great Response. My absence and the alterations in my scripts exclude me." It looked up at Neb, and its jeweled eyes leaked rusty tears. "I do not grieve for myself, Nebios Homeseeker, for it is my joy to give the dream back to itself. And I do not grieve that my brothers have left me behind; I would have done the same. The response must be made. I grieve that so much of the light was lost before we heard the dream. Before it taught us that Sanctorum Lux is far more than the books and scrolls of the past age, a far higher calling than what our creators intended us for."

The cryptic words settled in, and Neb sorted them as best he could. "Where have the others gone, then?"

"They have followed the dream onward. You will follow it, too, in your path toward Home." The mechoservitor opened up its chest cavity and reached long, metal fingers inside. "In my memory scrolls you will find a complete inventory of all my brothers destroyed here."

Then, the metal man began pulling out metal scrolls and tangled wires from inside, tugging at them as if they were the stubborn weeds of a garden. As it pulled, its lights flashed and dimmed, and its mouth flap opened and closed.

Neb took a step toward it, thinking he had to do something, had to somehow prevent what was taking place in front of his eyes. "How do I follow the dream?"

The mechoservitor, sitting in the ashes of the burned-out library, looked up. "The last cipher is the first day of the Homeseeker's Advent. You will know the rest within the song."

Still, those hands plucked at the wires and scrolls until they spilled out around the metal man. Neb suddenly found himself weeping at the sight of it but did not understand why.

The metal man tipped onto its side, its hands slowing as they pulled at its innards. The bellows chugged slowly now, as well, and its eyes were specks of light buried deep in the glassy jewels. A slight sound escaped the mouth flap, and Neb leaned closer to hear it. The sound built as the metal man gave it the last wind of his artificial lungs.

The canticle was unmistakable, and when it was released into the vast tomb of burnt books, it whispered and echoed with a life of its own. Then, with one last wrenching tug, the metal man yanked out one final scroll and pushed it toward Neb.

As its fine copper wires detached, the music died.

Neb looked upon the suicided mechoservitor as the last of the song echoed through the room and felt something twist and snap into place within him—a Rufello lock on his soul that opened him to something he'd not seen within himself. *The last cipher is the first day of the Home-seeker's Advent.*

He had come here seeking Sanctorum Lux and had found something different to search for. And he knew he could scour the burned-out remains of this Great Library, but Neb would save that work for others. They would find nothing here.

Instead, he would return to the locked well and place his ear to it. He would listen for the ciphers in the song and find the source of the dream.

It requires a response.

Somewhere, metal hands fashioned this so-called response, and Neb knew he was called to follow them. It was as if nothing else mattered. As if everything that could possibly matter depended upon finding the dream and obeying it.

Reaching down, he pried the last scroll from the mechoservitor's fingers.

Then, giving himself to the song, he rose and left the metal man's chosen grave.

Chapter 23

Lysias

Lysias ran his hands through his hair and squinted at the reports on his makeshift desk. Outside, a wind whistled across the plain where Windwir had once stood, and cold from it leaked into his tent despite the furnace that glowed in the corner.

This was a miserable, desolate place, and it broke his heart to be here again. The images of that first dreadful sight were burned into his brain, from Sethbert's wide-eyed, gleeful expression as the Overseer watched the fire fall over wine and cheese right down to the smoldering, stinking forest of bones Petronus and his army of gravediggers had ridden into with their shovels and wagons. It was a reminder of a genocide he had helped cause by trusting the wrong man with his loyalty. In the end, it had cost him. It had also cost the nation he loved above all others.

After the Ninefold Forest invitation had been received, he'd spent two weeks preparing his honor guard and organizing their winter march north. The Foresters had worked hard to be ready for the rest of the Named Lands, erecting what he suspected was the same massive tent they'd used when they'd hosted the Androfrancines' last council. They'd also carefully established quarters for each of the kinclave in attendance, their Second Captain of the Gypsy Scouts working with each military liaison to assure that no nation was placed improperly in the elaborate network of relationships, all precariously balanced with the recent troubles to the north.

When the council had convened three days earlier, the new Gypsy Queen, Jin Li Tam, had invoked the Articles of Kin-Clave regarding the call to council and—as hostess for the event—had taken petitions for the agenda. It was no surprise that matters in the Marshland quickly eclipsed Entrolusia's interests in the kin-clave. Rumors flew the camp of Y'Zirite resurgence and coup d'état. The young Marsh Queen was placed on the agenda, along with Meirov of Pylos and the dour-faced steward of Turam. Petronus had made his petition as well, along with Erlund, who supported the old Pope's call for a public trial. And then, because it had been some time since a kin-clave had been called, other issues were voiced. In the absence of the Androfrancine Order, the matter of access to the Churning Wastes through the Keeper's Wall was on the agenda. Representatives from the various counties of the Divided Isle petitioned the Ninefold Forest Houses for the return of Androfrancine land titles in their territories. It was a long list. Longer than Lysias could keep track of, particularly with his mind on other matters.

You should go to her. She is not hard to find. Somewhere in the Foresters' city of tents, his daughter sat with the young Gypsy heir. He'd gotten confirmation from his spies in their camp, even had word that she was healthy and well cared for. That should have been enough for him. But it wasn't; he longed to see her.

More than that, he longed to atone somehow. For many things, he now realized, beyond his parenting. The quiet snow fields of Windwir's buried dead whispered his sins to him. And at night, when he dreamed, he saw the coldness of Vlad Li Tam's eyes as he passed the cloth-wrapped weapon and forged confession across to him during the night of their clandestine meeting. He heard the muffled cries as he and Grymlis helped Sethbert's cousin, Pope Resolute, exit this life and make way for an end to a war they could not win by force but might survive by intrigue.

Petronus had been wrong, surely, to try Sethbert summarily and without regard to kin-clave and Entrolusian law. But Sethbert, regardless of why or how, had brought down Windwir—and boasted of it—and then, after breaking the back of the Delta's economy, had forced a war upon the Named Lands that even now spun out consequences of violence faster than a Tam could weave strategies. This unrest now to the north with the recent Marsher skirmishes far from their usual territories, the civil wars that still brewed in Turam and Pylos and the recently ceased hostilities on the Delta were all certainly outgrowths of Sethbert's actions. Because from his vantage point, before Windwir fell and the Androfrancines were taken out of the role of shepherd—and before House Li Tam packed up its network and vanished—the Named Lands had been safer.

Before Sethbert brought back the blood magicks of Xhum Y'Zir.

And I helped him do it.

He'd thought that rainy night last spring, nearly a year past now, he'd done his part to make that right. He'd worked with Tam, planted a forged suicide note that was actually more truth than lie, from all he could see. The note had implicated Sethbert and his cousin Resolute in the destruction of Windwir. Certainly, Resolute had been deceived and manipulated. That was clear. And Sethbert had made a great show of having evidence supporting Androfrancine plans for subduing the Named Lands, but when the Overseer had been called upon to produce it on the night of his arrest, he'd not been able to. And then the Overseer had fled.

No, as far as Lysias was concerned, Sethbert had gotten what had been coming to him and the wrong man was now under scrutiny. If there was a villain here besides Sethbert he suspected it was Vlad Li Tam and not Petronus.

Lysias rubbed his eyes now and tried again to read the reports before him. But it nagged him now, and he felt something clawing inside of him, demanding that he pay it heed.

It is never too late to do the right thing. He remembered these words from his father, long ago. They were the very words his daughter, Lynnae, had recited to him when she allied herself with the Democrats and their dangerous philosophies.

Whistling for his birder, he pulled a scrap of parchment and started triple-coding a message. When the birder came and went, taking the note with instructions to send it under the white thread of kin-clave, Lysias pushed aside his reports, drew down a fresh piece of paper, and started making his notes.

Within the hour, he'd written down his every recollection of that night in Pylos and then that later night in Resolute's guest quarters. Last, he wrote his recollection of his attempt to arrest Sethbert.

The more recent memories cataloged, he went back further, into the days of the war and days just before Windwir fell.

Some part of him knew that it didn't matter, that there was no way

Petronus's kin-clave would find Petronus guilty. He was a gifted orator and had the graves of Windwir as his stage for this present drama. He was also a strong king and perhaps the most innately talented of the papal line when it came to statecraft.

Lysias did not do this now to save Petronus. Of that he had no doubt.

But he hoped, perhaps, he might save some part of himself.

When the bells announced the resumption of council proceedings, Lysias stood, scooped up his sword and helmet, and left for the palatial tent with his bundle of notes tucked beneath his cloak.

Winters

Winters sat to the side of the council and watched Jin Li Tam preside over another day of questioning and discussion. It had been hard for her to keep her attention on these strange matters of New World statecraft. The Marshfolk had their own approach to council, but with less bluster and bravado and certainly less pomp. They made their decisions largely by consensus, and as queen, her primary role had been that of dreamer and, during time of war, sermonizer. And because the Marshfolk had remained set apart and without kin-clave until their secret and one-sided alliance with the Ninefold Forest, she'd not had any opportunity to see the intricate system of rules and rituals at work in a formal meeting. Certainly Tertius had educated her in these matters, but even the former Androfrancine had glossed over portions of it as unimportant and unnecessary for the work ahead of her.

So now, she sat, trying to remain still and listen. She stayed quiet and she watched. And most of all, she tried not to worry about her people—an impossible task. There had been no word since the Gypsy Scouts had brought Seamus to her, and the ride to Windwir—and away from her troubled tribes—had killed something inside of her with each league. It had even eclipsed her sense of separation from Neb, though when they'd first swept onto the plains to approach the growing city of tents, she'd been reminded of that first meeting, that first kiss, those stolen strolls along the northern line. But the memories seemed small things now in light of what happened among her people.

She heard Jin Li Tam's gavel and looked up as the Gypsy Queen called for order. The woman looked tired but regal, her copper hair pulled back from her face and held in place by platinum combs. Her blue eyes were clear, and she stood behind the podium watching the crowded tent. "We now resume the matter of Petronus, King of Windwir and former Holy See of the Androfrancine Order." Jin Li Tam nodded toward the table where Petronus and Esarov sat. "The petitioner may continue his declaration."

Esarov stood and bowed. "Thank you, Lady Tam." He stepped out from behind the table. "Over the last two days, you've heard Overseer Erlund and his governors discuss the matter of Sethbert's death. The council has seen and questioned witnesses to the Androfrancine Council. You've also heard Petronus himself speak. And there is no doubt: This man *did* personally and summarily execute Sethbert." The man's eyes narrowed, and Winters saw that he was staring hard now at Jin Li Tam. "You yourself, Lady Tam, bore witness to the events of that council and have spoken to them before us. But I would ask a further question of you." He turned, looking to the crowded tent, and lifting up a piece of parchment.

Jin Li Tam looked nonplussed. "Ask your question, Esarov. You've the floor and need no permission from me."

Winters leaned forward. She could hear something rising in his voice and noted that as he asked his question, he faced the audience. "Very well, Lady Tam, I will be direct: It has come to my attention that Petronus's actions were heavily influenced by House Li Tam— manipulated directly by your father, according to a highly placed officer in the Entrolusian army. According to documents I've recently received, Arch-scholar Oriv—also known as Pope Resolute—did not commit suicide as we have all believed. His death was coerced in collusion with your father, Vlad Li Tam." Here, Esarov looked to Erlund. "Sethbert's family was involved at some level, though the extent of this is not fully known. They wished to end a war they could not win and prevent the Delta city-states from sliding into civil war. Resolute's suicide letter—the very letter implicating Sethbert—was forged by one of the sons or daughters of House Li Tam, and an Androfrancine weapon was provided. A member of Oriv's own Gray Guard—a Captain Grymlis—assisted in the matter." He paused, turned back to the podium, and continued with a slight smile upon his face. "My question to you, Lady Tam, is this: Were you aware of your father's culpability in these matters along with Petronus?"

Winters watched Jin Li Tam's face. At Esarov's initial words, she'd blinked but maintained her composure. Now, her face turned red with

anger. "My father," she said with a low voice, "is culpable in *many* matters. What exactly is your point in these observations, Esarov?"

Esarov opened his hands and held them out. "Only this, Lady: The
Desolation of Windwir is the greatest tragedy in Named Lands history. Nothing like it has been seen since the days of Xhum Y'Zir and
his Age of Laughing Madness. And as the Francis have taught us,
these wounds go deeper than our awareness can know." He turned
now, and began pacing the room, making eye contact with the leaders
gathered there. He stopped at Meirov, and Winters saw the cold wrath
upon her face. "The Fivefold Path of Grief can take us down a winding
road, lead us into decisions and actions that in hindsight may be ex-
cessive but at the time, feel necessary." He continued pacing. "Already,
they ask one another in the taverns: 'Where were you when Windwir
fell?' We are not gods—most of us do not even believe in gods—and
there is no powder or magick to clear the head in the midst of such
trauma and violence." He stopped, back at his table now, looking
down at Petronus. "We all acted as we were compelled when Windwir
fell. Right or wrong. But to single out one man when so many others
could join him here seems premature and unjust to me."

Winters looked out over the room. The faces were a blur of grief
remembered and anger refueled. Jin Li Tam leaned onto her podium.
"What are you proposing, Esarov?"

Esarov smiled. "I am proposing a full investigation, authorized by
kin-clave and with the full cooperation of all nations, into the destruction of Windwir, any and all acts leading up to and following that
event, including oath-testimony by your father, Lord Vlad Li Tam,
and all others relevant to the subject at hand. We try everyone—not
just one man. Or"—here he paused and Winters heard the whispered
voices sweeping the room—"we mourn our dead, move forward and
rebuild our nations, restore balance to the Named Lands, heal the
broken kin-claves and work together to assist Queen Winteria with
the resurgence that has grown up in her territories. Either course is
proper, but do not think for a moment that what we do today even
scratches the surface of truth and justice."

Winters shifted in her chair, and as she did, the Firstfall axe shifted
in her lap. For the briefest moment, she thought she saw movement
reflected in the polished surface of its blade.

Then, suddenly, they were at Third Alarm as a mighty wind shook
the tent, and a young woman entered as Gypsy Scouts fell back from
her magicked escort.

"I bring you tidings of peace and grace," she said as she raised her hands. She wore gold-scaled armor, and her brown hair was braided with bone and shell and stick. Her face bore similar markings to Ezra's—the painting was more careful, using dark earth tones that accentuated her large brown eyes. She was unarmed. "Forgive my tardiness," she said. "I've been tending to matters of salvation. I had hoped to join you at the very beginning." The girl looked first to Winters, and when their eyes met, she smiled with warmth and affection. "Winteria," she said, inclining her head. "A strong and prophetic name."

She knows me. Winters studied the woman and quickly returned the nod, hoping her eyes would leave hers if she did. There was something in them that frightened her. Something masquerading as love.

The others were standing now, and Winters watched as scouts from the Delta and Turam applied their powders and vanished while drawing their blades. Gypsy Scouts, unmagicked for now, moved in closer to Jin Li Tam and Petronus, their hands upon the handles of their knives.

"I petition the council for audience," the woman said.

She saw Jin Li Tam wince. "Silence the alarm," she said, turning to the girl. "You have come into our kin-clave of peace, uninvited, with magicked escort that I can only assume stands ready to commit violence. Who are you and what is your business among us?" The Gypsy Queen's level of calm amazed Winters.

"I am about the business of our redemption and atonement, Great Mother," the woman said. "I am Winteria bat Mardic, first and true heir of the Wicker Throne and Queen of the Machtvolk."

Winters heard a stifled gasp and realized it was her that gave it.

Petronus

Petronus looked to the newcomer and then to the Marsh girl Winters. The resemblance was uncanny, though the woman who announced herself was easily five years older. She carried herself with a confidence and abandon that he could read easily in her posture and stride.

"My escort is indeed magicked—you would have not admitted me otherwise—but if we intended violence," she said, "we'd have made those intentions clear without introduction and without losing the advantage of surprise." Around them, he felt the tension crackling like electricity in a storm. The woman smiled. "May I have audience?" she asked again.

Jin Li Tam frowned. "You already have it."

The woman who shared the young queen's name bowed. "Thank you, Great Mother." She looked to the others and her voice rose. "The salvation of a people is difficult and painful work. Kinship must be healed. Blood must be let. Sacrifice must be made." As she spoke, Petronus watched her eyes travel the room, settling last upon Meirov of Pylos. The rage upon Meirov's face gave him pause, and for a moment he thought she might lunge forward to attack the woman with bare hands. Of course, it would be her death sentence if she did. He remembered the strength and ferocity of just one blood skirmisher and knew this so-called queen must have dozens of them with her and perhaps a hundred more nearby. She would not have walked into a kin-clave otherwise.

The woman continued. "You believe that you gather here upon the plains of our handiwork to judge the Last Son of P'Andro Whym and to hear my sister's plea for help. But this is not true. You are here—called and set apart—to bear witness to the grace and mercy of House Y'Zir and the Crimson Empress whose advent is nearly upon us."

Jin Li Tam's eyes narrowed. "You speak in riddles."

"No," the woman said firmly, "I speak of prophecy and destiny for those who have ears to hear. She raised her voice: " 'And it shall come to pass that the city of P'Andro Whym shall become a pyre and in the shadow of that pyre, a child of great promise shall be born to make ready all people for the advent of the Crimson Empress and the Homecoming of House Y'Zir.' "

The words were unfamiliar to Petronus, but they had the ring of age about them. And they had a similar tone and cadence to other words he'd heard not so long ago. *Thus shall the sins of P'Andro Whym be visited upon his children.*

The woman continued, and her smile warmed when she fixed her eyes upon Petronus. "Last Son," she said, "you know what I speak of. You chose this time and place for a reckoning you have felt calling you for some time now. Is this not true?"

Yes. He found himself nodding. "I have felt it," he said in a quiet voice that only he and Esarov could hear. Some Franci corner of him spun the Rufello ciphers on this lock, but a deeper voice pulled at his will like a tide. *How can she know this?*

Petronus glanced around the tent to see what others were doing.

Surprise and confusion still dominated most faces. Jin Li Tam watched carefully, her eyes moving from the woman who called herself Winteria, to the guards positioned at various points around the tent. He saw the briefest flash of fingers and hands moving to give orders. The Marsh girl Winters sat still, her eyes wide and her mouth open—it was obvious to Petronus that she was as surprised as anyone by this sudden turn of events, but the resemblance between them was unsettling. Last, he caught Ignatio's eye and saw him lean forward to whisper something into Erlund's ear. When the spymaster leaned back, his eyes locked with Petronus's and he understood the smile some twenty days earlier in the council chambers on the Delta. *He is a part of this.*

The Machtvolk Queen walked to Petronus's table, trailing her fingers across the surface of it as she strolled past. He caught the heavy scent of blood and mud and ash from her and from her invisible escort. "The time for kin-clave is past," she said, "and the time of kin-healing is upon us all."

Even as she said it, there arose a clamor beyond the tent. It was as if a thousand voices gathered just outside, raising up in a shout all at once, and then a frightened-looking girl entered the tent, a baby clutched in her arms. Behind her, an old man followed with upraised hands, singing loudly in an ecstatic burst of glossolalia. Around them, snow flurried as magicked skirmishers swept into the tent around them, forming an unseen wall between the audience and the infant.

Erlund's general—Lysias, Petronus remembered—plunged forward and called out a name that was lost in the gasps and cries that filled the tent. Invisible hands pressed him back. And the loudest cry sounded from the front of the room, where Jin Li Tam clung to the podium with ice in her eyes and a snarl upon her lips. "Release my child," she said, "and I will spare your life."

The Machtvolk Queen laughed, and Petronus felt the chill of it along his spine. "You are in no position to command me in this matter, Great Mother. Your boy's life lies in the hands of the Last Son of P'Andro Whym."

Jin Li Tam cleared the platform in one leap, and Petronus watched as a wall of force caught her up and held her, invisible hands grasping at her arms and legs as she bucked and twisted. Petronus heard a disembodied voice. "Don't struggle, Great Mother. We hold you for your own good."

The girl holding Jakob sobbed now and clutched at him as the old man stretched out his hands to take him from her. Jin Li Tam shrieked her rage then, and when soldiers suddenly surged forward, unseen wind knocked them back and down. Then, Jakob rose up in the prophet's arms for all in the room to see. "Behold," the old man said, "the Child of Promise."

It was Petronus's first close look at the child. He was gray and smaller than he should be, his eyes squeezed shut against the light. He hung motionless in the old man's hands, his head rolling to the side.

The older Winteria looked to Petronus and drew a knife and a ring from a pocket beneath her armor. He looked at them and blinked. *How did she come by those?*

He'd not seen either since that day he'd dropped them onto the floor of the tent and left to wash Sethbert's blood from his hands.

"You know these, then?"

He nodded. "I do."

She placed the ring upon the table. "I've told you that the child's life is in your hands. Do you believe me?"

He studied the line of her jaw, measured the certainty in her eyes. "Yes," he said. "I believe you."

"Rise, then, Last Son, take up your ring and face your reckoning."

He stood, his eyes never leaving the infant, and took up the ring. It was still brown with dried blood that he felt peeling away as he shoved it onto his finger.

He walked around the table to stand before her. She smiled at him. "You called this council of kin-clave for the matter of your guilt in the death of Sethbert as King of Windwir and Holy See of the Androfrancine Order. I charge you with more than this, Petronus, Last Son of P'Andro Whym. I charge you with two thousand years of blasphemy and bullying. I charge you with regicide and deicide." She paused and looked out over the others in the room. "I charge you with home-stealing and light-hoarding."

He looked to the baby and then back to the woman. "Who are you to make these charges?"

"I am the Bond-Servant of House Y'Zir, sent to prepare for the advent of the Crimson Empress. I am the Machtvolk Queen Winteria bat Mardic, the Home-Taker."

"I do not recognize your authority in this matter," he said, nodding toward Winters. "Winteria bat Mardic is the ascended queen of the Marshfolk."

"You do not have to. My authority is in this moment and this knife." She smiled. "And things are not as they seem. My little sister and I may share a name, but make no mistake that our father's throne is mine by right of birth."

He noticed out of the corner of his eye that Jin Li Tam's hands were moving. *Do not play into her hand,* she said in the Whymer subverbal. *There must be another way.*

He nodded so that she would know he understood her message, but he had no intention of changing course now. She held the knife in the same way he had, hidden beneath his robes, while he waited for the right moment. *This is my reckoning,* he thought.

"What do you require of me?" he asked.

She smiled. "I require a plea of you, Last Son."

Petronus looked at the infant. "And if I give you what you require the child will be unharmed?"

She laughed. "What you give, you give for Jakob and for us all." If he hadn't known better, he'd have thought love shone out from her eyes. "What you give, you give even for yourself."

His eyes narrowed. Some part of him wanted to flee now, and his bladder suddenly demanded release. He remembered the place where he had stood when it was Sethbert, remembered the look in the dethroned Overseer's eyes when he realized the knife had cut his throat, and he felt remorse again for the price he'd exacted—the price he had paid—in order to euthanize the Order and its backward dreaming.

It had been the right thing to do, he realized, even as now he *knew* this was the right thing.

"Then I offer my plea," Petronus said. "I am guilty."

The woman smiled.

He did not think he would feel the knife, but he did. It was a dull ripping with sudden cold against his open throat. He felt his knees buckle and saw his own blood.

Thus shall the sins of P'Andro Whym be visited upon his children.

He saw Esarov moving around the table, his face twisted in rage. He saw Erlund's stunned look and the ecstasy upon his spymaster's face. And he saw the baby, held high like a standard, so that his shadow passed over Petronus.

A wind of blood to cleanse; a blade of cold iron to prune.

He heard the cries of those who bore witness, he heard air bubbling through his wound, and above it all Petronus heard the Child of Promise raise up his voice and wail as if with great sorrow.

Then, the Last Son of P'Andro Whym smiled at his reckoning and embraced the light that reached for him.

Jin Li Tam

Jin Li Tam tore her eyes away from Petronus's twitching form at the sound of her child's cry. Her body and mind flooded with emotion as the weight of the day's events finally broke her.

It had begun with the bird. Weeks late, a reply from Rae Li Tam had arrived before dawn, pushed into her fumbling hands by the captain of the watch. She'd read it by firelight and wept.

The note was brief, but she recognized the handwriting as her sister's, and the triple-coded response was in the standard script of House Li Tam. *There is no cure. I grieve with you, Sister.*

Beyond those terse words, there'd been no further information and no word from Rudolfo, either, in weeks now. She'd kept the messages going out to him in the hopes that one would find him. None had—or if they had, he'd not responded.

She'd carried the note with her in her pocket and had spent the day crying in her tent when she wasn't presiding over the kin-clave.

Still, she'd steeled herself for her duties, though the weight of that knowledge crushed her. Rae Li Tam was perhaps the best apothecary in the New World, and if she said there was no cure, Jin Li Tam believed her. Not even the promise of Sanctorum Lux could hold her despair at bay.

So she had hidden her sorrow and faced her day.

And now, the tent stank of blood and mud and ash as Petronus kicked his last on the canvas floor. Her son wailed—great sobs that made his tiny body convulse in the gnarled and filthy hands of Ezra the Marsh Prophet. In his short time with her, Jin Li Tam had never heard him cry so forlornly, and it went deeper than any scout knife.

The so-called Machtvolk Queen glanced at her and then knelt over Petronus, flipping him over. "Do not despair, Great Mother. Salvation is upon us all."

Then, she opened the old man's blood-soaked robe, baring his pale chest.

Jin Li Tam willed herself to struggle, but somewhere between her brain and her body, the message fell flat and she hung limply in the arms that held her.

The woman's hand moved with confidence and precision, running the knife over Petronus's chest. His glassy eyes stared upward, his arms spread cruciform.

When the mark of Y'Zir was complete, the woman looked up to Jakob. "Bring the child of promise to me," she said. Then, from beneath her armor, she drew out an iron needle and a small glass phial on a silver chain.

Dipping the needle into Petronus's blood, the woman unstopped the phial and slid the needle into it, depositing a single drop. She stopped it up and stood, approaching Jin Li Tam. Behind her, Ezra cradled her crying son.

"Your child is going to die," she said, leaning close enough that Jin could smell the honey of her breath. "Ask me to save him and I will." She replaced the needle and shook the phial in her fist.

Jin Li Tam swallowed. This was a darker mysticism than the Marshfolk had shown before, and some part of her mind reeled away from it. "You cannot save him. He is sick." She felt panic growing within her.

She smiled. "Ask me to save him," she said again, "and I will."

Then, she turned and unstopped the phial she'd shaken. This near, Jin could see the black fluid that beaded in the bottom of the phial. "You cannot save him," Jin said again.

Using the needle again, Winteria bat Mardic drew out a single drop from the phial. She shook the needle over Petronus, and the drop fell upon the wound in his neck. Jin Li Tam gasped at the smell of ozone that filled the room and felt the fine hair on her arms and neck lift up as the wound in Petronus's neck began to knit itself together. His body began to drum upon the floor as his legs kicked and his hands pounded. The Machtvolk Queen sighed and stepped over him to avoid his flailing.

But even as he flailed, Jin Li Tam watched his eyes as they rolled in his head and watched the pallor of his skin flush with new blood. He sat up gasping, his eyes wild, still covered in his own blood, and reached trembling hands up to the ragged scar upon his throat, the careful mark upon his heart.

The woman turned to Jin Li Tam, holding up the phial. "Behold the grace and mercy of House Y'Zir," she said, extending the phial toward her. Her eyes narrowed. "Ask me to save him and I will, Great Mother."

And in that moment, nothing else mattered to her. The eyes of the Named Lands were upon her and she did not know them. She saw only her son and the miracle now offered. All her life, she'd watched her father use his children to shape the world. She'd stood by the graves of many of them, expendable arrows shot with intent into the heart of the Named Lands. And though some part of her cried out against the abomination she now faced, a louder part clamored life for her son at any cost.

I am not my father's daughter after all.

She felt the hands relax upon her, and she knew what must follow.

Do not look to the room, she told herself. She knew what she would see there. A mixture of wrath and fear and wonder. Instead, she forced herself to her knees before the Machtvolk Queen and took the woman's feet in her hands.

"Save my son," she said, weeping. "Please. If you can, save him."

Nodding, the woman turned and dipped the needle once again, taking the last drop of that dark fluid upon it. While Ezra the Prophet cradled him close, the Machtvolk Queen shook the needle over his tiny mouth. The black bead fell upon his lower lip and Jakob, firstborn of Rudolfo, ceased his crying.

And when the Machtvolk Queen Winteria bat Mardic took him and passed him to his mother, Jin Li Tam already saw the gray fading from his face and hands, replaced by a healthy pink. His eyes, clear and wide and brown, were open and focused upon her and he smiled.

In that moment, she heard a voice cry out from the entrance to the tent and looked up to lock eyes with Rudolfo.

Weeping with joy and shame, she clutched her son to her breast and wondered what price she'd paid for this miracle.

Chapter
24

Rudolfo

Rudolfo felt his legs turn to water and staggered back against the Gypsy Scout behind him. The man caught his king and steadied him upon his feet.

What he'd seen staggered him.

They'd landed where Windwir's docks had once been, and the *Kinshark* had no difficulty finding a deep-enough berth close in to shore. The iron vessels—those that had not left with Charles for the Churning Wastes and Sanctorum Lux—had turned back leagues ago when their deeper keels threatened to run aground on a river that the Androfrancines no longer dredged.

From the beach, he'd run to the tent, an invisible wall parting before him as he did. He would have walked, his feet unsteady from weeks at sea, but seeing the Ninefold Forest flag turned for distress hastened him.

And now, he stood slack-jawed. He'd reached the entrance to the tent as Petronus fell and kicked his last. And he'd stood to the side, transfixed, as the woman—the one called Ria—first brought back that dead Pope and then restored Rudolfo's son.

"I don't know the cure," Rae Li Tam had told him during one of her more lucid moments as the blood magicks consumed her. She'd spent her last days going over her small library and writing notes.

She'd created lists for Charles of which books to find when he reached Santorum Lux. But even then, Rudolfo had known the chances for a cure must indeed be slight. To travel so far with so little result only to have it handed to him felt unfair. And to have it given in such a way. He knew it was blood magick—it had to be. Only deep bargaining in the Beneath Places could bring about that kind of power. Somehow, and for some purpose he could not quite fathom, this woman had healed his son, had saved his life.

But at what cost? He remembered the blood pipes. He remembered the smell of death and the screams beneath the knife.

Now, watching his wife as she huddled on the floor and held their son, the magnitude of the afternoon's events settled upon him and he wanted badly to sit down, but he resisted gravity. He opened his mouth to speak, but the woman spoke first.

"Lord Rudolfo," she said, inclining her head, "bear witness to this, for a time shall come when you are asked to give an accounting of this day."

He blinked at her and said nothing.

She pointed to Petronus, who sat to the side, rubbing his throat in wonder with a lost look upon his face. "The last son has been forgiven the sins of his father and shall be released into exile. Look to me, Petronus." When he looked up, she smiled at him. "Leave the Named Lands. Go east into the Churning Wastes from whence you Ash-Men came to steal our Home. Stay there. Life is your gift. Return at your peril."

Rudolfo's eyes narrowed. "Who are you to command him?"

She smiled and swept the room with her hand. "I am one who has proven that her Blood Scouts can strike when and where she chooses." She paused to look to Meirov, and Rudolfo followed her. The Queen of Pylos shook with rage. "I am one who has proven that age and station do not give me pause from the course I am called to."

"You are a murderer and an abomination to our people," another voice said, and Rudolfo first noticed Winters, who stood now and brandished her Firstfall axe of office.

Ria laughed. "And you are a child, Winters, playing at queen with your dreams and your books and your white-haired Androfrancine boy. Bring the axe and come with me, little sister. Climb the spire and stand with me while I proclaim myself. Join me and we will take back our Home and make it what Lord Y'Zir promised us it would be in his Gospel. Take the mark upon you and find joy in servanthood and in Home."

Rudolfo watched the anger upon Winters's face and recoiled from it. Hanric's loss had twisted deep in her, and the dark look she now gave Ria spoke of buried violence within her such as Rudolfo would not wish to face in a foe. "This is not the dream of our people," Winters said. "This is not *my* dream."

"Dreams change." Ria's eyes narrowed as she continued. "And so do the hearts of men and women. How long do you think your friends, your family, met in secret and worshiped in secret, preparing for this day? Quiet evangelists teaching and preaching what was to come to pass. The silent prayer of decades, awaiting the column of fire in the sky that would mark the advent of the Age of the Crimson Empress and an end to the home-thieves' hold upon our land."

Windwir. Could they have somehow had a hand in it? Brought about the fulfillment of their own prophecy? House Li Tam was certainly involved—Mal Li Tam obviously in league and in bed with this woman. Rudolfo found himself caught up in Ria's voice and forced his eyes away from her and back to the girl. Winters stepped forward, and he saw her white knuckles upon the handle of the axe.

"I am the Marsh Queen, Winteria bat Mardic," she said in a low and even voice. "I do not know who you are, but I am my father's only daughter."

Ria laughed. "Ask Seamus if that is so, Little Sister."

Rudolfo watched Winters take another step and saw the rage growing upon her face along with her resolve. When she lunged forward to swing the Firstfall axe, Rudolfo knew it could not connect. Her feet were not well planted, and the weapon was too heavy and awkward for her to lift it with any speed.

Invisible hands seized the girl, knocking the axe from her hands. Lifting her up, the Blood Scouts held her as she shrieked and kicked at them.

Ria stepped closer, stooped and lifted the axe easily with one hand. Within its reflection, Rudolfo saw the Marshers that held the girl and measured the distance himself.

He stopped when Ria leaned in and kissed Winters upon the forehead. "Come with me, Sister. Take your place beside my wicker throne."

The girl found her composure. "I will not come with you," Winters said in a low and even voice.

Ria's shrugged. "You are my sister. I will not force you." She smiled. "The truth will call you unto itself in its own time. Come to me when you are ready, Winters, and I will show you a new dream." Then she turned and took in the entire room. "Hear this and know it well: These lands were given to the Machtvolk for their service on the night of Xhum Y'Zir's death. The lands from Windwir's Rest and north-ward are mine, and I will watch my borders very well." She looked to Rudolfo. "The kin-healing of House Li Tam binds us to your wife and child. And though the Machtvolk stand above these matters of kin-clave, kinship is another matter altogether. Our peoples were the first in this New World and the only that were granted deed and title by the Wizard Kings who kept it set apart. Will you live in peace with us and let us mind our own?"

Rudolfo looked around the room, saw that the wonder had passed now and only fear and hatred and surprise remained upon the faces of those gathered. As if they weren't sure what to do with the informa-tion they now held. As he watched them, he avoided his wife's eyes. He knew that he could not look into them and face Ria's question. He looked back to the Machtvolk Queen where she waited for a re-sponse.

Rudolfo took a deep breath.

What do I say? Which way now to turn in this Whymer Maze he'd fallen into? Suddenly, his right path was not so very clear. *And I cannot choose a war that I cannot yet win,* he realized. An uneasiness grew within him, and he felt expectation on the chill air as she repeated her ques-tion.

"Will you live in peace with us and let us mind our own?"

For now, he thought. *But my words must be careful.*

"It is my desire," Rudolfo finally said, "to live in peace with all people." Especially now, he realized, standing upon the grave of Wind-wir. But he knew even as he said it that his desire for peace would ever be in conflict with his need to create a safe world for his son, a world that held to the light and eschewed the dark.

Ria nodded. "It is enough for now. The truth will come to you in time, as well, Rudolfo, and you will bare your heart to the mark of the Crimson Empress with joy." She looked to her sister, then to Jin Li Tam and Jakob.

And then Winteria bat Mardic, Machtvolk Queen, turned and left with her escort of Blood Scouts.

Only then did Rudolfo look to his wife. She held Jakob close to herself, and the baby laughed and squealed, his face pink and ani-mated with expression. He followed the line of her forearm, around the curve of her wrist, to the slender fingers that stroked the thin dark hair of Jakob's tiny head. His eyes traveled the line of her neck and jaw, then settled upon her face. And when their eyes met, he saw despair and relief commingled there with surprise and with tears, and he knew in that moment that he loved the forty-second daughter of Vlad Li Tam and would spend his life on her behalf. That she truly was formidable and fierce and fair and that the child they had made would be the same, despite the price they had paid or the consequences that might follow after.

Weeping, Rudolfo raced to his family and gathered them into his trembling arms.

Neb

Neb looked across the canyon to the small cluster of tents and slowed to a walk. They were scout tents in the rainbow colors of the Ninefold Forest Houses, and there were horses tethered in a copse of stunted scrub-trees. But there were also other tents—a second, smaller camp erected in the midst of the forest tents. Spitting the last of the root onto the ground, he tugged his waterskin loose and took a long drink.

Every part of him felt alive, and it had since that first night he'd listened to the canticle within that ring of glass mountains. After locking and leaving Sanctorum Lux, he'd spent his first night alone in the Churning Wastes with his ear pressed to the iron cap that sealed away the source of the metal man's dream. He'd awakened the next morning refreshed, found a small and hidden spring to refill his waterskin and bathe. Then, he'd set out at a run for D'Anjite's Bridge and found the strength to run straight through.

Wind whipped up at the foot of the bridge when he approached it, and he felt the movement of magicked scouts around him. A small brown bird emerged from an invisible belt cage and shot across the chasm to the watch captain's net before anyone spoke.

"Captain Aedric will want to see you," a Gypsy Scout said.

Neb nodded. "I need to speak with him." He watched the camp stir to life once the message was read, and he thought at one point he saw Aedric. "Are Renard and Isaak well?"

"They are. Our medico splinted the Waste Guide and he's up on a crutch now. The Androfrancine is tending to Isaak's leg."

The Androfrancine? He wondered at this but did not ask.

A white bird shot out from the camp, swallowed into a sack that Neb could not see. But he remembered this part of his training very well. How to catch the bird and read the knots tied into its thread.

"Let's go then," the voice said, moving onto the bridge. "You scouts mind your post. I'll bring him in."

Neb followed. They crossed the bridge at a jog, and the guards at the other end, unmagicked, moved aside for them. Within the camp, Neb saw Gypsy Scouts intermingled with a handful of men and women dressed in the silk clothing of the Emerald Coast.

The Gypsy Scout must have read his face. "House Li Tam," he said. "They brought Charles to us by sea at General Rudolfo's request."

Neb blinked. "Father Charles is here?" It made sense that he would be the Androfrancine fixing Isaak's leg. He'd seen the old Arch-Engineer in the Great Library tinkering among his mechanical re-creations, and he'd even heard the old man speak once on the nature of the light in regards to mechanical science.

"He came after the metal man and Sanctorum Lux," another voice said. Neb looked up and saw Aedric approaching. "We happened upon them on our way to find you and Isaak."

He put his arms around Neb and squeezed him. "Are you well, lad? Where's your metal friend?"

Better than well. He heard the song again behind him and over his shoulder. "He's . . ." He searched for the word. Could a mechanical be dead? "He destroyed himself. I left him at Sanctorum Lux."

Aedric's eyes widened, and now Neb became aware of others gathering around them. He saw Charles approaching and behind him, Renard limping along upon a crutch. "You've found it then?"

He nodded and swallowed. He watched the light of hope spark in Aedric's eyes and then gutter at the despair he no doubt saw upon Neb's face. "It's gone. They burned it all."

Aedric flinched. "Who burned it all?"

Neb looked to Father Charles. "The mechoservitors did."

The Androfrancine's brow furrowed. "That's not possible. It is completely outside of their scripting."

Neb thought about the song and the dream it birthed. *Should I tell them?* If he told them, it would not stop there. He said nothing, though a part of him grieved at the lie of omission. He glanced up and saw Aedric's eyes upon him. The First Captain nodded slightly as their eyes met and he frowned. "We'll find out soon enough," Aedric said. "We ride for Sanctorum Lux at dawn."

He knows I'm not telling everything. Neb looked away, his cheeks hot.

It requires a response. A response given in secret to confound the enemies of the light—those who wished to snuff it out. Those who brought down Windwir. Those whose eyes and ears were upon the Named Lands now, though Neb was not certain how he knew it. He simply felt it and trusted that feeling.

This place has changed me.

And Neb suddenly knew that he would not be going with Aedric—that his time among the Gypsies was over as quickly as it had begun. Instead, he would return to the iron cap and learn the cipher and take the source of the dream to himself. He would learn the ways of the Waste from Renard and follow the dream until it took him Home. Nothing else mattered. Not Winters, not his adopted home among the Gypsies or his future as an officer of the Forest Library. He felt it in his feet where they stood upon this desolate landscape.

He lost himself within the calling and only brought himself up from it when the others began moving away, leaving him with Aedric and Renard. It was Aedric's hand on his shoulder that finally jarred him into the present.

"Rest up," the First Captain said. "There's hot food in the Tam camp, and you can find a fresh uniform among the men. Tomorrow will be a long ride."

Neb shook his head. "I can't go with you."

Aedric's eyes narrowed. "You are an officer of the Gypsy Scouts, Lieutenant Nebios, and you will be riding with us tomorrow as such."

I am Nebios ben Hebda, the Homeseeker, he thought. He shook his head again. "Tell Rudolfo that I'm sorry," he said, "and that I'm grateful for all he's done." He let his eyes meet Aedric's then, and this time he did not look away at the anger he saw there. "I'm grateful to you as well."

With careful fingers, Neb reached beneath his arm and untied the tattered scarf of rank that hung there and extended it to Aedric.

The First Captain took it. "You are making a mistake, lad."

"It would be a mistake for me to stay," Neb said, and even he could hear the strength in his voice as he said it.

Aedric regarded him thoughtfully and finally nodded. "I will bear your message to the general personally." His hard eyes softened. "And have you thought about the girl, your young queen?"

Neb swallowed. His own sacrifice to the dream. "Tell her I am called to find our Home."

Aedric gave him one final look, nodded again, and walked away without another word.

Renard smiled at him. They were alone now. "You've heard it, then," he told him.

Neb blinked. "You've heard it as well?"

"No," Renard said. "But your father did."

"I have to go back to it," Neb said.

Renard nodded. "We will. I can't run, but I can ride."

Neb looked around the camp. He would need to say good-bye to Isaak at some point and secretly pass to him the memory scroll his metal cousin had intended for him. And he would want to eat with the men. But after that, he thought, it would be good to take the root and stretch his legs.

To let the history of this land seep into him through his feet as he ran toward that buried song.

His calling stirred within him, Nebios Homeseeker felt the joy of it pulling him and he smiled at it.

Jin Li Tam

Jin Li Tam brushed her long hair out and watched Winters holding her son. Her initial fears of the newborn had faded, and the same instincts that guided Jin as a new mother guided the young girl as she explored one of the wonders that her body could someday produce. She watched and forced a smile.

My son is saved; I should not need to force my joy. But she did. She saw her hands upon the Machtvolk queen's feet and heard the catch in her voice as she pleaded for her son's life. It shamed her, and yet she felt relief flooding her when his skin turned pink and when he found his laughter and his lungs; and even now, when she heard him giggle with Winters, she brushed up against a miracle.

And Petronus, too. She'd watched him die and then return from the dead.

She heard a clearing of the voice and looked up, startled.

Her father stood at the tent flap. He avoided eye contact with her, averting his eyes. "I know that I've earned every bit of your disfavor," he told her, "but I beg audience with you, Daughter."

As he stepped into the light, she could see the scars upon his face—wounds nearly healed and yet angrily red. She'd heard what had happened in her brief hours with Rudolfo before he'd left to try to salvage some kind of kin-clave among the others. She furrowed her brows now and tried to find anger for her father; she could not.

He's had his reckoning. And she knew that someday, because of who she had begged to save her son, she would have hers. "Come in," she said, "and meet your grandson."

Winters nodded before Jin Li Tam said a word and brought Jakob back to her. "I will think about what we discussed," the girl said.

Jin Li Tam smiled. "Do. I know you would be welcome. You would have a home there."

Winters returned the smile and inclined her head. After she left, Jin Li Tam motioned her father to a chair. "Sit. You can hold Jakob."

She watched her father wince when she said the name. *Good,* she thought. She did not think it out of bitterness but because he should understand the price that was paid. Jakob had been Rudolfo's father's name—a man her own father had killed using one of the Tam sons as a weapon.

Vlad Li Tam took the baby into his arms. He held the child for a few minutes in silence before he looked up at her. "Your husband told me once that if ever he were a father he would not use his children as pieces in a game." He took a deep breath. "This was the same day that he vowed to kill me the next time he saw me because of what I had done to his family."

"You deserve to die for that." She said it without thinking and in a matter-of-fact tone.

He surprised her by nodding. "I do. But the next time he saw me, he did not kill me. He saved me and what remained of my family . . . *our* family." He looked at her, and his eyes were suddenly hard. "I know you've thought yourself a strategic piece in some game of mine, and it is true. I raised you for this, shaped you for this day. And now I know that my father did the same to me. That I was a tower in his game, scripted like your metal men to perform a function. To make you and Rudolfo." He leaned forward and kissed Jakob's forehead. "And to make you, too, Jakob."

She remembered well the note he'd left for her beneath the pillow of her guest bed in the Summer Papal Palace, warning her of war to come and ordering her to bear Rudolfo an heir. But why was he telling her?

Now when their eyes met, she could see that his were full of tears. "I regret every harm I caused another's child or father or mother," he said. "The grief of it consumes me now, and when I sleep at night, I hear only poetry and screams—only it's not my children but someone else's, and I have been the cutter, weaving a spell in blood and believing it would save the world."

She felt tears pulling at her own eyes, and it made her angry. Sadness often did. Finally, she gave voice to her question. "Why are you telling me?"

He sighed. "Because I think sometimes you are afraid you will be like me."

She remembered her exhilaration on the ride with the Wandering Army, remembered what it felt like to dance with the knives and bring down a Blood Scout in her wrath. "I don't want to be like you," she said.

And then he smiled and handed Jakob back to her. "You are not like me, Jin Li Tam. And I am proud of that." He stood, and she saw a strange look pass over his face. "Do you remember where you got your name?"

She nodded. It had been a long time since she'd thought of that. "From the D'Jin of the Younger Gods, swimming in the deepest darks of the haunted oceans."

He nodded. "I saw one before your sister pulled me from the sea," he said. "It sang to me."

Jin Li Tam did not know what to say. So she said nothing and simply stood.

Her father bowed to her. "He is a beautiful boy. He will be formidable and strong."

She returned the bow but again could find no words. Her father had changed, and her brain spun now to decipher what he'd become. *Because he's been broken.*

And though these past months had worn her, they had not broken her. Seeing what her father had become, she did not want to ever experience it.

After he left, she slipped into her sleep shift and laid Jakob into the crib beside her bed. Rudolfo would be up late into the night and would probably not sleep until sometime after dawn. He would be working to save what kin-clave he could with Pylos and Turam, though she was certain his effort there would be fruitless. Still, he would try because he always saw the right path and chose it. She would not see him tonight, though some part of her needed to. Some part of her that she was unfamiliar with wanted to smell him, to feel him warm and near her. He'd been away for too long. Still, he was an influential man. He could belong to the Named Lands tonight and she could hope for tomorrow.

She did not realize that she slept until she felt a warm hand encircling her, stroking her bare stomach beneath her shift. She felt the messages pressed into her soft skin as gooseflesh rose upon her. *My sunrise.*

She stirred awake and inhaled the scent of Rudolfo's hair. "I can't stay long," he whispered into her ear. His hand moved again. *My truest path.*

"I'm glad you're home," she told him and rolled over to pull him into her arms.

And for a time, she let go of her worry about what came toward them from the gathering storm clouds and savored this moment as a gift of great value.

Lysias

Lysias stared at the scout magicks and the poisoned knife before him and willed focus into his hands and feet for what was to come.

He'd been suspicious before Vlad Li Tam called for him. He'd seen the look of ecstasy upon Ignatio's face when Petronus fell beneath the woman's blade, and it had set him to thinking.

A conspiracy large enough to bring down Windwir would involve infiltrations at key levels across nations, and the Marshlands had fallen too quickly for it to have been a fledgling movement.

He'd arrived to the *Kinshark* just after dusk and listened to Vlad Li Tam reading from a slender volume. The man had changed, latticed now in scars and meek of voice. Initially, he made no eye contact and kept to his book. He was nothing like the arrogant, confident man Lysias remembered from the night they'd met near the ruins of Rachyle's Bridge. Vlad Li Tam had given him the means to end the war by bringing down Resolute and Sethbert, and later that night, Lysias and Grymlis had helped Resolute to his end.

The broken man had read him several pages, then met his eyes briefly. The rage and anguish there nearly matched what Lysias felt as he heard the words.

Now, he lifted the knife and opened the pouch. He'd not been under the scout magicks since his days in the Academy, but he remembered well how it felt. He threw the powders at his shoulders and his feet, then licked the bitterness from the palm of his hand, bracing himself for what was to come. His stomach lurched, and he vomited onto the floor of his tent.

Everything bent around him, and the world moved beneath his feet. The sounds of the camp outside grew to a roar, and his own beating heart kept time like a marching drum.

He sucked in his breath and felt the strength moving through him.

Setting off at a run, he took the course he'd walked out carefully earlier that afternoon when he'd decided what he must do. There was only one answer, though after he gave it there would be no turning back.

Still, he would take this right path.

Ignatio's tent was guarded lightly, but not by soldiers. The spymaster used his own men for that, and Lysias did not mind dispatching them. Before their bodies stilled, his hand was upon Ignatio's mouth and his blade was at his throat.

"I know who you are and what you've done," he whispered into the struggling man's ear.

He called up Vlad Li Tam's voice now, reading from the book. About the cult in the north and Tam agents planted within the Order, about Y'Zirites in high places. About the daughter of an Entrolusian general who was to be widowed and bereft of her child in order to nursemaid another. About a blood bargain made to spare that Gypsy Prince's life and prepare them all for the advent of a Crimson Empress. As he remembered, he felt the rage, and in that rage, he found resolve.

"I know what you've done, Ignatio," he said again, "and you pay for it tonight."

Ignatio bucked against his grip, and Lysias used his own body weight to keep the man pinned. He pricked the knife against the skin and waited for the kallacaine to take effect. He held the spymaster tightly as his struggles slowed, and then just as he went slack, Lysias reached for the pouch of scout magicks and tipped the remainder of the powders into Ignatio's open mouth.

As he faded from sight, Lysias lifted the paralyzed man onto his shoulder and staggered out into the snow.

He moved carefully through the camp, staying close to the shadows and rehearsing his petition to Rudolfo. After tonight, he was finished on the Delta. He would hope for mercy from both the Gypsy King and his own daughter.

And he would hope that tonight's work would redeem him in his own eyes, too.

He reached the river quickly and laid Ignatio down in its shallows. He placed him on his back and drew close enough to the spymaster that he could just barely see one wide and frightened eye close to his own. "You killed my daughter's child, you blood-loving shite," he said in a low and matter-of-fact voice.

After, he tipped the man over onto his face in the water and stood over him. He placed a boot upon the back of Ignatio's head and pushed him firmly to the bottom of the shallows.

He stood silent for a time, holding him there, until he was certain of his work.

Then Lysias pushed the body into the current and turned back for the Gypsy Camp.

Chapter 25

Vlad Li Tam

Vlad Li Tam leaned on his shovel and tried not to look at the canvas-wrapped body. Still, eyes took him there against his will and then filled with tears—also against his will. The sun rose east of them, turning the distant Keeper's Wall purple and pink.

They'd sailed with her in the *Kinshark* specifically for this, but he'd wanted to wait until sunrise. So he'd visited his new grandson and then slept, tossing and turning against the noise of his dreams. Then, he'd arisen to wake Baryk, and they'd carried her and their tools north of the camp to bury her away from all but the eye of Rudolfo's magicked scouts.

Later, he would speak with the Gypsy King, though a part of him dreaded it after two weeks of avoiding Rudolfo's watchful eye.

He cleared as much dirt as he could from the hole he'd started. Across from him, Baryk waited with the pickaxe ready. The others had offered to help, but he and Baryk had refused them. Instead, the bereaved husband and father worked together to carve out a grave for Rae Li Tam here among the dead of a city and a way of life that were no more.

It was the only proper choice that they work together, even as they had sat with her to watch her slowly die, still wrapped in the blood magicks that forced them to see her only in memory.

Even at the end, when the pain kept her weeping, she'd given herself completely to the work of finding a cure for her nephew and had died while Baryk napped beside her, an open book upon her invisible chest.

Vlad Li Tam felt the grief stabbing at him and looked up, nodding to Baryk. The gray-haired warpriest swung the pick down, breaking up the frozen ground for Vlad's shovel.

Again, he tried not to look to her, stitched there in the canvas, and he failed. *I remember your first steps,* he told her in the deeper places he rarely visited. *And your first words.* He remembered her last words, too, though he'd not known at the time that they were such.

He'd sat beside her that last night before she died, and she offered no poetry, no celebration of her love. Instead, she squeezed his hand. "Grow your pain into an army," she told him.

And he knew that he would. Later this morning, he would meet with Rudolfo and he would petition him to take their scarred children and care for them. He would show him the volume—a secret history of the Named Lands that even he had not known about. One in which House Li Tam cultivated an Y'Zirite resurgence in the Marshlands, quietly seeding it with the promised fall of Windwir until, by treachery and intrigue, they toppled that great city.

A resurgence that brought back blood magicks and had cast a great spell of power made from his anguish and from the blood of his children and grandchildren, such that it could heal the baby and raise Petronus from the dead—more miracles that pointed to a dark and rising gospel in their midst.

He would not have believed it if he had not read it coded in the book.

He'd believed at first, mistakenly, that perhaps they'd engineered the cult themselves simply to destroy Windwir. But deeper than that was the matter of faith. His father actually *believed* the so-called Y'Zirite Gospel. The volume was riddled with references to it. As much a study of scripture as a strategy for bringing out their present circumstances. But why?

To establish the throne of the Crimson Empress.

No, he thought, it could not be faith alone, some blind adherence in mysticism. He could not see his father in that light. There had to be a prime mover beyond him that he was in service to. And it had to be tangible and rational. Whatever the truth might be, the Crimson Empress was real.

Somewhere, someone played Queen's War with the Named Lands, and his First Grandson and this kin-healing Machtvolk Queen were but pieces in a greater contest. And Vlad Li Tam would find his actual opponents and repay them.

It did not matter if the blood of his family saved his grandson or saved the very world. They who called for it and they who took it would pay for that taking.

So he would tell Rudolfo what he knew. And then he would ask him for money. And with that money, he would outfit what remained of his iron armada and go back to that island, though the thought of it broke his heart. Weeping, he would take it apart stone by stone and learn what he could from it.

He would grow his pain into an army, and while he did, he would learn his foe as well as he could. He would patrol the waters to the south, keeping an eye out for schooners of unfamiliar line and trim, made from a dark wood unfamiliar to the New World's first family of shipbuilders. He would do all of this, and he would watch the water for ghosts while he did so.

Again, his eyes pulled him to Rae Li Tam, and he felt the sorrow moving through him like water.

She'd given her life to save him, taking in the blood magicks so that she would have the speed and strength to find him and pull him from the sea. He'd not anticipated that, and her sacrifice, at the end of so many other deaths, broke the old man's heart.

I have changed, he realized.

He'd sent many of his children to their deaths to move this river or shift that mountain. He'd sent them to the beds of tyrants and into prisons with thieves and killers. He'd made them murderers and torturers and liars and whores.

Never again, he vowed.

Baryk rested on the pickaxe now, and Vlad Li Tam worked his shovel. They went back and forth like that until the hole was just so. Then, they put down their tools and took up their beloved.

The tears flowed freely now, and he did not despise them. *I will grow my pain into an army.*

He looked across and saw that Baryk also wept. *He builds his army, too.* We all do.

It would be a mighty army, he realized, that each of them grew. It would be a terrible reckoning for whatever hand had moved those pieces against Vlad Li Tam's family.

Gently, and in silence, they laid Rae Li Tam into the ground and readied their hearts for war.

Winters

Winters knelt before Seamus, holding his hands in her own. He blinked at the mention of the woman who shared her name, his face showing his surprise.

She'd finally come and awakened him in the middle of the night when her questions and nightmares would not let her sleep.

"She claims to be my sister," she told him. "She said to ask you about her."

"It can't be so," he said, his voice quiet and low.

She read wonder in his voice, and her eyes narrowed. "What do you know, Seamus?"

He drew in his breath. "I know that it can't be so," he said again. "She couldn't be. . . . I helped your father bury her. The fever took her in the first month." He looked to her. "Unless . . ."

Yes, she thought. It was possible. She'd watched the drop from the phial bring Petronus back. She'd seen the second drop heal Jakob. The dead could be raised.

Or, she thought, a death could be faked. Petronus again came to mind.

"And her name was Winteria?"

Seamus nodded. "Yes."

She sat with this and tried to take it in. Why wasn't this in the Book? She'd seen not a hint of it through all her father's writings . . . and his closest friend, Hanric, had said nothing of it to her. "Why was her death kept secret?"

Seamus's eyes were hard now. "Her birth was kept secret as well. Only a handful of us knew, and your father swore us to silence. Your mother was kept in isolation from the time she first conceived."

"But why?" she asked again.

He shook his head. "I do not know."

"Do not know or will not tell?" She raised her voice and heard the bitterness in it. "Seamus, I abjure you to tell me what you know."

He shook his head. "I know nothing, my queen."

Winters stood, and she felt a wave of nausea roll over her as the truth settled in. "If you speak truth, then I am not your queen."

And without another word, she slipped out of the tent and into the frozen night.

Turning north, she slipped past the Gypsy guards and wandered toward the treeline at the edge of the ruined plain.

This was familiar ground. Not so long ago, she'd walked this plain with Neb as he patrolled the gravedigger's defenses. Where was he, she wondered? Her dreams were empty without him. Violence and blood and dark birds filled them, and there was no comforting word in it for her. Still, she clung to her memory of him and longed to walk with him again. Longed for him to tell her that everything would be fine, that home still arose though she was no longer certain that it did.

And she missed the dreams. Not the ones of late that unfolded now behind her eyes.

In that future, the light swallowed her Book of Dreaming Kings. And a song—mad Tertius playing it upon the harp—led her love away from her and deeper into desolation. Her secret sister—back from the dead, it seemed, and sharing her name—built shrines to Wizard Kings long dead and cut their mark into her people and their children, openly pledging themselves in service to the Crimson Empress whose soon-coming they preached.

The Marshfolk were gone. The Machtvolk had returned in their place. And now she was gone, as well, and another Winteria would climb the spire and announce herself Machtvolk Queen and Bond-Servant of House Y'Zir.

Until this day, she'd never felt an orphan, because she'd always had her people. And even when their sudden fall to the Y'Zirite heresy had shaken her, until she saw her sister, until she recognized her own eyes, her own mouth, her own nose upon the older Winteria, she'd not truly believed she'd lost them.

But she had. And beyond the loss of her name, her people, her dream and her love, Winters had also lost her faith, she realized. She felt the hole where it had been and wondered how it had vanished so fast. And she wondered how or if she would ever get it back. She doubted it.

But just as when she'd lost Hanric and before him, her father and her mother, she would take this loss into herself and would drink the pain of it.

As the sun rose, she turned to the east to watch it and knew what she would do. She returned quietly to camp and left again with a small bundle beneath her arm.

She walked upriver until she was out of eyeshot of the camp and she stripped carefully, feeling the cold winter air move over her, causing her to shudder.

Teeth chattering, she waded out into that river and quickly scrubbed the mud and ash from her body. She pulled the braids from her hair and sent the bits of stick and leaf floating downriver. Then she scrubbed with the bar of strong soap until the numbness of the cold water drove her back to shore. She dried off with a rough cotton towel from the Ninefold Forest supply wagon and dressed herself in a calico dress and boots.

Buttoning her fur coat against the cold, Winters turned her back to the north and returned to camp.

Tomorrow, she would ride with Lynnae and Jin Li Tam and Jakob. She would take up her work in the Ninefold Forest, helping to integrate the refugees into the city that grew there. Jin Li Tam had suggested that it would be meaningful work while she determined her next steps.

She wanted to feel excitement, but curiosity was the best she could muster. Her mind was elsewhere, working her crisis of faith like a tongue upon a missing tooth. Finding meaning and sorting facts out from the knotted mess of it all. The dreams had been real. The glossolalia had been real. And everything had changed now. She wanted to know why, and she wanted to know what she was meant to believe now. She could not even find the passion to be angry or bereaved over it.

Somehow, Winters knew, she would sustain this loss and find treasure in it. Perhaps something better than the faith she had lost would grow up in its place.

Perhaps I'm meant to be a Gypsy wife after all; perhaps home was never any farther away than that. Would that be so bad? And would it be wrong to hope for it? And to hope that someday, she would have a child who laughed and blew bubbles in his sleep?

A child with eyes as piercing and blue as a summer sky above the Dragon's Spine.

Like Neb's eyes.

Sighing, Winters slipped back into her tent and fell into a light sleep, her nose twitching at the clean smell of soap on her skin and hair. As her sleep deepened, she dreamed about her white-haired boy, even though it wasn't him but a memory of him. He held her by the campfire and told her that everything would be fine and well again in its proper season.

And above them, the blue-green moon sang both of them to sleep.

Petronus

Petronus left in the early hours while the sky was dark and the stars and moon were veiled lightly by wisps of clouds. The sun was red and low over the Keeper's Wall when he paused and looked down the hill to the snow-blanketed ruins of Windwir. He traveled lightly with a horse and pack, both marked with the crest of the Ninefold Forest.

He'd met with Rudolfo briefly that afternoon, but the brooding Gypsy King had obviously been scattered and spread thin by the challenges before him. They'd talked briefly in private, and when Rudolfo had suggested secreting him away in the forest, Petronus had shaken his head and pressed for the Gypsy King to give him what he needed to quietly slip out of the Named Lands. Reluctantly, he'd called for his hostler and for a supply captain who could write out letters of credit and introduction for him.

Rudolfo had made a great effort, Petronus thought, not to look at the ragged scar. But in the end he had stared, and wonder had touched his eyes. Petronus frowned at the memory of it.

A realization struck him as he sat atop his horse looking down at Windwir and the camps around it. *I may never see this place again.* It grieved a part of him, but there was another part that felt relief. This was his first time back since the grave-digging. Walking that plain, seeing the rubble buried in snow and the raised ground of the trenches they'd filled with Windwir's blackened bones was a cold blade that cut him deeply.

Below, he saw a figure by the side of the river just north of camp. From his vantage point, he could not tell who it was, but it looked to be a woman. She removed her clothing and waded out into the cold waters, dunking herself beneath them and scrubbing hurriedly.

His hand moved absently to his heart, feeling the raised skin of scar tissue there. *I wish I could cleanse this from me.*

But he couldn't. Now, he carried a mark. A token, with the scar upon his throat, to remind him that his life had been taken and given back to him in a greater reckoning than he could have ever known. An autograph upon someone's dark handiwork. A living miracle bearing witness to the power of the Wizard Kings.

He left now with only those marks and a few items of clothing. And it hearkened him back to another day he had slipped away alone. On the day he'd killed Sethbert and had then seen Vlad Li Tam's evidence of the threat against Windwir, he'd ridden out from the Seventh Forest Manor to return to his shack on Caldus Bay and begin his work gathering up what data he could.

But now, he left with no work to drive him forward, and perhaps that was a good thing. Until Windwir's pyre, he'd lived quietly for thirty years, marking his time by the fullness of his nets and the companionship of the kind-hearted people who kept his secret and welcomed home their prodigal Pope.

Maybe quiet would come to him again. He hoped so. But already, his mind spun. Why had he been brought back? What was the significance of Rudolfo's heir? Who was this Crimson Empress, and could she be the external threat he'd been convinced they faced? He thought it likely that she was.

In the moments before administering her blood magick upon him, the Machtvolk Queen had added his own blood to the phial, according to Rudolfo. He'd certainly studied what little of the alchemy of blood magick they understood, but there were reasons why those magicks and spells, bargained for in the Beneath Places with the ghosts of long-dead gods, were forbidden. They were songs crafted out of the blood of others.

And over the years, he'd seen the parchments—fragments of this spell or that—but he had never seen a blood magick that could reverse death.

Petronus shook his head and saw now that the girl below was dressing hastily upon the shore. He turned his horse east and left her to her privacy.

He would take his time riding for the Keeper's Gate, and when he arrived he would show the Gypsy Scouts stationed there the letter that authorized him entry. Then, he would go alone into that place and make what home for himself he could.

But as he rode east, a handful of horses separated from a copse of evergreens, and he recognized a gray standard he'd not expected to see.

When the riders approached, Grymlis rode at the head of them. Behind him, resplendent in the uniform of the Gray Guard of P'Andro Whym, rode five men he recognized and three he did not. The silver buttons upon their jackets cast back the red light of the rising sun, and a sudden rising breeze caught the edges of their standard and unfurled the crest of Windwir onto the morning air.

"Father," Grymlis said, saluting when they were within earshot.

Petronus sighed. "I thought I ordered you back to the Ninefold Forest, into Rudolfo's service?"

Grymlis smiled. "You did, Father."

Petronus looked over the men. The new ones were younger and had the look of the Delta upon them. "You've no doubt heard about my present situation."

Grymlis nodded. "I have," he said. "And welcome back."

Yes. He'd paid for his crimes with his life and then had his life handed back to him. He'd been made a spectacle, part of a story that would be told from town to town, city to city, in hushed tones and wonder, lending credence to the Y'Zirite Gospel. More than that, he also suspected he'd been brought back to force Jin Li Tam into a corner, and that frightened him more deeply than even his own return from the dead. Seeing the power of the Y'Zirites' blood magicks manifested by Petronus's resurrection, she had begged an ancient foe for the life of her child and it had been granted.

It was the beginning, he feared, of greater darkness in the land of his birth and first life.

Still, circumstances demanded that he leave and do quietly what could be done offstage and away from the eyes of the north. He realized then that Grymlis was speaking, and he forced his attention back to the old Gray Guard captain.

"I'm sorry," he said. "My mind wandered."

"Understandable," Grymlis said. "I was telling you that there are others, as well, who will meet us at the Keeper's Gate."

Petronus felt his eyebrows furrow. "Others?"

"Androfrancines are no longer welcome here," Grymlis said. "They killed the few that remained in the Summer Papal Palace. Caravans en route to Rudolfo's forests have been attacked—again, Androfrancines massacred and left unburied for the crows. The only place untouched has been the Ninefold Forest, but some of us believe it's only a matter of time before that changes. And now, the Gypsies owe a debt to these Marsher heretics." He shifted in the saddle. "I've word out of our exodus; we'll wait a week at the Keeper's Gate for any others who would join us."

At one time in his life, Petronus would have been angry at the disobedience of his orders, at the assumptions and actions being taken by the man before him. But the events of recent weeks had shown him that life was a nonmetrical song at times, one that went where it needed to for the melody without respect for the rhythm of history and tradition. Truly a canticle that one danced to as best one could. He would trust Grymlis to dance it, and he would not isolate himself from those who chose exile with their fallen father over a hidden life in a land that had turned on them so utterly in such a short time. Rudolfo's kindness notwithstanding, he saw a day coming when no Androfrancine would be suffered to live in the Named Lands. And more than continuing, he feared the pieces had been set to this board in such a way that the Y'Zirite resurgence would not just survive but *thrive* in the rich soil of desolation prepared for it.

Finally, he nodded to Grymlis. "Then we will wait there for them." He looked to the other men. "We will carve a home in the Churning Wastes, and we will offer ourselves to Rudolfo as his eyes and ears in that place."

And we will find a way to undermine those tangled and bloody roots that threaten to choke our light.

Petronus touched the scar at his throat briefly, then touched his breast. Then, without looking back, he whistled his horse forward and rode east beneath the red fist of the rising sun.

Chapter
26

Neb

Neb let the winds of the Churning Wastes move over him where he lay and turned himself again so that his other ear pressed to the cold iron cap.

Renard snored gently at the edge of the clearing, weary from the jostling ride he'd made. But Neb had not been tired. The canticle would not let him sleep. He'd lain awake here in this place for a night and a day, listening to the song and working through the ciphers in his mind.

It was nonmetrical, and the hands that plucked at the harp strings moved with a precision that he could hear clearly. It played and it played, with no beginning and no ending that he could discern, though he knew it had to have both.

And when the moon had risen that first night and the song's strength increased, he'd found that the nuances of note and measure concealed numbers and those numbers coincided with the notches and dials and levers of the Rufello locks upon that great iron cap.

Still, he had not known how it was that he could hear them. During the daylight hours Renard had joined him but heard nothing, not even the faintest note of the song, when he stretched himself out upon the ground alongside Neb.

So Neb kept at his work and left the Waste Guide to his rest. Soon enough, the Gypsy Scouts would reach this stopping point along their way to Sanctorum Lux, and Neb did not want to be here when they did. He wanted, by that time, to have the source of the dream within his hands. They would go north to Renard's people so that the Waste Guide could heal. And while he healed, Neb would find this dream the metal man spoke of.

He sighed and pressed his ear even closer to the iron. The numbers were hard to find, but they were there. Already, he'd puzzled out four of six lock ciphers. And now, his fingers found the fifth and worked it, too. Deep inside the iron lid, he heard the clacking and ticking of gears that moved a bolt aside.

He paused there and remembered the metal man's words. *The last cipher is the first day of the Homeseeker's Advent.*

He knew that one without listening to the song, but he'd still saved it for last. Sometimes Rufello's locks had to be worked in sequence.

Biting his lower lip, he calculated the numerical date of his birth based on the Whymer calendar and twisted it into that last dial. When he finished, he heard nothing below him—no gears, no raspy sliding of the bolt. Furrowing his brow, he rolled onto his back.

He'd lost track of all time here. It had been daylight the last time he'd paid any attention to his surroundings. It was nightfall now and the sky was clear. Stars throbbed above him, their cold light casting an eerie glow upon the mountains that surrounded him.

It hadn't worked. But why?

He tried again, but with the same result.

And then the moon rose and the song reached its crescendo with the rising. He stared at it, heavy on the horizon, and wondered at the size of it. He could see the lines where land ended and sea began and, squinting, he could even see the man-made line of the Moon Wizard's tower, desolate and abandoned upon that poisoned and empty world that rose above them to remind them of that long-ago war that had killed the last of the Younger Gods who huddled afraid upon that blue-green rock.

Neb started. *Of course.*

He knew now, and he recalculated the number, not by the Whymer calendar but by an older one that had gone out of use. A calendar measured by different landmarks in time than those of P'Andro Whym and the disciples who gathered and shepherded the light along with the orphans of a broken world.

When he converted the date of his birth into the ancient numerology of the moon calendar of the Wizard Kings, he heard the movement of grinding gears as the last bolt slid free.

Neb rolled aside and squatted, regarding the unlocked hatch in the ground. He gripped the edge of it with his fingers and put his strength into lifting the iron cap. It groaned slightly but swung open upon oiled hinges. Glancing to Renard, he decided against waking the man.

This place was made for me to find it. He knew this was true. Even as he knew that his father had had a hand in it. Soon enough, Neb knew that he would understand to just what depth his father had known and prepared against this day.

An iron ladder, bolted into the side of the stone well, descended before him. Bathed in the blue-green light of the moon, he climbed down into the earth. He climbed until the darkness swallowed him, but he did not fear. The song was there with him, around him, cradling him, and he knew that it waited below him.

He was not sure how long he climbed before his feet found the solid floor of the well. He looked up to see the moon framed in the round opening above.

It was too dark to see the small box with his eyes, but his ear knew where it was, and he went to it. Fumbling it open, his fingers found the cool, smooth metal object within, and he lifted it out carefully. Tinny and far away, the song played out from it and he lifted it, holding it against the backdrop of the dim light from above. The song grew louder, and beneath it, Neb heard the croaking of frogs and the distant burbling of a brook.

Beneath his fingers, he felt the line of continents and mountains upon the crescent-shaped object. He held it to his ear and felt the solid comfort of how it fit there.

It requires a response.

Slipping the crescent into his pocket, Neb climbed out of the darkness and into the moonlight. When he reached the top, he closed the cap and locked it. Then, he stretched out upon the cold iron and pulled the object from his pocket.

He knew what he would see, but he did not know how he knew it. Still, holding it up against the moon, he saw the sliver for what it was and compared the rough map of its surface to the blue-green orb that hung in the night sky behind it.

They matched. It was the moon.

Starlight and moonlight swirled in its silver surface, and it was a metal that he'd seen before. The same strange and ancient steel that formed the Firstfall axe of Winters's office. Bringing it down, he rested the silver crescent between his shoulder and the side of his head, cradling it against himself so that his ear was pressed up to it.

This is the source of the dream. Hidden within that "Canticle to the Fallen Moon" lay Neb's destiny, and he welcomed it.

He must have drowsed because he dreamed. Only it was a dream he'd had before and not the dream of the metal men that he longed for. And this second time he dreamed it, it was more clear, more detailed than previously.

He remembered it well—it was one he did not mind repeating. He and Winters were naked and tangled in one another. They were older, but not by much. The sheets were soaked with their sweat, and his limbs and his eyelids were heavy with exhaustion and spent passion. They lay beneath a silk canopy in a tropical forest overlooking a sea. Above that sea a brown and blue world arose and filled the starry sky. It made the moon he was accustomed to ridiculously small by comparison.

"This is our home," she whispered in his ear as she rubbed a stomach swollen with life to come.

It was a good dream; a dream that felt true.

He stirred himself awake briefly and wondered if some dreams were promises—deposits made upon a future that destiny could carve for them if they listened to its canticle even in the darkest nights and danced to its calling by moonlight.

I am called to find that home; this song will bear me to it.

And as the canticle played on, Neb wrapped himself in destiny like the warmest of blankets and hoped against hope that dreams could be made true.

Jin Li Tam

Jin Li Tam stood at the base of the gangway and waited. She'd received her father's note and had spent the day pondering what to do. Finally, she'd decided to come and see him one last time before he sailed on an unmagicked *Kinshark* to rendezvous with his armada and sail south in search of answers and vengeance.

Rafe Merrique's first mate had gone to fetch him even as the crew readied the ship to sail. While she waited, she watched the campfires in the Gypsy camp. The other camps were gone now—the Entrolusians had left last, though they'd left a man behind, unbeknownst to their Overseer. Sethbert's most celebrated general, Lysias, had petitioned Rudolfo for asylum earlier in the day, and her husband had assented when she'd told him that he was their nursemaid's father.

"I will find work worthy of his rank," Rudolfo had told her after.

Pylos and Turam had left before the others. Rudolfo had given his best effort to restoring peace with them but to no avail. She had known that it would be that way. She'd seen the look of wrath on Meirov's face, the venomous daggers of her eyes, when Jin Li Tam's son had been healed and given back to her.

She heard her father's footsteps on the gangway and looked to him. He walked slower and his shoulders were weighed down. He held a packet of papers in his hands. "I didn't think you would come, but I'm glad that you did."

She nodded. "I received your note."

He stepped closer and passed the papers over to her. "These are all your sister could think of to help Jakob." She took the packet and looked down at pages crowded with ink. "I know it's irrelevant now, but she spent her last days looking for a cure, and I thought you should have them."

Jin Li Tam blinked. *Looking for a cure?* "But I received her note, Father. She told me there was no cure."

"By the bird?"

She nodded, and Vlad Li Tam shook his head. "The birds have become unreliable, Daughter," he said. "They cannot be trusted." Behind him, she heard the whistle of "all hands," and he looked over his shoulder. "I've shared what I know with Rudolfo. Our messages are compromised, and birds are being diverted; forgeries are misdirecting us. Your husband is going to task the mechoservitors with establishing new codes."

She nodded. "That would be prudent."

The first mate reappeared now. "We're ready to sail, Lord Tam."

Her father nodded. "I'm glad you came," he said.

Then they embraced and he climbed the gangway. She watched while they raised it and left before the anchors rose.

As she returned to the camp, she pondered.

The note was a snare. The realization struck her like a fist. She'd received the note that morning. It was in her pocket when the Y'Zirite, Ria, interrupted their council. She had put her foot into it and it had done its work.

There is no cure. No, but when she saw a cure before her very eyes—saw Petronus rise up from the dead—and heard the Machtvolk queen's words, she'd had to act. The forged note from her sister was the snare that had caught her, luring her to a decision that had been so easy to make.

Ask me to save him and I will.

And kneeling, she had taken the devil's feet into her hands and wet them with her tears, begging for the life of her son.

When she reached her tent, she did not recognize the girl with her calico dress and long brown hair who waited for her there. But when the girl stood, her awkward and coltish posture betrayed her. "Winters?"

The girl smiled, and Jin Li Tam marveled at the transformation. She thought at first she might ask but then decided against it. She had more pressing matters. She needed to see her son. Winters curtsied. "Lady Tam."

Jin Li Tam looked around the room, an uneasiness growing quickly to alarm. "Where are Lynnae and Jakob?"

Winters blinked. "Both with their fathers. Lynnae is talking to General Lysias. And Rudolfo took Jakob to walk the perimeter."

Jin Li Tam released her held breath and forced calm. Why had she felt panic? What was it that made her need her son so badly in this moment? She pushed the question aside for later and looked back to Winters. "Tell Rudolfo I'm looking for him if he returns before me."

Winters nodded, and Jin Li Tam slipped back into the night.

Singing started up around the campfires, and she made her way north to the line. Rudolfo would walk from the south to the west, then to the north and east—she would hope to catch him on his return.

As she walked, she thought about this sudden need she had for her son and the panic that had arisen within her. Certainly it made sense after him so recently taken by the Blood Scouts and after seeing him sick for so long. Of course she would fear losing him after these threats.

But what of the need she had tonight of all nights to hold him?

She worked the maze as she walked and found her answer quickly. It was because she knew that the look of him, the smell of him, the softness of his skin beneath her hand would remind her that what she'd chosen had been the only good and reasonable path she could take. That the little life she had made with Rudolfo was worth any debt she could incur, even if it was to those who'd murdered her family, left Windwir desolate and seeded violence and chaos into the Named Lands.

But it was more than needing a reminder that she'd made a good choice, that she'd known and taken the right path. It was a reminder that there was still good in this broken place and that even in times of great darkness there could be moments of excruciating light and unbreakable hope.

Like light in the eyes of a husband home from the sea. And hope in the smile of an infant sleeping in his mother's arms.

Jin Li Tam moved across snowfields bathed blue and green, and when she reached the line, she found the soldiers there and whispered encouragement to them.

Walking the perimeter, she stopped here and there to greet the men and ask them if they were ready to ride on the morrow, ready for waiting beds and lonely wives, ready for home and hearth. The men bowed to her and called her queen as she went, and after she passed, she heard them whispering in low and respectful tones.

But she pushed aside the voices behind her and moved forward through the snow, her eyes searching for the moon-washed, striding figure of her Gypsy King and her ears listening for the sound of Jakob's laughter.

Rudolfo

There was singing now from the campfires, and Rudolfo stepped in from the line to hear it. He stared down into the face of his son and returned the smile he saw there. It was an odd moment, this, a father walking the line with his son. It brought back memories of similar walks with his own father, though he'd been old enough to not need carrying. He cocked his head and listened to the song on the wind. It was an old Gypsy tune about the year of the fallen moon sung in a minor key—slower than the version his mother had sung him.

How long since she sang this to me? He could not remember, and he felt a tug of loss when he sought her face in his memory and could not find it. But he remembered these lyrics. They spoke of love requited, though with sacrifices made, of bargaining pools in the basement of the world and ghosts that swam a haunted sea. It was a song about tears and separation, desperate hope and misguided faith. It was a song about the love between a Weeping Czar and a Moon Wizard's daughter.

Jakob laughed, and Rudolfo laughed, too. "You like music, then. So did your grandmother."

He resumed walking, but now he left the line and made a new path in the snow. He looked down into his son's face again. "I've awaited your coming for some time," he told the infant. "I'm glad you've come."

And so unexpectedly. At the end of a river of blood, in the shadow of desolation, an heir to the Gypsy throne. And to the light, as well, Rudolfo knew, for the Great Library he built would be the legacy he left his son.

A dark cloud passed behind his eyes as he thought of his own father and another legacy. Last year, he'd closed down Tormentor's Row and disbanded his Physicians of Penitent Torture. At the time, he'd intended more, but it had been enough. Now, after seeing the graves of House Li Tam and the stained cutting tables, after touching the warm pipes of the Blood Temple, he'd known that he could not let that last vestige of his forefathers' darker ways continue.

Especially for the children who would now make their home with him.

Earlier that day, he'd met with Vlad Li Tam; he'd heard the man's concerns and listened to his request. It had been surprisingly easy, and in the end he'd agreed to fund his work. That request had not surprised him, but the one regarding the children had.

I am a collector of orphans. The children, now scarred with the mark of House Y'Zir, would make their home in the Ninefold Forest, and it would not do to have any structure there that might remind them of their captivity. So after that meeting, Rudolfo had called his birder and sent orders home. Not one stone to stand upon the other, and no cutter's knife unmelted and reforged into something that could cause no harm.

Tormentor's Row would be torn down and its stones built into the library. Perhaps into a wing named for his father.

Of course, there were his other orphans.

He'd not recognized Winters when he'd taken Jakob from her. All that dirt and grime had hidden a pretty girl on the edge of womanhood. She would join them now and wait for his other orphan, Neb, to come back to her from the Churning Wastes.

And there was Isaak. If this place wouldn't break his metal heart, Rudolfo would wish him here now to hear him talk about the library they built and the light they saved.

Rudolfo heard a low whistle behind him and knew it at once. He

turned and saw Jin Li Tam approaching. The wind whipped up, catching the light powdering of snow that had not frozen yet. It swirled
around her feet.

"How is he?" she asked, stepping close to them.

"He's sleeping, I think," Rudolfo said. He passed his son into her
waiting arms and noticed the depth of her sigh once she held him to
herself.

They turned, and Rudolfo suddenly realized where they stood.
The snow-covered mounds, the view of the hills to the east and the
south. He took a few steps forward and stood at the edge of an impact
crater, listening to the ghosts that whispered to him there.

Jin Li Tam walked to the edge and stood beside him, looking out.
"This is where the Great Library stood," she said.

He nodded. "It is where we found Isaak." He paused, turning the
more painful memory over in his mind. "It's also where I brought
Gregoric the night he died."

He remembered what the Francis said about one loss connecting to
another, and he knew it was true. He could lay his finger upon the
thread of Hanric's loss and follow it back to Gregoric's. From Gregoric's, he wove his way back—through the Desolation of Windwir, an
unfathomable chasm of loss—to his father's and his mother's, and to
the older twin who would have inherited the Ninefold Forest if someone had not moved that river.

I could have killed the man responsible and instead I saved him.

And yet it did not unsettle him. It was the right path, and he could
not question it. And truly, though he despised the pain of it, he knew
that his father-in-law's actions had also brought as much life as they
had death.

In the shadow of desolation, he had found a formidable wife; and
in the middle of his road, he now had a son that he could raise up to
be a strong and fair king.

He looked to them and noticed the knives she wore. He chuckled
and brushed the hilt of one with his thumb. "I see you've found these."

She looked down and blushed. "I did. They were in your desk. I . . .
I liked the way they felt in my hands."

He smiled. "They were my mother's," he said. "My father had them
made for her as a wedding gift. I intended to have them polished and
sharpened for you."

"Knives as a wedding gift?" she asked.

Rudolfo shrugged. "They are fine blades."

She laughed and leaned close to him. He slipped an arm around her. "I can think of better gifts," she said. "But they are indeed fine blades."

They stood silent, then, watching the night around them. In the morning, they would strike camp and make their way home ahead of the winter's last snow before spring. When he returned, Rudolfo knew that a desk buried in paper awaited him. There were refugees to help acclimate. And the library construction would be gearing up with the promise of spring. Soon, the sun would be out and the bookmakers' tents would be filled with mechoservitors as they wrote their books and filled the basements with volume upon volume in a river that threatened flood. Added to that, there was the threat that grew to their north and west with the advent of the Machtvolk and the dark gospel they preached—and the trouble he now smelled to the south in Pylos and Turam.

And what of this Crimson Empress?

There was enough work ahead to keep him up nights in his den wandering a Whymer Maze of paper. He would gradually grow accustomed again to the feel of a desk and a chair beneath him instead of a horse or a ship. And of a warm, shared bed instead of a solitary cot.

And mixed in with the work, there would also be a Gypsy wedding to plan and a child to show his Ninefold Forest Houses so that his people could meet the next Gypsy King.

He would keep living despite the dead he buried. He would love his wife and his son, and he would spend himself for the light he'd gained from his time in darkness.

Even in Desolation, Rudolfo thought, life asserts itself.

Unbidden, the song from earlier found his lips and he began to sing it. Jin Li Tam looked to him, her eyes wide to see him sing, and he could not blame her. The last time he'd sung had been the Firstborn Feast when she'd been abed with their child. And the time before that? It was so far back that Rudolfo could not remember.

But he sang now, and the strains of it echoed out into the night.

In the distance, a wolf howled.

And above them, the full moon watched and lent them its watery light.

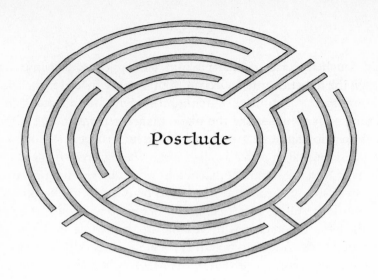

Postlude

The Watcher laid down his pen, pushed back his unfinished gospel, and walked to the mouth of the cave.

Sunlight called him forth and he followed it, drawing a long silver flute from the folds of his robe.

Holding it to his mouth and placing fingers just so, he forced air into it and called the kin-raven to himself as he'd called so many other birds before.

He waited for the dark messenger, and when it landed heavily upon a boulder, it regarded him. This one had much life yet in it, and it gladdened the Watcher to know it.

"Bear a message home," he told the kin-raven, and waited while the bird cocked its head and opened its beak to receive his words.

"The Last Son is in exile—spared to fulfill the scriptures—and the kin-healing of Frederico's line is complete. The Child of Promise has his forty years, and the Great Mother has indebted herself to your grace. The secret faith is now preached in the open, and the Macht-volk arise from their sorrow to take back their given home."

The Watcher paused. "Time is of the essence," he finally said. "The Age of the Crimson Empress is at hand."

He raised the flute to his lips and blew again, this time softly. Spreading its great wings, the kin-raven lifted and sped south.

The Watcher watched it as it flew, and when it was nothing but a speck upon the horizon, he turned and went back to his cave. He would finish this gospel, and perhaps when he did, he would walk through the forest near the Machtvolk shrine and listen for the hymns they sang there.

Clanking and clacking, the ancient mechoservitor slipped back into the shadows and took up his waiting pen.

Acknowledgments

Novels are a soup cooked with many hands in the kitchen and I'd like to thank some of those chefs who've helped me bring *Canticle* together.

First, my wife and partner, Jen West Scholes: She's been a great ear for me as I've verbally processed the challenges, both in the writing and the writer himself, and has been a great support in all things. Thank you, darling.

I've also got a team of pretty amazing first-readers (along with Jen): Jay, John, and Jerry—the three of you, once more, have seen me through another novel, lent your eyes to the first draft, and managed to help keep my head from falling off or exploding in the writing process. Thanks, guys.

Also, big thanks to Aimee Amodio, not only a great reader and cheerleader for the series, but also a fine Gyspy Webscout, taking good care of www.KenScholes.com for a pittance and a walk-on part in the book. And thanks to Alethea Kontis, Mary Robinette Kowal, Aliette de Bodard, Kalissa Canyon-Scopes, and Lee Dudley, who also took their regular shifts at encouraging and pushing me forward through the process of writing this book.

Along the way, I also get to work with some exceptional people. Jenn Jackson, thirty-second daughter of Vlad Li Tam and agent extraordinaire, thanks for all you do to keep my career moving. And then there's Tom Doherty and his fine crew at Tor: Tom, your belief in this series is a great encouragement to me, and I'm delighted to be in the Tor family.

My editor, Beth Meacham, gets a double helping of thanks from me. Your work with me, Beth, through all of the school buses that have shown up since we started, has made all of the difference. I knew you'd be great for my writing; now I see you're great for the writer, too. Thanks for all you've done to keep me sane, focused, and moving forward in spite of *Everything*. Also, big thanks to Melissa Frain for her work to get *Canticle* on the street. And then there's Patty Garcia—thank you for all you've done on the publicity for the series. You're a hoot to work with and excellent at what you do. Thanks, also, to Irene Gallo for once more bringing the amazingly talented Greg Manchess back for yet another great cover—and much gratitude to you, Greg, for once more stunning me with your work.

Robert, I've dedicated this book to you for the role you played in bringing me into the genre, encouraging me along the way to write down those stories, and introducing me to the role-playing games that honed my storytelling muscles. It's a good way to celebrate thirty years of brotherhood.

And thank you, Dad, for calling me the day I finished the draft of *Canticle* to tell me how much you loved *Lamentation*. Your high praise that day and your excitement about the book is one of my best memories of our time together here. I miss you and love you.

There are so many more to thank, especially those of you who've taken the time to write and let me know how much you enjoyed what we started with *Lamentation*. It really does fuel the fire. So thank you for that.

It's true that I write the stories for myself, but I also write them for you, Dear Reader, and I'm grateful that you've come back for a second helping. I hope you had a good visit in the Named Lands this time around, and that you'll join me in *Antiphon* to see what happens next with Rudolfo, Jin Li Tam, Isaak and the rest of the gang.

As always, the errors and omissions are entirely mine. I hope you will forgive those that may have slipped past the guard.

Ken Scholes
Saint Helens, Oregon
March 2, 2009